EARTHSHAKER

EARTHSHAKER

VICTOR OF TUCSON ✝ BOOK 7

PLUM PARROT

Podium

To my readers – thanks for witnessing Victor's exploits!

Cover design by J Caleb Design

ISBN: 978-1-0394-5556-6

Published in 2025 by Podium Publishing
www.podiumentertainment.com

Podium

EARTHSHAKER

1

THE STATE OF THINGS

Lesh's enormous two-handed cudgel, Belagog, whistled through the air with enough momentum and weight to pulverize a granite boulder. He wasn't trying to break a boulder, though; he was trying to smash Victor's skull. Unlike a boulder, Victor wasn't planning to stand still for the tremendous blow. He stepped forward and to the left, inside Lesh's swing, moving much faster than anyone his size had a right to do. Lesh immediately saw his mistake, and his eyes widened as he lifted a clawed foot to rake Victor's thigh in a bid to buy himself a fraction of a second and a few inches to recover.

Victor's epic axe skill showed as he adjusted his hack. He'd been aiming at Lesh's exposed ribs, but he swooped the blade downward, and Lifedrinker screamed, black smoke billowing from her smoldering edge as she took aim at Lesh's outstretched knee. Victor wasn't berserk, but he was running Inspiration of the Quinametzin. He had his strength and agility boosted with Sovereign Will, and Lifedrinker was imbued with a shard of his spirit. Lesh saw the blow coming, but he couldn't evade it. Still, he twisted, following the momentum of his two-handed swing, trying to minimize Lifedrinker's impact.

When she cut into Lesh's knee, despite the dragonkin's potent defensive spells, his dense, scale-covered flesh, and his quick reflexes, Lifedrinker bit deeply, slicing into the meat of his thigh, and Lesh grunted and roared, "Gods be cursed! Again?"

Victor laughed and lifted Lifedrinker. She boiled the blood off her blade, sending it into the air as more black smoke. "First blood!"

Lesh growled but lifted Belagog to his forehead, bowing to Victor. "Well done, Lor—Victor. Perhaps another . . ."

"That's it for me today, Lesh, sorry." Victor let his Inspiration drop, and as he began to relax and talk, Lifedrinker calmed as well, the smoldering heat of her blade fading. He and Lesh had been sparring almost every day since the colony's founding, and Victor enjoyed it, but he was spending far too much time on the practice field for his taste. Between bouts with Kethelket, Lesh, and Valla, he sometimes found an entire morning slipping between his fingers. There were so many other projects he wanted to work on—things like studying the spellcrafting books Valla had gotten from Tes, experimenting with new affinity weaves, and most importantly, helping the colony to grow so that they could open up world portals.

"That one will sting for a while." Lesh rubbed the cut on his leg, but Victor wasn't worried. Lesh was the only opponent he never really tried to pull his attacks on—the big dragon-blooded warrior healed almost as fast as he did. Big was an understatement. Lesh stood nearly ten feet tall and was even stockier than Victor. They both enjoyed fighting each other because if Victor didn't enrage himself to titanic proportions, they were pretty closely matched in strength and size; it was the only time Victor could go all out and not reduce himself with the Shape Self spell Tes had given him.

"You told me it was fine if Lifedrinker ignited. I didn't complain when Belagog cracked my collar bone . . ."

"I'm not complaining!" Lesh shook his head and spat some black tar-like saliva at a grouping of nearby stones. It sizzled for several seconds. "I'm paying you a compliment!"

"Ah, all right. Good, 'cause you know, it's fun for me when we go all out like that, right? I can feel myself improving, too."

"Aye, me as well." Lesh looked to the west, toward the Silver Sea. They were atop a hill, not more than a mile from where Victor had planted the Colony Stone, and they had a good vantage of the various ongoing construction projects. He gestured to the southern edge of the budding colony where Earth Casters were working to erect massive stone pillars in a rectangular pattern. It was the framework for something Rellia called a travel pavilion. "I heard they'd set up the first portal to that city many of you hail from. What is it again? Parshi Gables?"

"Persi Gables. Yeah. I guess we have a connection to Rellia's estate there now, which means we'll see a big influx of new colonists. I think she's planning to get the portal to Gelica up and running today or tomorrow, too."

Lesh nodded, thumping Belagog headfirst into the soil. He leaned on the metal haft, and Victor watched the head sink another four inches into the well-packed ground. "Which will speed the growth. Perhaps you'll soon have access to world travel. You must be pleased."

"I'll be pleased as long as we can get Edeya some help before it's too late."

"She seems stable. I believe you were correct; the witch who snatched her spirit has no immediate plans for it. Either that or she waits for the girl's body to die so she can get the last fragment she left behind."

Victor frowned. Thinking about Edeya always put him in a bad mood, largely because it reminded him of his guilt. Lifedrinker had cooled sufficiently, so he held her over his shoulder, and his new harness snatched her, the enchanted leather straps wrapping around her and pulling her snugly against his back. The volcano had destroyed his old harness, and Rellia had commissioned this new one for him. She had, of course, brought several talented Artificers along on the campaign.

Lesh had seen Victor's mood turn sour. "I don't mean to pester you with unpleasant thoughts. I only bring up the topic because I'm eager to help. I'm eager to see your friend made whole."

"Ah, yeah. No, I appreciate that, Lesh." Victor had resigned himself to the fact that he'd have a small entourage when he traveled to the "hub world," as Lesh described it. Naturally, Valla intended to go with him. Lesh insisted that he had to follow Victor no matter the destination, and then there were Edeya and Lam; the self-made noblewoman would hardly let Edeya out of her sight.

In the two weeks since the founding, Victor had gotten to know Lesh pretty well. At first, he'd tried to talk the dragonkin into going home. The giant warrior spoke fondly of the many battles he'd won, the social standing he'd gained, and the wife he'd left behind. To Victor, it seemed crazy to throw all that away to follow around a man you'd traveled through the universe to kill. To Lesh, it was the only honorable choice—if he couldn't kill Victor, then he had to follow him. He had to learn from him, and he had to make an ally of him. Victor didn't see the logic but chalked it up to cultural differences. The simple truth he couldn't argue with was that Lesh was stronger than anyone else he knew, at least on Fanwath, and Victor figured he'd need the help where he was going.

"Are you going to study your spells?" Lesh was used to Victor using that excuse to end their practice sessions.

"Not today. Today, I'm going to see the Shadeni clan off. Yesterday, Rellia and Lam finally signed off on their settlement location, and Tellen doesn't want to waste any more time; he's eager to get some structures built before fall."

"Ah, yes. The people with the red skin?"

"Right, though not everyone with red skin is part of their clan." Victor started walking toward the sea and the bulk of the new construction. He was still living out of his travel home, and it was set up in the courtyard of the keep Rellia had been building around the Colony Stone. He waved one last time to Lesh, and the man's green reptilian eyes narrowed as he grinned and nodded.

"I'll get you next time!"

Victor shook his head and chuckled. "We'll see." He and the others who'd been using the hilltop for sparring had worn a trail in the hillside. As he walked down it toward the little gravel pathway that would take him more directly into the settlement, he took in the view, letting his eyes traverse the various projects Rellia and her engineers had begun. The travel pavilion was impressive on its own, but it seemed insignificant in the shadow of the keep being built atop the central hill.

Magic made everything faster, but it was especially apparent when it came to building large structures. The Earth Casters were pulling massive stones from the quarry the surveyors had found in the mountains to the south and, again using magic, were carving and transporting them to the settlement much more quickly than even modern construction equipment might have done back on Earth. Victor had to admit that he didn't know much about large-scale construction, but he'd watched some big buildings go up in Tucson, and he'd seen how it took months before the outer shell looked like an actual building. That wasn't the case here.

The keep's foundations had been dug and filled with stone footings in a single day—hundreds of yards of trenches, dug down twenty feet or more to solid bedrock, then filled with stone footings magically melded together without the need for mortar. Days after that, the outer walls had been built with enormous metal gates fit for an emperor's palace put into place. Rellia had commissioned the gates back in Gelica, and they'd been carried in one of the capacious supply wagons.

Victor appreciated her preparedness, especially with regard to how quickly she'd built the keep wall around the Colony Stone. If for some reason they were attacked, they were already in a position to defend the stone. The keep itself wasn't going up quite as quickly. It took planning to build the foundation, digging out the basement levels and ensuring the infrastructure was in place for water and sewage. These were all things that had interested Victor, and they'd eaten away many afternoons as he wandered around observing, asking questions, and, of course, meeting with Rellia and Lam to "approve" this or that project.

They were still governing the colony as a triumvirate, though Rellia and Lam had plans to change that in the coming month, as the friends and family members of the legion came through the portal in their thousands. Victor didn't know all the details, but he knew there'd be a sort of elected republic, but elections wouldn't be open to just any citizens; voting citizens had to hold land in the Free Marches, and those holdings would determine the weight of a person's vote. Naturally, Rellia, Lam, and Victor, being awarded the most land from the conquest, would have the most influence, but it was a commodity that could change hands.

Rellia was sharing a large portion of her claim with Lam, and the three of them, Victor included, were awarding parcels to the veterans of the conquest, including the Naghelli, Shadeni, and all of the support personnel. To Victor, it didn't seem like much; the most significant awards for general troops were only a hundred acres, and some support personnel would only receive a single acre. People like Borrius would receive thousands, and some of the nobility from Rellia's family would see more than that, but those were all coming out of her share. Victor was going to have a stretch of land numbering in the tens of millions of acres.

Because Victor had recruited the Naghelli and Shadeni, he'd agreed to award them land from his share. On the one hand, he didn't care because he had plenty, more than he'd ever wanted or could conceive of using. On the other hand, he didn't care because he liked the idea of having them close. He liked Kethelket and his people, and he felt they deserved it; it felt good to give it to them. The same went for the Shadeni, only doubly so.

Victor had lobbied with Lam and Rellia for a large tract of land that ran along most of the southern mountain range and then up the coast of the Silver Sea. There was an old-growth forest near the mountains and plenty of seaside hills where he might build a keep with a view. Grasslands stretched for a hundred miles north of the hills and forests, and Victor liked the idea of having so many different sorts of land to call his own. More importantly, he thought they'd accommodate his friends nicely; the agreement he'd come to with Tellen granted the Shadeni a million acres of grassland and forest to call their own. Kethelket and his people were eager to claim some territory in the mountains near the forest, and Victor thought that would be fine.

He couldn't take all the credit for choosing his lands—Valla had come up with the idea of building a road and maintaining a garrison at the southern pass. It would put him, or more likely whomever he left in charge, in control of further exploration into unclaimed territory. His lands would meet with Rellia's, which began near the Sea Keep and encompassed the primary settlement.

When he and Valla had made their proposal, Rellia hadn't been hard to convince. She wanted the northwestern lands, primarily because she wanted to be in control of the Colony Stone and the pass to Ridonne. Lam also had been easygoing; she had her eyes set on vast tracts of farmland that abutted the eastern mountains. All in all, so far—Victor had the urge to knock on some wood—the fledgling colony and its triumvirate of leaders had been running smoothly.

As he contemplated the state of things, Victor rounded the last hill before the expansive, cleared area where Rellia's engineers were laying out the new town square. With the sea as a backdrop and surrounded by the scaffolding of a dozen new buildings, he saw the Shadeni wagons and the bustling activity of nearly a thousand people as they readied their caravan. Some butterflies began to stir in his belly as Victor thought about meeting with Tellen, Thayla, and their family. He'd hardly spoken to Chandri since she'd recovered, and he might not be a genius when it came to reading women, but he felt as if she harbored some severe animosity.

"I wish I knew why," he said aloud. Victor had no problem finding fault with himself; he blamed the disastrous final battle and the assault on the Glorious Ninth on himself, but he couldn't find anyone else who'd admit to harboring the same opinion. He wouldn't blame Chandri if she were angry with him about that, but he didn't think that was it. "Whatever," he grumbled as he reached into his Core and let some Energy out to cast Shape Self. He shrank down to a more comfortable six and a half feet and hurried his steps toward the front of the caravan, where he saw his old wagon and the two vidanii, Thistle and Starlight. If nothing else, he was eager to see Deyni.

He hadn't made it ten steps before jogging footsteps approached, and he turned to see Nia running his way. The former thrall of Baron Dunstan had come through the battle unscathed, and she'd been working as something of an aide for Victor in the weeks following the colony's founding. It hadn't been his idea; she'd approached him and asked to swear into his household guard, something Valla found very amusing, but also, after she'd relaxed and thought about it for a minute, a good idea—Victor would have to establish some sort of governance and militia for his territory.

Nia was sharp and determined, and there was just something Victor liked about the scar-faced, dark-eyed woman. Her personal tale was tragic, but she never seemed down or tired or less than enthusiastic about any hard work. "Lord Victor!" She held up a thin leather-bound volume. "You've received a response!"

"Ah! Really?" She held the Far Scribe book Victor shared with his cousin, Olivia. He'd written to her about their victory and about their plans for the Free Marches, but he hadn't received an immediate response. Afraid he'd put the book into a ring and forget about it, he'd given Nia the task of checking for a response twice daily. He slowed his pace to a stop and waited for her to catch up, then took the book. "Did you read it?"

Her eyes flew wide with shock, and her tone bordered on outrage, "I would never!"

Victor laughed. "Relax! I'm not accusing you, and I never said you couldn't. Still, I guess it's good you didn't. Thanks for your discretion."

"Of course!"

"Well, let me check it quickly before I get tied up with the Shadeni." Victor flipped the pages to the last written-in one and began to read:

Victor,

Well done with the Free Marches! Congratulations! I'm sorry it's been a few days since I received your message, but I was rather busy with a challenge of my own—something we can talk about next time we're together. My response was further delayed by my having to communicate with First Landing via another Far Scribe book. It took a few days to relay the significance of your victory and for the ~~Council~~ *Parliament to come up with a proper response to your good news. Forgive the cross out—I'm still getting used to the new system.*

Along with the new government, First Landing has expanded. It seems we've unlocked the option to purchase Town Stones from the Colony Stone, so two new settlements are being developed out there in the frontier. As much as I was against it, some of the low-affinity species we rescued from another world—this is a very long story I'll share with you sometime—have decided to found their own town half a day's journey north of First Landing. Thanks to the Colony Stone providing the Town Stone for them, they'll be a member of our budding, as-yet-unnamed, and unofficial—more on this in a moment—new country.

Similarly, we've purchased another stone to make the mining community south of us official; the people have decided to name it Clearwater because of a lovely little stream that flows through the canyon. You can imagine the Ridonne Empire won't be pleased if they catch wind of our steady growth. You know that my friend, the aptly named champion of our people, Morgan Hall, traveled to the capital, Tharcray, to treat with them, right? Well, that's another very long story, and it's not resolved yet, but Morgan's last message to us was something along the lines of "The Ridonne have their hands full." Still, he cautioned us to stay in the frontier and to keep a low profile as we continue to expand.

You know humanity, Victor. We're working to replicate much of the tech we lost to the System with Energy-based versions, and frankly, if Morgan's right and the Ridonne are too busy to bother with us for much longer, I feel we'll be in a position to demand our place in this world when they finally get around to us. That's without considering you and your allies in the Free Marches. What a great name for a country, by the way!

So, on to the business at hand. I'm going to be tied up with some academy work, a special project for my sponsoring professor, for another month before I can take a break. The ~~Coun~~ Parliament has appointed a very good man, Alec Green, a dear friend of mine, to visit you as an ambassador. You mentioned that your friend Lady Rellia will be opening portals from Gelica and Persi Gables to your new settlement. I was going to send Alec to you with one of Morgan's Tower Portal Stones, but we, too, have some Artificers who've finally reached the skill level required to create them.

Would it be possible for Alec to travel through Persi Gables to you? If so, he'll bring a Portal Stone, and we can set up a direct connection to First Landing. If we did that, you could visit! Wouldn't that be great?

I've rambled on enough for now. I'll await your response about Alec and directions for how he might access the portal in Persi Gables before I get lost on another tangent.

I'll look forward to your reply.
With affection,
Olivia Bennet

"Jeez." Victor snapped the book shut. "I thought I was already busy."

2

A SHORT GOODBYE

Victor squatted down to better look into Deyni's dark turquoise eyes. He remembered the first time he saw her; he'd been behind bars, waiting for his big duel with Rellia. He'd noticed how her skin was more purple than red and how her hair and eyes were different from the Shadeni he'd met—most of them had red-toned eyes from pink or magenta to deep crimson. He reached toward her, picked up one of her long, greenish-blue braids, and held it between his fingers. He knew now that her coloring had much to do with her father, an Ardeni man she'd never met. "You know what?"

"What, Victor?" She always grinned when she spoke to him, as if she was anticipating him teasing her or, at the very least, saying something silly.

"I never put two and two together, but have you noticed how your hair and eyes are similar to Valla's?"

"Lady ap'Yensha?" Deyni's eyes opened in wonder, and Victor knew she was picturing Valla as she looked now with her glorious wings and silver highlights.

"Yeah. I wonder if maybe you two share a common ancestor. I'm trying to remember, but I don't think I've ever met another Ardeni with such a pretty color in their eyes."

Deyni's skin was far too dark to show her blush, but her eyes squinted in a bashful smile as she looked away. "Stop teasing me, Victor!"

"I'm not, silly!" They were outside of Victor's old wagon, and he was waiting for Tellen and Thayla to come to see him—Chala had run to fetch them when Victor approached. He gave Deyni's braid a little tug and laughed. "Sorry if I embarrassed you. I've been thinking a lot about bloodlines lately, that's all."

"I wish I could have your bloodline!" Deyni puffed out her chest and began to stomp around, arms out to her sides, her hands balled up in fists. "I'd smash my enemies and throw the Ridonne off the nearest mountain!"

Victor laughed and, tired of squatting, fell back onto the grass, folding his legs in front of himself. "You're still angry about the Ridonne?"

"Of course! They killed my friends!"

"Well, the ones who did that have been punished. It's not healthy to hold onto a grudge, but it's probably smart to keep a wary eye on the north. We don't want them to surprise us someday."

"That's right! I'll help to guard the Free Marches!"

Victor plucked a long blade of blue-green grass and stuck the stem in his mouth. When he chewed the juicy end, it was almost sweet. "Mm! I can see why Thistle likes this stuff."

A new voice spoke up behind him, "I've seen you eat! You couldn't live off grass."

Victor turned toward the voice, squinting into the bright sun. Chandri stood there, the sunlight like a halo around her short spiky hair. For the first time in quite a while, she'd washed the war paint from her face, but she bore some new tattoos—a fanged skull on her throat and, along her jawline, a series of crossed bones. She had other older tattoos to commemorate her hunts, but these were the first she'd added since Victor had known her. "Hi, Chandri."

"Milord." She mock curtsied, and Deyni broke into a giggle.

"Well, I'm glad to see you smiling. I like your new tattoos." Victor pulled up the sleeve of his comfortable gray shirt, or tunic, as the people in this world kept calling it, and displayed the tattoo she'd given him. "You do good work; this one's lasted through quite a few racial advancements."

Deyni stepped closer and leaned in to look at the markings. "What does it mean?"

Chandri squatted beside her and pointed to the blade-tipped hand. "This is the hand of the monster Victor slew." Her finger traced upward to the spears. "These are the six hunters whose lives he saved." She touched the bright orange sun. "This is the dawn that came, though we'd all thought we'd die before we saw it." Her voice was soft and her touch very gentle, and Victor was suddenly hit with a deep, gut-wrenching sense of wistful melancholy.

Though it felt absurd, he couldn't help wondering what his life would be like if he'd embraced his feelings for Chandri and never returned to Persi Gables. For the first time, he thought he understood the emotion that lurked behind Chandri's outwardly smiling eyes.

"I wonder if I'll earn a tattoo someday." Deyni's innocent remark broke the spell, saving him from further contemplation.

Chandri sat down at his side and closed her eyes, lifting her face to soak in the sunlight. Without opening them, she said, "You'll have to be choosy about what tattoos to put on yourself; otherwise, you'll run out of room. You'll be a famous beast tamer and adventurer, right?"

"That's right!"

Victor laughed, reaching out to pluck another blade of grass. "And you, Chandri? Do you still dream of exploring beyond the Silver Sea?"

"More than ever. I think my brush with death has only deepened my desire to see more of the world."

"I get that."

"I hate it! I want you to stay with us." Deyni stepped behind Chandri and began to pull her fingers through her hair. "I'd braid it for you, but it's not long enough yet."

Chandri smiled and replied, "I'm not going to leave right away, and when I do, you can bet I'll be back often." She leaned back, clearly enjoying Deyni's attentions, and narrowed her eyes at Victor. "I wonder if Victor can say the same."

"Well, Victor?" Deyni continued to stroke Chandri's hair as she locked eyes with him.

"The only thing I can promise is that I want to visit you. I want to spend time with you. Of course, I'll try. My first priority is helping Edeya, and I don't know what that will take. I bet I can visit after she's better, though."

"Just visit?" Chandri asked, relentless in her desire to keep him on the spot.

"Come on, Chandri. You know I've got other things calling me. Challenges I need to pursue, people I've made commitments to."

"People? Commitments? I only hear rumors; you haven't told us much." Now Victor heard a touch of bitterness in her tone, and he began to sense a clue to her recent distance.

"Is that what you've been bothered about? I thought you were mad at me about the attack . . ."

"What? I'm not mad at you!" Chandri scrunched her eyes shut and leaned back toward Deyni, who was listening and watching Victor's face while she massaged Chandri's scalp. "I would like to know more about you, though. I'd like to be more than an afterthought . . ."

"Come on, Chandri! We've been over this, haven't we? You're important to me! I'm sorry I've been so preoccupied, and I know I should spend more time with you." Victor paused, looking at Deyni and winking. "And other people."

"It's not just spending time; I know you're busy. I just think it would be nice if we spoke about more meaningful things more often. Like, just whom do you have commitments to out there?" She waved a hand toward the sky, and Victor figured she meant out in the world or perhaps beyond it.

"Yeah!" Deyni nodded and winked at Victor, and he almost laughed, wondering if she had any idea what he'd meant by his earlier wink.

"I'll give you an example. I mean, you already know about Edeya. I visited another world where an evil Warlord has dominated society for a thousand years or more. He's almost destroyed a species of titan there, and I befriended some of them. I sort of promised to return and try to restore them to their former strength. It's a big job because they had an artifact called an Ancestor Stone where they'd somehow preserved their titanic bloodline and the powers that come with it. The Warlord shattered it, and finding all the pieces will take a lot of work. Look!" Victor held up his wrist with his silver bracer and the single pink fragment of the Ancestor Stone. "I have one piece, but I have to find sixteen more."

"And it has to be you?" Deyni pressed, apparently taking over the questioning for Chandri, who'd leaned further back, soaking in the sun while Deyni played with her hair.

"Right now, I'm the only 'titan-blood' who's been to their world and offered to help." He shifted and looked past the wagon to the bustling activity of the Shadeni clan as they hurried to finish their travel preparations. He wondered what was taking Tellen and Thayla so long. "Anyway," he said, trying to wrap up the topic neatly, "you both should know this feels like home to me here on Fanwath. Especially with you and other people I care about here. I'm going to build a house or . . . something near to where you all settle, and of course I'll visit when I can."

"A house?" Chandri opened her eyes. "I thought that keep to the south was on your lands. The one guarding the pass."

"Yeah, but I haven't laid eyes on it, and I want to be near the sea, anyway; I'm not sure I want to move into a castle up there in the mountains. Besides, the lands I granted to your clan aren't far from the sea. According to Rellia, there's an easy ride over some grasslands and low hills, and then there you are."

"Victor!" Thayla called out, breaking into a jog over the patchy grass. Tellen wasn't with her, but her smile was bright, and she seemed untroubled.

"Mom!" Deyni gave Chandri a quick kiss on the forehead, then let go of her hair and ran to greet her mom.

"She's so sweet," Chandri said, sitting up to watch Deyni run. "I'm truly happy that Thayla and Tellen found love."

"Yeah." Victor nodded, suddenly a little choked up. "I'm glad that Deyni has you, Chandri. I hope you realize how much she looks up to you."

"Huh. Seems like you don't realize that *everyone* looks up to me!" Her tone was bright, and Victor had to give her a double take.

"Hey! There's the old Chandri I knew." His words made her smile, and though it looked as if she might want to reply, Thayla and Deyni arrived and plopped down in the grass.

"Sorry it took me so long! We've been drawing plans for our new settlement, and some of the families are arguing about . . . things. It's not easy for a community used to a nomadic lifestyle to trust that they have nothing to fear, no reason to believe an army will try to take their homes or property. Many want to keep to the old ways, and we're trying to find a compromise."

"Oh, don't worry about me. I just wanted to say goodbye; I thought you were heading out today."

"We are! We'll likely continue the debate on the trail." She paused, looked around for a few seconds, and then looked him right in the eyes. "Victor, how long do you think you'll stay here? Don't you need to establish your home? Set up some land grants to build up your income? You need to have a garrison or something in your keep . . ."

Victor held up his hands and groaned. "Thayla! You sound like Rellia and Borrius. I guess it's safe to say that I'm going to be terrible at this governing business, at least for right now. I'm probably going to appoint a governor. Someone to run the place and set up just the sorts of things you're asking me about, at least for now."

"And you're certain this person will respect your wishes and the promises you've made to us and the Naghelli?"

"Of course, I'll be certain about that! More importantly, Rellia knows what I've given you, and she supports it completely. Lam, too!" He gestured to the wagons. "The land grant I've written for you is legally binding and endorsed by all the stakeholders in the Free Marches. Your lands are completely yours.

Once the landholder republic is established, you'll only have to pay taxes for services that benefit the whole of the Free Marches—game wardens, roads, a standing military to protect the border, etcetera." Victor laughed and shook his head. "I wouldn't know any of that if I hadn't had a dozen lectures from Rellia over the last couple of weeks. Anyway, the governor I put in place will have to abide by the rules. Your lands are yours. I've relinquished all claims."

"And if you don't return?" Thayla frowned and leaned forward to grasp Victor's hand. "I'm not trying to be a problem, but this is the sort of argument we're hearing from our people, the ones reluctant to build a permanent settlement.

"Thayla, you have your deed, in writing, sealed by me, Rellia, and Lam. No matter how land is split down the road, your deed was written and approved by one hundred percent of the landholders in the Free Marches. I know you're worried that something will happen, but if for some reason I die or get captured, your rights won't go away. Valla says I should set up a trust or something so that, even if I never returned, my share of the Free Marches will continue to be governed the way I would like."

"Thank you, Victor." Thayla nodded. "That will help with our arguments, to know that even if you disappear, things will continue as you've promised. I know our deed entitles us to the lands, but we'll be surrounded by yours. Regardless, I pray that you won't disappear. Do you think we could share a Far Scribe book?"

"Yeah, definitely! We'll do that, and I'll also give one to my governor. We'll make sure things continue smoothly here whenever I'm away." Victor was glad to see the conversation moving along; he felt as though they were going in circles, but he supposed it made sense considering the history of the Shadeni with the Ridonne. They'd been displaced many times and often despite promises to the contrary. He offered Thayla another smile and looked past her to the largest cluster of Shadeni, imagining Tellen at the center, busily trying to calm people's worries. "Do you think he'll be able to break free?"

"Tellen? He'll say goodbye before we roll out, but he's going to be with those elders for a while. I'm sorry, Victor."

"Nah, it's no problem. I'd offer to speak with them, but I doubt it would help. Would it?"

"No, they trust you. It's just a general distrust of circumstances that has everyone worried. It's no secret that you plan to leave soon. How's Edeya, by the way?"

"The same. I wish I could do something for her. As I'm sure you know, it's frustrating not having someone here who's more knowledgeable about the subject. I mean, as little as I know, I'm finding that I know more than most when it comes to spirits and spirit Cores."

"Believe me, I know. Old Mother used to talk about how she wished she could offer you more guidance, but it's an affinity type that's been greatly maligned in this world. Most of what she knew, she taught herself. I hope that you'll be able to learn more when you travel, and ancestors willing, bring that knowledge home to us."

"Please, Victor!" Deyni said, scooting closer to Thayla so her mother could wrap an arm over her shoulders.

"You better believe I will, Deyni. We'll give you everything you need to grow your Core into something special." He glanced at the sky, judged the sun to be just a bit past its midpoint, and said, "Since Tellen's tied up, I think I'll run a different errand. I left an artifact in the Sea Keep and want to pick it up. If I can't figure it out here, I'll bring it with me when we travel."

Chandri perked up at Victor's words, sitting up straight and blinking her eyes against the sun's glare. "What sort of artifact?"

"It's a crown made of dark stone with weird runes all over it. Dunstan, the wampyr lord, was wearing it when I killed him. I didn't want to put it in my storage ring because it felt powerful, and I'm not sure why, but I had a feeling that it might be, you know, conscious."

Thayla nodded, distracted while she worked on fixing one of Deyni's braids. "So you hid it in the keep before you left?"

"Yeah."

Chandri jumped up. "I'll go with you!"

Thayla frowned and opened her mouth, but Victor could almost see the second thought cross her mind as she reconsidered what she'd been about to say. "That's up to Victor. We can spare you for now."

"Yeah, sure." Victor clambered to his feet as Deyni also jumped up.

"What about me?"

"Oh no, sweetie! I need your help with Starlight and Thistle. We must brush and feed them before we harness them to the wagon for days and days." Thayla snatched Deyni's hand and pulled on her to help herself stand.

Victor squatted down and held out his arms. "Give me a hug, you little huntress. I'll surely see you again before you leave, but I can never get too many hugs."

Deyni didn't need to be asked twice—she crashed into him and wrapped her arms around his neck. While he squeezed her, she whispered in his ear, "Promise this isn't a forever goodbye."

Victor felt that familiar lump in his throat and the sting in his eyes as tears tried to fight free. He wasn't sad or upset; he was just happy to have such an innocent, sweet person giving him her love. He hadn't been lying when he said he felt his home was there with the people he cared about. "No, *mija*, it's not forever. I promise. This is just a short goodbye." He didn't hesitate at all to break his earlier commitment about making promises.

As he realized how much he wanted to return, how much he cared about Deyni and so many others, another realization hit him—the reason he hadn't been very excited about the news from Olivia that an ambassador and a portal stone to First Landing would be on the way was because, to him, they were just strangers, regardless of their origin. He was more eager to see how the Naghelli made out than he was with First Landing's prospects. He supposed that would change as he came to know them. He hoped he might make friends there and figured he ought to work to build a relationship with Olivia.

Sighing, he gave Deyni one last squeeze, then stood up and pulled some Energy out of his Core to summon Guapo. As the mustang burst out of the pool of sparkling glory-attuned Energy, he turned to Chandri and grinned. "Ready to see how fast this guy can run?" Guapo interrupted her answer by rearing onto his hind legs and whinnying mightily. Victor laughed and slapped his rump. "You big showoff!"

3

AMBASSADOR

Victor sat in the grass beside Edeya, watching Valla, Polo Vosh, Kethelket, Lam, and Lesh have a wild practice melee a short way down the slope. He'd already been in half a dozen brawls that morning, and it was his turn to sit out with the incapacitated young woman. It had been Polo's idea—having "last one standing" contests once a week. There were rules, of course. Victor wasn't allowed to go berserk, two hits from any source meant you were "out," and because of the wild nature of a free-for-all, no blows to the head or neck were permitted. That was just for starters; others also had limitations on their powers. For instance, Kethelket couldn't use his full shadow speed, and Lesh couldn't belch acid.

Victor snorted a quick laugh, gently squeezing Edeya's tiny limp hand in his. "He hates it when I say that, *chica*. 'Belch.' That's what it looks like, though! He doesn't breathe acid out in a spray. It's more like he coughs up a big glob of the stuff." Victor had spoken a lot to Lesh over the last few weeks, and he'd come to understand that Lesh's decision to reject the System's quest to kill him had been primarily because he'd witnessed Victor breathing his ancestor's fire. Breath Cores were a big deal among Lesh's people—they weren't born with them and had to evolve to gain one. Once done, the stronger a dragonkin's breath, the more respect he or she might earn. Apparently, Lesh had never seen anything like what Victor had done to Eric's army of reavers.

Victor laughed as Polo roared in frustration, stomping off the field with his great axe hung over his shoulder. "Too many fast ones in there. I'd gain more with a long fight against that dragon friend of yours."

"This was your idea." Victor chuckled and patted the grass beside him. "Take a load off."

Polo glanced at the sun, saw it was nearly midday, and shook his head. "I would, Victor, but I'm already pushing it. Rellia's finally going to sit down with me and talk about my land grant. I've got family arriving in a day or two through the new portal, and we'll be surveying for a suitable building site."

"Oh? That's exciting, isn't it? I don't remember you talking about your family, Polo. Will I get a chance to meet them?"

"Aye! Of course! Perhaps I'll invite you to see the building site, or—" He paused, eyeing Edeya's motionless form. "If you need to leave soon, maybe when you return, I'll have a proper dining hall and kitchen constructed."

"Okay. Whichever works out, you know we'd love to come by. You're right about Edeya, however. I'm hoping we'll have world portals accessible sooner rather than later. As people come through from the cities and claim their citizenship, the advancement options on the stone are opening up quicker than ever."

"Aye. I heard as much from Rellia when I was pestering her about my lands." Polo squinted toward the sun again and raised his voice to be heard over the clash of weapons, shouts, and curses as the nearby fight escalated. "Tell me, Victor, what have you decided to do about your holdings? Borrius mentioned you approached him about governing for you, but he's going to be busy with his own claim."

"Yeah. I'd hoped he'd be interested, but he wanted farmland, and I guess Rellia put him further north, near Old Keep. He doesn't want to split his time visiting my properties." Victor shrugged. "He told me he'd speak to some qualified people he knew."

"Aye, that's why he brought it up with me." Polo laughed, shaking his head. "Not because he thought I should do it, mind you, but because he knows I am good friends with a man named Gorro ap'Dommic—he's currently acting as the steward for my estate near Tharcray. Well, he was until I put him in charge of its sale. He should be arriving through the Gelica portal in a few days."

"Oh yeah? Borrius thinks he's the man for the job?" Victor shifted, leaning back to look up at the big furry Vodkin more easily.

"Yes, and I won't need his services on these new lands; my family and I will have things well in hand." Polo turned toward the melee and laughed as Lam threw her hammer to the ground in frustration, stomping toward them. "Gorro is a very experienced steward. I hired him right after Lam and I cleared the Dolondric Ruins—I was flush with treasure, and he'd just left the service of a Ridonne who'd granted the estate he was managing to a cousin. He's been at it for decades—got his start in the Legion, of course; that's how Borrius knows him."

"Kethelket cheats!" Lam announced, flopping onto the grass beside Edeya.

"Ha!" Polo laughed, and Victor just grinned, plucking a blade of grass to chew on. "In any case, Victor, shall I send him to see you when he arrives?"

"That'd be great. Thanks, Polo."

"A pleasure." The Vodkin bowed at the waist toward Lam, a comical maneuver for a man as bulky as he, and then waved. "I'm off to see Rellia, then." As he turned to leave, he hollered at the three combatants left on the field, "Good luck!" Then he strolled down the grassy slope toward the ever-growing settlement.

"What was that all about?"

"He's recommending someone to be my governor. Is that the right word? He said the guy was a steward. Maybe I should be calling him that."

"No. Not with lands as extensive as yours. The person you hire will need to manage settlements, attend political meetings, and maintain your militia. Governor is the right term." Lam leaned forward and shouted, "That's it, Valla! Keep his flank!"

"You want her to win?" Victor grinned around the blade of grass.

"Of course! She eliminated me, so if she wins, that makes me look better." Lam sighed, turning to examine Edeya and lifting a handkerchief to wipe at the corners of her eyes. "This breeze is making her eyes water. That damn circlet doesn't make her blink often enough."

"Shit. Does it control that much? I thought her blinks would be automatic."

"No. She'd be unconscious without it. Even her breathing is shallow and barely enough to keep her alive without it." Lam tucked her handkerchief away and gestured toward the slope leading down to the settlement. "The stone's Level Eight, and you know Rellia's literature says we should start seeing world travel options at Level Ten. Will you be ready to leave as soon as it opens up?"

"Yeah, I'll be ready. It could be sooner, you know; we're only a few steps away on the advancement tree. Rellia's been steering the colony's development toward our goal. By the way, I've been corresponding with my cousin, and she says the human Colony Stone is almost Level Twenty, but they don't have any options for world travel yet. I guess they've been very general about their advancement, not focusing the way we have." It had been a week since

Victor's first message from Olivia, and since then, they'd written back and forth several times.

"That makes sense. We're missing many System-developed infrastructure items—we're building our own walls, our own plumbing and sewage system, our own roads, and so much more. We could have spent advancement points on all of those things, had them done instantly and probably a lot more seamlessly integrated with the landscape."

"Yeah, but we're getting all sorts of intangible benefits going down the tree toward world travel—Energy storage, mapping, trade beacons, communication relays, the astral observatory." Victor pointed to the enormous white tower jutting up from the sea's edge. It looked very out of place among all the half-constructed structures, but it was undeniably awesome. Victor liked how the top was made of some kind of crystal, and he knew that the more prominent facets were lenses. He'd been in it a few times, peering through the weird brass and crystal scopes that could be aligned and moved to face the different external lenses. It was fun and interesting, but in the end, to him, it was just like looking through a telescope, and he'd never been into that sort of thing.

Lam nodded. "That one took much of our savings, but it ranked the stone up from five to seven. Perhaps the next . . ." Lam was cut off as Lesh jogged over to them and flopped onto his back, shaking the ground enough to jostle Edeya and send her toppling backward. Lam caught her, scowling at Lesh. "Have some care, you thunderak!"

Lesh looked at Victor and narrowed his green, reptilian eyes. "Thunderak?"

"Uh, giant lizards they use to pull heavy loads." Victor grinned, finding the moniker rather apt.

"Pardon my bulk, Lady Lam."

Victor nudged the giant man's shoulder with his boot. "Who got you?"

"One from Kethelket and one from the angel."

Victor chuckled at Lesh's nickname for Valla—Victor had started it, calling her an angel. When he'd described what he meant by the word, some of the others had taken it up. Valla certainly fit the bill with her big silvery wings and beautiful countenance. She'd paid one of the better armor artisans who'd come through the Gelica portal to adjust the enchantment on her wyrm-scale armor, giving it the ability to open holes to accommodate the wings sprouting from her back. With that armor, her shiny silver helm, and, well, everything else about her, she either looked like an avenging Valkyrie or, yeah, some kind of angel.

"Anyway," Lam said, pointedly looking over Lesh's thick body toward Victor, "we just need the travel beacons, the astral cartography crystal, and the portal enclosure. Whether we need Level Ten or not, I think we'll be there soon."

"Yeah. As more citizens arrive and we continue to collect Energy, our advancement credits build up pretty fast. Still, another Energy bead infusion might not go amiss. I'm still holding my million from the conquest . . ."

"You'll need that," Lesh said, rolling to his side and lifting his head on an elbow as he watched Kethelket and Valla weave their lightning-quick dance. "There's no telling what things will cost in the world hub, and you know, the System won't let you travel for free just because you rule these lands."

"Yeah." Victor sighed, shaking his head. Nothing was ever easy. "Right. Well . . . Oho! Good job, Valla!" She'd done some sort of rolling maneuver using her wings, curved before her like a moving shield, and come around behind Kethelket, giving him a swift gash on his left calf. "Is that the match?" he asked Lesh.

"Aye! They each had one mark already."

Victor stood up and reached down to take Edeya's hand. As he gently tugged it, she stood up—the artificed circlet she wore made her very compliant, moving with gentle prompts from her caretakers. Lam also stood and took the young Ghelli's hand from him as Valla strutted over the grass, her sword, Midnight, resting on her armored shoulder and a very self-satisfied smile on her face. "I heard you grousing!" She laughed, pointing at Lesh, still lying like a small hillock on the grass. He didn't respond, just grumbled and yawned.

"Nicely done, Valla." Victor looked past her to Kethelket and nodded when their eyes locked. "Not bad for your farewell match."

"Oh, that's right!" Lam looked up from where she'd been straightening Edeya's coat collar. "Your people will fly tonight?"

"Aye! We've resupplied and rested and are eager to begin the construction of Nighthome. We've three Ghelli families already committed to joining us, Lam—veterans from the conquest, eager to help mend old rifts. I hope you and Edeya will visit when you're back."

"I'm sure we will, Kethelket. I'm just as eager to bandage over old wounds."

"Who's this?" Lesh rumbled, and Victor turned to follow his gaze. An Ardeni man wearing Rellia's house livery was running up the well-worn path from the settlement.

"Hmm." Victor frowned. "Rellia should be meeting with Polo." The whole group grew quiet as the man made his final approach, his breath huffing heavily as he came to a stop twenty paces away.

"Lord Victor! A man is requesting you! He's just come through the portal from Persi Gables."

"Oh yeah?" Victor looked at the others, all staring, waiting to hear more. "See you all a bit later. If we don't speak before you leave, Kethelket, you know how to get ahold of me." The two of them had exchanged Far Scribe books. He shook his hand, and Kethelket stared into his face, suddenly serious.

"Of course. Thank you again for letting us select such a fine location for the new town."

"Are you kidding me? Your people earned it. It'll be nice having such good neighbors, anyway."

Before he and Kethelket could go further down their mutually congratulatory path, Lam called out to the messenger, "Who is it?"

"Oh, um, it's a man from the human colony in the Ridonne frontier. Alec Green." The messenger looked at Victor almost apologetically.

"That'll be our ambassador from the humans," Valla explained when she saw Lam's blank expression.

Victor let go of Kethelket's hand and turned to the messenger. "Let's go, Valla; you can make sure I don't say something too stupid."

"You think she can save you from that?" Lam chuckled, and Lesh snorted, shifting his bulk to wink at her more easily.

"All right, all right. Don't make me drag you both out there for a quick thrashing." Victor grabbed Valla's hand and started walking down the slope. He gestured to the messenger. "Lead the way."

"Farewell!" Kethelket called.

"Don't make promises you don't intend to keep!" Lesh rumbled.

Lam didn't say anything more, but Victor could feel her smiling eyes following him and Valla as they walked down the slope. "They've lost all their respect now that the war's over."

"Oh, don't begrudge them their laughs. They only tease you because they know they can't compete with you in other ways." Valla tightened the grip on his hand and lifted it to her chest, pulling it close as she cupped it with her other hand.

"Like neither will ever have someone like you? How'd I get so lucky? Have I mentioned I love you?" Victor almost laughed when he saw the messenger's hurried but stiff, awkward gait. He was clearly embarrassed to hear their conversation. Victor decided to spare the poor guy and change the subject. "You've really gotten good at dealing with Kethelket's two-weapon style."

"I know! He's a difficult opponent, but I've made some good gains over the last weeks. It helps to have your inspiration active while we spar. Well, and let's not forget he's only using a fraction of his full speed."

"Even so. Your grace with those wings is really something. I notice you're using Midnight one-handed more and more; have you ever thought about a second blade or maybe a shield?"

"Perhaps someday. I enjoy having the option to grip her hilt with both hands for more powerful swings."

"Well, I don't know jack about sword fighting, so I'll leave that to you."

"Jack?" Valla laughed as they stepped off their gravel path onto the new cobbled roadway that led east out of town.

"Uh, it's short for jack shit, and no, I have no idea where it comes from."

"Colorful."

Victor, currently only a little taller than she, looked into her smiling eyes above her flushed, pale blue cheeks and paused to lean down and kiss her on the lips. As always, she reciprocated, and Victor marveled at his luck for the second time in just a few minutes. When he straightened up, he said, "Does my word choice embarrass you?"

"No! I love how you can sound stiff and formal as though you're channeling Borrius one minute and then break into a string of curses that would drain the color from a soldier's face the next." They'd stopped, and the messenger had taken a few steps before realizing it. Victor could feel him turn to observe them. When Valla refused to look away, Victor stared into her silver and teal irises and wondered if it was true about eyes—could he see her spirit in there? He almost thought he could, which made him want to try harder, but her smile widened, and she gave him a playful shove. "Come on, *Lord* Victor! The ambassador is waiting."

"Fair enough. Messenger! Where'd you leave the ambassador?"

"In the new gardens adjacent to the travel pavilion, my lord."

"Ah, good choice. Near my travel home?"

"Aye." He gestured to the road. "Shall we continue?"

"Proceed." Victor laughed at his formality. He was fairly sure of the answer but asked, "Were you part of the campaign?"

"No, my lord. I'm a member of Lady ap'Yensha's household staff. I came through the portal from Gelica."

"Ah. Well, welcome to the Free Marches."

The man paused, turned, and performed a short but slow, deliberate bow. "I'm eternally grateful for the opportunity to make a life here, my lord."

When the young man turned and continued walking, Victor followed, suddenly sobered by his show of respect. He'd been about to judge the messenger, almost mocking him mentally for calling him "lord" when any of the men and women who'd fought in the campaign would have been addressing him as "sir." He chastised himself—not every man or woman was cut out for war, and those who'd come through the portals to join the colony were just as valuable right now as anyone else; without their numbers, their contributions, the growth would have been much, much slower. It would have taken years to open the deeper advancement options on the Colony Stone.

"Something on your mind?" Valla asked, still holding his hand with both of hers.

"Nah. I just have a lot to learn, Valla. Every time I think I'm getting a grip on things, I realize how much I don't know, how much of what I think I know is wrong."

She smiled and leaned her head against his shoulder, speaking softly. "And that makes you a good leader. The worst kinds of leaders are those who think they know everything and refuse to admit when they're mistaken."

When they arrived at the gardens, the messenger bowed and took his leave, and Victor led the way through the curved pathways, his boots crunching on the deep bed of round, rust-colored pebbles the herbalists, Nature Casters, and engineers assigned to them had imported. Beds of new flora—herbs, flowers, and plants of a thousand different varieties—lined the walkways, and a fountain burbled at each junction of paths. It wasn't pristine yet; dirt and mud marred the marble stepping stones and benches, the beds were only about half planted with their future occupants, and trellises were still under construction. Still, it was a good deal more done than when Victor had decided to move his travel home in, placing it at the end of one of the far-flung paths.

They found Alec Green sitting on a bench, admiring a little fountain shaped like a bulbous flower with long thorny stems adorned with tiny, delicate songbirds. The water trickled out of the pale yellow stone flower petals and dribbled pleasantly into the basin. Alec was a slender, average-looking fellow, but his sandy-brown hair was neatly combed, his short beard well manicured, and his soft brown eyes full of wonder as he took in the sight of Victor and Valla as they rounded a bend in the path. He jumped to his feet, straightening the lapels on his plush, velvety gray jacket. "Victor?" He stepped toward them, holding out a hand. "I'm Alec Green from First Landing."

Victor grinned and reached out to wrap the man's slender hand in his own, giving it a—to him—gentle squeeze. "Nice to meet you, Alec. This is Valla ap'Yensha." As soon as he released the man's hand, Valla took it.

Alec smiled and stared, perhaps a little dumbstruck, into Valla's eyes. "Nice to meet you!" Still shaking Valla's hand, he forcefully turned back to Victor. "I've heard a lot about you—from Olivia Bennet and also people in Persi Gables. Ha! From the tales, I'd expected you to be twenty feet tall!"

"Oh," Valla laughed, "sometimes he's nearly that tall." When she winked, Victor had to laugh—poor Alec's face said he didn't know whether or not he was being teased.

He decided to bail him out and change the subject. "I'm glad you've come to represent the other humans, Alec. I want to build a relationship with your colony, but if we can advance the stone enough, I'll be leaving soon. It's good that I'll get a chance to introduce you to everyone around here before I go."

Alec took a step back and looked Victor up and down. "You're leaving?"

"I have a friend who needs to travel to a more advanced world, one with more world portals open."

"Ah! Olivia said something like that in her messages, something about you all focusing on advancing your colony to open world travel."

"Yep."

"You couldn't travel from one of the other cities?"

Victor sighed. He didn't want to get into a lengthy explanation, so he tried to summarize things quickly and with some finality. "The Ridonne haven't opened much world travel for their subordinate cities, and if I went to Tharcray and asked to use their Colony Stone . . . well, let's just say the journey is long, and I'd as likely as not start a war I don't think we have the stomach for right now."

"I see. Well, perhaps my proposal will be of interest."

"You come with a proposal?" Valla asked, wrapping her fingers around Victor's elbow, leaning into him a little while she smiled at Alec.

Alec nodded, grinning. "We'd be willing to kick in a substantial sum of Energy beads toward your stone's development if you could do us a little favor."

4

THE PROPOSAL

Victor felt a sudden urge to direct Alec toward the Sea Keep, where Rellia was currently managing her operations. He'd been speaking to the guy for less than a minute, and he was already talking about favors. Victor knew relationships between towns, countries, and political factions were built on mutual benefits, but he'd hoped to just talk to the guy and show him around, not start wheeling and dealing immediately. His scowl must have been more evident than he'd intended because Alec held up his hands and after a quick shaky laugh said, "Let me stress, it's not a big favor. I mean, it's not for you, but for us, and it might mean the difference between continued existence and destruction—Olivia's words, not mine."

Valla squeezed Victor's arm, her cool fingers pressing into his biceps. "Don't worry about him, Alec. He's always frowning like that. Why don't we show you to Victor's home, and you can tell us about this favor over a cup of tea and a crumble cake one of Victor's admirers gave us?"

Victor chuckled at Valla's description of the cake one of Dunstan's former thralls had baked for him. "Actually, that's a good idea. I bet you'll be interested to hear about the woman who baked it. She's a human from a world other than Earth."

"Oh?" Alec's eyebrows rose, his surprise evident.

Victor nodded, gesturing toward the path that would lead to his travel home. "Yeah. I'm not sure if it's a coincidence or . . ." Victor laughed at himself, shaking his head. "No, never mind that. It's definitely not a coincidence.

The System chose vampires and their undead minions to invade these lands. The world they came from was settled by Death Casters who'd fled Earth when the Energy stopped flowing there."

"Ah, seriously? So, your 'conquest' was against invaders from another world?" Alec turned when Victor gestured to his left. Straight ahead, down a long flower-lined gravel lane, sat Victor's jade travel home. "Oh, what an interesting dwelling!"

"It's Victor's travel home. He'll build something more substantial eventually." Valla led the way up the steps, and Victor stood back, holding the door as she and Alec stepped inside.

"Ah! Dimensional magic. We have a few structures employing it back in First Landing, but not so heavily as this one! Well, other than Morgan's tower, I suppose."

"Morgan . . ." Victor frowned, scratching his chin. "That's the one who went to Tharcray, yeah? Olivia told me about him."

"Right."

"How'd that go?" Valla asked, taking the lead down the hallway toward the dining area.

"Um, he hasn't brokered any sort of lasting deal, but he did manage to get some assurances that the Ridonne don't care too much about us at the moment. They're dealing with some inner strife and political issues concerning their presence in other worlds. In fact, Morgan's gone off-world, which threw our little community for a bit of a loop . . ." Alec trailed off as he stepped into the dining hall and the adjacent kitchen area, his eyes taking in the big table, the bright daylight streaming through the kitchen windows, and the vaulted ceiling with the skylight. "What a space! I'd never have guessed looking at the exterior."

"Take a seat there with Victor, and I'll put together a snack." Valla didn't wait for any objections, walking past the table and into the kitchen.

Victor rapped his knuckles on the table's smooth surface. "Anywhere you like, Alec."

"Thanks." Alec sat down in the chair closest to the head of the table on the near side, so Victor moved around to sit across from him. As soon as he'd taken his seat, Alec hit him with some questions. "You're saying you had to fight invaders from another world to win these lands? I thought the conquest would just involve fighting monsters or, well, 'natives' is the right word, I guess."

"I'd have a hard time justifying something like that, but yes, the System made that part easy by filling these lands with undead monstrosities." Victor shook his head, grinning wryly. "Don't you think it's interesting to learn that there used to be Energy users on Earth powerful enough to flee through portals they created?"

"It's more than interesting. It conflicts with what we thought we knew of the System. Morgan was the first human to wake here on Fanwath, and according to him, the System didn't recognize humanity right away. It makes you wonder how broad the System is and how often each part of it communicates with the others. Does it send out updates once a month, once a century? Does it need to do that, or does it just know everything that's happening everywhere all the time? Sounds more like God than a 'system,' if so."

"Yeah. I'm pretty damn sure the System isn't God." Victor chuckled and looked over his shoulder to check on Valla. He hated being responsible for entertaining strangers.

"What makes you say that?"

"Uh, the fact that there are plenty of species that existed and worked with Energy long before the System came around. My ancestors, for instance."

"Ah! That's one of the things you might be able to help us with. How about I go over my little proposal? Is it too soon? I hope I'm not overstepping . . ."

"Nah, it's fine." Victor was annoyed, but he also was happy to let Alec talk for a while. It would give Valla time to rejoin the conversation.

"Well, Olivia indicated in our communications that when she's brought up the idea of you coming to First Landing, you've been less than enthusiastic. She's a bit of an outlier among our citizenry, what with her unusually high affinity with multiple attunements and her unnatural proclivity for mastering new magic." Alec held up a hand and laughed. "Don't get me wrong—from what we've gathered, dealing with some unpleasant nobility and the locals in our neck of the woods, it seems humans generally have high Energy affinity, but Olivia's a standout. I'm bringing this up because she's often banging the drum about how important advancing in levels and gaining power is when she comes to town, and her words are often less than enthusiastically received."

"Yeah?" Victor was having a hard time figuring out why he should care.

"Yeah. I mean, there are some who are pretty gung ho about leveling and exploring, but oftentimes, their abilities and enthusiasm don't exactly match up. Take me, for instance. I was pretty happy just running a business in town; I opened the first tavern and made a killing. I expanded the business, and now I've got a full-blown hotel—well, 'inn' is probably more accurate. I'm a Level Eighteen tavernkeeper." Alec smiled, shaking his head at a pleasant memory.

"When I first told Olivia that was my class, she laughed and laughed. She'd already been at Fainhallow, you see, and was studying about classes with a great deal more . . . gravitas, shall we say?"

"Uh-huh." Victor nodded, glancing again for Valla and sighing with relief when he saw her approaching with a tray. "Here we go. You're going to love this cake, Alec."

"Oh, I'm certain you're right." He paused his discourse to watch Valla set down the tray with three steaming mugs, a crock of whipped butter, and the sweet, nut-and-fruit-loaded crumble cake.

"Help yourself." Valla smiled and sat at the head of the table between the two men.

"Don't mind if I do." Alec grinned, took one of the mugs, and then slathered a slice of the cake with some of the soft creamy butter. Once his little plate was before him, he sipped the tea, smiled, and sighed, then took a bite of the cake. "Mm!" His eyes glazed over as he chewed. Valla helped herself, and Victor, of course, carved off a generous slice. The conversation was put on hold for a few minutes once they were all working on their snack, and Alec continued to exclaim about how good it was.

"So," Valla said, pushing her plate away. "You were telling Victor that there are some ambitious folks among you, but they're a minority? Is that the right way to explain things?"

"Ah, no, not exactly. I was about to use myself as an example of how most of us are ambitious but not in the way that makes us personally powerful. I'm very interested in seeing my business grow, gaining wealth, and buying properties. Back on Earth, such success would eventually have made me a powerful person. Here, according to Olivia and our few run-ins with less than savory folks, I've learned that that kind of success can be very fleeting. Everything I have can be taken away in a snap." To illustrate, Alec snapped his fingers. "I believe it, Olivia believes it, but many of the people in our settlement think that our government will protect them and that they can continue to focus on finding success as they've always done."

"Well, they're not exactly wrong." Victor shrugged, not seeing the problem. "It's the same in native cities; not everyone is out challenging dungeons or going to war. Plenty of people build businesses or lead small service-oriented lives."

"Right, but according to what I've learned from Morgan's correspondence and Olivia's studies, this world has been rather sheltered. Haven't the Ridonne limited travel beyond this world? Haven't they themselves grown powerful beyond even the 'heroes' who make their living facing dungeons and whatnot? Isn't it only a matter of time before a more dangerous world connects to this one? What if a true powerhouse comes through and makes some real trouble for us? If I can read between the lines well enough, that's what's happening in Tharcray. I think the Ridonne have stunted the growth of this world to their own detriment. I believe they've encountered something they're struggling with, and due to their imposed limitations, the rest of the populace isn't in a position to help them."

"I mean, I don't know what you've heard, but the 'trouble' the Ridonne have been having might just be me . . ."

"Oh, I heard about your encounter with their Legion. Talk of it was all over Persi Gables when I passed through. That's not it, however. Morgan contacted us about the Ridonne's 'troubles' a good four months prior."

"Why so cryptic? Can't he just tell you what's up?"

"I would think so, but he's . . . incommunicado."

Valla set her steaming cup down and cleared her throat. "Okay, Alec, we're losing sight of what you actually want."

"Right! I was hoping that Victor, and you, of course,"—he nodded at Valla—"would speak to our populace. I was hoping you'd sit down and have a sort of town hall where you speak about what you've seen on other worlds, or from other worlds, and why it's important to . . . what's the word they use, um, cultivate power? That's it, cultivate. Why it's important to build up a Core, to gain levels, and advance your bloodline."

Victor grunted, shaking his head. "It seems pretty damn obvious to me, Alec. You really need me to tell people why power is important?"

"Our people are stubborn, Victor. We've got a hundred engineers working on reinventing automobiles and airplanes using Energy-driven engines. We've got people making repeating cannons, landmines, and machine guns. I mean, it's great, but Olivia says one 'elder' being could wipe them all out, that someone who'd achieved Tier Ten or, hell, even Tier Five could probably ignore most of the war machines we can come up with. What's worse is that our Artisan Class citizens are far outstripping the cultivators—we've learned to build portal stones, for instance. What's going to happen when we open a connection to a high-tier world, and someone truly powerful sees our potential as, well, as slaves?"

"So you want me to come there and scare them?"

Alec laughed, shaking his head. "I mean, that might work, but Olivia had the idea that you could just talk about your time in, um, I have it in my notes, but what was the name of the world where . . ."

"Zaafor?" Valla supplied.

"That's it! She says you met many powerful beings and that you had to flee because of a villainous warlord or some such. Is that right?"

Victor sighed and nodded. "Sure, Alec. You're right that opening your-selves up to advanced worlds and powerful people before you're ready is a real risk. In fact, I wouldn't be surprised if the Ridonne's tight control over world travel has a lot to do with that, but that won't stop travel in the other direc-tion. The System can be a real bitch, but it won't send a 'challenge' here that's much beyond you. That doesn't mean a powerful individual or, yeah, warlord couldn't find their way here. If they did, if they opened their own gateway without the System's help, then they could easily dominate this planet."

"So, just a town hall?" Valla pressed, trying to pin down the commitment Alec was looking for.

"And perhaps a demonstration. Our Artificers have been building war machines—Energy-driven automatons. Think of a tank crossed with a robot. There's a faction in our government who think we're already strong enough to take on the Ridonne, that they're just backward medieval tyrants whom we can steamroll like Patton taking on a Roman legion."

"Patton?" Valla frowned, slowly turning her cup between her palms.

"He's talking about people from Earth."

"Oh, I'm sorry, Lady ap'Yensha! I was trying to draw a comparison between a modern military with guns and heavy artillery versus an army using spears and swords." When Valla continued to frown, her eyes betraying her confusion, he added, "I mean, I'm sure Victor has described our world to you a little, yes? We didn't have Energy or magic, but we had technology far beyond what you see on Fanwath. We had weapons that could strike a person down instantly from great distances. We had bombs and missiles that could destroy entire cities. Olivia worries we'll go down that road again, become too sure of our capabilities, and then run into someone with deific powers. Victor here might be able to give our populace a taste of that. That's all I'm saying."

Valla nodded and, to Victor's delight, continued leading the conversation. "If you want Victor to do battle with your automatons, you'll need to tell us what you'll put on the table."

Alec nodded. "I understand you want to advance your Colony Stone."

"That's right. We need to advance at least two more ranks before we can open world travel."

"That's what we can help you with. We've stockpiled a lot of Energy beads through our own development and from trade with neighboring towns and villages. I have it on good authority from our development committee that a million beads will go a long way in the early Colony Stone ranks."

"Is that what you're offering? A million beads?" Valla didn't betray much, but Victor knew her well enough to hear the excitement in her voice. A million beads would probably get them where they needed to be.

"That's right. What do you say?" To Alec's credit, he didn't break eye contact with Valla to gauge Victor's response. It was probably a good thing, because Victor was sold and didn't have a good poker face.

"Victor and I will visit your town and answer your questions, and Victor will destroy your automatons for one and a half million beads."

Victor almost laughed, surprised to hear Valla being so cutthroat. However, Alec didn't laugh and didn't even look surprised. He smiled, nodded, and said, "It's a deal, but you've reached the limit of my negotiation authority, so please don't push it any harder."

"Okay, Victor?" Valla looked at him for the final word.

"Hmm, I guess. I don't mind beating the shit out of some robots, but I'm not really excited to be on the spot answering questions on a stage. I'll do it for Edeya, though."

"Edeya?" Alec was smiling ear to ear as if he'd just made the deal of the century.

Valla began gathering the empty plates, stacking them on the tray. "Our friend. She's the reason we need to open world travel as soon as possible. That said, Ambassador, when shall we depart for your town?"

"I left the portal stone with the steward of your, um, travel pavilion. I'm ready to go whenever you'd like, though I'd hoped to meet the other leaders here and perhaps establish a residence—I intend to participate in the community you're building."

Victor pushed his chair back and stood up. "It's early still. Let's take him around. Rellia and Borrius will want to meet him. We'll get him a room in the inn, and then—" Victor paused for breath and to lock eyes with Alec. "If you're feeling up to it, we can go to First Landing in the morning. I'm sorry to rush things, but I feel like I've put my friend's welfare on hold long enough. She needs help, and if you're offering the Energy to advance the Stone, I'd like to do my part as soon as possible."

Alec, too, stood, slowly nodding his head. "The inn, hmm? Well, it'll do for now. Will I be permitted to build an official embassy eventually?"

"Definitely. If Rellia won't allow you one here, then you can build it on my lands."

"Your lands? They're separate from these?" Alec looked confused, and Valla chuckled. She stood and moved beside him, taking his elbow and steering him toward the front of the house.

"There's much you need to understand, Ambassador. I don't know how much Victor told Olivia, but these lands, the Free Marches, are more vast than the entirety of the Ridonne frontier. Even after gifting deeds to his allies, Victor's share of the conquered lands numbers nearly thirty million acres. That's assuming we don't continue to expand, pushing into the untamed lands further south." Victor listened to her as she and Alec walked ahead, his mind struggling to stay focused as he thought about everything Alec had told him.

The idea that humans had come to this world and were immediately trying to recapture the way of life they'd left behind didn't surprise him, but it certainly bothered him. Of course they'd try to make planes and tanks and machine guns. Of course they'd see Energy as just another fuel source, a way to power their tech. He hoped they weren't all focused on such things. They couldn't be, could they? Some among them had to have awoken Spirit Cores. Surely some of them had learned to see their inner selves and auras. There was so much more to Energy than, well, energy. It was the essential, vital force of everything and the connection every cultivator had to the universe. If a person didn't see that, didn't internalize and process the gifts Energy could grant, they'd never understand. Victor would have to show them. He'd have to give them a glimpse of the power of a sleeping god.

5

FIRST LANDING

Victor sat on the stone bench in the new travel pavilion and watched Valla speak to Alec Green about the structure. They were waiting for the other members of their "delegation" to First Landing, and he was trying to relax, trying not to think about having to answer questions in front of hundreds or maybe thousands of strangers. He'd opted not to wear his armor, at least not at first, and he felt comfortable in his silky gray button-up shirt and soft, slim-fitting black trousers. Valla had gotten them for him from a tailor she knew—a man who'd come through the portal from Gelica. He appreciated that they weren't overly fancy but simply very well made from materials that were clearly a cut above what he'd been wearing for most of his time on Fanwath.

His new silver-toed black boots were polished to a glossy sheen, and Life-drinker rested comfortably behind his shoulder, held snugly by the new magical harness that matched his belt and boots. All in all, he felt good because he knew he looked good. Valla said that was important when you were speaking in public—to look and feel good about yourself. In all honesty, Victor knew he shouldn't be worried; he was Quinametzin, and all he had to do was relax his hold on his alter ego a little, and he'd have no trouble speaking on just about any topic in front of just about anyone.

"We've built a similar structure ourselves, though we've been calling it a portal hall—so far, we've only set up a portal to Persi Gables and now to your settlement. Olivia will undoubtedly pick up a portal stone to bring to

Fainhallow next time she visits home." Alec was nodding, rubbing his chin, staring at something across the open-air structure. Victor followed his gaze and saw that he was looking at the shimmering mirror-like portal to Gelica on the other side of the pavilion. It wasn't usually open, and Victor watched as what looked like a large family began to come through, gathering on the stone dais on this side of the portal.

"Looks like more new citizens," he grunted.

"Ah, yes." Alec nodded, watching as one of the yellow-robed concierge staff Rellia's people had appointed hurried forward to greet the new family and guide them to the settlement registration center.

"Here comes your aide, Victor." Valla pointed as Nia strode through the big archway that led toward the center of town. The former vampire thrall had changed quite a lot in the weeks since the end of the campaign, and Victor could see she'd made an effort to look nice for their visit to First Landing.

Nia had exchanged her black clothing and leather for a knee-length flowing blue dress with long sleeves trimmed in lacy blue gauze. She still wore high leather boots, which Victor thought was kind of cool, but he wondered what the locals thought of her style. She'd washed out the black oil or grease or whatever she'd used to slick her hair back but still styled it in braids adorned with polished ivory charms and jewels. Victor could see she'd recently scrubbed her face from the rosy pink hue of her cheeks and the somewhat inflamed nature of her many scars.

When she approached, Nia bowed quickly and nervously, her eyes darting from Valla to Alec and then settling on Victor, reclining on the bench. "Lords, Lady." Victor found it strange to see her standing beside Valla. In the old days, when he'd been an average human back on Earth, he would have thought Nia was tall, imposing, and despite her scars quite beautiful. Beside her, though, Valla looked like a demigod coming to walk among mortals. She towered over the woman, her silvery pale blue skin glistening in the diffuse sunlight that filtered through the trellised roof of the pavilion.

Valla's hair was delicately styled, held in tight, elegant curls with jeweled combs. She wore the silver choker Victor had given her with its carved sapphire runes. And, as if to highlight her Ordeni skin tone, she was dressed in flowing, silky, silver and blue robes that as far as Victor was concerned clung to her in all the right ways. He shook his head, forcing himself to quit staring at Valla, and stood up. He nodded at Nia and smiled. "You look nice, Nia. Thanks for agreeing to come with us."

"Of course, milord."

"I know it's a habit, but you don't have to address us as lords and ladies, Nia," Valla said, saving Victor from having to say the same thing for probably the twentieth time. "If you take a permanent position in Victor's household, you can use that honorific, but for now, we're all members of a delegation to First Landing, and there's no need for such deference." Victor thought Valla was being nice, and he was sure that was her intent, but Nia's face paled, and her eyes widened as she looked toward Victor.

"I thought my position was permanent!" She stepped past Alec, looking up to lock eyes with Victor.

"Oh, I didn't . . ." Valla started to say, but Victor waved his hand, chuckling.

"It's just a miscommunication, Valla. Nia, of course, as long as you want to work for me and help me manage things here, I'll have plenty to keep you busy. I think Valla simply means we haven't established any formal agreements."

"Then, as the lord of the lands on which I serve, I will address you as such." Again, she bowed at the waist, and Victor saw a smile behind her blue eyes. He looked at Valla and shrugged slightly. She arched an eyebrow, perhaps amused by Nia's persistence.

"Where the hell is Borrius?" Victor turned in a circle, looking at all of the entrances to the pavilion, wondering if the old general was coming from a different direction. He'd asked him to come along primarily because the man loved to hear himself talk, and Victor figured he'd take some of the pressure off him in the town hall.

"I'm sure he'll be along. Relax, Victor. We're still early." Valla moved to stand beside him, clasping his hand. Her wing brushed his shoulder, the feathers twitching and shivering against him as she shifted. Her feathers were incredible things; they almost tinkled metallically as she moved. He'd spent many a long evening with her, feeling those wings, playing with her feathers, and he knew they were incredibly resilient, though they were light as air. Valla had gotten very comfortable with her new appendages and moved so gracefully that it was hard to remember how awkward she'd been at first.

Alec shook him from his reflections by asking, "Is he the last member of your party? Borrius, um, what was his surname?"

Valla answered him, "Borrius ap'Gandro—he's a former commander of the Imperial Legion, a legate, and now a landholder and nobleman in the Free Marches. We feel he'll be invaluable when it comes to explaining the dangers of having a populace controlled by more powerful Energy users. Whatever you know of the Ridonne, I can assure you, Borrius knows more." Valla pointed over Alec's shoulder. "Here he comes with his aide, Lieutenant

Darro." Victor exhaled a pent-up breath as he watched Borrius and Darro stride into the pavilion. Of course, they wore their military uniforms.

"Well met, all," the old commander said, striding up the marble path. "Am I tardy?"

"Not at all, sir!" Alec smiled and strode forward, offering his hand. "I'm Alec Green from First Landing, and I'll be serving as an ambassador to your fine settlement here. I'd hoped to meet you yesterday, but Lady ap'Yensha indicated you were busy with other matters."

"Ah, yes, quite. It's a pleasure, young man." Borrius took Alec's hand in his and gave it a firm shake. Handshakes weren't as common on Fanwath as on Earth, but Borrius was a well-traveled man and wasn't put off by the custom. "Well? Shall we? Are we waiting for any others, Victor?"

"Nope. We're all here. Alec?"

"I'm ready if you folks are." He stepped onto the nearby dais where the travel pavilion attendants had set up his portal stone and approached the big marble archway. Victor could see the portal stone at the center of the arch—darker than the surrounding stones and adorned with silver-inlaid runes. "Let's see, I think I'm just supposed to put my hand here." Alec placed his hand on a cluster of runes on the side of the arch. "Then I, what? Do I just feed it some of my Energy?"

"That's right." Valla stepped up beside him. "Just as you would use any magical item—for instance, a glow lamp."

"Right, right." Alec closed his eyes momentarily, and then Victor felt the surge of Energy as the portal stone activated and a shimmering blue sheet of Energy filled the archway. It rippled and crackled almost like electricity. It didn't look like any of the other portals he'd stepped through, and he wondered at that—was a portal's appearance dependent on the person who'd created it? Was it affected by the destination?

"Interesting," Borrius said, perhaps thinking along the same lines. "That Energy feels like a mix of air and water attunements. Do you know the Artificer who crafted that stone?"

"I do! Boris Saltzki—he's our highest-level Artificer." Alec jerked his thumb at the shimmering electric doorway and grinned. "I suppose I should be the one to demonstrate it's safe, huh? I'll see you all on the other side!" With that, he stepped through in a sizzling shower of blue sparks.

"Huh." Victor chuckled and stepped up to the archway. "Well, I didn't expect to be nervous about the portal."

"I'm sure it's fine." Valla smiled encouragingly.

"Right." Victor took a deep breath and stepped through. He felt the magic tickling his flesh as he passed through. When his foot set down on springy wood and he walked into a brightly lit hall the size of a high school gym, he looked around, taking in the scene. He'd been right about the floor—polished, pale wooden planks covered the expansive space, running to white plaster walls that rose to a high vaulted ceiling held up by beams of the same pale wood. It was a lovely building, but very empty. The only adornments were the massive Energy-powered chandeliers that hung from the rafters.

"This is our new portal hall," Alec said, taking Victor's shoulder and directing him away from the portal. "Don't want your friends to bump into you when they come through."

"Right." Victor turned and watched as Nia and then Valla came through the portal, blinking in the bright lights and looking around the space.

"Sorry, there isn't much to see in here," Alec said. "It's brand new, and we figured we should keep lots of space open for delegations or trade materials going through the portals." As he finished speaking, Darro and Borrius came through with a shimmer of blue electric sparks. "That's all of us! Just a moment while I close the portal." Alec held his hand to the side of the archway, and then, with a sizzling *pop*, the blue gateway disappeared. "There we go! Well, I know it was early morning in your settlement, but it's the middle of the night here. How about I show you to my inn, get you settled, and then we can go over your schedule? I've been communicating with the committee responsible for setting up your town hall and the 'military demonstration,' as they're calling it, and a representative will meet us at the inn."

"Sounds good to me." Victor shrugged and took Valla's hand. He had, as usual, altered his size to be close to hers, which was still quite tall by human standards. He'd been anticipating a lot of strange looks as they walked through town and was almost relieved to find that there was a significant time change. When they followed Alec outside through the big double doors of their portal hall, he was surprised. He'd been picturing First Landing as a quaint little village, but from the raised ground on which the portal hall sat, he had a rather expansive view of a sprawling, busy-looking town. He almost wanted to revise that and consider the place a city, but he could see it wasn't as extensive or populous as Persi Gables or Gelica. Still, it was a good deal more than he'd expected.

"Impressive!" Valla said. "I thought you'd only been here a few years."

"Oh, we have, but we've been hard at work, and our open policy with new citizens has helped us to proliferate." Alec pointed down the cobbled road toward a distant cluster of tall buildings. "That's the center of town—we built outward from the Colony Stone, which is on a hill you can't see thanks to that big rectangular building. That's my inn." He gestured past that to a distant row of lights that encircled the town. "Those lights are on the top of the wall. We've outgrown that wall but kept it as a second line of defense. We have a bigger one about a mile out and have begun expanding the residential areas into that outer circle."

"How many people . . ." Victor started to ask.

"Well," Alec chuckled, "we started with about five thousand humans. The first year was kind of harsh—we had a conflict with some local, um, low-affinity types and lost a few hundred. The children have more than made up for that, however. We're prospering. Um—" He glanced at Valla and smiled. "I'm not sure if you wanted this much information, but we've found that humanity is quite compatible with Ardeni, Shadeni, and Ghelli as far as, well, children go. We've had quite a few people from neighboring towns and villages settle here, and we took in a large number of refugees . . ." Alec groaned and rubbed a hand through his short brown hair. "Oh, brother, I'm rambling. The point I'm trying to make is that upwards of twenty thousand people live in First Landing."

"Very interesting," Borrius said, stroking his chin. "I can see the lights of airships if I'm not mistaken."

"Oh, yes! We've got three cargo ships and seven warships."

"No planes yet?" Victor asked, remembering Alec's words from the day before.

"There are some, but they're still inferior to the airships when it comes to cargo capacity and durability. The engineers are excited about their progress, though." He started down the cobbled road. "Come on, I'll show you to the inn. By the way, I'm sorry we don't have a big welcoming committee here for you—Issa didn't think you'd appreciate that."

"Issa?"

"Oh, Issa ap'Roald. She's the member of Parliament who's heading up the committee that organized my appointment as ambassador to the Free Marches and your visit here." He started walking as he spoke, and they all fell in around him. They were the only people on the narrow, slightly winding road leading down from the portal hall. However, Victor could see hundreds of lights in the buildings around them and, farther down the road, some sparse pedestrian traffic.

"You have an Ardeni on your ruling council?" Valla asked.

"Ah, yes. Issa's been a part of this community since near the beginning. She's engaged to Morgan Hall—would be married, certainly, if not for his prolonged absence. Still, the people here generally love her, and she didn't have any trouble getting elected to one of the Parliament seats. She's also an impressive crafter. She'll meet you all in the inn when the sun's come up."

"If you don't mind me asking, Alec, and please don't take this the wrong way, but why do you think Issa thought we wouldn't like a welcoming committee?" Valla wrapped her fingers around Victor's elbow, walking in step with him as she spoke.

Alec looked over his shoulder and smiled, nodding toward Victor. "Hmm, well, I suppose it's due to Olivia's correspondence. She sort of indicated that Victor here was reticent to visit and wouldn't enjoy a bunch of fanfare. Was she wrong?"

"Not at all," Victor grunted.

"Excuse me, dear boy," Borrius said, quickening his stride to walk beside Alec. "I've only had a cursory briefing about why we're coming here aside from meeting a community similarly in poor favor with the Ridonne, but I do have a bit of a concern itching the back of my brain."

"Oh?"

"Yes, well, you see, Victor seemed to think that we're meant to speak to a large gathering about the dangers of allowing oneself to fall behind on Energy cultivation, about the dangers of growing complacent in a universe full of powerful beings who could make their presence known on our little backwater world."

Alec nodded. "Um, that's accurate, I suppose."

"Well, what sort of opposition should we expect? It stands to reason that if the people here need convincing, there must be others working to shore up the opposing argument, namely that your current trajectory is the way to go. There must be some profit involved, I'd think."

"Ah, yeah." Alec nodded enthusiastically. "I see your point, Lord Borrius." It wasn't lost on Victor that Alec was buttering the old commander up. "It's not exactly profit in riches that they're after, but there is a faction here trying to profit politically by arguing against Olivia's frequent warnings and trying to marginalize those on Parliament who side with Issa."

"As I thought," Borrius said, turning to Victor and winking at him in an utterly uncharacteristic move. "We're being used as pawns for someone's political gain. I hope the rewards will be adequate."

"Ah . . ." Alec seemed a little lost for words, and he glanced at Victor and Valla, then turned back to Borrius. "I don't know if it's exactly like that, but I won't deny that there's a faction of very good people in this settlement who will definitely benefit if you can shut some of the louder know-it-alls up."

"Well, Alec." Valla chuckled, breathing in through her nose and twitching her wings as a cool breeze passed over them. "You can rest assured that if there's one thing Victor's good at, it's shutting up know-it-alls."

6

FACTIONS

Green's Inn and Suites was much more like a hotel on Earth than the inns Victor had seen in the cities of Fanwath and Zaafor. It had a lobby separate from a bar and restaurant and, in a show of Earthling ingenuity, an Energy-powered elevator. It was a five-story building, and Alec put everyone in suites on the top floor—it was evident that he'd built the hotel with growth in mind because it felt relatively empty. Victor and Valla had a corner suite with lots of windows, and they both enjoyed looking through the crystal-clear glass as the town woke up around them.

"I'm surprised at how diverse the populace is," Valla said, looking down at the busy central hub of retail businesses. They were built around a lovely red-brick street that surrounded a hill at the center of the community. Steps led up the sides of the hill to a garden-like plaza that surrounded the Colony Stone. People were opening shops, sweeping sidewalks, and bustling to and fro, getting ready for what looked to be a busy day of commerce. Victor could see what Valla meant—fewer than half the people walking around down there were humans.

Victor nodded. "I guess, with only five thousand original settlers, they had to open their doors to the natives of Fanwath if they wanted the community to grow quickly."

"Isn't that strange? I understand they all came on one ship and that it was likely crowded, but you'd think they'd send more people to settle a new world."

"Yeah, I don't know anything about that." Victor shrugged. "They weren't expecting to run into the System or arrive on a world full of other people. Maybe if they'd actually been allowed to land their ship and if they'd been alone . . ." Victor trailed off, acutely feeling his lack of knowledge on the subject. "Shit, I should ask Olivia more about this stuff. I should be more interested in her. She's always asking for details about me and my experiences, and I haven't been good about showing an equal interest in her." He gestured out the window. "In them."

"Well, something tells me you'll learn a lot about these people today."

"Yeah." Victor looked to the horizon at the pink, yellow, and orange-hued sunrise and said, "I thought that lady was coming to meet us at dawn."

"That's not an exact time, though, is it? Is dawn when you first see the sun? Is it now, when the sun is halfway visible? Is it the hour or so after it's just risen?"

Victor didn't take the bait. "Let's go down to the lobby. I want to be ready." He walked to the door, crossing a plush, intricately woven rug featuring multicolored flowers on an olive green background. The hotel suite was nicely appointed and much more familiar in style than some of the furnishings he'd seen on Fanwath. The difference was especially evident in the art—their suite was adorned with paintings of objects and landscapes, but not a single person, a stark contrast to what was common on Fanwath. Rellia's villa, for instance, had walls covered with portraits of family or historical figures. The bathroom was another big change—somehow, the humans were making porcelain. Victor hadn't realized how much he'd gotten used to seeing brass and copper tubs and toilets.

In the hallway, he paused to knock on doors, alerting the rest of their party that they were heading down to the lobby, and a few minutes later, they rode down in the weirdly smooth, silent elevator. "I don't think this thing is on a cable," Victor said, stepping out and turning to regard the elevator as the polished brass doors slid shut.

"A cable?" Valla frowned.

"Never mind. Let's sit over by the fire while we wait." Victor led the party to the grouping of couches near the big stone fireplace across the lobby from the reception desk.

On the way, Borrius stepped over to the young Ardeni man who staffed the desk. "Ahem, young fellow. Please let Ambassador Green know that we're sitting together there by the fire."

"Of course, sir."

Victor smiled at the exchange, glad he'd brought the old commander along; he was perfect for this sort of thing. The couches were comfortable, the room was cozy despite its vaulted ceilings, and they all sat, making small talk for several minutes. Victor enjoyed the lull in activity, though it felt as though he was wasting time, and part of him wanted to stand up and seek out the people he was supposed to speak to and get it over with. Still, he sat back and tried to be present, listening to Valla as she attempted to bring Nia out of her shell a little.

"I know it's not a pleasant memory, but can you tell us about your home a little? Your people originated from the same world as those who've settled here. Does anything seem familiar?"

"Aside from them being human, not much. I suppose . . ." She looked around, frowning. "I suppose the aesthetic is a little familiar. I grew up in a village without an inn, but I know the cities of the great lords have hotels and restaurants. I haven't seen enough of the town to say more."

"Have you thought about what you'll say today? About the 'great lords,' as you name them?"

"I didn't name them that." Nia scowled, but then she seemed to remember whom she was speaking to, and her eyes widened as she stammered an apology. "I'm sorry! I didn't mean to snap; my bitterness found its way off my tongue. The great lords of Dark Ember are called that by decree, and if those such as myself were to name them otherwise, we could be killed or worse for the offense."

"Don't apologize." Valla leaned forward so she could reach over to take Nia's wrist, giving it a gentle squeeze. "You're rightfully bitter about what they've done to you. Still, my question stands."

"Oh, um—" Nia paused and licked her lips. They were dry and cracked, and Victor realized that if he was nervous about speaking in front of a bunch of strangers, Nia was probably feeling a thousand times worse. "I suppose I'll talk about how it felt when they passed through town. How . . ." Her description was cut short as a cheerful voice called out from the front of the lobby.

"Folks from the Free Marches! I see you're eager to get started. This is Issa ap'Roald, a member of our Parliament and the head of the committee responsible for your visit today."

Victor turned toward the hotel doors and saw Alec striding toward them, accompanied by a stunningly beautiful Ardeni woman with gleaming yellow eyes and hair that hung like spun threads of gold. She was impressively tall for an Ardeni and moved with a grace that spoke of many racial advancements. Where Alec was dressed in a nicely tailored brown and cream suit, Issa wore a silky blue kimono-style dress with a tight high collar and sleeves that covered her arms down to the backs of her hands. It hugged her figure, and the single smooth garment from neck to ankles accentuated her height.

Victor stood up, as did the rest of his party, and he stepped forward, extending a hand. "It's nice to meet you."

Issa took his hand warmly between both of hers, and the smile she offered him was reflected in her bright eyes. "It's so nice to meet you finally, Victor. I've heard much about you from Olivia, and I've been hoping for your success in the Marches."

"Um, thank you." Victor felt lost for words, annoyed with himself again for not asking Olivia more about the people of First Landing. He felt he should know more about this woman. Valla cleared her throat gently, saving him from standing there like an idiot. He let go of Issa's hand and gestured to Valla and the others. "This is Valla ap'Yensha. She represents the most influential family in the Free Marches."

"Lady ap'Yensha, it's my pleasure to make your acquaintance." Issa took Valla's hand, and it was obvious that she wanted to ask more as her eyes locked onto Valla's silvery turquoise wings.

"My pleasure." Valla smiled, and the two women clasped hands for several seconds before they let go and turned back to Victor.

"This"—Victor reached behind Valla to grasp Borrius's shoulder—"is Borrius ap'Gandro. His military leadership is renowned on Fanwath, and he's here to share his experience and knowledge with your people."

"Well met, madam." Borrius shocked Victor by taking Issa's hand and kissing it, bowing with a flourish.

"You honor me, sir!" Issa chuckled a little nervously if Victor were any judge. Perhaps to save further embarrassment, she looked at Darro and Nia. "And these two? Are they also landholders from the Free Marches?"

Victor knew Alec must have already told her who was in their party, so her question, while polite, bothered him a little. Was she playing politics already? "That's Lieutenant Darro; he's Borrius's aide, and this is Nia, daughter of Efa, a woman from Dark Ember. She has much to share about the dangers of allowing a single faction to gain too much power in a world."

"Wonderful! Thank you both for coming!" Issa surprised Victor by taking Darro's hand and then earnestly shaking Nia's. "I know you've traveled far, though with the portals, it doesn't seem so. There's still time for you to eat or rest for an hour or two before the town hall; we've scheduled it for mid-morning. I just wanted to meet you before the big event so I could answer any questions you might have."

"Victor won't ask, so I will," Valla said, smiling as she glanced sideways at him. "What sort of demonstration do they expect from him? I mean against your automatons?"

"Well—" Issa looked at Victor, and her smile seemed almost nervous. "I have to say, we can cancel that if you'd like. Olivia's description of you and your exploits left a different impression than I'm getting right now. With what she told them and the, perhaps misguided, desire to prove that they're ready for anything, the Defense Department has arrayed quite a force on the parade grounds." She looked at Alec and frowned slightly as she continued, "It might be better for our cause to await Morgan's return to highlight their mistakes."

"And how would that affect our payment?" Borrius asked, demonstrating his priorities.

"Oh, well . . ." Issa started, but Victor held up a hand and cleared his throat, interrupting her.

"Don't sweat it, Lady Issa. I'm reducing myself significantly right now."

"Hmm?" She looked at him with a cocked eyebrow.

"Victor learned magic to make himself more comfortable in the quaint dwellings of wee small folk." Valla hid her smile behind her hand as she explained.

Victor couldn't help hamming it up a little as he put an arm around Valla's shoulders, wings and all, "Well, it's not just so I can fit through doors more easily; I also can hug you better like this, yeah?"

"Yes." She nodded, no longer hiding her smile. "There's that, too."

"Well, in that case, I'll let you be the judge of your readiness." Issa spoke with her hands, gesturing to illustrate her words as she continued, "They've arrayed something like twenty of the 'tank' automatons on the field. I've also heard rumors of two 'juggernauts.' They're like giant person-shaped constructs built of wood and metal and highly charged with Energy. I've seen them demonstrated before, and . . . I'm not sure I'd like to do battle with one." She paused and looked around. They were all still standing in the lobby, and though the hotel was quiet, it seemed she was feeling a little self-conscious about standing there. "Would you all join me for breakfast? I know it's not breakfast time for you, but . . ."

"I'll excuse myself, my lady." Borrius bowed and turned to Darro. "We have some work to do for my estate back in the Marches, and we can make good use of this time."

"I'll go to my room until you need me, if you don't mind," Nia said to Victor. He nodded. "You're welcome, you know . . ."

"No, thank you, Lord Victor. I'll use this time to meditate."

"Well, Victor and I will join you, Lady ap'Roald," Valla said, taking the lead.

"Just Issa, please." She smiled and gestured to the arched opening of the hotel's restaurant. "Are your kitchens open, Alec?"

"Always!" He led the way, and Issa and Valla followed.

"See you guys soon," Victor said, nodding to Borrius and Nia. A few minutes later, he was sitting at a small table near a window with Valla and Issa; Alec had begged off, saying he had hotel business to manage before the big meeting. A waiter had brought over steaming cups of coffee with a tiny pitcher of thick cream, and Victor was savoring the drink, watching Issa eat pancakes and listening to the two women talk.

"I hope you don't find it rude, but I'm very curious about your bloodline, Lady ap'Yensha," Issa said between bites.

"Please, if I'm going to call you Issa, you must call me Valla. Hmm, my bloodline stems from an ancient ancestor, a Rihven. Have you heard of them?"

"Rihven . . ." Issa's eyes unfocused, and Victor could see she was searching through her memory. "I'm afraid I haven't."

"You're well versed in the Ridonne, though, I'll wager."

"Oh yes. Obviously." Issa snickered as though the two women were sharing a joke.

"You know about the Vessi, yes?"

"All but gone, no thanks to the Ridonne." Issa nodded and took another bite. "Are you sure you two aren't hungry?"

"I'm always hungry." Victor laughed. "But I don't want to eat so soon before the meeting. I'd probably spill syrup on my shirt."

"Victor!" Valla sighed. "Your shirt is enchanted to clean . . ."

"I know, I know." Victor sipped his coffee. "I'll eat when I'm done beating up all these *pinché* robots Issa's people have set up for me."

"That sounds like something Morgan would say." Issa laughed.

Valla gave Victor a knowing look and continued speaking. "Well, back on the topic of the Rihven, you know that there were three species of people that came from our homeworld, yes?"

"From Alurath?"

"Yes. Before the joining—the Ardeni, the Shadeni, and the Ordeni."

"Oh, yes! The Ordeni were almost gone before the joining; the Ridonne were at war with them. Didn't the Yovashi finish them off?"

"Right, the Yovashi were from Kthella—the homeworld of the Ghelli. You could say that when the System merged the worlds, they didn't exactly get along with the new species they were confronted with. The Ordeni especially threatened them, being at least equally gifted with Energy usage." Valla stopped, sipped her coffee, then chuckled, shaking her head. "I'm sorry for the history lesson; I promise I have a point."

"No, please go on!"

"Well, as you no doubt know, we people from Alurath are quite compatible physically; if a Shadeni loves an Ardeni, they have no trouble bearing children."

"Of course." Issa nodded.

"Before I found my bloodline, I was, as far as I knew, Ardeni. I discovered, though, a distant ancestor who was Ordeni. Through her, I brought forth this Rihven bloodline. It's the equivalent of the Ridonne and the Vessi bloodlines."

"Ah! I love this sort of discussion! Wouldn't you say, then, that the Ordeni aren't really gone? I'm sure millions of Shadeni and Ardeni have Ordeni ancestors!"

"That's right!" Valla smiled and leaned back, sipping her coffee. "I'd like to go to Tharcray and liberate the texts in the Imperial Archives. I'd like to learn more about the Ordeni, to learn more about everything the Ridonne have tried to bury or erase from the public record."

"We should . . ." Victor started, but Valla sighed and shook her head.

"Someday, maybe. We have other priorities."

Issa nodded at Valla's words, setting her fork down. "Do I understand correctly that you're seeking to open world travel so you can get to places the Ridonne have blocked?"

"Yes! We're hoping to open up a hub world where we can learn more and perhaps travel farther."

"A pity the timing is off, but that's just the sort of thing my Morgan is working on."

"He's off-world?"

"Yes. He bargained with the Ridonne, and, for a favor, he's been granted passage. This was before we learned of your troubles with them, before we realized the extent of their corruption." She frowned and shook her head. "I hate to make excuses for my ignorance, but I'm from Tarn's Crossing, a frontier village, and my knowledge of world affairs was sorely lacking. Sadly, that's the case for most of us who aren't living in the bigger cities. The Ridonne have done well in spreading their version of history."

Issa's face betrayed some worry or tension, and Valla leaned closer, her voice soft and sympathetic. "Have you had contact with him? Morgan, I mean."

"Oh, goodness! Does my worry show so much? Morgan is very resourceful, and when he contacted me, and asked for my blessing to undertake the journey, he set the appropriate expectations. Don't trouble yourself a second longer worrying about me. I'll be fine. Now—" She turned to Victor. "Victor, I don't normally speak bluntly about political motives, but I want you to know that my reasons for lobbying for your visit weren't wholly altruistic."

"I figured." Victor shrugged.

"It's true that these people need to understand what a powerful cultivator can accomplish, but just as importantly, for me, there's a faction here in First Landing who must be taken down a notch. If they lost some political face, it would benefit Olivia, me, and others who think like us. I want that to be clear before you go into that town hall. I won't have you thinking me duplicitous."

"Well, if that's the case, maybe you should tell me about this other faction. What sorts of beliefs do they have that you think are problematic?"

"For one, most of them think I should have been excluded from the election. I'm the only nonhuman in Parliament. For another, they believe in recapturing the technology they left behind on Earth as a priority that supersedes all others—gaining levels, cultivating, trade agreements, exploration, nothing matters to them more than their 'lost tech.' They advocate for human expansion and supremacy, and though I think it isn't such a terrible idea, they are actively working to build a vessel that can travel into orbit where they believe their ark ship still flies. There are a hundred thousand human embryos on that vessel."

Victor snorted. "You think that's not terrible?"

"Well, not the recovery of the embryos, no, not in and of itself. Everything will depend on which faction wins control. Things are very divided here. There's a reason the low-affinity species Morgan and his friends rescued have left First Landing to found their own village a day's travel from here. Publicly, people say it's because they wanted their own homes, their own farms, and their own traditional buildings, but there were many people here who made them uncomfortable. I think it had more to do with that."

Victor looked from Issa's earnest face to Valla's frowning, contemplative expression and growled, "Wherever people gather, you'll find assholes. There are assholes among the Ardeni and the Shadeni, and yeah, of course, there are going to be some assholes among this many humans. I like you, Issa, but I don't really know you, do I? I won't promise that I'll be on your side right away, but if anyone at that town hall says something as stupid as what you just described, if any of them try to tell me that humans are better for some reason or another, I'll be glad to set them straight. Olivia tells me humans have a high average affinity, but that's nothing compared to dragons or"—Victor shuddered as he involuntarily remembered his encounter with Fox and Three on the spirit plane—"some of the scarier individuals I've run into."

"That's all I ask, Victor. I just hope it wasn't a mistake to advertise your 'demonstration.' There's a faction led by a man named Norton Holmes who's very influential with the Defense Department here, and, well, I'm worried about what he's going to throw at you. There are rumors about a special project."

"Oh? Are they playing for keeps, then? Like, no holds barred?" As he spoke, Valla shifted and grimaced, reaching under the table to put a hand on his wrist, almost as if she thought she had to restrain him.

"I . . ." Issa tilted her head, contemplating. "I believe they're going to try to convince you to sign some sort of contract indicating that they'll not be held responsible for your death."

"Ha!" Victor shook his head as his burgeoning rage subsided, replaced by amusement. "I guess it's only fair. I was going to make you—or them, I guess—sign something saying I won't be responsible for the damage I do."

7

TOWN HALL

Victor stood on the stone, stage-like dais and looked up at the rows of benches made from the same material. They rose in ranks up the slope of a kind of natural depression. The people of First Landing had built an outdoor amphitheater on the outskirts of their town near the foothills of a small range of mountains that helped to form the valley in which the settlement had been founded. High granite cliffs formed the stage's backdrop and helped redirect sound to the audience. However, the runes inscribed in the magical devices at their feet pulsing with Energy made it clear that more than natural acoustics were at work.

The tiered seating wasn't as bad as he'd feared—he figured maybe five hundred people could fit comfortably in the little amphitheater, and upon their arrival, about a third of the benches were empty. He supposed he wasn't too surprised. It wasn't as if he and his companions were celebrities. They were people from another community coming to answer questions and talk about things that, to him, seemed pretty mundane. He doubted he'd come to watch something similar if he were in their shoes. Their seats, comfortable wooden chairs, were arranged in a loose semicircle in the middle of the stage, and as they sat down, Alec stood before them, back to the audience, nodding and smiling.

"Everything all right? As I explained earlier, we've arranged for people to ask questions and for you all to answer. If a question isn't directed at an individual, we'll leave it to you to decide who answers. If there's something you don't want to respond to—there shouldn't be, but we can't vet every person—feel free to pass and ask for the next question."

"Am I to understand," Borrius said, leaning forward, clearing his throat, "that we aren't to deliver a prepared speech? I believe I was misinformed." He turned to glare at Victor.

"I never said you had to prepare a speech!"

"Uh . . ." Alec smiled and lifted his hands, tamping down at the air as though to cool hot tempers. "I don't see how it wouldn't be helpful to be prepared! I'm sure many questions will touch on the topics you wrote about, Commander ap'Gandro." He looked at a wristwatch, the first Victor had seen anyone in this world wearing, and added, "We're actually a bit behind schedule. Will it be all right if I introduce you? Just stand up as I say your name, and when we're done, you can all sit together. We have speaking stones embedded in the aisles, so only someone standing on one will be heard clearly—it will keep people from shouting out questions haphazardly."

Victor nodded. "It's fine. Go ahead." He looked to his left, smiling at Valla, and then leaned forward a little so he could see Nia beyond her. "You'll be great, Nia. Don't worry."

"Thank you, Lord Victor." She clasped her hands together and tried to smile, but her nerves made the expression look more like a grimace. Victor wasn't worried about being overheard as they spoke—just as the audience had speaking stones to use, identical devices were on the stage before each of their chairs. Alec had explained that they had two modes, blue and yellow. If they weren't glowing yellow, the audience wouldn't hear their voices. Apparently, they worked to dampen sounds as much as project them. The speaking stones were about ten inches in diameter and relatively flat. To Victor, they looked more like dinner plates than stones. If he'd understood Alec correctly, all they had to do to change the stone from blue to yellow was to rest a foot upon it.

His contemplation of the sound-projecting artifacts was cut short as Alec began to speak, his voice stridently rising off the stage to cut through the murmur of the crowd. "Good people of First Landing, I welcome you all to this town hall, the first of hopefully many, as we seek to increase our knowledge and understanding of the System-controlled universe—a universe we are new to, despite the centuries of study we and other scientists have conducted back on Earth. When we embarked on our incredibly long voyage to Tau Ceti, we couldn't have imagined what we'd find. Every day, we learn something new about our environment, and each tidbit of precious knowledge reveals ten more mysteries.

"Some of you are frustrated with our current situation, while others are enthralled by this vast expanse of new frontiers, this great void in understanding waiting to be filled. To that end, members of the Concordia Forum have worked to bring some fascinating guest speakers before you today. They've given up precious time to travel here to answer your questions, and I hope you'll all join me in welcoming them with warm hearts and open arms to First Landing. Please, before I introduce them individually, join me in giving them all a round of applause."

Victor smiled and nodded as the audience began to clap. He looked at his companions. Nia blushed and looked down. Valla was impassive, and the old commander smiled, nodded, and soaked up the adulation. Darro had been spared the stage; he sat in the front row beside Issa, along with some other members of Parliament. They'd introduced themselves when Victor's party first arrived in the amphitheater, but he'd already forgotten their names. As the clapping died down, Alec continued to speak. "As you know, these guests come to us from the newly formed republic of the Free Marches, where they battled the undead invaders from the world of Dark Ember to win lands free from the Ridonne Empire's influence.

"Now, as I've told our guests, most of the people of First Landing, especially you all who've shown an interest in this town hall, are well versed in the details of that conquest and invasion, so I won't bore you by rehashing it. I'm sure there are those among you who've prepared questions for our guests on that topic, so there's no sense repeating everything now. As I introduce each of them, I'll keep things brief; we'll have plenty of time to get to know these people over the next couple of hours.

"First, allow me to introduce Borrius ap'Gandro, a former commander in the Ridonnian Imperial Legion." As Borrius stood and performed a half bow, Victor wondered at Alec's use of the term Ridonnian—was that the correct phrasing? He'd never heard anyone from the Ridonne Empire label themselves as such. Borrius sat down, and Victor braced himself, but he apparently wasn't going in order of seating. "Next, please welcome Nia, a young woman, a survivor and freedom fighter from the world of Dark Ember!" Nia hesitantly stood, glancing at Victor with a puzzled expression as the audience clapped more enthusiastically for her than Borrius.

Victor frowned, slightly annoyed by Alec's very liberal interpretation of Nia's situation. Freedom fighter? Clearly, he was trying to sway the public opinion about the speakers he'd gathered for them. Nia sat down, and Alec said, "Beside Nia is Lady Valla ap'Yensha, a powerful person in her own right, but also the heiress to the most influential family in the Free Marches."

Valla stood up and, surprising Victor, stepped onto the speaking stone, clearing her throat. The audience had already grown hushed as she stood to her full stature, towering over Alec. She spread her wings slightly, and their lustrous metallic sheen as they rustled in the morning breeze was probably the source of the audience's stupefaction. "Pardon me, Mr. Green, but I'd like to clarify one thing: Victor Sandoval is the most influential landholder in the Free Marches, not my family." She smiled radiantly, bowed with a flourish, and sat back down, removing her foot from her speaking stone.

"Ah, thank you, Lady ap'Yensha. Your timely correction brings me to our final guest, a man many of you have already heard spoken about in Parliamentary sessions—Victor Sandoval." Victor stood up and nodded to Alec, whose eyes focused on him as he continued to speak. "Victor is a new citizen to Fanwath, just as we are—a traveler from Earth!" Despite Alec's assurance that many of the audience members already knew about his origins, there was quite a hubbub at his proclamation. Victor could hear the murmur of conversations, could see people speaking openly to their neighbors, but the magic of the amphitheater kept the noise from impacting Alec's introduction as he continued. "Victor was summoned to this world; he didn't travel via spacecraft. His welcome to Fanwath was a good deal harsher than ours, even considering our troubles with the Urghat.

"Despite that, or perhaps because of it, Victor has grown in power and prestige beyond anything we've accomplished here in First Landing." He laughed at the faint sounds of outrage or disagreement coming from the muted audience. "You don't have to take my word for it! I'll elaborate with some facts about the man: He's reached levels of personal power that none of us here can begin to comprehend. He's conquered armies led by the Ridonne and traveled to another world where he rose to fame in a matter of weeks, besting champions in their arena and battling creatures larger than the shuttles you all took to board the ark ship.

"Victor Sandoval helped to lead the army that drove the invaders from Dark Ember from this world, and as Lady ap'Yensha just assured you all, he's now the most influential landholder in those liberated lands. Even saying all that, you don't have to believe me! Believe the man himself, standing here ready to answer your questions about the true nature of power in this, our new reality." Alec turned and, with the audience, began to applaud Victor.

Victor might have protested if someone asked whether he enjoyed the adulation, but the truth was that he ate it up. He stood tall, teetering on the brink of canceling his Alter Self spell but managing to keep it together until Alec stopped clapping and turned back to the audience.

"Now, I'll yield the floor to you, citizens of First Landing. You know the procedure. Form lines at the speaking stones, and we'll allow our guests to answer you one at a time."

Victor sat down, noticing the sour expression on Borrius's face as he did so. "Something wrong, Borrius?"

"Oh, nothing. I'd hoped to have a chance to take the stage without you. I'll forever be clouded by your shadow while we share it."

"Ha," Victor chuckled, amazed as usual by the man's conceit. "Try to keep your chin up, old man. I'll make sure you get to answer plenty of questions."

"Old man? Ha! You know I purchased a racial upgrade from the campaign store. I'll eat that, and the next time we meet, you'll see what a handsome fellow I am." Victor couldn't tell if Borrius was being droll or serious, so he just snorted, amused either way.

"Ahem," a woman's voice rang out over the audience, and Victor realized the first citizen had stepped up to the speaking stone. She was a tall, thin woman with long brown braids, wearing peach-colored overalls and a long-sleeved white shirt. "I was wondering if you consider the Free Marches to be at war with the Ridonne Empire."

Victor grinned at Borrius. "Now's your chance!"

Borrius stood, clasped his hands behind his back, and stepped onto the speaking stone. "An excellent question! Are we at war? Not openly, no. The Ridonne, who led their Legion against us as we made our way to the Untamed Marches, acted without imperial sanction. Their armies were destroyed, and Victor here meted out justice most severe to the perpetrators." He nodded, stroked his jawline, and added, "I would say that our relations are cool and that we keep a watchful eye to the north, but we are not at war."

As Borrius bowed and took his seat, a portly bald man stepped up to the stone. "Victor, er, Mr. Sandoval, is it true that you're the highest-level person on Fanwath?"

Victor barked a short laugh at the man's bluntness. He stood up and stepped a foot onto the speaking stone. As it turned yellow, he said, "That's an interesting question. First, I'll offer a little advice: Be careful with such a blunt question about a person's level. In some circles, that could get you in trouble. Most people would think it's rude, but there are those, for instance, many of the people on Zaafor, who would thrash you or, at the very least, challenge you to a duel."

"My, uh, my apologies . . ." he began to stammer, but Victor held up a hand and continued.

"I'll answer you, in any case. I might be the highest-level human, but I'm not sure. As for the highest-level person, I can definitively say no. There's at least one person on this stage who's at my level. I've never been to Tharcray, so there might be many people there who are at a higher level. I hear that's where all the old masters go to live, primarily because the Colony Stone there allows them to visit other more powerful worlds. Considering some of those folks are more than four hundred years old, yeah, they might be higher level." Victor shrugged, stepped off the stone, and sat down.

"Pardon me, sir, but if you aren't the . . ."

"That's your question, Gerald. Give the next person a chance," Alec interrupted. Gerald, a bit red in the face, stepped off the stone and moved back to his seat while a thin, dark-skinned woman wearing a tie-dye blouse and pants that looked very much like blue jeans stepped forward.

"Hello, Mr. Sandoval. Since you're standing, I have another question for you." When Victor nodded, she continued. "I'm Andrea Belgrade, and I've been studying and trying to compile a list of Core types. I saw from Gerald's question that you find invasive questions rude, but would you mind if I asked a little about your Core? I believe it will be enlightening to this assembly."

Victor tapped his toes onto the stone and responded, "I don't mind."

"Thank you! From Olivia Bennet's briefings, many of us who've had an interest have learned a bit about you. As Gerald indicated, one thing we learned is that you're higher level than most or all of us here. Another is that you spoke to her in your correspondence about cultivating Energy for the advancement of your Core. Would you feel offended if I asked what type of Core you have? Your affinities?"

"Heh." Victor didn't have to raise his voice; the speaking stone carried his softly spoken reaction perfectly to every ear in the amphitheater. He shook his head, amused and dismayed, unsure how to proceed. Here he was, confronted with hundreds of people, and they wanted to know things that were rather intimate, things that could lead to him being harmed by his enemies. He supposed the best way to handle it was to explain. "First, I can see you all have been a little sheltered out here in the frontier. I'm surprised Olivia, at least, hasn't spoken to you about etiquette when it comes to sharing things like affinities, levels, skills, etcetera. If she has tried to explain and you all haven't taken her seriously, let me say that you should listen. You don't want people in the wider world or beyond to know about your affinities."

He wanted to pace about as he spoke, but he had to keep his foot on the stone, so he settled for stretching his neck while he gathered his thoughts. "For example, during our war against the invaders from Dark Ember, one of my enemies learned too much about my affinities and managed to entrap me. That action led to the deaths of hundreds of good people, people who were counting on me. You have to believe that there are those who will use you in any way possible to advance their agenda, whatever it might be. You should have learned something like that from your experience with ap'Gravin. Olivia told me he almost kidnapped half your population!"

The woman didn't back down. She only nodded, holding up a hand to forestall Alec's objection. "I understand that, Victor, but this town hall is about learning, and I think we could learn much from you. Without telling me your affinities, then, will you talk about your Core type? According to Olivia, that cat's out of the bag, yes? This is a relevant topic, and I'll illustrate that with a quick follow-up." Victor suddenly realized what she was getting at. She knew his Core type and wanted to make a point about it, but sought his permission to speak openly.

"Ah, I understand. I appreciate your consideration. I have a Spirit Core." He looked around at the people sitting on the stone benches and tried to gauge their reaction. The murmuring buzz of conversation had increased, and he saw some blatantly dismissive expressions from quite a number of people. A couple of men near the upper exit actually stood and began to leave.

"Do you see the ignorant reaction some of my fellow citizens are having to your statement, Mr. Sandoval? Not a single human in First Landing has a Spirit Core, yet they were rather abundant with the so-called 'low-affinity' species, which until recently were living among us. Despite the novelty of Cores in general, and our great dearth of understanding, there are those among us who believe they know enough to dismiss an entire category as inferior and less evolved. What say you?"

Victor frowned and rubbed his chin. His Quinametzin pride was annoyed, and he was toying with the idea of casting Iron Berserk and demonstrating his "inferiority" to those pitiful people, especially the men who'd stood and begun to leave. He thought about canceling his Shape Self spell and letting his full aura roll out over them, crushing them into submission with his Aura of Command. Instead, he shrugged and smiled, speaking more calmly than ever, letting his deep voice rumble smoothly out to the audience. "Plenty of people have underestimated me. Plenty have thought to punish or kill me with their superior affinities, only to be ground to dust, forgotten as a footnote in the history of my conquests."

8

THE OPPOSITION

At the crowd's reaction to his words, Victor immediately began questioning his decision not to put some weight behind his statement. Maybe he should have let his aura loose and allowed the people in the audience to understand that his words weren't empty. He'd struggled with his Quinametzin pride, though, and won, and now he wouldn't change course. Many people had shot to their feet, crowding toward the speaking stones. There were four of them, with four different queues, but orderly patience had been cast aside as some of the audience members apparently took Victor's words about "grinding his enemies to dust" as a threat.

Despite the noise-dampening magic in the amphitheater, the buzz of the crowd was loud enough to make the people at the front of the lines feel they had to shout. The stones amplified those shouts, so they felt they had to contend with each other, creating a chaotic din in which Victor began to revel. It almost sounded like a battlefield to him, and something of a mad grin spread on his lips as he stood tall on the stage and watched the chaos unfold. Alec wasn't so content to let his town hall fall apart. He stood and, red-faced, began to shout. Whatever magic the amphitheater employed allowed his voice to cut through the clamor.

"Quiet! Order! Keep your seats! We have a process here, and you all know it. Victor will be happy to answer follow-up questions, and as you can see, he means no harm with his words." Alec gestured to Victor as he stood calmly atop his speaking stone, arms loose by his sides, a—perhaps disturbing—smile on his face. "Order! Quiet! One at a time!" Alec continued to admonish the crowd until, after four or five repeated requests for order, the buzz finally began to die down. Alec pointed to the man at the front of the centermost line of waiting townsfolk. "Richard, you were about to leave, and now you're at the front of the line. I see the people behind you are content to allow you to hold that spot, so why don't you ask your question."

Victor could see what Alec was doing. It was evident that more than half the audience hadn't liked his response. It was also apparent that they had some ringleaders among them, and this guy, Richard, was one of them. If Alec let Victor deal with his questions, he probably figured the town hall could move on to more productive topics. As Richard, a thin man with very broad shoulders wearing clothing that wouldn't have been out of place in an ancient Rome revival, cleared his throat, Victor stared down his nose at him and folded his arms. "Ahem, yes, Victor, is it? Right, well, would you mind clarifying what you just said? Was that meant as a threat to First Landing?"

Victor looked around the audience and saw that most of them had settled down, and the queues had returned to orderly lines near the speaking stones. He looked down to the front row where Issa and other high-ranking guests sat. She was impassive, though he thought he saw something of a smile in her eyes as she watched him. However, her neighbor, an older man with swarthy skin and hard eyes wearing a very Earth-style suit, looked more than disturbed. Victor figured he'd try to turn the tables on the guy asking him questions. "I was talking about people who sought to do me harm. Did you take that to mean you?" As he spoke, he unfolded his arms and tried to look relaxed and reasonable.

"Perhaps you could enlighten us. Whom have you been grinding to dust during your time away from Earth? Why should we be entertaining a violent warmonger?"

"Are you entertaining me?" Victor's smile faded, and his eyes began to glower, his restraint on his pride fading far more quickly than he'd anticipated. "So far, I'm unamused. To answer your question, I was brought into this world as a slave, and I killed most of those who wanted to keep me that way." Victor was, of course, simplifying things, but he wasn't feeling charitable with his words just then.

Alec had seen enough, and it was clear he was starting to worry that the town hall would devolve into a shouting match again. "Do you have a question for our guest, or are you going to badger him? The topic at hand, I believe, is Spirit Cores."

"Certainly." The man adjusted the sash-like belt around his waist and straightened up, clearing his throat. "We've learned through our study that the use of Spirit Cores is relegated to the low-affinity species of this world because they are directly tied to emotion. As anyone who's studied history can tell you, emotion isn't what successful nations are built upon. Why should we take advice from you, a man who is, admittedly, a slave to his emotions?"

Victor chuckled, shaking his head and rubbing his chin as he tried to unpack the loaded question. Again, he felt frustrated being tied to the speaking stone; he was a man who liked to move and especially so when he was trying to think. Finally, after several long seconds during which he could hear the faint buzz of the audience growing impatient, he replied, "First, I'd say that you need to revisit your studies. Spirit Cores aren't tied to emotions, but our emotions connect us to our spirits. Notice I said 'our.' All of you have spirits, but those of us gifted with a Spirit Core are able to harness that Energy. I'll say one final word on this matter publicly: A person with a Spirit Core isn't a slave to their emotions but rather one who must learn to master them. If not for my many hours of torturous introspection, I would have lost myself to one emotion or another during this town hall, for instance." Victor nodded as though confirming his words to himself, then he sat down.

"But that's not . . ." the man started to say, only to be cut off by Alec.

"Let's keep things moving, folks." He pointed to another queue and said, "Raif, what's your question?"

"Ahem, yes. I was wondering if we might hear some more about this invasion that took place. How did an army arrive on Fanwath from another world? How many soldiers were there? Why was it imperative that you do battle? Rumors I'm hearing are that mere thousands of people were fighting over millions of acres. Couldn't negotiations have taken place?"

Valla stood up. "I'll take this one." She stepped onto her speaking stone and with a clear, unemotional voice, said, "That's an interesting question, and I can see why you'd ask it, being that you and your people are from a world untouched by the System. Those of us who've lived our lives under the System, though, know that while it may seem like a deity at times, it does not, in fact, care about us, or if it does, it cares in the way a mother boyii hound cares about her young—survival is the only important goal. If there's only food for three pups and she has four, she will abandon the weakest one.

"Think of the System as that harsh mother hound. It sees growth as the most important thing, and to foster that growth, it will pit its 'pups' against one another. In the case of the invasion from Dark Ember, the System chose invaders who were fundamentally incompatible with us, opened a portal, and allowed them to funnel tens of thousands of their people into the land we were marching to settle. To foster the competition, the System offered rewards for conquest along with the high stakes of knowing that if one side failed, it would spell doom for their kind on this world."

Valla clearly wasn't done speaking, but the man interjected. "How can that be? What sort of doom? We've not seen any evidence of world-ending weapons on this planet. No nuclear technology or plague or . . ."

"Sir, if you'd allow me to finish, the answer to your question may become clear." Valla paused, but the man nodded, waiting, so she continued. "Firstly, if you've not seen any world-ending magic or plagues, you've not been here long enough. They exist. Secondly, these invaders were just such a thing—a plague given sentience. They were undead, and not only did they seek to subjugate all the peoples of Fanwath, they sought to turn the very land into a haven for their kind. As they spread . . ."

Valla continued to expound on the dangers of the undead, answering many follow-up questions about the System, about conquests, about portals, and her evidence for the System's harsh nature. It seemed that the people who wanted to press for more and more detail were never satisfied, and Victor began to remember how frustrating it could be to argue with those who'd already made their minds up about something. The entire town hall was a bit of a sham in his mind. Issa's people thought a certain way, her competition thought another, and they both sought to make the other look stupid. It felt as if Issa was the more rational, correct one, but Victor couldn't help feeling used.

While Valla spoke, he wondered if they were just wasting time. Looking around the audience, the same people looked as incredulous as when he'd first riled them up by talking about how he'd crushed his enemies. He was beginning to understand why Issa had talked her opposition into setting up a "demonstration" of their war machines. It was going to take the slap of harsh reality to make them see reason. ". . . perhaps Nia, here, will better be able to illustrate that point." Victor snapped his mind back to reality as Nia, nervously clenching her hands together, stood up to speak.

"Hello," she said, flinching as her voice echoed through the amphitheater.

"Ah, hello, Miss Nia," Alec said, trying to smooth the transition. "Allow me to repeat the question—would you say the, um, 'great undead lords,' as Lady ap'Yensha called them, are equivalent to the Ridonne faction of the Empire?"

"I . . ." Nia paused and licked her lips, glancing at Victor. He nodded at her, and he could almost see the determination take shape in her eyes as she steeled herself and kept speaking. "I haven't met your Ridonne, but I've heard tales. The soldiers I've fought with, they told me about the Ridonne Lords Victor fought, and they sounded fierce indeed. Still, those soldiers said Prince Hector was worse, that his bone dragon alone was enough to send a Ridonne lord running. Well, Prince Hector was a lickboot on Dark Ember, a 'princeling,' the great lords called him. So, to answer your question, aye, the great lords are like your Ridonne, but only 'cause they rule over a world. If they were to come here, the Ridonne would be on bent knee within a day."

Victor grinned as he watched the crowd's reaction. The suppressed hum of conversation rose in volume, and several people tried to speak using the stones at once. Alec calmed them down, and then Victor listened as the following ten questions seemed to be aimed at getting Nia to admit she was exaggerating. She wouldn't budge. The town hall went on like that, and Victor tried to stay seated as much as possible, giving his companions plenty of opportunity to speak. Borrius did an excellent job dragging out the responses to questions about the Ridonne Empire, its ruling practices, and its military capabilities.

Valla spoke at length about Zaafor and Coloss, but she grew frustrated at one point trying to describe the disparity in strength between the Warlord and his war captains, so she asked Victor to help explain things. He stood up and talked about how the Warlord kept his Colony Stone under tight control, issuing tokens for its use and keeping the best rewards for himself. The real lesson wasn't there, though; it was in how the Warlord himself was stagnating, so Victor tried to explain. "What you all need to understand is that the Warlord, despite spending more than a thousand years working to improve his Core and gain levels, was kind of stuck. He'd reached the limit of what he could do in his world. I believe that's a good lesson for you, if I understand Lady ap'Roald's concern."

"Pardon me?" the man at the speaking stone asked. Victor didn't remember his name, but he was a member of the First Landing Parliament. He looked fit, and if Victor were guessing, he'd say the guy had eaten a racial advancement or two. "Is that the concern *Lady* Issa has? What nonsense. How can staying in one world stagnate a person? Innovation doesn't cease because you've not ventured forth. Rather than support Issa's stance, I believe you've undermined it. This man, the 'Warlord' you speak of, exemplifies how trying to gain power through Energy cultivation is a fool's errand. Rather, we need to demonstrate to these backward peoples what technology is capable of. If someone like this 'Warlord' presented a threat to us, how would he fare versus a missile strike?"

Victor snorted and shook his head. "You aren't listening. The Warlord worked for millennia to improve himself. He grew powerful enough to rule his world, and, if he came here, he could conquer this one easily. You can't stop a guy like that with guns or bombs—you'd never see him coming! Forget him, though; he was nothing next to a dragon I met . . ."

"A dragon? What's next? Are you going to join in on the hysterics of Dr. Bennet about fairies and . . ."

"Ah," Alec said, speaking over the man, his master speaking stone making his voice impossible to ignore. "That's just about the end of our time, and I feel it's a good note to end on—Lester, you speak about the superiority of human technology, and as you know, Victor has agreed to participate in your party's demonstration. By his own admission, Victor has a long way to go before he's at the Warlord of Coloss's level, so it should be a good indication of how ready our defenses are when it comes to powerful invaders." Several people tried to speak using the stones, but Alec did something to turn them off, fiddling with a device he held.

Victor noticed the stone he stood on was also no longer glowing, and he turned to Valla. "What a bunch of assholes."

"Oh, I don't know," Borrius said. "I sat in many sessions of the Imperial Senate, and this was far less contentious. Politics is an ugly business, Victor."

"Was I all right?" Nia asked before Valla could formulate a response to Victor's declaration of assholery.

"You were great." Victor held out his hand, and Valla took it, standing up beside him. As the audience began to file out, men and women wearing blue and gray uniforms and carrying bulky musket-like guns walked in from the stage's wings. They stood at the aisles, ensuring everyone left and that Victor and his companions weren't accosted by people wanting to get some one-on-one questions in. "These people really have already made guns." He sighed as Alec walked over to them with Issa.

"I'm so sorry," Issa said before Alec could get a word in.

"Nonsense," Valla said, smiling. "As Borrius just said, politics are ugly."

"I'd so hoped to have something more academic in this town hall! When Olivia proposed it, she'd thought you'd have time to detail your experiences and, through them, convince people of the need for cooperation and mutual edification. I didn't think we'd have to talk in circles again and again while the

P and Ds tried to discredit you. Alec, how did they get so many representatives in the queues?"

"I don't know. I'm sorry, Issa. We interviewed everyone, but they must have lied."

"P and Ds?" Valla raised an eyebrow.

Issa sighed, shaking her head. "They're the opposition party to everything we try to accomplish. Progress and Dominion—a platform for recapturing their Earth technologies and expansion through, as the name implies, dominion. It's ugly!"

"Excuse me," a smooth masculine voice said from off to the left. Victor looked to see a familiar figure—the guy in the business suit. He had two men walking behind him, and they both carried weapons that looked very much like fancy handcrafted machine guns. He wasn't very tall, but he looked reasonably fit beneath his suit. He had a full head of wavy dark hair, and his equally dark eyes twinkled with amusement as he chuckled, approaching them all. "Oh, dear, that wasn't anything like we'd hoped, was it, Issa? I had so many questions we never got round to. I hope we might sit down together before you all leave."

Issa sighed and gestured to the newcomer. "This is Darren Whitehorse, a member of our Parliament and one of the leaders of the P and D party, along with Norton Holmes."

"Right, right." He nodded, extending his hand to Borrius. "My apologies, I should have introduced myself. I'm sorry for some of the more hostile-seeming questions, too. I'm afraid old Norton has the party rather whipped up about this whole affair." Borrius shook his hand, and Victor regarded him. The man looked smug and very secure in his position, likely due to the large men with guns standing behind him. Maybe it was Victor's ranks in intelligence, maybe it was his gut, or maybe it was just more obvious than it should have been, but he connected some dots.

As he shook the man's hand, purposefully barely squeezing, he said, "I think I can see why a political party would want to push an agenda like yours."

"Oh? What an interesting greeting. What agenda do you mean?"

"Isn't it obvious? When people learn about the strength they can unlock through Core, level, and racial advancement, when they learn there's competition for resources to improve those things, they'll do what they can to suppress the interest of others."

"Ah, hmm." Darren frowned, then shrugged. "An interesting take, sir, but that's not the case here. In any event, a crowd is gathering on the northern wall, and the demonstration is ready. Are you still willing to put yourself on display? My people are eager to show everyone what we've accomplished."

"Mmhmm. After that 'town hall,' I've got the urge to break something." Victor smiled, put an arm over Valla's shoulders, and gestured toward the stairs leading out of the amphitheater. "Shall we?"

"Of course, of course. There is just one small matter we need to discuss on the topic of liability. We're rather worried that your allies and"—he glanced at Nia and narrowed his eyes—"followers will seek retribution should something untoward happen to you during the demonstration." He held out his hand, and one of the machine-gun-toting soldiers handed him a rolled parchment. "Would you mind agreeing to an Energy contract indemnifying us?"

"Hmm? Oh, that shouldn't be a problem. I believe Borrius has one for you as well. He'll review your contract while we walk." Victor looked at the solemn-faced old commander. "That's right, isn't it, Borrius?"

"Indeed. We wouldn't want First Landing to grow angry if you destroy their war machines."

"Right, right." Again, Victor gestured to the stairs. "Shall we?"

"Yes, right this way," Issa said, leading their small procession off the stage and up through the now empty amphitheater.

"Oh, but . . ." Darren Whitehorse hurried to walk beside Victor as he took the steps two at a time. "Wouldn't you want to read the contract?"

"Borrius will read it. He's written and signed hundreds of them." Victor looked at the man, offered him a sly wink, and added, "Wouldn't want to strain my primitive mind on all those words, you know?" He would have said more, would have maybe tried to pick a fight with the guy, but Valla squeezed his biceps where she held his arm as they walked, and he convinced his inner titan to hold back—it was almost time to break some shit.

9

A PRELUDE TO VIOLENCE

I don't get how an Energy contract is going to help here," Victor said, looking at the document in Borrius's hands. "If I die, how is a bargain I struck going to keep my 'allies and followers,' as he put it, from seeking revenge?"

"Ah, well, it's quite a complicated contract. As you complete it, you'll be required to list three individuals who will suffer an Energy-fueled backlash of sorts should punitive action be taken against First Landing as a result of your demise. Before the contract is complete, their signatory party will have to approve the names."

"Nah, that's bullshit. I'm not putting others at risk. Go back to them and work something else out." When Borrius frowned, Victor heard his words and tone echoing in his head and tried to soften them. "I know it's not your fault, and I appreciate you helping with this. Can you please try to negotiate something else? I'm afraid I don't have the tact."

Borrius nodded, his frown smoothing over. "Of course." He turned and approached the group of First Landing representatives—members of Parliament and their aides—about twenty paces away. They were standing atop the southern ramparts of First Landing's outer walls. Now that the sun was well up, Victor had to admit the walls were pretty spectacular. Much about the settlement was impressive. After the town hall, they'd taken a leisurely walk with Alec and Issa as guides. Despite knowing that Darren Whitehorse and his "Progress and Dominion" party were waiting for them, Issa insisted that they see some of the infrastructure the colony had been hard at work implementing.

The roads were the first thing Victor noticed—they were straight, flat, and orderly, laid out in a pattern that made him realize just how different the cities of Fanwath were from those he'd known on Earth, an admittedly small sample. In Persi Gables, for instance, the streets were narrow, winding, and very difficult to navigate if you weren't a native. In First Landing, once Victor had learned that the tall metallic tower was on the southern side of town, he never had any trouble figuring out where he was. It also helped that the center of town was on higher ground, with streets leading away from it like spokes on a wheel. Avenues circled "Bronwyn's Hill," every one of them crossing the two central boulevards. No matter where a person was, they could walk along one of those gently curving roads, and eventually they'd come to Broadway or Main.

Victor wasn't impressed with the creativity in their street names, but he couldn't argue with the practicality of the layout. As they'd walked, Issa pointed out the streetlights powered by Energy, which wasn't a big deal to Victor, but when she pointed to weird copper posts on every corner and said they were "communication hubs," allowing nearby homes and businesses to connect to a telephone system, Victor had to give props to the artisan-engineers who'd come from Earth.

The other standout was the cars. Victor had seen vehicles powered by Energy in other cities, especially Coloss, but the humans had gone a long way to recapturing the look of modern automobiles from Earth. They had metallic bodies and glass windshields and were painted in bright colors. More than that, they were aerodynamic, had some kind of rubbery material for tires, and were equipped with brake lights and turn signals. Nothing like them existed in the other cities of Fanwath.

Standing atop the gigantic whitewashed outer wall, Victor could look back toward the town, across a large expanse of mostly empty land where residences were being constructed, to the older earthen wall that surrounded the central built-up part of First Landing. Jutting above it, on the gently sloping ground, was the gleaming brass tower that Issa said was her home. It was tall and imposing, considering it was made of metal, and it made for a good landmark. Issa had explained that the System had awarded it to Morgan Hall for completing some kind of dungeon.

"What are you thinking?" Valla asked, turning toward him and leaning an elbow on the chalky white crenellation. "Seems you're avoiding looking out at the field. Are you getting nervous?"

Victor scoffed, shook his head, and then smiled at her. "You're joking, right?" He turned to the field beyond the high wall and looked at the twenty shiny steel tanks. There was no mistaking that they were tanks. They had treads, not wheels, no windows, and they all sported a turret with various types of protruding tubes—clearly weapons.

"They're large and made of thick, enchanted metal. Are you sure you can damage them? What if you injure Lifedrinker?"

"If I were a normal person or, well, even a low-level cultivator, I'd be worried. I'd say they have to weigh ten or twenty tons each, and I bet the Energy weapons these guys have cooked up are impressive. They figure they can blast some airships out of the sky and steamroll some little soldiers, but they've never seen a titan. Anyway, don't worry about Lifedrinker. I have another axe I've been holding onto, one I got from Karl the Crimson while you were sleeping the days away back at the Sea Keep."

She darted out her hand, pinching him on the side of his pectoral. "Sleeping the days away?" He winced and laughed, and she relented, chuckling along with him. "Well, you never showed me an axe."

"We got kind of busy after you woke up." Victor winked at her, and her laugh got louder, her cheeks flushing just a little as she squinted at him in the bright sunlight.

She nodded toward the rampart behind him. "Here comes Borrius."

Victor turned and smiled at the dour-faced old commander. "What's the verdict?"

"I have managed to strike new terms with them. They ask that, in lieu of you signing the contract, Valla does. She must agree that the Free Marches will not hold them responsible for your demise, else she will suffer Energy depletion."

"Not a chance—"

"I'll do it. When does it expire?"

"In two hours' time. They think that will be plenty for the demonstration."

Victor frowned at Valla and shook his head. "I don't want you getting tied up in this BS."

"It's nothing, Victor. We need the quick supply of Energy beads if we want to help Edeya soon. If you were to lose, I wouldn't blame them anyway. You've agreed to this with open eyes. It bothers me a bit that they don't trust our honor, but I'll sign the stupid document."

Victor stared at her for a long moment, then turned to Borrius. "You're sure nothing sneaky is in the language?"

"Nothing at all, and that Darren Whitehorse fellow will be signing my contract, the language of which explicitly states that he is not being duplicitous." He paused, shook his head, then added, "I suppose I should state that they insist on a single line in the contract that gives me some doubt."

"Yeah?" Victor raised an eyebrow.

"Yes. The terms of the contest are that they can bring to bear 'all defense machinery on the field, visible or otherwise.'"

"Huh?" Victor looked out at the twenty shiny tanks, squinting as he scanned the field for anything else. "Something invisible?" A thought occurred to him, and he summoned his little magical spyglass from his ring. Scanning through it at the tanks, he saw they had no halo at all. Either the magic of the spyglass thought he was right and they wouldn't be a problem, or it didn't work on non-living machines. He figured it was the latter.

"Or hidden inside the machines?" Valla speculated.

Borrius nodded and shrugged. "Or under the ground. Does it concern you?"

"Nah." Victor put his spyglass away.

"I thought not. Shall we?" He gestured toward the group of First Landers.

"All right." Victor wasn't happy about Valla signing the contract, but if it only lasted two hours and all she had to do was not seek retribution, he couldn't see how it was a problem for her. The real issue was that Darren and his people thought they needed it. Why were they so confident that Victor was going to die? Were they simply underestimating him, or was he the one doing the underestimating? He'd seen plenty of videos featuring tanks back on Earth. He'd seen them drive through buildings, smash cars and trucks like they were made of cardboard, and of course shoot their cannons, destroying all manner of things. Was he being stupid? Could he take on twenty tanks, even as a titan? Victor chuckled at the lack of concern he still felt. Maybe his Quinametzin pride was making him stupid, but he wasn't worried.

"Amused?" Whitehorse asked as they approached.

"Yeah, I guess so." Victor shrugged.

"Victor, you don't have to do this," Issa said, stepping around Whitehorse to get closer.

"Like I said earlier, I'm looking forward to it. I haven't had any exercise in a couple of days." Victor heard muttering and incredulity from the crowd behind them. He'd met a lot of the members of Parliament and some other government officials, but if he were being honest, Victor didn't feel like memorizing all of their names. Maybe if he came back after helping Edeya and stuck around for a while, he'd make more of an effort, but right now, they were just a bunch of politicians to him. Issa and Alec were friendly faces,

Whitehorse was kind of a prick, and that was about the extent of his desire to get to know these people.

"Excellent." Whitehorse smiled, and to Victor, he looked like a cat getting his ears rubbed. Why was the guy so damn happy? "Let's sign these documents, and you can use the lift there to descend to the gate." He pointed to the large freight elevator they'd built into their wall. Victor stepped back and let Borrius and Valla handle the paperwork. He leaned against the wall and stared out at the field, wondering what Whitehorse was hiding. He supposed the tanks could be full of robots. Maybe they really didn't understand the difference between a Tier Three or Four human and a Tier Six Quinametzin. Did they think they could overwhelm him with numbers? He smiled in anticipation.

"That's a very hungry grin on your face, Victor." Issa had quietly come to stand beside him.

He looked into her bright golden-yellow eyes and saw concern. "Hey, relax. It'll be fine."

"I just want you to know that Darren's engineers have been hard at work preparing for this demonstration. They've really talked it up. You can see"—she gestured down the walkway atop the rampart, past the roped cordon and security guards, at the enormous crowd gathered to watch the event—"that they've been running a promotional campaign. He thinks this will catapult his party into primacy."

Victor shrugged. "Okay, well, I don't intend to make them look good. I mean, it can't have been cheap to make those things. I almost feel a little guilty."

She looked at him, tilting her neck to take in his height fully. "You're a big man, no question, but not much taller than my Morgan. He has powerful magic, and I'm sure he could destroy these machines. At least one of them . . ." She frowned and trailed off. When Victor didn't respond, she blurted, "I've seen how thick the enchanted metal armor on those things is! How can you hope to damage them with that axe?"

"This axe?" Victor pulled Lifedrinker from her harness and held her toward Issa. "I'd never abuse this beauty by making her smash up some dumb machines. No, she's too good for this sort of thing." Lifedrinker buzzed in his grip, pleased by his attention. Her Heart Silver blade gleamed in the sunlight, but she was cool—not a hint of heat or smoke drifted out of her. Smiling, he slung her back over his shoulder, and her harness snatched her up, pulling her tight to his back. "Don't worry, Lady Issa."

"That's that," Darren announced, coming to stand beside Issa. He was grinning from ear to ear, displaying very nice straight white teeth. "I appreciate your willingness to help us demonstrate the effectiveness of our machines. As I'm sure your representative, Mr. ap'Gandro, informed you, should things prove difficult and you wish to save your own life, simply run for the gate, and we'll let you in. The contest will then be over."

"Mmhmm. And you guys?" Victor looked at him, still grinning, still excited at the idea that he'd soon be breaking things.

"Us?"

"Yeah, how will you signal for me to stop? Breaking your little machines, I mean."

"Little, hmm? Well, don't you worry, Mr. Sandoval. That's not an eventuality that we're concerned with."

Victor cocked an eyebrow at him and then shrugged. "You signed the contract, yeah? I'm not paying for 'em."

"Of course, of course." Whitehorse had the nerve to squint slightly in amusement and wink at Victor. Victor felt a little heat start to leak out of his Core into his pathways; if he hadn't been ready before, now he really wanted to smash some shit.

"So, you want me just to go out there and stand in the middle of the field? Are you going to signal when to start?"

"Of course! We'll fire a flare to make it clear, but the machines will also begin. Please be on your toes, sir, and remember my offer to cease hostilities should you run for the gate." Whitehorse smiled and turned, gesturing toward the elevator, but Valla, who'd followed him over from the document signing, stood in his way.

"I'd like your assurance that you'll stop the machines if I ask you to as well. What if Victor can't break free?"

"Valla . . ." Victor started to protest, but Whitehorse responded immediately, effusive in his eagerness to please.

"I will happily agree to that! No one wants to see Victor lose his life today."

Victor sighed but decided to let it drop; if it made Valla feel better, he was fine with the condition. Since he wasn't arguing, he hopped atop the whitewashed crenellation and, amid the gasps and startled exclamations of the crowd, said, "I'll head down. Don't start till I wave." He didn't wait for a response; he simply stepped into the air and let himself fall nearly a hundred feet to the hard-packed gravel ground. As the wind whistled past his ears, he severed his connection to his Shape Self spell, expanding from something near seven feet tall to nearly ten.

He doubted anyone on the rampart could see the change now that he was below them and some distance away, but it was important because once he was back to normal, his Titanic Leap ability allowed him to land from the great fall without any discomfort. Even so, his impact was loud, and the ground rippled beneath his feet, a dust cloud bursting up around him. Victor had good hearing, along with all his other senses, and he could hear the gasps and exclamations from atop the wall. He smiled in his dust cloud, wondering what they thought.

As he caught himself enjoying the reaction, he felt a little guilty, a little childish. He hadn't even hugged Valla or said goodbye, so intent had he been on catching the First Landing folk by surprise. "Ah, fuck it. I'll see her soon enough." With that, he started forward, striding out of the slight depression he'd created and onto the field. At ground level, the tanks were bigger than they'd seemed from the ramparts. "Shit," he muttered, looking at the twenty gleaming colossal vehicles. They were probably ten feet high at the tops of their turrets, maybe just as wide and twice that in length. "These things are going to take a pounding." Victor scanned through his storage ring, looking for Karl's axe. "Don't be upset, *chica*; I'm just going to use this other axe for a little while, just to smash some big tin cans."

Issa watched the young human drop from the ramparts and smiled as most of the people around her responded with alarm. She knew better; even she could survive that fall, and she'd yet to reach Tier Three. Undoubtedly, someone who was, if the rumors were to be believed, higher than Tier Five wouldn't be overly harmed by such a drop. The fact that Valla didn't so much as flinch was a good signal that nothing was amiss. Still, it illustrated how much the people of First Landing had to learn. Many of them clearly thought he'd just leaped to his death. When he impacted the ground, and the sound traveled up to their lofty position like a brief rumble of thunder, that was another matter.

"Is he all right?" she asked, peering over the crenellation to the cloud of dust that obscured the man from view. "That sounded like quite an impact!"

"He's heavier than he looks." Valla smiled at her reassuringly. "He's fine." She looked over her shoulder at the startled, even panicked, faces of the governmental delegation. "He's fine, everyone. Don't worry."

"He walks!" someone cried from the audience farther down the wall where the large crowd of onlookers had gathered. A smattering of applause broke out, and even a few cheers as Victor strode out of the dust cloud, walking as though out for a stroll into the middle of the field of short blue-green grass. He looked tiny compared to the giant metal automatons Darren's people had been toiling so hard to build over the last months.

"He'll eat that up," Valla said, sighing as she leaned over the crenellation. Her words said one thing, but her smile said another.

"You truly love him." Issa's face flushed, and she quickly added, "I'm sorry, that's none of my business."

"It's anyone's business who wants to know. I love Victor Sandoval with all my heart."

"Yet you're not worried?"

"He's worried me before. I was worried when he faced off against a thousand undead reavers. I was worried when he chased a mad Death Caster up the slopes of an active volcano. This doesn't worry me much."

"Well," Darren said, speaking up from Valla's other side, "I'm very sorry for any harm that may come to him. You heard me warn him. Please be ready to throw in the towel for him." Issa hadn't heard the expression before, but she could figure out what he meant. She was sure Valla did as well. He cleared his throat, and Issa could tell he was getting ready to signal the start of the demonstration, but then he coughed and started to laugh. "God! Look at the foolish man. That axe is larger than he is! Can he even swing it?"

Issa jerked her eyes back to the field and Victor. He still stood in the center of the field, but a few things had changed. He wore a black and red armored vest that shimmered as the bright sunlight reflected off its scales. Atop his head was a thick dark metal helmet that covered the top of his face, shielding his eyes behind angry, angular slits. He also now held the handle of a weapon. An impossibly massive black metal axe rested on the ground behind his shoulder, on which he held its handle. The handle had to be fourteen or fifteen feet long, and at its end, half buried in the grass, was a chisel-like axe-head that probably weighed a thousand pounds.

"Oh," Valla said, a slow smile spreading her beautiful lips, "he can swing it."

10

TIMING IS EVERYTHING

Victor hefted the handle of the giant axe, grinning at the way he had to strain just to lift it onto his shoulder. The massive axe-head was still resting on the ground behind him. He figured if the axe were made of steel, it would weigh a couple thousand pounds. The blade stood up from the ground more than a yard, and the spike on the backside was buried in the soft soil another foot, sunk there by gravity when Victor summoned it from his ring. The fact of the matter, though, was that the axe wasn't made of steel. It wasn't iron. It was some alloy or magical metal that neither he nor any of the men and women of the ninth could identify. It was far heavier and denser than an iron-based alloy, but it wasn't soft like lead or gold—they'd ruined hammers trying to test the edge.

Without his Iron Berserk, Victor could lift the axe and swing it, but it was unwieldy, and the momentum of the great weapon would throw him off balance. No, he'd found that to use it effectively, he needed the size his Berserk granted him and the strength from his Titanic Rage feat. He twisted his hands on the metal axe haft, grinning at how his fingers could barely wrap around the dark metal. He wondered what the silly bastards up on the wall were thinking. Did they think he was insane? Did they wonder how he'd swing such a massive implement? He was having a good time keeping them wondering.

When he'd released his Alter Self spell, he'd done it as he fell away from the crowds, far beneath them. His hope was that they wouldn't be able to discern the fact that he'd suddenly grown. No other people were on the field, and the axe was enormous, so he figured they thought he was still the same size he'd been. He loved the idea of pounding those tanks into scrap without revealing his full titanic form. He loved it so much that he was going to try to fight them without berserking, just to see if he could pull it off. "Yep, *chica*," he said, looking at his shoulder where Lifedrinker's haft jutted up, "I'll just start off slow. It's better I don't get too pissed off anyway, right? Wouldn't want me to lose my shit and smash through that wall." He chuckled, shaking his head, starting to daydream, but then he realized they were probably waiting for him to signal that he was ready.

Victor smiled and muttered, "Timing is everything," then lifted his right arm in the air, waving it back and forth. Almost immediately, an answering *boom* sounded from the far corner of the wall, and a sparkling red flare flew into the air, arcing over the field. Victor had good reflexes when it came to starting a contest. From the ancient-seeming days when he'd been a wrestler and waited for the whistle or beep to the death battles in the pits, arenas, and colosseums, he'd always been quick to jump into combat. This was no different, and he literally leaped into action. He squatted, flexed his powerful thighs, and gripping the massive axe as if he was trying to uproot a streetlamp, he launched into the air toward the centermost tank on the field's eastern edge.

The axe ripped a massive divot out of the ground, trailing dirt and grass as he flew through the air with it hanging behind his shoulder. Soaring through the air, he began to bunch the wire-taut muscles of his shoulders and arms, getting ready to swing the tremendous weapon over his shoulder as he descended. Of course, he was channeling Sovereign Will into his strength and vitality. Of course, he'd pulled that hot, familiar rage-attuned Energy from his Core and into his pathways, casting Channel Spirit to fill his arms and the massive axe with its furious heat. Considering the axe's black metal and the trail of dirt, it was hard to see, but if one were discerning, they might catch the hint of a faint red halo limning the weapon.

As he reached the apex of his leap, some thirty yards in the air, and began to descend, Victor saw the automated Energy-driven tanks had reacted to the signal, or perhaps some remote operator had. He didn't know how smart the things were on their own. Regardless, they'd all rumbled to life, their treads glowing with yellow Energy, their turrets turning to try to track him, but only a few had enough vertical mobility. Victor had no idea what they might fire out of their many differently shaped barrels, but he didn't find out right away;

he'd gotten the jump on them—Victor laughed at the pun—and before they could react enough to stop him, he fell like a flesh-and-metal comet on his chosen victim. With a roar loud enough to be heard over the rumble of the many machines, he jerked his gigantic axe over his head. His feet hit the turf with a muffled *boom*, and he smashed the weapon down on the tank.

Karl's axe, focusing thousands of pounds of metal on a wedge-shaped cutting edge, split through the shiny tank like a hatchet hitting an aluminum can. Victor had placed his blow on the front quarter of the machine, just in front of the turret, and the axe tore through the armor, the metal gears, and whatever else was inside, all the way down into the ground. In a spectacular shower of rainbow-hued sparks and flames, the machine began to come apart at the seams. Victor would have loved to watch the show, to see the various liquids spurting forth, to listen to the pop of magical crystals and fuses, but he knew better than to stand around when nineteen other enemies were targeting him.

As the concussive sounds of cannons being fired echoed around him, Victor jerked on the enormous axe and started running toward the machine to his left. The shots weren't aimed at where he currently was, thankfully, because the axe didn't want to come free. Victor's momentum was brought to a screeching halt as the blade caught up in the smoldering, smoking metal of the ruined tank, and, despite the vast disparity in their relative mass, Victor began to drag the vehicle through the grass. He only made it a few feet before it became too much for him, the treads buried a foot into the soft soil. Still, as it bit into the ground, the axe jerked free, and Victor veritably flew through the grass toward the next tank as it set its sights on him.

"Jesus Christ!" someone off to her right exclaimed, confirming, if Valla had doubted the fact, that these people came from Victor's home world. The outburst had come when Victor launched himself into the air and smashed one of the machines before any of the automatons could react. She couldn't help her small smile and slight nod, approving of Victor's showmanship. He was holding a lot back, but it was probably wise; Borrius thought these humans had something in reserve, and she agreed.

She watched Victor struggle to pull his axe out of the wreckage of the first machine, saw him actually pull the massive vehicle a short way through the grass, and then sprint toward the next one as the axe broke free. All the while, colorful explosions were bursting in the air as the other war machines fired, belatedly, at the places Victor had been as he soared toward the first broken construct. "Quite a spectacle," Issa said beside her. "Reminds me of a harvest celebration back home."

"That axe," Darren Whitehorse said from the other side of her, "it must weigh thousands of pounds to do that to our tank. How does he move with it like that?" He sounded genuinely incredulous. Hadn't he seen the magic people could work in this world? Hadn't he listened to Victor's cousin? Was he so dense?

Before she could respond, Issa did. "I suppose he's put much of his Energy cultivation into improving his physical attributes."

"But . . ." Whitehorse said, wincing as Victor destroyed another machine, this time cleaving the axe in a sideways arc so it broke free with its own momentum. "But, we've had citizens put their leveling attributes into strength; the ones who've focused on that exclusively have reached limits, unable to add more past a ceiling. A ceiling, I might add, that is far less than what would allow anyone to do that!"

"Have you truly refused to listen to what people have tried to explain? Victor has advanced his race to the point where the ceiling for his attributes is far beyond what a normal human or"—she winked at Issa—"Ardeni could reach."

"He's large, but it doesn't explain it. It's not logical! How can he swing that weapon without flinging himself off the ground?" He winced again as Victor, using his weapon's momentum, sprinted across the field toward the advancing row of tanks on the other side. In his wake, the automaton he'd just destroyed was further ruined by the explosions of belated friendly fire. The ground erupted in clouds of smoke and soil as the other machines tried to track Victor's movement but fell short.

Valla peered down her nose at the man, her regal brows narrowing. "Did you not hear him hit the ground when he leaped off this wall? Did you not feel the stones beneath your feet shudder? You underestimate Victor at your own peril."

"He's destroyed two of twenty, and surely he's growing tired. No one can run that fast carrying a weight like that for long." As if he could hear Darren's words, Victor suddenly exploded into the air, performing another impossible leap, the enormous axe hanging behind him as he traversed the second half of the gap between him and the oncoming machines. The ground where he'd launched himself exploded in a series of massive concussions. The soil was pockmarked with craters, and colorful smoke rose in small clouds. Had the machines been too slow-witted to realize he'd leaped? They'd all fired on the last spot he'd stood as though he were still there.

As another tremendous crash echoed up the wall from the field, Valla jerked her eyes away from the smoking, cratered field to see Victor had buried the axe into the center of his target, crumpling the automaton. He'd hit it squarely on the round swiveling part with the cannon barrels, and it exploded, sending Victor and his axe flying through the air. He lost his grip on the weapon and smashed into the field, bouncing and flopping while the axe hit the ground with an audible *thud* and sank into the soil, unmoving. Gasps sounded around her, and further away, down the wall, where the townspeople had gathered, she heard some cries of alarm and, disturbingly, some applause.

"Ah, a pity," Whitehorse said, a smug smile twisting the corner of his mouth. "He seems to have underestimated the explosives within the turret housing. I'm sorry, Lady ap'Yensha."

"Valla will do, sir. Please don't apologize. I doubt Victor is much bothered by that little tumble."

Whitehorse jerked his eyes away from the field, looking at Valla incredulously. "He was just exploded! You saw him flopping on the ground." He looked past her to Issa. "Lady Issa, perhaps you should counsel our guest. I fear she's in . . ."

"He's up!" one of the other members of Parliament crowed. Valla squinted at him, trying to remember his name—Ballad? Bannard? Something like that. She followed his and everyone's gaze back to the field where Victor had stood, looking around with a slightly dazed expression. She wondered if now was the time he'd cast his Iron Berserk spell or summon his banner. Perhaps he'd conjure one of his totems to distract the many machines turning their barrels his way. She saw him moving oddly, his shoulders moving up and down while he rested his hands on his knees. A slow smile crept over her lips as she realized what he was doing.

"Is he all right? Shall I cancel the demonstration?" Whitehorse sounded hopeful.

"He's trying to breathe!" another man said.

"No," Valla said, raising her voice to be heard by all nearby. "He's laughing."

"Ha, what a *pendejo* I am!" Victor laughed, sharing his amusement with Lifedrinker. "I should know these things might explode." Before he could say anything more, he heard the deep *boom*s of the tanks firing at him, and he instinctively jumped into the air. He tried to angle his reflexive leap toward his fallen axe, but he wasn't facing quite the right way, and he couldn't turn once he was airborne. Still, he cleared the area in time to avoid getting pelted with whatever projectiles those things were firing, and when he landed, he turned and sprinted for the gigantic weapon.

He was a little battered, his arms cut and scraped, his face and neck raw from the explosion. His entire body was a little sore; when he'd crashed into the ground, it hadn't felt great. Still, his armor and helmet kept the brunt of the explosion from really affecting him. His feats and affinities made him almost immune to fire. "If I couldn't berserk, I'd feel like hell tomorrow." Victor smiled grimly as he grabbed ahold of the tree-like axe handle. When he pulled on it, he realized the blade had buried itself a good six feet into the soft ground. Jerking and tugging, he grew a little annoyed. His shoulder was sore, and he knew those cannons were retargeting him. As they fired—*thum, thum, thum, thum*—his frustration got the better of him, and he released his tight control on his Core and let his rage flow into his pathways. Without a second thought, he cast Iron Berserk.

"He's gotten himself in a pickle now. That axe is too much for him in his battered state!" Darren Whitehorse smiled at Felicity, his aide and one of the best engineering experts in the colony. She nodded to him, habitually pressing at the space on the bridge of her nose where her glasses used to be; she no longer needed them, but her brain hadn't caught up to the fact.

"He'll have to abandon it, or they'll fire upon him there." She leaned close, looking left and right, perhaps trying to time the rudimentary intelligence she'd helped program into the tanks. "Right about now . . ."

The long range cannon–equipped tanks interrupted her with their *booms*—*thum, thum, thum, thum*. Darren watched the big man still struggling with the axe. It was hard to see his expression at this distance, but he imagined he was frustrated and exhausted. Undoubtedly, that explosion had hurt. He had to be exhausted, ready to quit. Perhaps that was why he didn't jump again, why he didn't flee. Was he really too tired? Was this the end? Darren wouldn't relish seeing the haughty, beautiful woman beside him in mourning, but he also wouldn't mind taking her down a notch. What would Issa say? Would she finally bend a little, admitting that what they brought from Earth, their technical know-how, made them worth listening to?

With those thoughts racing through his mind, Darren clenched his hands into fists of nervous anticipation and watched as the big man disappeared in a cloud of colorful smoke, turned-up soil, and fiery gasses. The four long-barreled tanks had struck direct hits, and already the others were firing—mortars, fire canisters, and short-range cluster munitions. "Yes!" Felicity hissed, clapping her small hands together. "Direct hits!"

Darren was watching as she spoke, and sure enough, the smoky ground zero of the first shots suddenly erupted with fire and more smoke as the dozen other tanks landed their hits. "Ouch! Again, my apologies, Lady . . . Valla. I do wish you'd have surrendered for him."

She didn't respond, but when Darren looked at her, he saw for the first time that she'd pressed her lips into a firm, flat line. She was worried. His heart began to race at the idea. Had they just killed him? The hero of the Free Marches as that fool, Alec Green, had been billing him? Had Darren really just orchestrated his death? The idea was both terrifying and thrilling. He'd truly advanced his agenda with this display. Who would stand against him? This demonstration would certainly sway the voters, and the next election would be a landslide . . .

Like something out of a monster movie, a roar ripped through the smoke and dust, echoing over the field and up the wall. It shook the very mortar in the stone crenellations, and Darren found his knees buckling as they started to tremble involuntarily. "What the . . ." he managed to say through lips suddenly dry, with a tongue that felt as though it had been salt cured. But then the roar sounded again, and this time, it ended in a mad bedeviled laugh that threatened to loosen his bowels. *Something* fell on him with that sound. Something like a blanket of pure oppressive dread. He had to clutch at the crenellation to keep from falling, and he realized he wasn't alone. Many people on the wall had fainted or fallen, pressed down by that palpable field of hatred, fury, and fear.

"What . . ." Felicity tried to say, her voice trembling and thready. "What is . . ." She had to stop and lick her lips, also hugging the smooth lime-washed wall to keep from collapsing.

"That's Victor's aura," the tall angelic warrior woman said, her voice perfectly steady. "He must have summoned his banner. You'll see it after that smoke clears. Judging by that mad laughter, I'm afraid that he's likely gone berserk, too. I don't think any of your machines will be salvageable."

11

A CLEAR MESSAGE

Victor couldn't have timed his Iron Berserk better if he'd tried. He'd just felt the swelling, burning, furious surge of rage-attuned Energy pour into his body when the first explosive shells struck. One hit his chest, another the crown of his head, and two exploded at his feet. His wyrm-scale vest took the impact with aplomb, the intricate layers of Tes's enchantments helping to disperse the force of the impact and utterly ignoring the conflagration that erupted as the shell smashed apart. Victor was jostled, certainly, but he wasn't knocked over.

As for the shell that struck him atop his head, he hardly felt that. The Kethian Juggernaut helm was a hundred times more dense than whatever metal casing the humans had fired at him. The explosions nearby shook the ground and threw dirt on him, but all that did was further enrage him. Something itched at his throat, fighting to get out of his lungs, and Victor opened his mouth to let it loose—a roar that echoed off and rattled the stones of the nearby wall. Victor suddenly didn't know why he was holding back, and with a rather mean-spirited laugh, he summoned his Banner of the Champion and let loose any semblance of control he still held over his aura.

More shells and canisters hit him, unleashing fire and heat. Sparkling, weaponized Energy of various flavors rippled through him, shocking him, freezing him, burning him, though never enough to really harm him, never enough to do more than momentarily make his flesh a little raw before his hyper-paced healing washed away the discomfort. Part of Victor was amused, yet part of him was angry—who were these gnats to sting him so? Did they not know their place before one such as he?

As the smoke of the bombardment cleared, Victor saw the black metal haft of his axe thrusting up from the ground near his hip, so he snatched it up, ripping it out of the soil where it had lain buried. It was a big axe, true, but nothing he couldn't easily swing. He looked through the haze of smoke and ash, saw the glowing Energy limning the treads of a tank moving into position, and jogged toward it. Despite his relaxed pace, the vehicles tracking and firing at him struggled to time their shots, and he was only struck a few times before he smashed the huge slow-moving vehicle with the axe. It was trivial to destroy the thing—one hit, then two, and it was a pile of smoldering scrap.

While he dismantled the tank, he was hit in the back by several more explosive rounds. Something hot and wet splashed onto his neck, burning painfully, and the red haze of fury began to darken his vision. Though he wasn't in pain for more than a couple of seconds, the impudence of the incessant attacks and the irritation they caused him were beginning to take a toll on his clear thinking. He whirled, scanning the field, noting that four or five of the tanks had clustered together in their attempts to follow and aim at him. Grinning madly, Victor leaped into the air, aiming for the vehicles. None of the machines were able to effectively aim at and shoot him as he soared through the air, and when he smashed into the ground a dozen paces from the tanks, he stomped forward.

Victor stood before the group of Energy-driven war machines, lifted his axe into the air, and roared. His face flushed with his fury and the exertion of his bellow, and as it tapered off, he poured a massive surge of Energy into the pattern for his Wake the Earth spell.

Silence had fallen over the crowd atop the parapet, and Valla turned to regard the governmental delegation. Darren Whitehorse stood with his hands on the ramparts, his mouth ajar and his eyes wide and fixed upon Victor as he strode over to one of the tanks, shrugging off cannon shots, and then, as quickly as a grown man might swat an offending gnat, he pounded the thing into scrap.

When Victor had emerged from the smoke and focused his attention on the tanks, some of the weight of his burdensome aura fell away, and everyone had stood or straightened, much relieved. Now, that relief was replaced with a mixture of fear and awe as the full-sized titan demonstrated his physical power and resilience. Victor was pelted with more missiles fired by the remaining automatons, but they seemed to do little more than irritate him.

Valla could see it in the narrowed glare he gave the far line of machines when he whirled away from the one he'd just destroyed. He took two steps and then launched himself into the air, aiming for a cluster of the things.

"How . . ." Darren started to say, then trailed off, watching Victor's great bulk soar through the air.

"How is he not burned? How is his flesh not pierced? Those shells are steel jacketed!" the young woman beside Darren wailed in dismay. She reached toward her face, touching her nose, then grasped the sides of her head. Valla could practically see her mind racing through scenario after scenario. Then, as Victor roared again, faintly vibrating the rampart stones so bits of loose mortar and gravel bounced about, she cried, "We have to stop it! If we can't harm him, he'll just work his way through them, destroying everything!"

"He's using Energy, though," Darren said, nodding to confirm his own words. "He'll run out . . ." He might have intended to say more, but Victor stomped, and the world shook. Darren and most others atop the wall fell to the hard stones as the wall shifted alarmingly. Valla maintained her balance, but she had to work at it. It was a strange sensation having the ground roll beneath your feet; if she hadn't recently been involved in a battle near an active volcano, she might not have realized what was happening. The damage to the wall was significant—cracks emerged between the stones, parts of the crenellations toppled down to smash onto the ground below, and with a loud, grinding, ripping sound, the attached bronze-colored elevator pulled away from the stone, hanging precariously to the wall's inner surface.

If the wall was damaged, the battlefield where Victor fought was devastated. His spell had pulled great boulders up, surging out of the earth. It had split the ground with wide crevices that spewed hot steam. Half a dozen of the automatons had fallen in or been smashed by the boulders as they toppled, hot and steaming from their traversal through the ground. Through it all, Victor roared, jumping, charging, and smashing into the huge metallic vehicles. He seemed utterly unbothered by the bucking ground, dancing between rends in the soil, rolling stones, and blasting steam geysers.

The wall only shook for a handful of seconds, and as things grew still there on the ramparts, the citizens of First Landing scrabbled to their feet, using the less-than-solid stonework to steady themselves. Wide-eyed and gasping for breath, Darren Whitehorse helped his assistant stand, as yet unaware of the destruction Victor was wreaking out on the field. Valla looked over his head to the crowd of government representatives and saw many of them scurrying for a stairwell, ready to be away from the wall they'd once thought the pinnacle of solidity. She turned the other way and saw Issa taking charge of the civilians, trying to encourage them to vacate the structure as well.

"What the fuck!" Darren gasped as he finally looked over the rampart to see Victor squat, grasp the bottom treads of one of the construct machines, and deadlift it up, flipping it over sideways to tumble into a steaming fissure.

"He's . . ." the woman started to say, shaking her head and rubbing at her eyes as though she could banish the scene before her. "He's unstoppable."

"What about Project Omega?" Darren wailed, looking out at the smoking, ruined field.

The woman took a flat crystal slate from some storage device and began tapping her fingers on it. "Oh, God! It's not responding! What if it sank? Those fissures! They're right where it was buried!"

"Goddamn it! Stop that maniac!" Darren cried, turning to Valla with pleading eyes.

Valla smiled at him and then looked out at the blasted landscape. There were only two or three automatons that seemed to be whole. Victor was currently ripping one to pieces with his hands, his axe left buried in the wreckage of another. While he peeled the turret off his current victim, she said, "I can try. He's somewhat more reasonable while berserk than he used to be. I can probably calm him as long as he doesn't channel his Volcanic Fury."

"Do it! Do it!" Darren screamed. Valla almost stalled, almost insisted he speak to her with more respect and consideration. She wanted to rub his nose in things, reminding him he'd insisted he wouldn't need the means to signal surrender. She wasn't mean-spirited, though, and it looked as though the poor fellow had just had his view of the universe shattered—everything he'd believed upended in a matter of minutes. Rather than salt his wounds, she spread her wings and leaped off the wall, soaring toward the mad titan.

Victor hoisted the tank's turret, gripping the barrel like a handle, and with a spin and a grunt launched it into the air, flinging it to the northern edge of the cleared field to bounce and roll away into the plains beyond. He laughed, turning to regard the smoking, ripped "parade grounds." Only a few of the tanks were still functioning, and none were currently shooting at him. He was picking out his next target, getting ready to bound over the fissure-riddled ground, when he felt a presence above him. He reached a hand for Lifedrinker's haft, jerking his eyes upward, only to see Valla's glittering turquoise-silver wings reflecting the sun's light as she descended to land atop a rough boulder, facing him.

She shouted over the sounds of popping, crackling explosions as a dozen of the tanks burned, their ordnance losing its integrity in the flames, "They cry mercy, Victor!"

"Oh?" He grinned as his voice boomed out. "Shall I grant it?"

"Forget the automatons; you've wrecked this field and greatly damaged their wall. I think some mercy is in order." Valla smiled, and he could see the pride in her eyes. "Darren didn't say as much, but I'm fairly certain that when you moved the earth, it ruined their surprise. They had something buried, lying in wait, and you . . . sent it to the depths."

"Ha!" Victor grinned, brushing his hands together, sending black soot and dirt falling in a shower to the ground. "I'm done smashing things, I guess. It's good I didn't cast Volcanic Fury." Victor turned toward the gate. "I'll meet you inside. Tell 'em to open the gate, or should I jump the wall as one last lesson?"

"No, no. Perhaps you should cool your rage as you go. The people on the wall took a tumble when you did this." She gestured to the ripped ground and mountainous boulders. "They don't deserve to be further terrified."

"Ah, shit." Victor felt his rage seeping away as guilt took hold. He wouldn't mind seeing Darren and some of the other politicians taken down a notch or two, but he hadn't wanted to hurt anyone. "Are they okay?"

"I'm sure they are. It was just a bit of a scare." She spread her wings and waved. "See you soon." Then she launched herself back into the air. Victor sighed and lumbered over to the giant axe, touching it to send it into his storage ring.

He touched Lifedrinker's haft. "Well, *chica*, hope I didn't overdo things too much." As he walked toward the gate, he worked to pull his rage out of his pathways, sending it into his Core. He cut the connection to his banner and then to Iron Berserk. He also cast Alter Self, intent on reducing his size to his normal "comfortable size," and was surprised by a System message:

*****Congratulations! Your Alter Self, Basic has become Alter Self, Improved.*****

*****Alter Self, Improved: You have mastered the magic necessary to change an aspect of yourself, reducing your physical size and mass. This spell will last as long as you supply it with Energy, though it will reduce your maximum Energy pool so long as it is in effect. Due to the spell's reduction of your Core's potential, you'll find that your other abilities and spells are similarly reduced in efficacy. At the Improved Level, this spell can alter you further from your original size and shape while having**

a reduced impact on your total Energy. Energy Cost: Variable, 5000 minimum. Cooldown: Long.***

"Well, shit. That's cool." He stood there, rubbing some soot off his knuckles, waiting patiently as the opening gate revealed him. Issa, Alec, and Valla were the only ones in the tunnel, and they all looked somewhat relieved to see him back down to human proportions.

"What a show!" Alec crowed, pumping his fist. Issa smiled beside him, but she didn't speak right away.

Victor smiled a little sheepishly. "Was that all right? Sorry about all the damage. That was the first time I've used that spell, and I think I dumped too much Energy into it."

Issa nodded. "It was an effective lesson—a clear message. Thank you, Victor. As the crews work to salvage the constructs and repair the field, it will be a good reminder of how ill-equipped we are to face a truly powerful Energy user." She turned and started back through the long tunnel, and everyone fell in around her. As they walked, she continued, "The citizens were alarmed at first, but I hope you heard the cheers as you pummeled those machines. Your incredible show of power inspired many people. There's quite a crowd waiting near the inner gate to greet you. Would you mind fielding some questions from them?"

Victor shrugged. "As long as it gets me closer to collecting our pay and heading back home, that's fine."

"Aren't you exhausted?" Alec looked over his shoulder, eyeing Victor incredulously.

"From that? Nah, I've had sparring matches more tiring. I mean, to be honest, it was mostly just kind of fun."

Valla jostled him. "Don't be so dismissive, Victor! They worked hard on those machines."

"Well, Issa and I didn't"—Alec laughed—"but, yeah, maybe don't rub it in so hard when you see the others. Not that the P and Ds hung around."

"Darren looked like his heels were on fire as he retreated!" Issa laughed.

"On the one hand," Alec said, winking at Victor, "you cost the colony a lot of money; we've sunk much of our budget into building those tanks. On the other, you saved us from growing complacent, believing they could protect us."

Issa sighed, nodding along with him. "Or worse, if Darren and his cronies gained power, trying to use them to intimidate the older powers in this world."

"Such as the Ridonne?" Valla asked.

"Exactly." Issa smiled at Valla. "This was a costly but valuable lesson."

"Well, the Ridonne aren't a match for Victor—at least not the ones we've met, but they would rather easily trounce machines like that. Don't you think?" Valla looked up at him, catching his eye, and Victor shrugged.

"I think so. I mean, I doubt the couple I've fought were the strongest in the Empire. Borrius thinks there are dozens of them, too, so yeah, better not to pick fights with those *pendejos*. You folks aren't ready yet." Victor stretched his neck from side to side, wringing a series of pops out of it. "You know, it sucks, but the System didn't think I deserved any Energy for killing those tanks. I was kind of hoping I'd make some progress toward leveling."

"Uh . . ." Alec didn't seem to have an appropriate response.

"Do you cultivate for Energy and levels, Victor?" Issa asked as they stepped out of the tunnel into the sunlight. Victor turned to look at the wall, noting a lot of commotion off to his right. There, he saw the damage he'd done: Large spiderwebs of cracks ran through the stone of the massive wall, and the big, cleverly designed elevator was hanging at an angle, the metal tracks it ran on having separated from the stone near the top.

"Shit," he said, putting Issa's question to the side. "You're sure no one got hurt?"

"We're sure. Everyone is fine." Issa smiled at him, maybe glad to see he was concerned and chagrined.

They started walking again, and Victor saw the throng waiting by the next gateway. He felt a little excited at the idea of fielding questions to an enthusiastic crowd; it ought to be a lot different from the town hall, especially now that these folks had an idea of what he was capable of. "Um," he said, turning back to Issa, "I mostly level from killing my enemies. Luckily that's usually a monster or an undead asshole. I can cultivate, but I'm really undisciplined." He grinned at Valla, reaching to grasp her hand in his. "Isn't that right?"

"He's very disciplined about some things, but I will agree that his cultivation habits could stand some improving; he's found a workaround for leveling his Core, so he doesn't have quite the incentive that we mere mortals do."

"Workaround?" Issa raised an eyebrow.

"Mortal? Is . . ." Alec visibly gulped. "Are you not a mortal?"

Victor laughed and slapped the much smaller man on the shoulder. "She's being cute, Alec. Relax. As for my workaround, Lady Issa, that's a trade secret." He squeezed Valla's hand to indicate he wasn't joking around. He might like these two people, and he didn't mind sharing some knowledge, but he'd seen the lengths one asshole would go to try to steal his ability to gain power from eating the hearts of his foes. Who could say what a diabolical human mind might come up with if they knew such a thing was possible?

When they approached the crowd of citizens, Victor could see the guards or police or peacekeepers—he had no idea what they called their uniformed officers—had managed to get them all to stand behind ropes tied to stanchions on either side of the road, leaving the area directly before the inner gate clear for Victor and his escort to stand. Still, hundreds or maybe thousands of people lined the road, and an equally large crowd had gathered atop the inner wall. He could see Borrius, Darro, and Nia standing close to the gate on this side of the ropes and was a little relieved to see his traveling companions were still being treated well despite the destruction he'd wrought out on the field.

The crowd's excitement was palpable; many of them shouted his name or greetings, and quite a few burst into applause at their approach. Victor loved an adoring crowd, so he raised his arms and hammed it up while Issa moved forward a few steps, clearly waiting for the people to grow quiet before speaking. With a crowd like that, though, it was hard to get everyone's attention, and she didn't try for perfection, beginning to shout as soon as she thought she could make her voice clear over the noise. "Citizens of First Landing! I hope many of you could witness Victor Sandoval's demonstration on the parade grounds. He's graciously agreed to pause here today to answer a few of your questions!"

Victor grinned as more applause burst out, his glory-attuned Energy seeping into his pathways. He had half a mind to summon Guapo and put on a real show but decided to try to play it a little cool. He held up a hand, staring around at the thronging people, making eye contact with many. The noise began to die down, and when it was almost quiet, he said, in a loud commanding voice, "Raise your hands. If I point at you, ask your question." Immediately, a hundred hands shot into the air, and Victor laughed, looking the people over. When his eyes fell on a young man who reminded him of himself before he'd gained a thousand pounds of muscle, he pointed at him.

The fellow cleared his throat, then, in a high voice with a slight Spanish accent, asked, "Why aren't you gigantic all the time? Is it just a spell?"

Victor decided a little hyperbole was in order. "Other way around, *cabrón*! I use a spell to make myself small. You ever tried sitting in a chair when you weigh ten thousand pounds?"

12

A SURPRISING PROPOSAL

Victor sat in the formal dining room of Issa's home in the metallic tower on the edge of First Landing. She'd invited him and the others for dinner—a sendoff and thank you for their efforts. Only Alec, Issa, a man named Boris Saltzki, and a woman named Diane Royce were there to represent the growing colony, and Victor was fine with that. Still, it didn't stop Issa from feeling self-conscious about the little group. "I hope you don't mind that I kept things small," she said, leaning to her right, close to Victor and, beside him, Valla. "There were dozens, maybe hundreds of people clamoring to join us, and I couldn't think of a fair way to pare things down. Instead, I insisted that you'd want some calm after your heroics on the field and the frenzy of the crowd afterward."

"You used me as an excuse?" Victor grinned as Valla elbowed him in the ribs.

As he hammed it up, wincing and rubbing at his side, she said, "You don't know his humor. He's teasing. This is perfect."

"Well, I have some ulterior motives for keeping it small. I wanted to be sure that Boris and Diane had a chance to speak with you." Issa gestured to her left, where her two other guests occupied the spots across from Victor and Valla. Farther down the table were Alec, Borrius, Darro, and Nia. As Victor scanned the table, he started to laugh.

"Hey, Borrius. I just realized you and Boris have almost the same name."

"How astute, Victor." Borrius sighed at the interruption, then turned back to Alec and continued his description of an inn he'd been impressed by in

Tharcray. Leave it to the old commander to try to teach Alec about the hotel business.

"I've cooked something simple, but I hope it will remind you of home, Victor; it's one of the first dishes from Earth that I tasted when I came to First Landing. My friend Maria taught me how to make it." Victor saw her focus, and she spoke very carefully, trying to properly enunciate the vowels and syllables as she said, "*Enchiladas.*"

"*En serio?*" Victor's eyes opened wide with excitement.

"Yes! Seriously. I hope I did them justice, but I'm not too worried. I'm good with recipes, and Maria has tasted my efforts. I'm fairly sure she'd tell the truth if they weren't good."

"Awesome! Thank you, Issa." Suddenly, Victor's entire outlook had changed. He'd been sort of dreading sitting around talking over another fancy meal. Now, he had enchiladas to look forward to.

"It's my pleasure." Issa looked tickled by Victor's genuine enthusiasm. "Excuse me while I check on my children and then the food. I'll be back shortly. Diane, now would be a good time to speak to our guests about your research." She stood and walked away while Diane cleared her throat and looked at Victor and Valla. She was clearly nervous, struggling to maintain eye contact with either of them.

"She has kids?" Victor asked, saving the woman from having to speak first.

"Oh, you didn't know?" Boris chuckled. "Two little ones and a few older ones she's kind of adopted. You'd never know it, considering how hard she works, but yeah, she's one of the most generous, big-hearted people I've ever met."

"Sheesh," Victor sighed, leaning back. "Now I feel lazy."

"Ah!" Diane finally found her voice. "That's an excellent segue, Mr. Sandoval. I wouldn't call what you did on the field today lazy—in fact, it was the most eye-opening demonstration of personal power I've ever seen, and I've seen Morgan Hall in action!" She smiled again, looking nervous as everyone turned to her. She was a small, jittery woman with light-brown hair cut short above the ears and tapered at the neck—not too different from Victor's usual haircut. She had rosy cheeks and brown eyes, and when she blushed nervously, she reminded Victor of a schoolkid who knew the answer but was scared to say it in front of the class. "I've been, um, researching the Spirit Cores among the Urghat, Grugell, and Krystree peoples."

Victor frowned and glanced at Valla. "I've heard of the Urghat but not the others."

"They're all considered 'low-affinity' by the System, and so they aren't given access to the boons it grants—levels, skills, even the language integration skill. When we began integrating them into our society, I was on the team to help document their languages and cultural practices. That's when I made the connection about the 'low-affinity' species having a higher incidence of Spirit Cores than among other peoples." She gestured around the table. "In fact, Victor, you're only the second human I've heard of who has one."

"Yeah, I heard something similar during that town hall." Victor shrugged. He could tell she wasn't trying to be insulting, so he waited to hear her out.

"I've learned that those with Spirit Cores are revered among the low-affinity folks; they're seen as leaders and as a living connection to their ancestors. I believe such Cores used to be more common among other peoples, too—the Shadeni, Ardeni, and Ghelli in particular. Have you run across others with such an affinity in your travels?"

"Not many, but yeah. It was a Shadeni Old Mother—kind of a wise woman—who taught me most of what I've learned. Well, and a spirit fragment I found in an artifact deep under the earth." Victor glanced at Valla, scratched his jaw in contemplation, then added, "It shouldn't be a secret that Spirit Core affinities are tied to a person's character traits and emotions. They're the essence of who we are. Old Mother used to tell me that civilized folk—her words—worked hard to weed emotions out of their magic. That prejudice made it kind of rare for people to form a Spirit Core, even if it might have been possible for them. There are tons of Ardeni and Shadeni with simple Pearl Cores. They use basic unattuned Energy, and I bet many of them might have formed Spirit Cores but were steered away from them by a mentor."

"But why? It's clear that your magic isn't weak. Why would the magical schools and 'mentors,' as you call them, try to weed Spirit Cores out?"

Valla answered for him, her voice soft but thick with emotion as she remembered something disturbing, "Because they're dangerous." She glanced at Victor almost apologetically.

"It's all right. Tell her."

"People have dark sides to their spirits, and often they're the stronger affinities. You saw Victor unleash his rage on the field outside the wall, but what you don't know is that he had to work very hard to gain that kind of control. Once upon a time, anyone around him, even us up on the wall, would have been at risk. I . . . I doubt Victor wants to speak about it, but there are other affinities that are even more dangerous, more frightening."

"Ah!" Victor had heard the idiom about a lightbulb going off in someone's head, but he'd never seen it so well represented as at that moment in Diane's expression. "That explains everything—the stigma, the prejudice, the lack of such Cores among the city-dwelling folk. I can imagine how affinities based on negative traits or emotions could cause problems among people whose ties weren't as close-knit as a clan or tribal structure. Imagine someone with an affinity for paranoia running amok in New York City!" She turned to Boris as she spoke, and he nodded along with her.

"It's not just negative affinities that can be a problem," Victor added. When they looked at him with questioning expressions, he said, "Think of the damage someone with an affinity for love could do with the wrong intentions."

"You mean . . ." Boris's words trailed off as his mind traced dark paths.

"Yeah." Victor shrugged. "I could be a real asshole with some of my affinities, especially as my Core continues to grow in power." The conversation was put on hold as Issa returned carrying a big steaming casserole dish. Victor's mouth began to water as the unmistakable smoky scents of baked chili peppers, onions, and corn tickled his nose, waking up memories he'd left buried for far too long. He saw his *abuela*'s smiling face as she lifted a pot from the oven. He saw his cousins laughing around the big table in her kitchen. He felt a loss so keen that his eyes began to tear up, and he had to look down and squeeze them shut for a moment.

The dinner was delicious, and Victor had a lot of fun describing some of the dishes he missed from home. Issa's enchiladas were great, the best thing he'd eaten in months, but they weren't exactly like his *abuela*'s. It made sense—every family did something a little different. They weren't very spicy, and there was more cheese and greens than he was used to, but Victor couldn't imagine complaining; the meal was terrific.

As they ate, they spoke about Cores, about cultivating, and about how important it was to find natural treasures that would allow them to craft more powerful items and to improve their bodies. As Darren Whitehorse had learned the hard way, a person's strength, or any other attribute, could reach heights that the people in the human colony hadn't entirely realized. Overall, it was a pleasant meal with good food and company, and Victor felt much better about the human settlement than he had going into it.

They wrapped things up early—Issa insisted she had to spend some time with her children, and Victor and the others hoped to sleep in their own beds that night. With that in mind, Alec guided them back through town in the early evening to the portal hall. The people they passed on the way were pleasant, and several clapped and called out Victor's name. He felt they would have asked for an autograph if times had been a little different. They were even stopped by a few Parliament members who offered their thanks.

Unsurprisingly, they saw nothing of Whitehorse or his faction. As they approached the portal hall, Alec chuckled as Victor mentioned the contentious man's absence. "Oh, he's off with his aides trying to salvage something from his defense budget. He's going to get massacred in the assembly on Monday."

"Speaking of budgets," Borrius said, clearing his throat obnoxiously.

"Ah, don't you worry, good sir! I have your payment right here." Alec slapped a pouch that hung from his belt. "A lot of beads, but I think it's worth it, considering you probably saved us from just as much trouble. P and D will have to curtail their warmongering for the foreseeable future." He unfastened the pouch and handed it to Victor. When Victor trickled a bit of Energy into it, he was pleased to find the full sum of promised Energy beads within the dimensional container.

"You guys can make these?" Victor held up the bag.

"Beads? Or dimensional containers? Well, yes to both. That many beads would take us a long time to craft, but we earn a lot through our trade partners. We've apparently thought of some clever uses for Energy that hadn't yet occurred to the people in this world. The telephones, for instance—Tarn's Crossing paid us a tidy sum for a similar system. Boris is in talks with Persi Gables now that we have a portal connecting us. I think we're going to see some big paydays soon."

"You're coming back with us, yes?" Valla asked, stepping closer to Alec.

"Oh, I'll come through in the morning, if that's all right. I'd like to spend a little time with the hotel staff tonight. There are a few adjustments I want to make to the schedule."

"Of course, that's fine." Valla smiled, reaching out to clasp Alec's hand. "Thank you so much for this opportunity. Lam will be thrilled that we have the funding for the Stone's advancement. We're all very worried about our friend and want to start taking action to help her."

"Will you leave right away?"

Victor nodded, gesturing toward Nia, Darro, and Borrius. "Probably, yeah. We'll drop these folks off, and then I'm going to go down to the stone to see how much I can unlock with these." He jostled the sack of beads, though they didn't click together, and the bag felt empty—they were all in the dimensional space. He shook Alec's hand when Valla released him, and then the five of them waited while Alec activated the teleportation stone. The crackling blue portal appeared, bright enough to make Victor squint in the dim light of the hall, and with a wave, he stepped through.

He emerged into the dark, silent, cold air of the Travel Pavilion back in the Free Marches. It was well past midnight there, and the colony was fast asleep. With crackling bursts of light, his companions came through behind him, and then the portal shimmered and *popped* out of existence. "I almost expected some treachery," Borrius announced, looking around.

Nia nodded, hand on the hilt of her belt knife. "Me as well, Lord Borrius."

"Why didn't you say something?" Valla asked.

The scarred, angry-looking woman formed a rare smile, showing her surprisingly white straight teeth. "I didn't want to insult our host, and I trusted Lord Victor would see us through any deceit."

"All right, well, things went fine. I'm heading to the Colony Stone." Victor turned to look Valla in the eyes. "I have a meeting with that steward tomorrow, the one who used to work for Polo. If I can get him to agree to work for me, I'll be ready to leave. Will you find Lam and Lesh and fill them in?"

"I was thinking I'd find her, aye. She'll want to hear the good news." She stepped forward, offered him a quick kiss, and then started toward the door. Victor had just turned to pass some final instructions to Nia when the portal burst to life again with crackling blue Energy. He stepped back, snatched Lifedrinker out of her harness, and severed the Energy feeding his Alter Self spell, surging to his full, natural height. He heard Valla's wings crack open and Midnight sing as she drew the blade. Nia, grimacing with determination, drew her long, curved knife and hurried to stand beside him. A second later, a man stepped through the portal.

"Oh, God, don't hit me!" Darren Whitehorse wailed, holding his hands up, illustrating his lack of weaponry. "I come in peace!"

Victor growled and lowered his axe. "What the fuck, Darren? You're supposed to schedule activation of this portal using the Far Scribe book."

In a stunning display of obsequious groveling, the man fell to his knees before Victor, ducking his head so his long dark ponytail flopped over his shoulder. "I . . . I'm not authorized to use the portal. I've come to join you, to follow you, Victor. It's the only way I'll ever save any face. I have to learn what I've failed to grasp. My political ambitions are over—I've left my resignation from Parliament with a friend. Please! I have to learn!"

"Nah, that's not happening. I'm not babysitting you. There's just as much chance you'd die as learn something." Everyone's eyes were on him now, and Victor waved Nia, Darro, and Borrius off. "You guys can go. Nia, come see me in the morning, please."

"As you say, Lord." Nia slammed her knife back into its sheath, a look of something like disappointment in her eyes. She left, and Darro followed, but Borrius lingered.

The old commander cleared his throat. "Victor, you could do much for your people, I mean your kin from your homeworld, if you were to help this man. Assuming his intentions are true."

"They are! They are! Truly, Victor—you've opened my eyes! I know you can swat me like a gnat. I know I'm nothing to you. Let me learn! I've failed so many people and wasted so much time, Energy, and wealth! Please! I've left my aide; I've left most of my belongings—it's just me, and I swear I'll be no burden. I've brought enough money to fund my passage. Let me see what's beyond this world. Let me learn the truth about this new System-controlled universe. Let me bring something valuable home to our people. Let me spread true knowledge, not the nonsense I'd allowed to cloud my mind!" The man's pleas were desperate in their apparent sincerity, tears pooling in his eyes as he begged. Victor had never seen anything like it.

Victor looked at Borrius, then down at Darren, and his scowl sent a shudder through the man. To his credit, Whitehorse didn't look away. "First of all, those aren't my people. I like some of them, and I suppose I'm related to one of 'em, but these"—Victor gestured around, indicating Rellia's burgeoning capital—"are my people." He looked over his shoulder at Valla, but she simply shrugged. He supposed she'd have advice for him later when the others weren't listening. "Borrius, will you show him where the inn is? I'll talk to him in the morning." Scowling, furious annoyance threatening to push regretful words through his lips, Victor turned and stalked into the night.

He'd only managed a dozen paces into the garden outside the Travel Pavilion when Valla caught up to him. He was still full-sized, his long strides forcing her to jog as she said, "Calm down, Victor. Talk to me."

He slowed and glared down at her; for a moment, his anger was directed toward her, and she flinched. That expression finally got through to him, and the scope of his overreaction dawned on him. "Jesus, what's wrong with me?"

"I was going to ask that! So what if he came here begging to join you? Just say no. Why are you upset?"

"I . . ." Victor closed his eyes and thought about it. When it clicked, he chuckled. "I'd convinced myself that man was my enemy. Some part of me is pissed that he's here. Some part of me wants to rip him to pieces. Damn it, Valla, I have to get a grip on this Quinametzin anger. Pride? It's all a blurry hot mess in my head. I think I wanted him to suffer through his humiliation back home. I'm irritated that he slipped away and did the only really smart thing he could do—ask us for help."

"And part of you knows it's the right thing to do. If he was the primary obstacle to your cousin's politics, wouldn't it help her if we can educate the man? Wouldn't it promise a more hopeful future for your species here on Fanwath if he were to return and help her and Issa rather than rallying people against them?"

"Yeah." Victor sighed, then turned back toward the center of the colony. "I'll go feed the Stone. Let's talk about this later. Just because we help him doesn't mean he has to tag along. We could leave him with Borrius." Victor barked a short laugh. "Imagine that! Borrius would lecture him night and day!" Valla wasn't quite as amused as he was, but she hugged him briefly, and then Victor walked alone to the Colony Stone. As he went, his mind ran through the situation, and he knew he was full of shit; he'd probably bring Darren with him, if for no other reason than to watch his face when he realized how wrong he'd been. "What's one more guy following me around? I'll put Lesh in charge of him, *chica*." Victor laughed at the idea. "I gotta admit, though, the guy surprised me. I think Olivia will thank me if I keep him. Better he's here, learning a lesson, than stirring up more trouble for her."

13

WORLD TRAVEL

Victor handed the pouch to Gorro ap'Dommic, nodding as though the act sealed the deal they'd made. "On a hillside with a view of the sea." It contained the hermitage blueprints and all of the exotic building supplies it would require to build.

"Of course, Lord Victor. I'll hire a proper surveyor to select the most idyllic location for your home. In the meantime, I'll run things from my travel tent—it's quite luxurious, and the command table I liberated from the Legion when I retired will aid greatly in the logistics of mapping and plotting your lands as the surveyors complete their work. With the funds you've given me, I'll be able to hire your personal staff and begin forming the militia. You won't recognize the place when you return! I've got big plans for your town layout, beginning with the central fountain square . . ."

"Right, right." Victor held up his hand. "No need to rehash it all; I'm sure it's going to be great." The truth was the guy liked to talk, and Victor could swear they'd been over his plans for the town square three times in the last couple of hours. He didn't know why he had to establish a town, but Gorro seemed to think there would be homesteaders flocking to his lands, seeking property in the form of leases and grants, depending on what they had to offer. Gorro said his massive holdings would fund everything he needed if appropriately managed, and that all started with getting some tenants. If he were honest, Victor was kind of annoyed that he had to leave; it sounded like a lot of fun and a nice break from constantly fighting.

"Oh, yes, I'm sorry. I know you're in a hurry to get things ready for your journey." Gorro nodded to Nia, standing near the doorway leading out of Victor's library. "Do I understand correctly that Nia will be working for your household guard, not the militia?"

"That's right. I also want you to give special consideration to any other veterans from the conquest who want a position with either my household or the standing militia."

"I was under the impression that the bulk of the legion soldiers were receiving their land grants from Lady ap'Yensha."

"That's right, but, like I said, if any of them want to settle on my lands, work with them."

"Understood."

"All right. Let's head out, 'cause I need to pack up my house." Victor started for the doorway, nodding to the dark-haired, scar-faced woman standing there. Nia had been following him even more closely than before the trip to First Landing, and Victor wondered what she would do with herself when he and Valla left. As he passed, he said, "Nia, let's head out. I have to pack the house. Governor ap'Dommic is counting on you to help secure my new homestead and build up my household guard. You're up to it?"

"Yes, Lord Victor."

"I know you have some friends from Dark Ember, and you can hire any who want to come to work for me, but make sure you never turn away anyone from the Ninth. God, I wish Sarl was here." Victor saw Nia look down at the mention of the dead captain. Victor shook his head and forced himself to acknowledge that Sarl had been a lot more than a captain to him. "Not because you aren't doing good work, Nia, but because he was a friend, and I wish he could see what we've won."

"I understand." Nia's voice was soft, and glancing down at her, Victor saw her eyes were distant. She understood loss.

Outside the house, in the corner of the garden he and Valla had claimed, he found her squatting beside Uvu, scratching the big cat's ears and cooing soft praises. "He'll be all right," Victor said as he walked over to her, Gorro and Nia in tow.

"Yes, he will," Valla said. It's a paradise here for him—he's getting fat. I'm wondering if he'll find a mate, but so far, there don't seem to be any predators around, not even boyii hounds. I think the undead left quite a void."

Nia cleared her throat. "Lady Valla, I'm sure they'll start to creep back in now that the threat's gone and that miasma has dispersed. Your big cat might find a friend."

"Oh, he will, but sooner than you think. Nia, this is Uvu. Uvu, Nia." Valla grinned and stood up. "Give him a scratch, will you? I want him to follow you down south to Victor's holdings. If he's going to hunt and range about, I want him to do it from our home."

"Oh, Lady, I couldn't . . ." Nia shrank back, her pale face going paler.

Victor chuckled, but Valla reached out and snatched Nia's hand, tugging her closer to Uvu. "Nonsense. He already told me he likes you."

"Truly?" Nia's eyes were wide, and she licked her lips nervously.

"Oh, very truly. He can sense a person's intentions, and he thinks yours are good. Do you like to hunt, Nia?"

"I do, though the sheriff only allowed it if something threatened the lord's game."

Valla smiled and pulled the woman's hand a little closer to the cat. "Well, you're not on Dark Ember anymore. Uvu will hunt with you, and I think you'll become fast friends. Does that sound all right?"

Nia gingerly reached out to scratch the cat's enormous head between his ears, and Uvu chuffed, arching his neck and pressing against her hand. "He . . . he likes it!"

"Have you ever had a pet?" Victor asked.

"No, we weren't allowed such. The vampyrs would know. I tried to keep a fox cub once, but my mother, in a frenzy of terror, swatted my butt and took the animal out to the woods."

Valla rested her hand on Nia's shoulder and gently squeezed it. "Well, Uvu's not a pet, but he'll be a companion. You see, I don't want him to get lonely while we're gone."

"I will do my best to be a boon companion to him!" Nia's joy was palpable, and Victor felt good watching her. It reminded him that, despite his blunder that had cost so many soldiers their lives, he'd managed to do some good in the campaign. He caught himself thinking about how he'd been fooled into entrapping himself in the caldera, and as Khul Bach had counseled him, he turned his ire toward Victoria, or more accurately, Catalina. He was just minutes away from finally starting on the road to catch up with her, to bring her justice. The Energies in his Core swirled at the idea, eager to be let out, eager for him to do some bloody work. At least, that was his interpretation of his eagerness—it might have been the Quinametzin in him coloring his perspective.

"Ready?" Valla asked.

"Yeah. Let me get the house." Victor heard Gorro asking Valla questions about Uvu as he turned back to the travel home, but their conversation faded to the background, and he began to wonder what was in store for them. If they found someone who could trace Edeya's spirit tether, someone powerful enough to reach out and open a gateway to Dark Ember, what would it cost them? He assumed they wouldn't find Dark Ember as a destination when they reached the hub world. With countless worlds in a universe impossibly vast, the odds seemed slim.

When Victor had unlocked world travel on their stone, only five destinations had been offered. He had no idea how it worked, exactly, but it seemed they'd have to advance the stone a lot more to open up a broader list. Were the five worlds chosen by the System for them? Were they the closest? Were they of similar level? As he touched his house and gave it the command to shrink, Victor again lamented his lack of knowledge. Luckily, Lesh seemed to know quite a bit more than he or any of the Fanwathians— Victor wasn't sure he liked the term, but he figured it might be technically correct.

Lesh had looked at the list of worlds, pointed to the third one, Sojourn, and said it was likely a world hub. When Rellia had asked how he knew, he'd shrugged and said that worlds that worked hard to open all the travel options often prided themselves for it, seeking to name themselves in such a manner. He'd seen world hubs called Portalus, Veridian Gateway, Waypoint Crossroads, and Odessey. Knowing that, Victor had to agree that Sojourn was a good fit. The other travel options were Zikza, Ves, Monota, and Robal—each one an order of magnitude cheaper to travel to than Sojourn.

Victor stooped to pick up his house, clipping it to his belt. When he turned back to the others, they looked at him expectantly. "Well, this is it, I guess. Gorro, I can't thank you enough; it makes it easier to leave knowing my lands will be in good hands. Nia, I'm counting on you to ensure the Naghelli and Shadeni are treated well. Make sure you both keep in touch through the Far Scribe book. Depending on how far away we get, there will be some delay, but I'll respond as soon as I see any messages."

"As you say, Lord Victor." Gorro bowed and stepped back, eyes on Nia.

"Thank you, Lord Victor and Lady Valla. I feel like I have a home again, and I'll be sure to keep your lands clear of threats. The first thing I'll do with the budget you and Gorro approved is hire a few rangers."

"You're welcome, Nia. Uvu will help you range, too." Valla took Victor's hand and tugged him toward the path. "Come. Lesh and the others will be waiting."

"Right." Victor waved again, smiling as Nia saluted and Gorro bowed. Then he and Valla hurried through the garden toward Rellia's central keep on the hill, where the System Stone nestled in its bailey. The keep was still under construction, but the wall was in place and formidable. It wasn't as high as the one in First Landing that he'd nearly wrecked, but he knew it was enchanted with earth-attuned magics, and there was little chance he could collapse it. It gave him comfort knowing that Rellia and the people here in the Free Marches weren't quite as clueless as they might be if the Ridonne had their way.

The gates to the keep were wide open, and some soldiers Victor recognized were on guard duty—many of them had signed up for new commissions with Rellia, Borrius, and Lam. He was sure Gorro and Nia would end up hiring quite a few veterans for his household as well. Inside the courtyard, things were quiet. It was still early enough that only the cooks and the kennel master were up and about. The workers hadn't yet arrived to continue building up the keep, but Victor could see the scaffolding and the framework in place. It was going to be an impressive structure when finished.

As they'd leveled the Stone, the System had built, for lack of a better word, infrastructure around it. It still jutted up from the cobbled courtyard, but a low marble wall surrounded it, and a recessed stair led down, under the ground, to the lower level—the stone had expanded into the earth as they'd purchased more and more upgrades. It was in that underground level that the teleportation platform awaited. Despite the low traffic and protective wall, Rellia had guards on duty, watching anyone who approached the stone. They waved Victor and Valla through, though, without a second of hesitation.

The shiny filigreed silver gates at the base of the stairs were open, and Victor could hear the weird echo of a conversation taking place within—weird because the hollow stone chamber caused the voices to reverberate oddly, the sounds mixing and muffling. "Ah, I hear large feet clomping. Is that you, Victor?" Rellia's voice rang out sharply, and Valla looked at Victor with a knowing smile. She'd teased him the other day, referring to Rellia as "their" mother, and he'd almost had a fit.

"It's us," Victor said, walking around the stone partition that separated the stairs from the chamber beyond. Warm yellow light suffused the space as if shed by the very stone. Broad stone hallways led away from the central chamber where the dark rune-covered System Stone stretched from ceiling to floor. There was another level below them that had yet to populate with any functionality, but he knew it was only a matter of time before the people of the Free Marches expanded the Stone further.

Rellia stood there with Lesh, Lam, Edeya, and, irritatingly, Darren Whitehorse. Victor paused to take in the sight of them. Lesh was dressed, as always, sparingly, preferring, it seemed, to let his scales be his garb. Still, he wore black leather pants, boots, and a thick leather baldric from which his absurdly heavy jagged bludgeon hung. He was resting a massive hand on Darren's shoulder, and Victor could see they'd been talking. Darren wore gray suit pants, shiny leather shoes, and a tailored burgundy dress shirt. Over his shoulder, he'd slung a hand-tooled leather satchel, and Victor knew it was a dimensional container crafted by one of the Artificers back in First Landing.

Lam was dressed sharply in her military-style pants and jacket. She'd stolen the design of the Ridonne Legion officer uniforms but changed the colors— pale, creamy trousers, shiny brown boots, and a soft leather coat with shiny polished horn buttons over a gauzy mauve blouse. Her hammer hung at her waist, and her wings dripped golden motes onto the polished marble floor. Edeya, sadly, looked wan and limp, her wings sagging and her eyes staring blankly over dark circles. Lam had dressed her in silky blue robes, which looked comfortable, but he doubted Edeya would have liked them if she were cognizant.

"You two look ready for war." Rellia hurried over and grabbed Valla in a hug.

Victor shrugged. They were wearing their wyrm-scale armor—Valla had found an Artificer capable of altering it to allow for her wings. Her armor had tones of blue, while his had shades of red, but they were clearly crafted by the same person. It wasn't exactly a uniform, but anyone who saw them would know they were together. Besides that, Victor had Lifedrinker slung over his shoulder as always, and Valla wore Midnight at her waist. But it wasn't as if they had helmets and gauntlets on. "Should we not wear armor?"

"No, no. I'm teasing. This armor is so fine that you're sure to make a good impression." Rellia had to look up as she examined her adoptive daughter. Victor watched her and saw the pride in her eyes but also the angst and worry. She'd always meant for Valla to help her build this new nation, and now she was leaving.

Almost reflexively, he said, "We'll be back."

Rellia jerked her gaze away from Valla to look at him, and he saw her narrowed eyes soften. Then she opened her arms wide and hugged him, too. "I know you will. You've been so good for Valla, Victor. I'm not upset that you're leaving, especially because young Edeya here needs your help! She and I fought back to back more than once during this campaign, and I'll not see her fade and die with her spirit held captive on some distant world. You need to make her whole, and you need to find that traitorous bitch who did this. Don't let her get away!"

That was the most clearly anyone had spelled out his mandate, and Victor felt a spur of eagerness in his chest at the command. His voice was a growl, deep in his gut, and he saw Darren flinch back behind Lesh when he spoke. "Justice will have his due." The words weren't as impactful on Lesh and Darren as they were on the others—they'd seen Victor wearing the Inevitable Huntsman's guise, and their faces said they almost pitied Catalina when Victor caught up to her. He looked away from Rellia to the others and asked, "Everyone has their fare?"

The System was charging them each a hundred thousand Energy beads, or in Lesh's case the equivalent of Energy-rich metal coins. He hefted a dimensional pouch and rumbled, "Aye, but I'll need to make some money in the next world if we have to pay the System for travel again."

"I think that's true for most of us," Lam said. "I'm rich on paper, but it wasn't easy scrounging up the beads."

"If there's an emergency, and you must return in haste. Valla has funds she can lend."

Valla nodded, and Victor said, "So do I. Provided we don't spend it all getting help for Edeya."

"We shouldn't be paying the System," Lesh grumbled. "I had to find Fanwath, but there are those with the power to open gateways. They rarely charge as much as the System Stones."

"Right. Well, with any luck, we'll find someone like that on Sojourn."

Rellia jostled Valla's shoulder, still clinging to her with one hand. "Write to me immediately! I'll want to know what that world is like and that you're all right. Keep us informed on the details of your quest."

"We will, Mother."

"Um, I'll be happy to help in that endeavor," Whitehorse said, stepping out from behind Lesh to look up at Rellia. He held out his hand, and a neatly bound book appeared. "I brought several of these Far Scribe books, and I have no one to report to. Most in First Landing aren't interested in my correspondence at the moment, but hopefully I'll gain some favor with a detailed record of our journey and all that I can learn. I do have a couple of friends back home keeping our leadership apprised of my efforts."

"Thank you." Rellia took the book, offering the man a smile that, if Victor could believe it, made him look away like a blushing schoolboy.

"Right. Enough stalling. Let's get going." Victor stepped forward to the Stone and rested his hand upon it, navigating the menu with his mind until he saw the selection for world travel. He scanned the offered worlds again, saw nothing had changed, and selected Sojourn.

Travel to the world of Sojourn? The cost of travel from this Stone is 100,000 unattuned Energy beads.

Victor looked around the room, and when his eyes locked with Rellia's, he asked, "Any final objections? Last chance."

"No objections, but a request: Please be careful and keep Valla safe."

"Mother . . ."

"I'll try." Victor nodded, then answered the Stone in the affirmative. Suddenly, the world spun away with a weird rippling shift, as if he were sliding backward through a person-sized kaleidoscope. Just as the dizziness became overwhelming and he thought he was going to pass out or vomit, it faded, and the world snapped into focus. Victor found himself standing on a big metal circle made of bronze or some similar alloy. The circle was inlaid in a marble floor that stretched for hundreds of yards in every direction toward mountainous walls that rose to a cavernous ceiling suspended by magnificent ornamented metal arches.

Eight enormous circular windows of stained glass lined the ceiling, each depicting a different stylistic scene, from a shepherd by a stream to an unmistakable fire-breathing dragon. The hall itself was jaw-dropping in its gargantuan proportions and splendor, but the thing that had Victor dazed and quite frankly speechless was the thronging crowd. Thousands of people of all sorts milled about, walking to and fro, materializing out of thin air or disappearing just the same. People with suitcases, people in armor, people in fancy clothing, and people wearing nothing but tattoos.

And what people! If Fanwath's species were diverse, here there was an extraordinary spectrum of existence—giants and fairies, lanky skeletal creatures and squat teddy bear men, people that looked almost human, and others that reminded him of elves from video games. Victor was gaping like a fool, turning in a slow circle as his companions materialized around him. Perhaps because he was the most alone among them, Darren said what they all were thinking. "It doesn't seem like anyone noticed our arrival."

14

SOJOURN

Darren was disturbed to find his mouth hanging ajar again. He closed it with an audible *clack* of his teeth, his head swiveling left and right, his mind unable to choose something to focus on. Victor grunted, jerking his big thumb left and right as he spoke to the giant dragon man. "Are we good to just wander into the city? There's no check-in or something?"

The giant black-scaled fellow rumbled in reply, "I don't think so. I've never been to Sojourn, but the other hub worlds I passed through didn't require such."

The tall blonde Ghelli leading the other one, the frail, mentally vacant one, spoke up. "We should secure lodging and try to find our bearings from there. I'd feel better if we could speak and . . . think away from this crowd."

Darren saw his chance to demonstrate his worldliness. "Yes, it's not unlike Times Square or Heathrow Station back home. This hubbub is quite a shock after the quiet of Fanwath!" He found himself raising his voice to be heard over the constant background noise of the crowd. Victor scowled at him for his efforts, but Valla smiled, humoring his comment with a slight nod, though she clearly had no idea what he meant.

Suddenly, a great insect-man, something like a bipedal cricket, boomed at them in a basso voice, "Clear the arrival pad, please. Information services are there." He pointed to a tremendous arched opening on the distant side of the building, easily a kilometer away. "At the north exit." Victor took up the catatonic young woman's left hand while Lam took her right, and they hurried off the metallic disc. Everyone, including Darren, followed closely. The last thing he wanted was to be separated from the group, not in this place. The cricket man spoke again. "Use the lanes and avoid walking on the bronze pads—the System won't allow arrivals or departures if non-travelers are standing on them."

"Thank you, soldier," Lesh said, for some reason assuming the cricket was such. The label didn't seem to offend, though; he nodded his thick chitinous neck, then turned and marched away.

"Darren," Victor said, turning to face him, "can you make yourself useful and hold Edeya's hand? I don't want anyone to jostle her, and it's hard for Lam to manage alone." He held the girl's limp arm toward him, and Darren hurried to comply. It might not be much, but Victor's simple acknowledgment that he could be of use was enough to put some spring in his step. He took the young woman's hand in his, noting that it was paper dry and barely warm. How long could she exist in such a state? "Thanks," Victor grunted, then, in an uncanny show of power, he grew in size, easily matching Lesh's towering height. "I want to be able to see a little better."

"Ancestors! Do you feel the auras around us?" Valla asked, her wings ruffling in a shiver, or was it excitement?

"Only a little, and that says a lot considering their strength." Victor glared around at the party, even at Lesh. "Don't insult anyone. Some of these people remind me of the volcano." With that ominous warning, he turned and began leading the way to the distant archway. Darren waited for Lam to follow, pulling Edeya along behind the others while Darren matched her pace, doing his best to keep close to the frail, sickly girl's side. As Victor had requested, he was determined to ensure that no one jostled her. As he stumbled after the party, he tried to understand what they'd meant by the "auras" around them.

Ever since arriving on Sojourn, stepping into this massive, busy hall, he'd felt a weight on his mind, a kind of invisible pressure. Was that what they meant? Were the auras the overbearing sense of heaviness in the air? He'd assumed the sensation had something to do with the atmosphere or climate of the new world. They couldn't all be perfect for humanity, right? Some worlds must have too much gravity or air difficult to breathe. Still, maybe that wasn't it. Perhaps that constant shifting pressure was due to the power of the individuals walking about. He supposed it was similar to the weight he'd felt when Victor had destroyed his future back in First Landing.

"No," Darren said softly, shaking his head. He'd made an agreement with himself—he wouldn't blame Victor, and he wouldn't count himself out yet.

He'd asked the giant man to do what he did. He'd even goaded him with haughty pride. Darren snorted in derision, glad that the hall was so noisy lest the expression be taken the wrong way by one of his companions. He was derisive, yes, but it was aimed at himself. He'd been so sure the tanks could crush any person. He'd honestly been feeling guilty about forcing people to watch what had been, in his mind, tantamount to an ancient gladiatorial display—the barbarian versus the lions. How wrong he'd been!

Still, that aside, he supposed the shifting psychic pressure could be the auras the others spoke of. How did they know they were powerful? They felt the same to him. Perhaps that was it; everyone felt powerful to Darren with this pathetic status, which made it impossible for him to appreciate the difference. What had Victor said? He barely felt them, and that somehow indicated their power. Was it a matter of control? Darren lost his train of thought and almost dropped Edeya's hand when a creature that looked very much like a mauve elephant lifted off the ground ahead of them, buoyed by a bladder of sparkling rainbow gas that expanded from its back. It warbled a strange tune from its tusked mouth as it floated away toward a distant corner of the hall.

With his eyes following the floating creature—person?—Darren was made aware of the many other flight-gifted people traversing the heights of the hall. People with wings, people who simply seemed to float, and people on magical conveyances from rugs to chairs to wing-like capes. It was chaotic and dizzying, and Darren had to look down, focusing on Victor's back, to ground himself. For the first time, he was thankful for Victor and Lesh and their bulk; they cleared a path through the crowd that was easy to follow, keeping him, Edeya, and Lam from being overwhelmed. Even Valla hung back a bit, though with her height and stunning appearance, Darren had little doubt she could traverse the scene.

Ever since Victor had humiliated him, Darren had been taking hard looks inward to where he'd learned the seed of his Core dwelled. Back on Earth, he'd been a decently fit man, a good-looking fellow with an Apache grandfather, a Norwegian mother, and a penchant for organization. He'd been hired because of his contacts in the upper management of the Ark Program, and ostensibly for his experience in project management, but when they'd arrived on Fanwath, things had rapidly fallen out of his control. The System and that damned Colony Stone had erased many of his presumed duties. He'd found himself listless and had taken up politics to fill that void.

"Oof," he said, realizing he'd fallen behind and Lam was pulling Edeya away from him. He hurried his step to catch up and tried to refocus his musing. Where had he been? Oh, the Core! He'd never bothered forming one and was still, as his detractors mockingly pointed out, without any levels. Still, with some tutelage from Dr. Kerns in the early days, he'd learned to look "inward" and see the nascent swirl of Energy where he was supposed to form one. He'd grown busy, though, focusing on more mundane, Earth-based defenses, and as the months slipped by, he'd eventually grown too prideful—embarrassed, honestly—to ask for further help.

However, that pride was a thing of the past, thanks to the titanic man before him. No, Darren would ask for help. He'd figure something out on this trip that would help him regain some standing back home. Either that, or he'd find a reason to stop caring what they thought of him. So far, he wasn't regretful; this space alone was enough to grant him a new perspective. He was surrounded by beings resembling demigods, mythical heroes, and creatures. What was more, as they drew near the massive archway leading out of the north end of the structure, he began to see what waited outside, and again his steps faltered, and he almost lost hold of Edeya's hand.

"Darren, keep up!" Lam snapped, looking over her right wing, scowling down at him. Why was everyone so damn tall? Even the frail, sick one was nearing six feet.

He hurried his steps and nodded toward the archway. "Sorry, I just saw those crystal buildings and almost fainted." What was the point of pride among people such as these?

"Almost fainted?" Lam followed his gaze, and her scowl melted. "Roots!" Darren grinned at her outburst. At least he wasn't the only one amazed to see iridescent, shimmering, crystalline skyscrapers outside. He and Lam weren't alone in their stupefaction; Victor and the others, too, were staring at the view beyond the archway. More than the crystal towers, the very sky was a marvel—shimmering stars, seemingly too close to be real, rainbow archways upon which fantastical beings and vehicles traversed the heights, and glass-paved roads that wended in sweeping curves between the structures.

"Look at the train!" Victor said, and they all followed his pointing finger toward a sleek silver passenger train that traversed an elevated rail held aloft by glowing, floating platforms. It moved quickly and silently past the busy square outside and had to be five kilometers long from the first car to the last.

"Train?" Valla asked.

Darren quickly stepped in. "That's an antiquated term for a conveyance like that from our homeworld. It consists of many cars pulled or pushed by an engine car along a set track or railway." He stepped forward and pointed.

"Do you see the gaps between the segments? Those segments are individually called 'train cars,' and they're usually joined to each other via some sort of coupling."

"Thank you, Darren," Valla said, smiling at him. Darren almost melted on the spot, but he looked down quickly, nodding, his voice fading to a mutter as her attention stole his ability to think clearly.

"There!" Lesh said, pointing to a booth set into the wall of the grand arrival hall, as Darren had come to think of the place, near the exit. The party moved toward it, and Darren began to breathe again. He watched Victor drape a massive arm over Valla's shoulders, and his heart began to bleed with envy. It wasn't so much that he was envious of Victor's relationship with Valla, but more of him in general. What must it be like to wield such power, to have such ease around people who would have been heralded as deities back home?

As they approached the window and Victor stepped forward to speak with the humanoid, porcelain-skinned woman behind the glass, Darren had to give her a double take. She didn't simply have pale skin; her flesh was literally porcelain. "Welcome. May I aid you with information, traveler?" Her voice was high-pitched, musical, and carried a weird edge like a tuning fork being pulled over smooth glass.

"Um, yes, thanks," Victor said, and if Darren hadn't been in awe of the man, he might have slapped his forehead at the giant's poor diction. "We're new here from a much, um, smaller . . ."

"Lower-affinity," Valla interjected.

"Yeah, lower-affinity world. We've never been to Sojourn. Are there rules or something we should know about?"

"Again, my heartfelt welcome, travelers." The woman's strange sky-blue eyes peered around Victor to take in the rest of them, and her glass-like red lips tilted up in a smile. How could it look like pottery and yet move like flesh? Darren fought to keep his mouth closed. "You should know that Sojourn is a world for all. We value every individual, and there will be no tolerance of violence or crime in our streets." She gestured to the massive archway leading out of the building. "We are a city world, much smaller than normal worlds, but very populous and with doorways to many realms. Here, you can find a million billion items for sale, a million different species, and tens of millions of classers. If you seek knowledge or merchandise, you've come to the right place. If you seek travel elsewhere, you are similarly well positioned. If you seek entertainment or to provide it, this is the world for you. If your power be minuscule or great, you'll find ways to advance."

She paused, and Victor cleared his throat, perhaps thinking she had finished, but the porcelain woman began to speak again. "I see you are all within the iron ranks, and thus you should avoid attempting to traverse the high roads. There are those who will not tolerate the presence of others so low and, though we have laws against violent behavior, their might is beyond our ability to reproach."

"Iron ranks?" Valla asked.

Victor spoke simultaneously, "High roads?"

"Ah, I see you are, indeed, untraveled. Allow me to expound: The System Levels One through One Hundred are often referred to as the 'iron ranks' because they're seen as the forging process in which the raw ore of your bodies, spirits, and Cores are refined into something more precious. The high roads are the crystalline pathways in the sky where those who have passed through to steel and beyond traverse Sojourn. While you may mingle with such folks in private domains and some public facilities, we find it's best for the iron rankers to avoid them in the streets."

Valla stepped a little closer, inserting herself into the woman's attention. "Are those terms common in the universe, or are they specific to Sojourn?"

"They are common in our region of the universe. The classifications originated from Sojourn, but as millennia passed and we spread our influence to other worlds, many hundreds have taken up the terminology."

"Are you familiar with Fanwath?" Victor asked, surprising Darren yet again with his quick wit.

"Fanwath?" The porcelain woman closed her pale blue eyes with a *snick,* then opened them and nodded. "Yes, Fanwath connected with Sojourn three hundred and twelve years ago."

"Those fucking Ridonne," Victor growled, and Darren felt enough heat from his simmering rage to necessitate taking a step back.

"Please remain calm, sir. As I alluded to earlier, there are few laws in Sojourn, but we have a simple mandate to keep violence out of the streets and to respect each individual."

"He won't be violent, ma'am," Valla said, grasping Victor's arm at the elbow. Almost like a switch being thrown, the hot waves of palpable anger faded away.

"No, I won't, but that doesn't mean I can't think violent thoughts, right?" Victor chuckled to lighten his words, and the porcelain lady simply nodded, her weird, shiny red lips curving up in a demure smile. Victor cleared his throat, shook his head, and then asked, "Can you direct us to lodging fit for those of our level?" Victor glanced over his shoulder, and his dark brows narrowed when his golden-brown eyes settled on Darren. "Someplace where people respect individual rights. We have some . . . delicate members in our party."

"Of course." She pointed to a sigil of inlaid bronze beside her window. It seemed to shift as Darren stared at it until he realized it was a stylized *SJ*. Had it been so before, or had it shifted until his mind could understand it? What a wonder! "This is the official seal of Sojourn, and if you find an establishment bearing such a mark, you can rest assured that they've passed monthly audits to ensure that they uphold the high standards of Sojourn's business practices. I would highly recommend you avoid establishments without our sigil."

"Should we just go out and wander, or is there a map?" Lam asked, perhaps tired of waiting for Victor or Valla to get to the point. Speaking of silent people . . . Darren looked at Lesh to find the big man looking outside through the massive archway, his eyes glazed as he stared into space. He wondered what the dragon man was thinking about. Darren turned back to the window to see the woman handing Victor a sigil-covered document.

". . . for only one hundred System beads." Victor plopped a heavy sack of beads onto the counter, and the woman touched it with a black rod. Darren had seen similar; it would take the correct amount from the sack without anyone having to count them out. Victor stowed the pouch away, then nodded, muttering his thanks as he stepped back from the window. He started to move off with Valla and everyone else in tow.

Darren took a step, following, still grasping the now warm hand of the catatonic girl, but the porcelain woman spoke, nearly stopping his heart with her words. "Darren Whitehorse. It's not often that people without a formed Core find their way to Sojourn. Please take great care, for there are forces in this city that could snuff out your life with careless ease. I advise you to ask your master to escort you to one of the Genesis Centers so that you may develop some small level of resilience."

Darren, startled beyond words for a moment, turned to formulate a reply, only to find the woman looking down, reading a document. He was tugged along by Edeya, who was in turn pulled by Lam. He looked around the party, wondering what they thought of the woman's words, but none seemed to have heard her. Had he imagined it? Had she somehow mentally spoken to him? As Victor guided them on the glass-like sidewalk along the similarly crystalline cobbles, through thick crowds, and under the fantastic expanse of stars and crystal structures, Darren struggled to wrap his head around everything he'd heard.

Victor was an iron ranker. The idea that this man, this titan of unimaginable strength and destructive power, was too weak to travel upon the high roads in this city was almost more than he could grasp. The woman had hinted at the upper power structure. What had she said? Passed through to steel and beyond? If steel was after iron, what was next? Silver? Gold? Were there even greater heights? How could such power even be measured? "God, I was a fool," he said, and in a quirk of luck—whether good or bad, he didn't know—they happened to be standing on a relatively quiet corner while Victor studied the map, and everyone heard him.

Victor looked at him and raised an eyebrow. "Humbling, isn't it? I felt this way in Coloss, too, but shit, that place is a backwater compared to this."

Darren nodded, irrationally pleased by Victor's attempt to relate with him. "Um, Victor, is there any place on that map called a, uh, Genesis Center?"

15

A SUITABLE SPACE

Victor felt himself starting to relax a little as they moved away from the crystalline towers of the city center and into more normal-looking buildings with brick and stone facades. Something about being on those glassy streets under the high, shimmering roads, beneath people with godlike power traversing the soaring heights, had made him uncomfortable. He'd felt a kind of primal tension in his chest, a tightening of his muscles, and a fraying of his nerves. He wondered if that was how rabbits felt while a wolf stalked through the meadow. The analogy rankled—he was Quinametzin, and comparing himself to a prey animal was galling, but he couldn't help how he'd felt.

Looking back at the tall gleaming towers as they reflected the sun in rainbow shimmers, he could imagine it was a city of the gods, a place mortals weren't meant to tread, and something in him believed it. That, more than anything else, illustrated to him that though he was a big fish in a little pond back on Fanwath, here he was swimming in a vast dangerous ocean. He let his eyes drift from the glassy towers to the stars visible through the thin atmosphere and shook his head in bewilderment. "How is gravity the same? How can we breathe so well? Why aren't, I dunno, *pinché* meteorites or something smashing into this little planet?"

"I, too, wondered at the physics of it all," Darren said, mouth agape, eyes following the direction of Victor's bewildered gaze. Victor nodded, frankly impressed with the guy's ability to keep his cool. If Victor felt like prey among those powerful forces, how must that dude feel?

"Energy," Lam said, stepping closer to the building so a large antlered man and the petite woman he escorted could pass by. "It's so thick in the air. Can't you feel it? This world must be in the center of a river or ocean of it. I don't know how it works, but I've heard some worlds are richer with Energy than others. That's right, isn't it?" She looked at Lesh with her question.

"Aye," he rumbled. "It's denser here than I've ever felt. I suppose, when Energy is involved, some of the rules of the universe become more like suggestions."

Victor held up the magical glass map he'd purchased from the information kiosk. It functioned a lot like a very simple tablet back on Earth. He touched things with his fingers to center the view and could zoom in and out by tapping. The map it displayed was in color and even had a slightly three-dimensional aspect, making it clear how much bigger some buildings were than others. It also had a simple menu, and one of the headings indicated a lot more to the device. "This map has a guidebook section. I haven't opened it yet, but when we get to a hotel or inn or whatever, we can probably get a lot of our questions answered by looking through it."

"Are we close?"

"Yeah." Victor held the map lower so Valla could see, pointing with his index finger at a section circled in bright pink and labeled "Abundant Lodging." The information clerk had done that for him, showing him how to make annotations to the map with one's finger. It really felt like a high-quality tablet, something the rich kids up in the foothills back home might have in their classrooms.

"And the blue dot is us?"

"Well, the tablet. I guess it's connected to some kind of magical network." Victor shrugged.

Valla wrinkled her nose. "Network? Like the, what was it, telephones in First Landing?"

"I think that's probably right," Darren said, nodding. "It would seem the people of Sojourn have, once again, illustrated my provincial ignorance. To think I thought we could recapture our dominance away from Earth with a few tanks and bombs. Just standing here, in the shadow of those great towers, I feel the power steeped in them. Can you imagine if someone tried to let off a mundane bomb in there? Those beings could wave a hand and send the explosion away!"

"Try to stop that, Darren," Valla said, smiling down at the man. Looking at him, watching him frown in confusion, Victor wondered how old he was.

Thirties, probably. He looked as though he'd experienced some living, but he definitely wasn't middle-aged. Victor might think Energy was making him look younger, but he knew the guy hadn't even formed a Core yet, let alone advanced his race somehow.

"Stop what, um, Lady Valla?" He looked down, as usual, completely unable to lock eyes with Valla for more than a second. Victor wanted to laugh and tease him a little, but he held his tongue, also wondering about Valla's point.

"Thinking of how you'd attack every new place you come across. Isn't that what got you into trouble back in First Landing? Wasn't a tenet of your political party about dominion? Your people are new to the System and the part of the universe it rules. Domination shouldn't be your primary reason for exploration."

"Of course, I suppose, well, yes. You're right." Darren nodded and closed his mouth, and, once again, Victor had to give him props; it was clear he wanted to explain himself, wanted to make excuses for his outlook, but he was choosing to let it go.

"Right. Come on, then." He started across the street, walking on one of the ubiquitous arched pedestrian crossways in the city. There weren't traffic lights, but the roads were orderly and safe. The magical and mundane conveyances, from glowing bullet-shaped carriages propelled by Energy to mythical mounts with horns and wings, traversed the city on one-way streets. At the same time, the pedestrians walked on wide, smooth sidewalks and crossed streets overtop the traffic. Most of the intersections were circular, and it seemed there was some unposted law about taking them slowly, because he never saw anyone who appeared to be in a hurry. Glancing up at the flying vehicles and winged people and animals, he supposed rushing was left to those with the gift of flight.

Darren seemed to be following his gaze with his own. He spoke up, looking at Lam with his question. "Does it make you want to fly?"

"Hmm?" Lam looked at him past Edeya, whose hands they both held.

"The people soaring about up there. Wouldn't you rather join them than walk on the ground with us landlubbers?"

"Landlubber?" Lam snorted at the strange word. "Is that . . ."

"A silly word from home, aye." Darren looked at Victor, perhaps hoping for some backup, but Victor just looked at his map, ignoring the conversation. He was warming up to the guy, not exactly despising him anymore, but he didn't want to act like his buddy.

"I presume it means someone who can't fly?" Lam prodded.

"Oh, actually, it's meant to be disparaging toward people who don't like to sail the seas. It was a stupid word choice."

"Well, back to your question," Lam said, taking pity on the poor man. "I wouldn't mind flying a bit, but I can't soar the way Valla and those folks up there can. For now, I'm only able to manage short flights. Someday, maybe." She looked up at the sky longingly, and Victor saw something in her eyes that made him give her a double take. In his mind, Lam had always been "Captain Lam," the heroic, powerful, wealthy woman who'd bucked the social hierarchies and given Victor a chance to escape injustice. He admired and looked up to her, but here, she had wide hopeful eyes and seemed younger than he'd ever seen her. For some reason, he felt he had to protect her, and the idea was freaking him out.

They walked for a few minutes, everyone lost in their thoughts or speechless in the wonder of the strange city of Sojourn. Lesh was always quiet, but Victor could see he was also lost in thought, pondering the implications of the place and its people. As they rounded the corner and meandered down a gently sloping sidewalk cobbled with smooth red stones, their destination finally came into view. It was a big park square surrounded by tall, many-storied brick buildings. They were charming in their uniqueness, each building a different shade with slightly different architecture, but they were clearly all hotels.

Welcoming awnings and stylish wooden or metal placards announced them each. He saw names ranging from the Astral Loom Suites to the Prism of Dreams to the Whispering Wyrd Inn, and a dozen others besides. The park wasn't massive, probably only a few acres of grass and thin willowy trees surrounding a big white stone fountain with a dozen matching benches at the center. From their vantage on the elevated approaching street, they could see most of the buildings, the entirety of the park, and the crowds of people meandering about.

"Where do the vehicles go? I only see pedestrians," Darren asked.

"Looks like there's another road around the back of the square." Lesh pointed to the left down the street. Victor could see he was right; the wagons, carriages, and magical vehicles were all being diverted down a side street, and it was easy to guess that it would turn to parallel the now pedestrian-only roadway approaching the park.

"Any of those inns catch anyone's eye?" Victor asked, giving Valla a nudge. She'd been quiet, but she was always like that, especially when she wasn't alone with him.

"I'm partial to the one with the red gables." She pointed, and Victor squinted, trying to read the sign.

"Wayward Wanderer Inn?"

"I think it fits us better than some of those more fanciful names."

"Agreed," Lesh said with a note of finality.

Victor shrugged and started forward. "I'm not gonna argue. I don't care as long as it has big beds and bathtubs."

"Yes! With boiling water!" Lesh rumbled enthusiastically. Victor laughed, imagining the big guy reclining in a bath of water that would boil the flesh off a human.

"I know you've been busy with that map, Victor, but now that we've arrived, would you mind if I search for that place the guide suggested to me?" Darren asked, stepping quickly to keep up with everyone else's long strides. Victor looked at him and at Edeya, listlessly walking between him and Lam, and he slowed down.

He turned to Lam. "Sorry if I'm going too fast. Is this all right for Edeya?"

"It's probably good for her. I doubt sitting around is healthy for her body."

"Okay, good. Uh, yeah, Darren, you can check the map, but wait till we get to the inn. I don't want you to try to walk and read it at the same time. What if you bump into the wrong guy, and he flattens you?" Victor was half joking, but he was also quite serious. He could only imagine how dangerous it would be for Darren if the wrong person decided he'd done something insulting. "Also, I told you Lesh is your buddy while we're here, so if you want to check the place out, you'll have to work with him."

"Of course! Thank you, Victor."

Victor paused and turned to look down at Darren, glowering a little. He appreciated his attitude change and his attempt to be respectful but didn't want a companion acting obsequious all the time. "Darren, chill out with that stuff, will you? I'm not going to beat you up or anything. Just be yourself; you don't have to kiss my ass."

Darren's eyes widened with dismay, clearly fearing that he'd angered Victor despite his words. "I didn't mean anything . . ."

"He knows," Lam said, narrowing her eyes at Victor. Valla tugged at his arm, so Victor turned and continued walking. What was it with everyone? They acted like he was going to kill the guy. As far as he was concerned, after they got to the hotel, Darren was Lesh's problem. He'd already told the big dragonkin as much, and Lesh had agreed with such solemn acceptance that Victor had almost taken back the request. It was like he'd given out some kind of noble quest, and Lesh was determined to succeed beyond his expectations. Did he feel chaperoning the one-time politician would earn him some points with Victor? How would he feel if he learned Victor didn't really care what happened to the guy? That thought gave him pause. Was it true? Had he grown so heartless?

Victor found himself scowling, feeling kind of irritated with himself as they walked through the hotel's big glass and brass doors. He barely heard the hirsute doorman as he bowed and greeted them, pulling the massive door wide. He slowed his steps, enjoying the décor of the expansive lobby, and allowed Valla to take the lead, approaching the reception desk. Victor had never been to a fancy hotel on Earth, but he imagined it would look something like this. Marble floors, covered with lush blue carpets intricately patterned in a green floral print, ran through the expansive space to meet walls decked in lavish artwork—portraits, display cases filled with crystal and fine plate ware, and hanging tapestries that complemented the carpets.

Plants hung from the heights, along with the bright sunny lighting that emanated from high crystal chandeliers, gave warmth and vibrancy to the space. Victor took a deep, cleansing breath and tried to push his stress aside. They had things to accomplish in this place—Edeya's catatonic face was a constant reminder of that—but that didn't mean they couldn't enjoy themselves while they were at it. A tiny voice in a deep corner of his mind, one he'd been repeatedly shoving down since the battle at the volcano, whispered, "Should you really enjoy yourself after getting hundreds of people killed?"

Darren hung back with Lam and Edeya while the others spoke to the hotel clerk. He watched Victor staring into space, glowering, while Valla made arrangements for their rooms. He was happy to let them handle things; he'd spent most of the fortune he'd been hoarding back in First Landing to pay for his travel through the System Stone, and though he hadn't said anything, he desperately hoped they'd find alternative means of further travel. Otherwise, he'd have to throw himself on Victor and Valla's mercy again.

He wondered what Victor was so tense about. He'd seemed rather surly since Darren had arrived unexpectedly in the Free Marches. Darren had expected him to be annoyed and hadn't been surprised when he'd been reticent to allow him to travel with them, but it wasn't just Darren Victor had been short with. He'd seen the faces Lam and Valla made. Lesh, eager to please Victor, wasn't so easy to read. Besides, he scowled almost as much as Victor. No, he wasn't a good indicator of Victor's mood.

Darren wondered if it was simply the stress of being responsible for all of them. He had a vague idea that Lam, Valla, and Lesh were far from helpless, but he'd seen how they all looked up to Victor back on Fanwath. Was Victor perhaps feeling out of his depth, worried that he'd led them all into waters too choppy to swim through? Darren wanted to help but felt like an infant trying to advise nuclear scientists. No, he figured the best thing he could do was get himself out of Victor's hair and work on making himself less of a burden.

Lesh stepped away from the counter, holding a shiny brass key. He looked at Darren and said, "Come, fosterling, you will stay with me."

"I, uh, oh. Very well, thank you, Lesh." The dragon man narrowed his gold-banded green eyes and grunted, turning back to Victor.

"Lord Victor, I'll be ready for your call. Please keep me apprised of the situation." He nodded to Edeya meaningfully and then gestured for Darren to follow him, stepping briskly toward an ornate wrought iron and marble stairway.

Darren started to hurry after him, but Victor held up a hand. "Wait." Lesh froze, and Darren turned to Victor, unconsciously shrinking inward, flinching as though the giant might smack him. He was relieved to see Victor's face in a neutral expression as he held out the glass notebook-sized map. "Use this for now, but don't take it from your room. I'm going to want to look through it later." As Darren accepted the magical device, Victor looked at Lesh. "If you go anywhere, leave a notice with the desk here. We'll do the same."

Lesh nodded, then turned, beckoning for Darren to hurry. Darren clutched the tablet to his chest and hustled after the big warrior, jogging to keep up. When they approached the stairway, Lesh looked at Darren and asked, "Have you used a travel stair before?"

"A, uh, what?"

"This is a travel stair. It will aid your movement with dimensional magic. You must keep your destination in mind as you step, or you'll get lost."

"Lost on a stairway?"

"Exactly. We are on floor seventeen. Think of that number as you climb." With that, the giant turned, lifted his foot to the fourth step, and started up. To Darren's dismay, he vanished from sight after only one more giant step. Darren hurriedly started climbing the steps, picturing a big floating seventeen in his mind, and after three steps, he stumbled onto a landing.

"How the hell?" He looked around, surprised to find himself facing into a hallway with Lesh striding away from him. He hurried after him, and when they approached a door labeled 1755, Lesh stopped and pushed his key into the lock. The door opened with a click, and they stepped into their suite. Lesh put his fists on his hips and looked around, breathing deeply. He bared his many pointy teeth in a smile. "This is a suitable space."

Their hotel room must have been constructed with heavy use of dimensional magic. The ceiling soared some thirty meters overhead, and windows the size of tennis courts lined the far wall, providing an expansive view of the hotel square and park. Half a dozen couches were arrayed before the windows and the big freestanding circular fireplace. A large kitchen lined one side of the room, and doorways to the bedroom suites were on the other. All in all, it was decorated much like the lobby, with deep shades of blue and dark polished wood. It was luxurious on a level Darren had seldom seen, and on a scale he'd never encountered. "Amazing," he breathed, stepping into the massive space, savoring the thick carpeting as his feet sank into it.

"Elder," Lesh said, catching him by surprise.

"I'm sorry?"

"You need not apologize. Now you know; do not fail to use the honorific in the future when we are in mixed company." Lesh brushed past him toward the windows, and Darren stared at him, confused for several seconds before it clicked; back in the lobby, he'd scowled when Darren called him Lesh. He expected him to call him Elder?

"Um, do you mean I should always call you Elder, or do I say Elder Lesh?"

"Either will do, fosterling."

"You, uh, Elder Lesh, you know I'm an adult human, right?"

"Regardless. You are as helpless as a hatchling, and I've taken you into my protection. You are my fosterling, and you will address me with the proper show of respect." Something in Darren wanted to balk at the idea, wanted to argue, but another part of him felt admiration and gratitude for the giant black-scaled man. Calling Darren a "fosterling" was going a lot further than Victor had demanded. If Victor were the most powerful person in their party, Lesh would probably be second, though Darren wasn't sure of that; Valla was also an unknown entity. The point was that Lesh was a powerhouse, and if he was willing to foster Darren, that was a win in his eyes.

"Thank you, Elder." At his words, Lesh folded his arms over his chest and nodded solemnly, still staring out the window.

"Good. Now, fosterling, you will contact the man at the front desk and ask that the furniture in this suite be stored away. We have no use for it. A bath and a dry floor are all men such as we require."

"Oh." Darren looked around the room at the comfortable, luxurious furniture. He supposed sleeping on the floor wouldn't be so awful; at least they were well carpeted. "I'll do that right away, Elder."

"Yes." Lesh nodded, his black reptilian lips curving into a slow smile. "A large cave with a good view will benefit our outlook. Look out there, fosterling. Look at those people, at those buildings, at the stars beyond. See what there is within your grasp and be filled with inspiration. Think of the man who changed your life and took you in, assigning you to me. Think of how you will work to impress him and make him glad that you exist. That is our mission here, in this great city—to grow stronger so that we might aid Victor in his quests. Through his victories, we will have our own."

16

PROGRESS

Victor sat on the supple leather couch, looking through the enormous windows at the park and the city beyond it. Rather than a medieval magical world, it felt like a futuristic New York or Paris—he really had no clue, having never been to a big city on Earth. It was hard not to feel relaxed with that view in the comfort of his hotel room, but he managed. He was tense and annoyed and feeling like everything was too damn complicated.

When he'd gone from Fanwath to the city of Coloss, he'd been irritated to find that people there were generally a lot more powerful than those on Fanwath. He'd been expecting something similar when they traveled to Sojourn, but not on this scale. There were times he'd been talking to people on Fanwath—Borrius, Rellia, even the folks at First Landing—and while he spoke about being prepared and growing in power, he'd often wondered, quietly, why someone truly mighty, someone like Tes but opposite in temperament, wouldn't come to Fanwath and take the place over. Being here, walking around in the thick Energy, slinking through the shadows cast by the godlike powers up above, he realized that Fanwath wasn't worth noticing for these people.

"Do you want to talk about it?"

Victor looked up to see Valla stepping out of the bedroom. She'd been hanging some clothes in the wardrobe, something he didn't understand. He was fine keeping his things in his storage ring, but he supposed Valla liked to visualize her outfits. "Hmm?"

"Are you ready to talk about your mood? You've been . . . short with people." She walked closer to the couch, pausing to look out the window while he considered his answer.

"I just hate feeling so small, I guess."

She looked at him and frowned, making an expression that was half irritated and half sympathetic. "Firstly, love, if that's truly bothering you, then you need to take a step back and put yourself in everyone else's shoes. Secondly, that's not it. You've been distant since we beat the invasion, distant with me, and short with everyone else. You have bouts of good humor, but there's more bothering you, and it's only going to fester until you confront it."

"I don't know what you want to hear. I'm worried about Edeya. I'm stressed having so many dangerous . . . beings, I guess, around us."

Valla shook her head, sighing, then walked around behind the couch. He could hear her steps as she continued toward the door. "I'm going to get that guidebook thing from Darren. We need to figure out where to ask for help with Edeya."

"Want me to come with you?"

"No. Be back soon." With that, she stepped through the door, and he heard it click shut. Victor felt his irritation start to steep into something more like anger and clenched his fists, sitting there alone, feeling stupid and childish. Something in him wouldn't allow him to take all the blame, though. Was it his fault he felt stressed? He hadn't exactly been mean to anyone, had he? Hadn't he even told Darren to relax and stop sucking up? What was he supposed to do, kiss everyone's ass? Was Valla right about him being distant since the volcano? Again, what was he supposed to do about that? Forget about all the good people who'd died? Forget about Sarl?

Victor found he was clenching his teeth, his jaw bulging from the pressure, and forced himself to physically relax by taking a deep, slow breath through his nose. He stood and paced before the window. Even at his full, natural size, it took him five steps to traverse its length, and a part of him was impressed with the weird spatial magic that allowed the massive windows on the interior of the building while making them a tenth the size on the exterior. The thought didn't last long, though, in the storm of emotions raging in his mind. Looking deep, where he hated to gaze, he knew it was more than stress, anger, sadness, or disappointment that was messing with his mind; it was shame.

He'd put on a brave face and accepted everyone's insistence that it wasn't his fault that so many had died when Hector had sprung his trap, but what it boiled down to was that he didn't believe the platitudes. He didn't believe that Kethelket wasn't upset with him, not after losing nearly a third of all his people. When he'd joined the campaign, he'd brought more than three hundred Naghelli. Now, he was settling the lands they'd earned with something like a hundred and eighty. Even if Victor put that aside, how could he ever be okay knowing that more than seven hundred members of the Ninth and the reserve cohort had died in that attack?

People said things like, "If not for you, more would have died during the campaign," but the words didn't help. To him, Edeya had become the symbol of his failures. She was a constant reminder of what had gone wrong that night, and the sadness lurking in Lam's eyes only compounded that feeling. Lam put on a brave face and tried to keep hopeful about a solution, but Victor wasn't so sure. Catalina was cruel, sadistic even, and he didn't doubt that the part of Edeya she'd taken wasn't being treated well. He wasn't sure what a Death Caster would do with someone's spirit, but he knew it wouldn't be pretty. Even if they made her whole again, would she ever be the same?

His stewing was interrupted when the door opened, and Valla walked in carrying the glass tablet. She held it aloft and said, "A different person was working at the desk, a strange metallic being with four arms. I couldn't tell if it was a man or a woman or something else. Anyway, they were very kind, and when they heard me speaking to Lesh and Darren, they offered to send a runner back to the World Hall, as they called the place where we arrived, and fetch us another one of these. Lesh paid for it and said he'd wait for the replacement."

"That's cool." Victor sighed, shaking his head. "Listen, I know I'm not a great communicator. I don't know how to voice all the shit going on in my head, but I want you to know I'm sorry if I'm making you miserable."

Valla, too, sighed, and she walked toward him, pulling her wings close with an almost metallic rustle. "Come here." She opened her arms, but Victor didn't move. He wasn't feeling right, and receiving more comfort or kindness from someone wasn't what he was looking for; it wasn't what he deserved. That didn't deter Valla, though, and she continued toward him. When she stepped around the couch into the bright sun shining through the window, the light in her eyes was mesmerizing, and Victor almost didn't realize it when she took his hands in hers, looking up at him. "I noticed you're not reducing your size here."

"I . . ."

"You want to put more distance between yourself and us." She didn't ask; it was clear she thought she was right, and she might be. It was easier to stand high above Lam and Edeya. It was easier to avoid looking into people's eyes. "I know the source of your pain, and I know people have tried words to make you feel differently. Maybe you should try some words. Put to voice what's haunting you."

"What's haunting me? A thousand ghosts!" Victor snapped, jerking free of her grasp and turning back to the window. "A thousand people who died because I was a prideful idiot. Because I let that . . ." He trailed off, not wanting to start throwing out curses and invectives he might come to regret.

"You let her play upon your pride? You took some bait and, with every good intention, attempted something perilous? How many others could say the same? How many of us wouldn't put ourselves at risk if we thought it would save the lives of others? You made a bad decision, but you made it for the right reasons."

"Valla! The Naghelli are practically gone!"

"Would it be better if you'd never killed Belikot? Would they be better off?"

Victor turned to the glass, refusing to meet her gaze, and pressed his forehead against the cool surface. "So if I do something good, it excuses *hundreds* of deaths?"

"Get over yourself, Victor!" Valla snapped, apparently tired of coddling him. When he turned, eyes wide, surprised at the outburst, she continued, "How are you so certain no one would have died if you'd been there? Most of the deaths occurred when Hector descended with that bone dragon! What if you'd run off like me and Kethelket, pursuing and slaughtering the ghouls? He still would have landed on that wall. He still would have run amok among the troops while you fought your way to him. Should Kethelket and I carry the burden of those deaths because we didn't stand back with the soldiers? Now, tell me, if you'd pursued him up that mountain but hadn't had the breakthrough you were *forced* to make while trapped, do you think you would have beaten him so cleanly up in that volcano? Keep in mind that his veil star would have still been there. Keep in mind that the volcano wouldn't have awakened. Stop moping and grousing about what *could* have been when you've got so much to be thankful for! We won! We destroyed a vast army of undead and drove the invaders from Fanwath, and that was largely due to your heroics!"

"I . . ." Victor stopped, mouth hanging open, unable to formulate a coherent string of words. He'd rarely heard Valla speak so much at once and never with such ferocity. She glared at him for a handful of seconds, then turned and walked to the couch. She sat and began tapping her fingers on the tablet, scowling. Victor turned back to the window, staring out at the crystal city center in the distance, and, for the first time, he appreciated the beauty of it. For the first time, he didn't think about the beings walking the heights, wondering about their intentions. "It's beautiful," he said, voicing his thoughts.

Valla didn't reply, so he turned to her and watched her eyes scanning the tablet. Her eyebrows were drawn down in a scowl, and he wondered what it must have taken for her to yell at him like that. Had he really been so wrong? He moved over to the couch, casting Alter Self, reducing his size to something more on her level. When he sat, he was sure to leave some space between them. He watched her scanning through the guidebook information, pointedly ignoring him, and after a few minutes, he said, "You're right." Her finger paused for a moment, then went back to scrolling through the information. "You know, you're a lot older than I am. It's not really my fault that I don't see things as clearly as you do . . ."

"What?" She whirled on him, dropping the tablet to the carpet. "Did you just say I'm *old*?"

Victor grinned, leaning back as though taunting her, daring her to do something. "I mean, I'm just stating the facts . . ." She leaped on him, hands going for his throat, her wings spreading wide. Victor laughed and fell back, grabbing her around the waist and pulling her close. Her feigned chokes became caresses, became kisses, and then it was only a matter of time before they were pulling each other's clothes off and, in the shadow of the glittering, rainbow-lit city, they made love, or more aptly, had sex—wild, pent-up sex that left them both sweaty and drained and, at least in Victor's case, much clearer of mind.

Later that afternoon, after they'd cleaned up, Lam came to their suite with Edeya in tow. While she and Valla sat talking, Victor perused the guidebook. It didn't take long to find a listing of "Sojourn sanctioned" businesses, and among them, subheadings for practitioners of "spirit" and "portal" magic, among other promising categories. When he saw that, he looked up, tuning in for the first time to the conversation taking place.

". . . think it's kind of endearing. He could have become bitter or vengeful, but he's accepted his failure and chosen to better himself. In fact, I was the one who convinced Victor to bring him."

"That's all well and good, but are we sure Lesh is the right one to mentor him? What do we even know about that man's culture?"

"Uh, sorry to interrupt, ladies, but I think I have a lead here. This guide-book has listings for different kinds of businesses and dozens of spirit and portal experts. I figure if someone can't help Edeya here, maybe someone can help us find a way to get to Dark Ember. Or at least to send me. If I can get my hands on that bi—"

"Whoa," Lam said, laughing. The genuine humor in the sound and the light in her eyes reminded Victor of what an idiot he'd been earlier. She might be upset about Edeya, but there was great hope there, enough to let her enjoy the moment. And why shouldn't she be hopeful? While Edeya had life, there was a chance she'd recover. There was so much in this uni-verse he didn't understand, so much power he couldn't fathom. Who was he to decide something was hopeless? Those beings who'd inspired dread in him as he walked beneath those crystal towers were just as worthy of inspiring hope.

"Right. One step at a time. Do you guys want to go see one before it gets dark?"

Valla smiled. "This is a city, Victor. Darkness doesn't mean businesses close . . ."

"Right, well, dark was the wrong word. I meant late. Businesses do close, you know."

"I'm up for it," Lam said, illustrating her words by standing.

When Valla nodded, Victor said, "Let's pick a place first. I say we should visit a 'spirit practitioner' first. It would be good to have another opinion about what's going on with Edeya, and I wouldn't mind asking about, shit, I don't know, an instructor? What do you call it when you want to learn more about your magic?"

"A teacher, or master, or mentor, or . . ." Lam looked as though she meant to continue listing synonyms, so Victor held up his hand for mercy, laughing.

"Right, right, you know what I mean. Here are some of the names. He read from the list: Vyrt's Wonders of the Soul, The Love Loom, Empathy Echoes, Hope's Horizon, Chamber of Remorse, Harmony's Haven, Ether Echoes, Celestine's Crystal Gaze . . ." Victor trailed off, frowning.

"Is that all of them?" Lam prodded.

"No, there's about forty more, but I was just thinking that these names don't say a lot. We might as well just pick one, and if they can't help us, we can ask whoever runs that shop for advice on where to go next."

"Well, I'm partial to the, uh, hope one," Valla said, gesturing to her sword, Midnight Hope, leaning in her scabbard against the wall beside Lifedrinker.

"Right." Victor grinned. "Hope's Horizon, it is." He and Valla gathered up their weapons, and then, with Lam holding Edeya's hand, they walked through the long hallway to the magical stairway. When they approached it, a thought occurred to Victor. "Hey, how does Edeya use the stairs? Don't you have to think of your destination?"

Lam shrugged. "I just hold her hand, and she moves with me."

"Well, that's good. I guess if nothing else worked, I could carry her . . ."

"Not necessary." Lam laughed.

The map made it easy to navigate the city; it was like having GPS on your phone back on Earth. Victor led the way, but the sidewalks were wide, the denizens of the city were pleasant, and they didn't encounter any trouble as they made the short walk to the address in the guidebook. Their route took them back toward the city's center, but they stopped well short of the first crystal tower, finding Hope's Horizon to be a small shopfront on the side of a large building occupied mainly by a huge bookstore.

"Oh!" Valla said, grabbing Victor's wrist. "Can we go into the bookstore when we're done in there?"

"Yeah, for sure." Victor glanced at Lam. "That all right with you?"

She nodded, smiling at Valla's excitement. "I love books."

"Never saw you reading back in the mine . . ."

"Spent a lot of time watching me in my private quarters, did you?" Lam gave his shoulder a bit of a shove.

"See? That's what happens when I walk around all tiny like this; people think they can shove me around."

"Tiny?" Lam scoffed. "None of us are tiny." It was true; even if he reduced his height to be similar to Valla's, the three of them were all seven feet tall or more. Victor shrugged, then approached the business door. The bright yellow sun was dipping toward the horizon, providing a breathtaking sunset that filled the western sky with deep shades of red, magenta, and purple while darkening the rest of the atmosphere, allowing the already visible stars to shine more brightly in the blackness. He'd nearly walked into traffic twice, trying to stare up into that expanse as they traversed the city. With that in mind, he worried they were too late as he pulled on the door handle. It opened easily, putting his fears to rest, and they stepped inside.

Victor found himself in a small comfortable-looking shop with couches on the right-hand side, a counter on the left, and rows of trinkets and potion bottles on shelves behind it. A man with long wavy pink hair, massive pointy gray ears, and golden eyes that reminded Victor of a cat looked up from the counter. His eyes narrowed with interest. "Welcome in. Hurry now, don't let all the warm air out. Ah, ah, I see a bright Spirit Core among you, and . . . what's this? This poor girl's spirit is fragmented. Come, come, sit down. Let me have a better look."

17

PRYING EYES

The door to the suite clicked open, and Lesh's voice boomed out, "Fosterling!" Darren jumped, startled more by the volume than the sudden return of the giant reptilian man. Was that right? Were dragonkin reptiles? Were they dragons? Darren decided it would be best to guard his words and thoughts about the subject on the off chance that labeling them such would be considered an insult. He clambered to his feet and cleared his throat. "Here, Elder." He'd been lounging in front of the windows, lying on the carpet—the hospitality staff had come in with dimensional containers and removed all the furnishings. Lesh had been pleased by the wide open feeling of the room, but Darren found it strange; it felt hollow, and sounds seemed to echo and bounce off the naked walls.

"I have regained the information device. No, better; I have acquired a new one. We no longer have to worry about returning this to Lord Victor."

"Oh? That's excellent news! May I see . . ."

"You will take this and find the location of the Genesis Building. Is that not the name of the place the steward of the portals whispered in your ear?"

"Um, right, Elder. Genesis Center, actually." Darren hurried over to Lesh, as always daunted by the fact that his head only reached the enormous warrior's waist. Holding the device between a clawed thumb and finger, Lesh handed it down to him. "I cannot make myself small as Victor does to use this comfortably. I may require you to navigate here and there, depending on how long we stay in this city."

Darren took the tablet, nodding as he tapped the screen. When it didn't light up like the first one, he said, "Elder, I think you need to activate it." Lesh grumbled a sound, half sigh and half *tsk,* as he reached out with one of his three clawed "fingers," each as wide around as Darren's wrist, and pressed it into the glass. A half second later, it flared with amber light, and the map of the city appeared. "Thank you, sir, um, Elder."

"Good. As your education advances, I will teach you a proper honorific in the tongue of the dragons. For now, Elder will continue to suffice. Will it take you long to find the center? I've half a mind to bask in the afternoon sun." Lesh eyed the bright sunny section of blue carpeting in front of the windows.

"Only a moment, but we can wait to go if . . ."

"No. We will go now. I cannot condone your Coreless existence for a moment longer than necessary. If this grove or nursery cannot help you, I will guide you through the process, painful as it may be. First, however, we will give the teachers of children a try."

"I'm not so sure it's a place for children . . ." While he muttered his half-hearted objection, Darren scanned through the listing of businesses and public buildings. Somehow, it was organized alphabetically in words that looked just like English to him, and for the millionth time since waking up on Fanwath, he wondered how the System could do that. It had to be a complex spell or something that existed in their minds. Is that what "skills" granted by the System were? Could it take them away as easily as grant them? He tapped the name of the business and selected the "map" option, and then he saw, just like his GPS back on Earth, a faint golden line leading away from the hotel on the map toward the destination. It didn't look far. "I have it, Elder."

"Good! You see, fosterling? Your mind is quick; there may be a useful class for you."

As Lesh turned toward the door, Darren fell into his shadow, following behind. "Um, thank you." When they reached the sidewalk outside the hotel, Lesh paused and turned to look down his short tooth-filled snout at him, narrowing his mossy green eyes in the dark hollow beneath his prominent scaled brow.

"You will lead us. Fear not—I will be close behind."

Darren nodded and continued down the cobbled walkway past the park. Just as before, he was nearly dumbstruck by the sights, sounds, and smells of the magical city. The smell was a big one; it was clear from what they could see through their hotel window that the city was massive. It sprawled to the horizon, and its downtown, with the giant crystal towers, was easily the size of skyscraper zones in the big cities of Earth. That said, it didn't smell like New York. Darren had been there a few times for seminars, and the thing he always noticed, provided the weather was warm enough, was the ever-present underlying stench of urine. "The air is fresh, Elder," he said over his shoulder.

"Should it not be?"

"Well, I don't know why, but I'd often find cities smelled of garbage and waste on my homeworld." Darren shrugged; he really didn't know why. He supposed that when lots of people gathered, you got all kinds, and some of those would rather pee on the side of a building than find a restroom.

"Shameful. One who cannot dispose of their own waste should be banished." Lesh rumbled his proclamation offhandedly, and when Darren looked back at him, he saw that his big mentor was busily staring at a procession of veiled feminine figures. They were larger than humans, had four arms with blue and purple skin, and beneath their veils, bright lights shone from where their eyes should be. Darren tried not to stare as the twelve figures sauntered by, studiously staring at his map while he hurried.

"What interesting ladies," Lesh said after they'd rounded the corner. "Something about a hidden face makes me want to see it more. Do you feel the same, fosterling?"

"I suppose. The allure of the unknown or the mystery of what we cannot see . . ." Darren trailed off as he rounded the last corner and saw his destination ahead. It was a domed, crystalline building occupying something like four city blocks. The afternoon sun shimmered on the structure, making it appear bright white, painful to the eyes, near the top, and gradually darkening to a glimmering orange-red near the street level. "Beautiful," he breathed, beginning to walk again.

"Indeed. That's an edifice worthy of a visit, even if the services within are meant for the youth of this world." Lesh's cocksure certainty that the place was for children was almost amusing to Darren. He couldn't argue, though; he figured most adults who'd been born in a System world would have developed their Core and whatever other services the Genesis Center provided. It didn't help matters when, as they approached, a group of children—pointy-eared, colorful folk who reminded Darren of fairy stories—surged out of the central doors, corralled by a floating cloud-like being as they laughed and jumped, running with the exuberance of youth toward the sidewalk.

Darren didn't wait around for Lesh to comment, hurrying up the steps to the enormous glass, or maybe crystal, doors. When he approached, they swung open quickly and noiselessly, and Darren stepped into an oval reception area constructed of the same crystal substance as the building's exterior. It was domed and almost cave-like, with a dozen oval passages leading away in every direction. The lighting came from the crystal walls, ceiling, and floor—a soft blue-white glow that permeated everything. The air was remarkably crisp and fresh, and Darren folded his arms, gripping his shoulders as he registered the temperature, bordering on cold.

He was about to turn to Lesh to ask him for advice on where to begin when a cloud of misty light coalesced in front of him. It pulsed with a soft glow as a pleasant masculine voice asked, "Darren Whitehorse, welcome to the Genesis Center. Are you here to begin your journey toward Energy cultivation?" Before he could answer, the misty ball of light floated over to Lesh and said, "Lesh'ro'zellan, welcome to the Genesis Center. Is Darren Whitehorse your charge?"

"He is my fosterling."

The misty light bobbed up and down, then moved back to Darren. In his peripheral vision, Darren could see other such lights, speaking to other people in the hall. "Darren? Will you learn with us today?"

"Am . . ." Darren licked his lips, unsure what he wanted to ask. "Am I allowed?"

"Of course! The Genesis Center is funded and maintained by the generosity of charitable citizens of Sojourn. All of our instruction and counseling services are free to the public."

"You will learn here today, fosterling," Lesh rumbled, making his decision for him.

"If you're sure." Darren glanced up at the giant man. "Elder."

"Your elder is wise to give you time to study here, Darren. There's much that we can teach you. Lesh'ro'zellan, please retrieve your charge here tomorrow at noon; he'll be ready for rest and recovery by then."

"Good." When Lesh turned, Darren thought he would leave, but he stopped halfway, facing him. He took Darren's shoulder in one of his enormous clawed hands, turning him so they were face to face. "Look in my eyes, fosterling." Darren looked up. He hadn't even realized he was looking down. What was it about people like Victor and Lesh that made them hard to lock eyes with? No, it was more than those two; Darren felt the same about Valla. He'd thought it was her beauty, but could it be more? Could it be their raw power? Darren forced himself to keep his eyes open, staring into the mossy green, yellow-banded eyes, feeling the weight of the consciousness behind them. "Here, in this public place, I have declared that you are my fosterling. You are a member of my household. You will bring pride to my name." He didn't say it as though he was asking or telling Darren to "make him proud," but rather as a statement of fact. Darren felt his chest swelling as he stood up straighter. Had he ever had a boss or mentor put such faith in him?

"Thank you, Elder."

Lesh nodded and turned to leave without a backward glance. The floating ball of mist and light moved between Darren's eyes and his view of Lesh's diminishing form stalking down the steps outside the glass doors. "Darren, please follow me to your genesis pod." It moved slowly, as though to ensure Darren was following, then it gradually increased its speed until he had to step with brisk, long strides to keep up. It led him into one of the round crystal-lined passages, which meandered in a winding, unpredictable pattern as it slowly climbed into the enormous edifice. When they stepped into a small, perfectly circular room, Darren had no idea how far they'd come or in what part of the building he might be.

"This is your genesis pod, Darren. You will learn and practice here for your first day at the center. If your elder brings you again, you may return to a room like this or work with other students, depending on your progress today."

"Will, um, will I have a teacher?"

"I will be your instructor and guide today. You may call me Y-seven."

"Y-seven?" Darren had turned to address the light and was faintly disturbed to see the doorway was gone; he was in a round ball of faintly cloudy, luminous crystal. "Forgive my ignorance, Y-seven, but are you a life-form or a construct of some kind?"

"There is no need to forgive a lack of knowledge so long as the desire exists to learn. I am a member of the Orushra species, and yes, I am alive, though my body functions differently than yours. Speaking of body functions, Darren, will you require nourishment or a place to void biological waste?"

"I, um, not right now, thank you."

"Very good. Please move your body into its most comfortable position while still remaining alert. Many bipedal beings prefer to sit on the floor, for example. You'll find the crystal will accommodate your form."

Part of Darren wanted to ask for a chair, but when he'd fled First Landing and thrown himself on Victor's mercy, he'd made the conscious decision to be open-minded and agreeable. "I will sit," he said, kneeling and then sitting on his butt, trying to fold his legs before himself. His knees were a bit stiff, so he kept them up, wrapping his arms around them for comfort. The being hadn't lied; the crystal seemed to shift under his weight, and rather than a hard, unyielding glass-like crystal, he felt as though he was sitting on a warm soft cushion.

"Are you comfortable?" Y-seven asked, and Darren nodded. "Good. I can see much about you thanks to the divination glyphs woven into this structure. Still, it would be good if we had a conversation. Will that be all right?" Again, Darren nodded. "As I ask you questions and you answer them, feel free to ask me questions of your own."

"Thank you, I will."

"Darren, are you a child of your species?"

"No, I'm considered an adult man. Most people consider humans to be adults around the age of twenty years. I'm thirty-four."

"And yet, you've not formed a Core. Are you a member of a caste that isn't allowed the use of Energy on your homeworld?"

"Not exactly. You see, my people come from a world where Energy doesn't exist. I've heard stories from, well, from two sources now, that say Energy used to be rich on my homeworld but that, for some reason, it stopped flowing there."

"And with no Energy, the System is not present, either?"

"That's right."

Y-seven pulsed and throbbed with light for several seconds, then it said, "I will guide you, Darren. You are lucky to have been brought here. Truly, considering your lack of Energy, it's quite fortunate that you were taken in by such a formidable and kind master. There are many worse places you might have found yourself than here on Sojourn. Now, tell me, what do you know of Energy Cores?"

The strange-looking man hurried out from behind his counter and ushered their party over to his couches. Lam and Edeya sat in one, while Victor and Valla took the other. The couches were accommodating but still a bit small for comfort. Victor wanted to reduce his size further but knew it would probably irritate Valla, so he sat there, knees as high as his chest, and watched as the long-eared, cat-eyed man alternated staring at him and Edeya. "Quite a surprising visit! Sir, have you embarked upon your test of steel?"

"My, uh?" Victor frowned, looking at his companions, wondering if he'd missed something.

"Your test of steel. Are you yet in the iron ranks?"

"He is." Valla smiled at Victor, sighing almost wistfully as though longing for a day when someone wouldn't be impressed by him.

"Very good!" The man smiled, exposing too-large teeth, and wiped at his brow. "I was afraid I'd have to mind my manners to an absurd degree, but we iron rankers can speak frankly, no? My name is Erd Van."

"That we can," Lam said, leaning forward. "I am Lam, there are Valla and Victor, and this is Edeya. She's in a bad way, Erd Van. Can you help her?"

"This poor soul?" He stepped close to Edeya, peering into her listless eyes. "A moment!" He bustled around the counter, the tails of his patchwork coat flapping with his rapid movement. Victor heard bottles clinking and drawers opening and slamming shut, and then the man reappeared, hurrying forward with a disc-shaped blue lens. He stood before Edeya, peering at her through the lens. Victor felt a small surge of Energy, and then the lens began to sparkle with silvery light, throwing off rainbow sparks as he moved it around, peering at Edeya from every angle. After a while, he put the lens into his breast pocket and stood there, scratching the very short, very pink hairs on his chin.

"Well?" Lam prodded.

"Well, I'm sure you're aware that she's being made to appear far better than the reality of the situation. That circlet around her brow is giving her body some appearance of vibrancy, but were it taken away, I fear she'd wither and die."

"That's right." Victor leaned forward and gestured to Edeya. "Can you tell us anything we don't know? Can you help her?" He didn't mean to sound short with the guy, but something about his smug assessment rubbed him the wrong way.

"Only a fragment of her spirit is there! What happened? Was she attacked on the spirit plane? Was she attempting a breakthrough with a Khal'nav infusion? Did she do battle with . . ."

"A Death Caster," Lam said, frustration and hopelessness creeping into her voice. "She was attacked by a traitorous Death Caster who fled our world when confronted."

"Ah! That makes much more sense. Someone was trying to take her spirit, then, and was interrupted?"

"Yes." Lam's eyes filled with tears, and Victor knew she was reliving her encounter with Catalina. He wanted to sit beside her and offer her some comfort, but there wasn't room on the little couch.

"Do not despair!" Erd Van said, moving close to Lam and resting one of his small wiry hands on her shoulder. "The thing about spirits is that they

yearn to be whole. The greater part will constantly tug at the lesser fragments. This one would have fled this vessel if not for your stalwart vigil! You
being here"—he gestured to them all—"your spirits, along with the pull of
her body, a familiar vessel, are providing a counterbalance. With a strong
enough influence, you might be able to use the innate tether all soul fragments have with each other to snatch the rest of her from the clutches of that
Death Caster!"

"Really?" Lam's eyes sprang tears at his words, but they seemed to be
tears of relief or joy. Victor felt his eyes watering up in sympathy. "Can you
do that?"

"Me?" Erd Van held a hand to his chest and chuckled. "Oh, no, dear. I'm
afraid not. Even your friend here with the mighty furnace of rage and fear in
his Core wouldn't be able to, even if he had the know-how. No, I fear you'll
need to find a patron who's completed their test of steel and moved into their
lustrous veil. Someone of that level of power could probably overcome the
enormous imbalance between your friend's larger spirit and this fragment.
They may be able to exert the force required to help her spirit break free and
find its way home to her. Of course, there are risks, but there is hope. Sojourn
is just the place to find the right patron!"

While Lam and the others absorbed his words, he turned to Victor and
narrowed his eyes, staring at him for a long minute. "Do you not have a powerful patron already, sir?"

"Not exactly." Victor shrugged, not sure what he was getting at. Could
he sense Khul Bach? Was there something about his Core? It rankled Victor that the guy could apparently see his Core. How was he doing that? Was
it just that he was very sensitive to Spirit Energies? Maybe it was a skill or
ability with his class . . .

"I only ask because I can see wispy remnants—tendrils of left-behind
power—of spirits that have touched yours. Their connections to you seem
tenuous, but it seems they are still there, as though great beings are connected
to you through the spirit plane. I wonder if . . ."

Something came over Victor at that moment, and he felt his rage begin to
seep into his pathways. He surged to his feet and glowered down at the man.
When he spoke, it was him, his voice, his mind, but he felt the firm comforting influence of his ancestors guiding his tongue. "You may cease your ogling
of my spirit! I am Quinametzin, and my ancestors walk with me. Be wary
of insulting them with your prying eyes." Instinctively, he reached out with
his will, grabbed ahold of his aura that he'd been dutifully squeezing into

submission, and pulled it closer still, drawing a curtain of the furious, potent stuff around his Core.

Congratulations! You have learned a new skill: Aura Veil, Basic.

Aura Veil, Basic: Using your will, you have learned to obscure your Core and affinities from the prying eyes of others. Your veil is only as strong as your aura, and those whose will is greater than your own can pierce your concealment.

"My apologies, sir!" Erd Van fell to his knees, pressing his forehead to the carpet.

Victor might once have felt embarrassed at the obsequious display, but in his current state, bolstered by the haughty presence of his ancestors, it felt just right. He nodded to the man, ignoring the looks Lam and Valla were giving him, and said, "Your insult was innocent. You may relax. Tell us, Erd Van, can you direct us to someone who might be able to pull Edeya's spirit home?"

18

FAVORS

Victor, please." Valla gently tugged on his wrist, urging him to sit back down. "Give the man a moment to gather himself."

Victor glowered, and when Valla's eyebrows drew together, mimicking his expression of irritation, it felt as if someone had splashed cold water on him. He looked inward, at his roiling Rage Core, at the heat in his pathways, and he sighed, succumbing to her pull and sitting back down. Not trusting himself to speak, he folded his arms and made a point of not staring at Erd Van, who still knelt before the couch.

Maybe to change the subject or ease the tension, Lam spoke up. "Erd, or is it always Erd Van?"

The man sat up straight, smoothing his long pink hair back. "You may call me Erd at your pleasure, Lady."

Lam smiled and leaned against the couch arm, shifting to cross her legs more easily. "Can you tell me what you mean by 'test of steel'? I've never traveled to Sojourn before."

"Ah." Erd lithely stood, glancing at Victor as he did so, then almost eagerly looking back toward Lam. "The term originated here on Sojourn. Our founders had a flowery way of speaking and a poetic way of looking at things." When Lam's face didn't betray any understanding, and Victor and Valla remained silent, he continued. "It's all based around the idea that we're 'forging' our class during the iron ranks. You know, until the synthesis at Level One Hundred."

Lam frowned, looking over at Victor and Valla with an arched eyebrow. "Forgive me," Valla said, stealing Erd's attention. "The people in my world rarely ascend beyond Level Fifty. Those who do are secretive. Would you mind explaining this synthesis?" It wasn't lost on Victor that both women had phrased their questions saying "I" rather than "we." Were they worried his Quinametzin pride was still bristling?

"Oh, of course, of course! On System-controlled worlds, just as most races receive a class refinement every ten levels, at Level One Hundred, the System will guide you through a process in which you build a class based on the aspects of your previous classes that you've most fully mastered."

"We'll create our own class?"

"Yes, which leads to the test of steel, thanks to our founders' creative sensibilities. You see, most people, when they first build their class, end up with something at the 'base' level. In the ranks that follow, a person must sharpen and hone their 'steel' until it reaches a level of ascendancy, whereupon they can move into their lustrous veil, something I'm far less knowledgeable about. You see, for every one hundred iron rankers, there's likely to be only a single person working on their test of steel, and for every thousand of those, there might be one person in their lustrous veil. At least that's the old adage here on Sojourn. I'm sure the numbers differ from world to world. For instance, according to you, there may not be many outside the iron ranks in your homeworld."

"Or Zaafor," Victor said, looking at Valla.

She nodded. "Perhaps only the Warlord and his closest supporters."

Lam cleared her throat. "So, do I have it right in my understanding that the test of steel is not the same for everyone?"

"Yes!" Erd nodded enthusiastically. "Some people begin their test by creating a more advanced class, so their journey is shorter. Some jump multiple tiers at their first refinement, while others struggle to move out of the base tier. Everyone's journey is different."

"So you can't just grind it out?" Victor asked, and when Erd's frown signaled puzzlement, he elaborated. "I mean, you can't just keep gaining levels, eventually moving into the next stage?"

"Ah, correct, sir. There are many in the test of steel who have reached a level beyond which they struggle to grow, and their class is still in the lower tiers. They are collectively known as steelbound."

"Still more powerful than anyone we likely know," Lam said, shaking her head, grinning at the absurdity of it all.

"Oh, there are steelbound who can shift the tides of culture, who rule planets and systems, who . . ." He trailed off, glancing nervously at Victor. "Perhaps I could acquaint you with my mentor? He has passed through his test of steel, and though he disappears for decades at a time working toward his mysterious goals, he's currently in the city—he also spends years and decades in recreation, you see. It may be that your timing is just right, for I've scheduled a consultation with him next week. For a small fee, I'd be willing to spend part of my precious allocated time with my mentor asking about your friend's situation. He's the only person I know who can guide me as I approach my seventh class refinement, and I'm sure he'd have some insights." He nodded at Edeya.

"Couldn't we make an appointment of our own?" Lam asked, uncannily guessing the exact question Victor was about to voice.

"Yes, absolutely. You'll find his waiting list for consultations is something like three years out."

Victor groaned. "Seriously? Do you think he'll even help?"

"I think he'll be intrigued. I think he may . . . want to meet you, sir." He paused while he spoke as though weighing his choice of words.

"Why?" Victor had to fight hard to suppress the urge to snarl the word.

"Your Spirit Core, sir, is uncannily potent for an iron ranker, let alone one closer to the middle than the top." His eyes widened with horror at his words, and he hastily scrambled to add, "Forgive me! I saw much before you veiled off your Core! I don't mean to. You see, um, seeing into people is second nature to me. I have a legendary class called Soul Diviner, which grew out of my original Scryer Class. When I look at an unshielded person, it's actually quite difficult for me not to see things like that."

"Forget it." Victor waved his hand. He was smart enough to notice how he'd felt almost appeased by the idea that this guy's "master" might find his Core interesting. Impressing people was what his Quinametzin alter ego lived for.

"Even if he's interested in Victor, how does that help us? You said his next appointment is in three years," Lam said, lifting Edeya's hand, their fingers interlocked. "She's not going to make it three years."

"No, no." Erd waved placatingly. "That's how long it would take to schedule an appointment with him without a sponsor to make him aware of you. You see, he doesn't make many appointments. If he finds something interesting, believe me, he'll make time for it."

"All right. Do it. What kind of fee are we talking about?" Victor looked into his storage ring, the one where he kept most of his easily traded wealth—gems, precious metals, Energy beads, and the like.

"Well, you'll find that in Sojourn, favors are usually paid for with favors."

Victor felt his Core begin to bleed rage into his pathways, and he fought against it, buckling down with his will, forcing it back, concentrating on maintaining a neutral expression. He wasn't a bully, and he wouldn't let his bloodline make one of him, not without a fight. "I'm listening." He didn't look at Valla, but Lam's expression was surprised enough for both of them. She arched both her eyebrows and shook her head slightly, grinning crookedly.

"Well, sir, as you can no doubt discern by the deference I give you, not all iron rankers are built the same. I'm skilled with auguries, counseling, and guidance. I make good money helping people to overcome mental trauma, and in so doing, I continue to improve those aspects of myself that make such things come easily. As you might guess, such a peaceful existence, while pleasant and comfortable, especially here in Sojourn, doesn't afford me many opportunities for the true breakthroughs that will eventually allow me to surpass these iron ranks and then find success in my test of steel."

"And we can help you somehow?"

"Just so! I require an artifact, something that will allow me to impress my mentor significantly. If I can do that, he'll aid me with my particular affinity. However, the item I see is well out of my reach at the moment."

"But not out of ours?" Lam narrowed her eyes quizzically.

"I would think not. I have the location of the world on which this artifact is purported to . . ."

"Wait a fucking minute." Victor held up a hand. "You want us to travel to another world?"

"Oh, well, yes. I'd not need your aid if it were an item available on Sojourn. I will pay your fare and, if things go well, you shouldn't be gone more than a few days . . ."

"Sir, would you mind if we stepped outside to discuss your proposal?" Valla asked.

"Let's hear the whole thing first," Lam said. "What will it take to get this 'artifact' of yours?"

"What I require lies at the bottom of an insect hive. The insects are called ivid. Are you familiar?"

"Ivid? No." Victor shook his head.

"They're large—person-sized, though more like me than you, sir. They aren't intelligent, per se, not individually, but, as a hive, they function with a single mind, one that is formidable."

Victor groaned. "Do they fly? Do they sting? Like, what are we talking about here, man? Ants, bees?"

"I will provide you with a dossier on the creatures. I believe they all have six legs, though there are different castes—some are simple workers, others are tasked with warfare. As I said, they aren't intelligent enough for classes or sophisticated Energy manipulation, but they have instinctual abilities that can prove quite dangerous. What I require will be in the lair of the hive matriarch."

"The queen?" Victor shook his head, liking this idea less and less.

"They reproduce by laying eggs, you see, and every so often, one of their eggs will not hatch. Rather, it will enter a kind of permanent gestation. The unborn ivid in the egg becomes a being of nearly pure spirit, growing connections through the spirit plane to other realms of existence. I must acquire one of those spirit eggs in order to present it to my mentor. With it, he can enter into a ritual communion with the spirit egg and, over the course of years or decades, learn from it."

"How big is it?" Victor couldn't imagine they'd be able to put the thing into a dimensional container.

At the same time, Valla asked, "Surely you could hire someone better at thievery than we three? Someone who can hide and even teleport?"

"Ah! Astute questions! The egg won't be large, perhaps about like so." He held his hands apart from each other, miming an object about the size of a football. "As for more qualified adventurers, I'm afraid you'd be quite mistaken. Remember, together, the ivid hive creates a formidable mind—a mind which actively defends their realm from invasion. Portal or teleportation magic will not work to pierce their strange dimensional space."

"The hive is a dimensional container?"

"Of a sort, aye. It's almost like a natural dungeon, not unlike the System-controlled ones. I won't lie to you; I've needed a relic like this spirit egg for a long time and sent quite a few intrepid iron rankers after it, never to be seen again. In the years since the last excursion, I've had a rather talented Alchemist develop a concoction that may help. It's a perfume of sorts that you can spray to mask your presence in the hive. I sponsored a test by the Alchemist in question, and he returned with promising results."

Victor's frown deepened. "How promising?"

"Well, it seems to do a good job of preventing a hive-wide alarm due to an invader's presence, but some of the more alert ivid will still attack if they encounter the invader, um, you."

Victor abruptly stood. "We'll discuss this outside."

"No need; I don't mind stepping away. I hate for you to have to stand around on the street . . ."

"It's fine. Edeya could use the air." Lam, too, stood, pulling Edeya toward the door. That only left Valla, and she was quick to follow Lam out.

Before he pulled the door closed, Victor briefly locked eyes with Erd. "We'll be back in soon."

"Well?" Lam asked as he turned toward her. It wasn't chilly, exactly, but it wasn't warm now that the sun had slipped below the horizon. Victor never really felt cold anymore, but he worried about Edeya, so he stepped closer to her, putting one of his warm arms over her shoulders and pulling her against his side.

"Well, I think we've got a decision to make. Go on this guy's quest, which sounds nuts, by the way, in the hope that his 'master' might want to meet with us about Edeya's problem. Or . . ."

Valla interrupted, smiling as she tried to guess what he'd say. "Or we can waste time trying to find another demigod to listen to our tale?"

"Demigod?" Lam frowned.

"Victor calls those up there"—Valla pointed to the glimmering rainbow lights of the city heights—"such. He says it's like a person who's part god."

Lam nodded. "Whatever it means, it's an apt term if what that man said is true. One in a hundred iron rankers reach their 'test of steel,' and only one in a thousand of those makes it to the next stage? How many might be experts on the spirit like this man's master?"

Victor thought about the math, his enhanced intelligence making it a lot easier than he would have found it in the old days. He probably could have used a proper equation, but he just brute forced the division and multiplication a couple of times and said, "I guess if there are, I dunno, ten million people in Sojourn, that means there's only something like a hundred who've gotten out of their test of steel. If this guy has an in with one of them, maybe we should consider his offer." He pulled Edeya's frail, still form closer to his side and added, "I mean, I should. We won't all go."

"Now, Victor . . ." Lam started to say.

"I'm going with you!" Valla growled, grabbing the strap for Lifedrinker's harness that crossed his chest, pulling him close. "You will not leave me here!"

"Okay." She glared at him, and he said, more forcefully, "Fine! I was thinking I'd go with Lesh, but he could stay here with Darren and Lam."

Lam nodded. "And Edeya. I wasn't going to argue that I should go along; I won't leave her. I just didn't want you to go alone. You should take Lesh, too. I can keep track of Darren."

Victor shrugged. He wouldn't mind taking Lesh, that was for sure, and he supposed Lam was right; Darren would be all right without Lesh to hold his hand for a few days. "Right. Let's give Erd the good news and get the details."

Y-seven bobbed and floated around Darren, the wisps of his strange incorporeal form brushing his shoulders occasionally. The tendrils felt chilly and tickled the hairs at the nape of his neck, almost as if someone was gently blowing on them. "Describe what you see when you look inward, Darren." They'd been practicing something Darren had already sort of learned from friends back in First Landing. He'd contemplated trying to build a Core, trying to do the little quests and introductions to Energy the System had offered them all, but something had rankled in him, some stubborn desire to show the new world that they had what it took to succeed and flourish without the tricks. Looking back, he could see how shrill and tiresome his objections had become, and he felt ashamed.

"I see a black space, but not like a void. I feel like the black is bordered by something, like . . . it has structure. It's sort of warm. Even though I can't feel it, that's the impression I get. I can see a soft golden misty ball at the center of the space, though its borders are undefined; it's not a perfect sphere."

"Very good, Darren! Your inward eye is seeing clearly. You should be pleased; on occasion, I've spent days trying to guide novices through this process." Y-seven moved away from him, lowering toward the floor so he floated at Darren's eye level. "That was wonderfully quick and leaves us time to study your affinities. Would you like to learn what types of Energies you have a proclivity for? Knowing that will help us determine what sort of Core you should attempt to form."

"Yes! I would appreciate that, Y-seven."

"Very good. There are many methods to achieve what I just described, but I have a means that always seems to work well with candidates who can clearly see their nascent Core. That's the ball of misty golden energy you can see with your inner eye."

Darren nodded. "I've had colleagues tell me as much back home."

"Excellent. My method is simple for you. You must keep your inner eye open, staring at that Core and telling me what you see. I will be conjuring different types of Energy into this space; your nascent Core will react to some of them, most strongly with those you have an affinity for. Does that make sense?"

"Yes. What sorts of things will I see?"

"Mostly colors or movement. Just describe any change you see; I'll do the interpreting. Are you ready, Darren? Close your eyes and tell me when you have a clear view of your Core space."

Darren did as he asked—he'd taken to thinking of Y-seven as "he" simply because of his voice—closing his eyes, peering into the blackness of his eyelids, and then *shifting* his view to that place that didn't used to exist when he'd lived back on Earth. Suddenly, he was looking in at that soft glowing ball of formless Energy, feeling very much like he was there with it in a dark, warm chamber. "I see it."

"Good. I will begin in a few moments but won't speak again until we're done. Do not stop viewing your Core space until I say we've finished. Understood?"

"Understood." True to his word, Y-seven didn't speak, and the silence became heavy. Darren allowed his bodiless consciousness to drift around in the space where he could see his "nascent" Core, watching the very gently pulsing golden cloud, waiting for something to happen. After a while, when he began to fear he wouldn't see anything, some wisps of that cloudy golden stuff began to flicker and lift upward as if a draft was passing over them. Their golden tendrils darkened to red-gold, then to bright crimson, dancing atop the cloud like flickering flames. "Ah!" he gasped, excited. "My Energy looks like red flames! Part of it, anyway!"

Y-seven didn't respond, but the red tendrils began to fade, shifting back to gold and falling back into the cloud. Darren continued to watch until another change occurred. "The whole cloud of Energy just turned green!" Again, Y-seven didn't respond, but the change reverted, and soon, Darren was looking at the formless golden cloud again. After a while, that cloud began to shimmer and shift, remaining golden but moving almost like a whirlpool. He described the change, then the next, and the next, and soon he realized he might be there a while; apparently, Y-Seven was going to be quite exhaustive in his search for Darren's affinities.

He settled in, suddenly feeling impossibly fortunate. How big a boon was it to have an expert helping him with this process? How much could the people of First Landing benefit from something like this? A slow smile spread on Darren's face as he continued to watch his Core. He aimed to learn and intuit as much as he could. If nothing else, he'd have this to bring home. It might not elevate him to greatness among his people, but it was a hell of a lot better legacy than being the laughingstock who'd tried to fight a titan with some steel tanks.

19

MINOR AND MAJOR

Darren, you may stop concentrating on your Core space. We've finished the affinity assessment." Y-seven's voice cut through Darren's concentration, snapping him out of his semi-meditative state. He wasn't sure how long they'd been at it, but it felt like hours. He'd stared at his nascent Core that entire time. Mostly, it had sat there, unmoving, but quite a few times, it had reacted, changing colors, shapes, and movement patterns. Sometimes the changes were singular, and sometimes they were manifold. He wondered if the more significant reactions meant a higher affinity or if there was some other way to interpret them.

Blinking his eyes blearily in the soft white light of his crystal cell-like "genesis pod," he looked up at Y-seven, still floating before him, seemingly in the exact same spot he'd occupied prior to the assessment. "Will it take long to learn the results?"

"Not at all. I've already compiled a list of your affinities, minor and major."

"Oh? It's that easy?"

"For me, yes. Bear in mind that I've been at this for a long time. Would you like to take a break before we go over your lists? Do you require sustenance? Have you any biological needs requiring attention?"

Darren shifted slightly, realizing his knees and back had grown quite stiff. "I wouldn't mind a stretch and some water. Heck, I could eat."

"I don't have much data on your species, Darren. What sort of sustenance would suit you best? Do you consume the meat of prey animals? Can you eat the fruit of trees?"

"Yes to both, assuming they're carbon-based, I guess. Um, I'd prefer it if the meat wasn't raw . . ."

"Very good. You'll find a newly-opened passageway behind you. It will lead you to a private area where you might see to your biological needs. When you return, I'll have some food and drink for you."

Darren looked over his shoulder; sure enough, a round passageway in the crystal led downward. He stood, and after stretching for a moment, bending his waist and flexing his knees, he followed the passage. It meandered downward in a winding pattern for what felt like quite a distance without passing any other openings until he stepped into a round room, much like the one where he'd been with Y-seven. This room had some fixtures, though—a device clearly meant to function as a toilet and a free-standing sink beside it. The toilet had an appropriately sized seat over a bowl containing a stream of continuously flowing water, and the sink, too, didn't have valves but functioned more like a small fountain, water dribbling into a half-full basin. Both fixtures were seemingly grown from the surrounding crystal, smooth, opaque, and faintly luminescent.

He looked around, a little uncomfortable with the open doorway, but figured the only other person with access to the corridor he'd traversed was Y-seven, and he was waiting back in the genesis pod. Shrugging, Darren stood over the toilet and relieved his very full bladder, sighing with relief. He rinsed his hands in the sink, looking around for a towel, only to hear a *woosh* as warm air blew from a spout he hadn't noticed in the crystal wall near the sink. He held his hands in the air, enjoying the warmth while he rubbed his palms together, and then walked back the way he'd come.

When he returned to his "genesis pod," he found a low table dressed in a white tablecloth and occupied by a tall glass of water, a bowl of cut fruit, and a tray of sliced cured meats. Y-seven floated nearby, his lights softly pulsing as his pleasant rich voice greeted Darren. "Welcome back. I hope these refreshments will be satisfactory."

"That looks perfect, thank you." Darren sat before the little table and began to sample the fruits and meat. They tasted much like something he'd get back on Earth—melons, berries, and salty meats that reminded him of various types of pork. The water was cool and refreshing, and Y-seven waited several minutes, allowing Darren to eat in silence before he spoke again.

"Shall I list your affinities? We will start with the minor ones."

Darren swallowed his current bite, then asked, "Why spend time with minor affinities? Wouldn't it be wise to focus on the, um, major ones?"

"Not exactly. We have yet to form your Core, and certain affinities complement certain Core types. You might find that one of your major affinities will go hand-in-hand with one of your minor ones, both taking shape within your newly formed Core. It's important to note that while I can see if you are strongly attracted to certain affinities or only mildly so, I don't know the exact levels. Some of your minor affinities may be nearly as strong as your major ones."

"Ah." Darren nodded. "Thank you for explaining."

"My pleasure. Now, for minor affinities, allow me to list them, and then we can discuss the implications."

"All right." Darren sat back from his meal, giving Y-seven his full attention.

"Mind, fire, pride, dream, glass, magnetism, and bone."

Darren sat there, dumbfounded, for several moments while Y-seven allowed him to process the information. He could figure out what most of those meant, but he'd never heard of them in the context of Energy affinities. That wasn't entirely true—there were quite a few people with fire affinities back in First Landing. The others seemed so esoteric, though, and he wondered if it was simply because Y-seven was better at rooting out affinities than the tutorial the System had put the humans through when they'd arrived on Fanwath. "I think I understand the fire, but can you explain the others?"

"Certainly. While in your case it's only minor, a mind affinity can be quite powerful and also quite dangerous. In many civilizations, such an affinity is frowned upon. Simply put, a strong Mind Caster can influence the thoughts and actions of others." Y-seven paused, perhaps waiting for questions, then continued. "Pride is a spirit affinity, and should you choose to formulate a Core to take advantage of it, you'd find yourself limited when utilizing other types of Energies. After we discuss your stronger affinities, we can decide if that's a wise path for you. A dream affinity can be potent in its broad range of applications—divination, prophecy, dreamwalking, and illusion."

"But I only have a minor affinity?" Darren liked the sound of a dream affinity. The mind affinity sounded great, too, but something about it made him uneasy. He could feel the politician in him getting excited by it, and that frightened him. He'd worked hard the last few days to turn a new leaf, and the way his heartbeat had begun to race when Y-seven explained that mind affinity made his palms sweat with stress and excitement. He felt like a kid who'd opened a shoebox in his dad's closet and found a loaded gun.

"That's correct, Darren. We'll discuss your major affinities momentarily. Shall I continue elaborating about your minor ones?"

Darren nodded. "Yes, please."

"Magnetism is an interesting affinity in that it is a blend of earth and air and allows the cultivator to interact with certain types of metal quite profoundly." Darren nodded; magnetism wasn't so hard for him to understand. It brought to mind certain old comics and superhero stories he'd enjoyed as a kid. He doubted it was the same, but Y-seven's description made it seem similar. "Glass is a particular type of earth affinity, again, blended with the electrical aspect of an air affinity. Finally, there's your bone affinity—a specialized form of blood affinity. Many things are possible with bone-attuned Energy, from healing to mutation to golemancy."

"Golemancy?"

"The art of crafting and animating golems. I'm sure you can guess what material a Bone Caster would use to craft their golems."

Darren frowned. He had an idea of what Y-seven meant by golems, but he wasn't a hundred percent sure. Still, he didn't like the idea of spending his days manipulating bones, so he decided to let it go. "I get it, I think. Did I have as many major affinities?"

"Not quite. Allow me to list them: fear, chaos, lightning, and paranoia."

"What? Holy shit . . ." Darren trailed off, disturbed by the sound of his major affinities. What did it say about him that his strongest affinities included things like fear and paranoia? Was chaos any better? The only one that didn't give him an uneasy feeling was lightning. "I don't like the sound of those, Y-seven." He sighed.

"I can understand that those affinities convey certain negative connotations, especially to one whose knowledge of such things is limited. It's good that you are cautious, and I will strongly counsel you against pursuing some of these affinities, but at least one here bears serious consideration. May I expound on the subject?"

"Um, sure."

"Firstly, fear and paranoia are both spirit affinities. If you chose to create a Spirit Core, you could probably split it into three component parts, cultivating Energy attuned to fear, paranoia, and also pride. Having three differently attuned Energies to work with would open a wide array of skills and spells. However, we must consider that building a Spirit Core and focusing on cultivating those Energies will affect you on a fundamental level. It's called a Spirit Core for a reason—these affinities are tied to your most true inner self. Your particular spirit affinities are all known to impact a cultivator's personality in a less-than-ideal manner, especially without other more positive affinities to counterbalance them. Think of your Core like a power source— can you see how having a potent Core of fear and pride at the center of your being might negatively impact you?"

"Yeah. It doesn't sound ideal." Darren frowned, then asked, "Can you explain the difference between an affinity and an attunement?"

"Of course. An affinity is like a proclivity, a talent, with a certain type of attunement. You have an affinity for fear-attuned Energy. Does that make sense?"

"Yeah." Darren frowned, unhappy to hear that his spirit affinities were so negative. Since seeing Victor in action, he'd liked the idea of building a Spirit Core. He'd wondered how the larger-than-life man would react if Darren showed up with a Spirit Core. Would he respect him more? Would he be more willing to help him, more patient with his lack of power? "I must say, I'm not too excited about those affinities."

"In that case, let us talk about chaos and lightning, two rather rare affinities."

"Rare?"

"Indeed. People associate negative connotations with chaos, and usually for good reason, but that's generally because we think of chaos in terms of conscious beings and the madness we are capable of. Chaos itself is a fundamental pillar of the universe. Some argue that without chaos, there would be no order. Just as there could be no light without darkness. An affinity for chaos means that you can grasp hold of that illusive yet dreadfully powerful Energy and use your influence to alter reality itself. This is a dangerous but extremely potent affinity, Darren Whitehorse, and if you choose to pursue it, I'll need to insist on further evaluation and education here at the Genesis Center."

"I . . . see." Darren nodded, his mind suddenly awash with imagined possibilities, his disappointment in his spirit affinities forgotten.

"As for lightning, it's quite rare—a specialized air affinity. As you may know, air affinities have some broad utility with lightning, though far less potent than what a true lightning affinity can accomplish. For example, while a Wind Caster might call down a bolt of lightning or even conjure a lightning-filled storm, a true Lightning Caster might travel upon a bolt of electrical Energy. The difference may not seem profound, but it's akin to the disparate nature of a handful of sand and a vase of blown glass."

"Truly? So, almost like teleportation?"

"Yes! That is but one application of such an affinity, but not one you will learn quickly; such powers are reserved for those well into their iron ranks."

Darren sat quietly for a moment, contemplating the ideas of chaos and lightning. He kept thinking about the mind affinity, though, wondering how it might have changed things if he'd had it while pursuing a political career. He thought about his other "minor" affinities, wondering about dream—what if he could combine mind with dream? What if he could master more than one?

Y-seven spoke again, interrupting his meandering fantasy. Almost as though he were reading Darren's thoughts, he said, "There are Cores capable of harnessing more than one affinity. My reference manual indicates that lightning is technically an elemental affinity, and chaos has been known to function well when combined with elemental Energies."

"You . . ." Darren squinted up at the being of misty light. "You're reading a manual?"

"Yes. I have an extensive database in a special dimensional space, one that I can mentally access. It's an ability related to my specialized class."

"I see." Darren didn't see but didn't want to belabor the subject. He licked his lips and shook his head, banishing thoughts of trying to learn to influence people's minds and dreams. Hadn't he learned his lesson already? If he could have done something like that, if he'd managed to gain control of First Landing through such desperate, nefarious means, all he'd have done would be to make them too weak to fend for themselves. If Victor could demolish their war machines, what damage could be wrought by one of the more powerful beings he'd glimpsed in Sojourn? "Do you think that would be a wise decision? To try to capitalize on my two strong, rare affinities?"

"I do, Darren Whitehorse. For me to guide you in the formation of such a potent Core, however, you'll have to be evaluated by others in my order. Such knowledge is guarded, you see. You'll have to prove your character."

"My character? What if I refuse?"

"Then you may leave and seek knowledge elsewhere. This is not a prison, Darren."

Darren nodded. Something about that statement felt right. He was trying to change, was he not? Turning a new leaf was an understatement; he was rebuilding himself. It only made sense that something worth having wouldn't come easily. "I will take your tests."

"He's where?" Victor frowned at Lesh, trying to make sense of what he'd said.

"He's in this city's nursery, a place for novices to learn about Energy and Cores."

"Until tomorrow?" Valla, too, was trying to wrap her head around the idea.

"Yes." Lesh nodded, and his tone indicated he considered the matter settled. "I will retrieve him tomorrow at noon."

Victor shook his head. "Lam might have to do that for you. Is it far?"

"Not at all. A short walk. I am Darren's mentor, however, and feel it is my duty to . . ."

"We have a job, Lesh. To help Edeya." Victor nodded to Lam and Edeya, who were sitting on the nearby couch.

"Ah! I see. If I'm being called to duty, my fosterling will have to survive without me for the time being." Lesh turned to Lam and raised his voice. "Lam, will you please take responsibility for my fosterling until our return?" When she nodded, smiling, Lesh turned back to Victor. "What is our task?"

Victor grinned, trying to think of the best way to summarize Erd Van's request. He took a deep breath and rattled off, "We have to take a portal to another world, infiltrate some kind of monstrous insect hive, reach the deepest part where the queen lives, collect a magical egg, and get it back here."

"Blech! Insects? I deplore the things."

"Yeah." Victor shrugged, nodding. "Yeah, me too. Apparently, they're big, too, like the size of a person but, you know, with six legs, exoskeletons, magical abilities, and yeah, I guess some of them are venomous."

Lesh growled deep in his belly, but the sound faded quickly, and he shrugged. "Belagog will enjoy crushing their hard shells. What of the portal fees? My Energy-rich treasures grow thin."

Victor clapped him on the shoulder. "Our travel is paid for, *hombre*."

"If you have shopping to do, now's the time," Valla said, moving toward the door. "I'm going to buy healing and curative draughts. Do you want to come with me?"

Lesh nodded and stepped toward Valla. "I will accompany you, Lady Valla."

Victor watched them go, returning Valla's wave as she paused by the door. When they were gone, he walked closer to Lam and squatted to better look at Edeya. "She seems the same to me. I wish I knew what to do with her spirit. I wish I had more to go on than that guy's word. What if it's not as hard as he said? What if we don't need someone as powerful as his master?"

Lam frowned, creasing her brow, gently rubbing her thumb on the back of Edeya's hand as she held it. "If we weren't worried, if we weren't hurrying to save Edeya, we could spend more time asking around. I think you should do this job, get that egg, and while you're gone, I'll do more research and talk to more spirit specialists. If you return with the egg and we find we don't need Erd Van's master, we'll make him pay for it."

"All right, then." Victor nodded and stood up, but Lam wasn't done. She reached out and grabbed his wrist.

"Just don't get killed. If the hive seems impossible, then leave. Edeya would hate for you or the others to get hurt trying to help her. I'd hate to lose you all and have to try to help her on my own." Her voice sounded strained, and Victor could tell she was feeling the stress of the situation, pulled thin to the point of breaking.

"I know. I know you're going to be worried while we're gone; you'll hate being alone in this strange city."

"I won't be alone . . ." Lam smirked, and Victor knew what was coming, so he finished her thought for her.

"Oh yeah! You have Darren! Nothing to worry about." He and Lam laughed for a minute, and then he started for the door. "I'll check in with you before we leave. I'm going to do a little cultivating and check in with Khul Bach. You know, fill him in on everything that's going on." Lam's eyes narrowed momentarily as she tried to remember who that was. Victor tapped his bracer, his finger pointing to the pink gemstone. "The spirit in here. Remember?"

Lam snapped her fingers and nodded. "Ah, yes. The one from the world of giants and snake-folk. Yes, I suppose it's best you let him know you're off to yet another world, one filled with insects."

"Yeah, I guess. Maybe he'll have some advice." Victor shrugged and left, heading for the suite he shared with Valla. The truth was, he wanted some time to be alone and think about things. He would talk to Khul Bach, but he didn't anticipate the meeting lasting long. The old giant spirit wasn't much of a conversationalist. No, for the first time in a while, Victor was looking forward to some cultivation; he wanted to look into himself, to analyze the fear and anger he'd been feeling ever since his entrapment by Hector in the caldera. "Time to stop denying those feelings."

20

IVID

Victor, Valla, and Lesh stood on one of the copper discs inside the World Hall, each holding a token of travel they'd purchased from a counter near the entrance. More accurately, Erd Van had purchased them, along with some "tokens of recall." Victor had been a little surprised at the ease with which they'd claimed the tokens; either the travel attendant was very trusting, or she'd had some way to determine they were who they claimed to be. Whatever the case, they had their tokens, they stood on one of the "portal platforms," and now they simply had to activate them. "We're ready?" he asked, looking from Valla to Lesh.

Valla shrugged. "As ready as I can be. We have thirty different types of poison remedies, a dozen powerful healing draughts, besides whatever we each already had in our possession, and we've got the perfume Erd says will keep the bugs from noticing us."

"Can we really call them bugs? I mean, bugs are . . . small." Victor grinned, chuckling at his stupid attempt at humor.

"I will smash them just like bugs, should they come near." Lesh lifted Belagog to his shoulder in illustration. Victor had to admit he was glad to have the big guy along.

"All right. Let's get this over with." He concentrated on the chalky blue ball in his hand. As he sent some of his inspiration-attuned Energy into it, it crumbled away, swirling on an invisible current of air, spreading into a cloud that shimmered with Energy and flickered like a billion tiny lights.

The effect obscured his vision, and when it cleared, he almost fell over—he was in a different world.

The sky was tinted yellow, the air hurt his throat to breathe, and twin suns hung high overhead—one blue and brilliant, one red and glowering. He stood atop a hill, and in every direction, all he could see was short dry yellow grass. Suddenly, a sparkle of blue lights erupted beside him, and when they faded, Valla stood there. As he reached out to steady her, he heard the crackling pops of Lesh's arrival behind him. "Great dead gods!" the giant dragonkin grumbled as he coughed, slowly turning, taking in the sights.

"The air's terrible!" Valla said, choking out a sympathetic cough.

Victor nodded. "Yeah, it's not great. Honestly smells like cat piss. I can feel it sort of making my throat raw."

"It does!" Valla replied. "I've smelled that lingering stench after seeing Uvu relieve himself!"

"It's the hive," Lesh said.

"Where?" Victor turned in a slow circle again, but when he faced Lesh, the dragonkin was grinning a toothy smile at him. "Are your eyes that good? I can't see anything all the way to the horizon."

"Look closer, titan."

At his words, Victor looked down at the dry yellow grass under his feet, noting the fine white sand among its roots rather than dirt. "This hill?"

"Aye. I have a sense for this sort of thing, and I can tell you this mound is largely hollow. I can feel it in my bones. There's an entrance just below the surface this way." He started walking down the slope, and when Victor looked at Valla, she just shrugged again and began following the big warrior.

"You have a sense for these things?" Victor hurried his steps to catch up.

"Yes. Perhaps one of my ancestors dwelled beneath the soil for too long, but I have an uncanny knack for finding caves and navigating beneath the surface."

Still trying to acclimate to the harsh air, Valla coughed and spat, then wiping her mouth, smiled at the two men. "Looks like we picked the right companion to explore a giant insect hive."

"I led an army against the Kothids on my homeworld, so, aye, you did."

Valla shot Victor a glance, eyebrow raised, and he shrugged. He really hadn't had the chance to get to know the guy. Most of the time they'd spent together had been sparring, and Lesh wasn't exactly talkative. Taking Valla's cue, though, he said, "Lesh, man, I know you feel like you're doing the right thing following me around, but are you sure you should've left all that behind? Don't get me wrong . . ."

"I might have doubted myself once, but when you climbed the volcano, awash with the power of a mountain, my conviction grew resolute. There's much I can learn from you, and much we will uncover together. Already, we seek an artifact that may grant us an audience with a being more powerful than any to walk the craggy slopes of Ashenshoal."

In a blatant attempt to steer the conversation away from boosting Victor's ego, Valla asked, "Tell us about the Kothids."

"Kothids." Lesh spat in the grass, and it sizzled and smoked. "Serpentine insects. Some were the size of my arm, others the size of twenty dragonkin laid out end to end. They crawl through tunnels on hundreds of legs, bear an acidic bite, and have shells as hard as stone. Belagog and I earned the title Kothid Bane during the war. My Breath Core awoke during those long years fighting through their tunnels, pushing them back to their warrens beyond the Rukspagh Mountains."

Valla sniffed, rubbing at her watering eyes, clearly still struggling with the vapors in the air. "Sounds awful."

"Awful and glorious. I gained nine levels in that war and earned a fruit of evolution. Not as potent as a heart, but good. I gained many scales." He stopped, looking around and sniffing. They were about two-thirds of the way down the slope, and Victor couldn't tell anything different about the dead grass and sand under their feet. "Here. It's not deep." He lifted Belagog off his shoulder and up over his head.

Victor frowned, watching him, and before he could stop himself asked, "Is Belagog a he or a she?"

"Belagog? He doesn't speak much, but he's no lady." With that, he brought the massive, jagged, pole-like cudgel down onto the sandy hillside. It impacted the ground with a dull *thud* that rippled through the sand and dry grass, even five feet up the hill where Victor stood, making him take a step to keep his balance. Lesh didn't strike again but took a few more steps down the hill and stared at the spot he'd struck. Valla moved next to him, also watching.

Victor frowned, wondering if he'd missed something. "What are we watching for?"

"If this was a Kothid nest, one of them would investigate . . ." Lesh stopped speaking as something began to happen. The sandy depression where the cudgel had struck seemed to be growing deeper. It reminded Victor of sand draining out of an hourglass. Seeping down through some kind of opening, the depression growing ever larger.

"Did you break through?" he asked, stepping farther back, wondering how big the hole would become. It was already several feet across and probably three feet deep at the center.

"Perhaps . . ." This time, when he stopped speaking, it was because he jumped back, lifting his cudgel high. Victor could see why—long, dark brown, chitinous prodding limbs had pushed through the sand at the center of the hole he'd made.

"Ware!" Valla cried, snapping her wings wide and jerking Midnight from her scabbard. Victor didn't need the heads-up; he'd already pulled Lifedrinker from her harness and was channeling rage into his pathways, getting ready to cast Iron Berserk. The ivid, if that's what the thing was, didn't plan to wait around for them to react. In a shower of stinging, flying sand and yellow burning gas, it erupted from the hole, launching itself at Lesh. Victor stumbled back, blinded by the shower of sand and gas, but he didn't wait for his vision to clear. He cast Iron Berserk and released his aura, letting it fall around him as he summoned his Banner of the Champion—he wasn't going to take half-measures until he had an idea what they were up against.

Victor had only seen a glimpse of the carapace-covered monstrosity, but one thing was sure: Either Erd Van was a liar, or he'd been woefully misinformed—the thing was closer to the size of an SUV than a person. Suddenly, a gust of hot wind blew the stinging gas and sand away, and Victor could feel something of Valla in that wind; she'd summoned it. Lesh was struggling with the ivid. Belagog was caught between a pair of massive pincers, and Lesh was fending off another set of pincers with his free hand. Meanwhile, the giant insect pushed him down the hill, driving with its four other legs. Victor stomped forward, skirting the much larger hole, and, without further ado, hacked Lifedrinker through one of those legs.

Hot yellow fluid geysered from the hewn appendage, and where it hit Victor, it sizzled and burned, almost like acid. His Iron Berserk and titanic constitution handled the burn, making it only a painful annoyance, but he shuddered to imagine Valla getting doused with the stuff. His attack had sent the insect into a frenzy, and it whirled, letting go of Lesh to see what had harmed it. One of its shovel-sized, pincer-like claws snapped out at him, but Victor was fast when he was berserk, too fast for that claw. He dodged aside, hacking Lifedrinker down, splitting the claw's chitin and producing another spray of caustic yellow blood.

His distraction was just what Lesh needed—he lifted his enormous cudgel and brought it down with a terrible *crack* on the ivid's bulbous abdomen, splitting the hard shell and sending fragments to fall to the sandy ground amid a shower of hot acidic guts and blood. The insect went wild, mortally wounded but not nearly ready to quit. It leaped at Victor, but Lifedrinker was ready, and he was too damn big to be pushed around by a bug, even one that size. He snatched its pincer-bearing arm with his left hand and brought Lifedrinker down with the force of a falling anvil, right at the center of its head, between half a dozen eyestalks. She cracked the shell and buried herself to the haft, and Victor felt her throbbing and vibrating, digging for the veins of Energy within the creature.

The ivid's legs writhed, spreading and contracting as it died, but Victor held it still, one hand gripping the intact pincer, the other still holding Lifedrinker's haft. Lesh, ensuring the thing would truly die, pounded it three more times, nearly deshelling the monstrous insect as he broke its carapace apart. While it died and Lifedrinker took her due, Valla landed with a gentle flutter of her wings.

"I was going to call lightning down, but you two had it in hand. This thing is much larger than Erd Van indicated."

"Quiet!" Lesh growled, and Victor felt his prideful anger bristle. He almost told the guy off, but when he turned to him, scowling, he saw Lesh leaning down, one ear cocked at the ground. "Something comes. Troll shit! Many things come! We must fly!" With that, he turned and began charging down the hill. Victor yanked Lifedrinker from the insect's head, flinging the corpse aside. Then he looked at the hole and contemplated fighting; he was Quinametzin, and the thought of fleeing from bugs rankled.

He felt wind against his neck and turned to see Valla taking flight. "Summon Guapo!" she cried, then flapped her wings and dove toward Lesh, following him away from the hill. Victor growled, watching the two of them grow distant.

"Just you and me, beautiful?" Now, he could feel the shaking of the earth, and he began to wonder if he was being stupid. "Well, maybe I should follow them, you know, just to be sure they get away okay. I mean, if I get busy killing a swarm, what if they get caught up in it?" Lifedrinker hummed lazily; she was content with her meal. "All right." Victor concentrated and, using glory-attuned Energy, summoned a titan-sized Guapo from a pool of sparkling golden light. He'd just swung onto his back when something burst out of the sandy tunnel opening. Guapo began running, leaping down the hill in a single bound, and Victor looked over his shoulder to see not one, not ten, but dozens and dozens of the massive clawed ivid bursting out of the tunnel in a stream of black, hissing and clicking chitin.

Guapo devoured the distance between himself and Lesh, and when they drew near, Victor leaned over to take the dragonkin's arm, pulling him up behind him on the giant mustang's back. Lesh was a big heavy man, but in his berserk state, Victor pulled him up as if he were a child. "Watch them!" he yelled over his shoulder.

"They yet pursue us! A dark swarm that streams forth from the tunnel. Hundreds." After a few more seconds of running, Lesh amended, "Thousands!"

"Get that *pinché* spray!" Victor urged Guapo to stop; they were a few miles ahead of the swarm by then. "Valla!" he yelled. "Come here!"

"I have it!" Lesh said, holding up one of the containers of liquid Erd Van had given them. It was in a quart-sized bottle with a bulbous pump spray attached, and Lesh began dousing himself and Victor with it. He pumped out a dozen spurts, basically clouding Guapo and his passengers in the thick oily substance. It smelled terrible—pungent and eye-watering. It reminded Victor of urine and mothballs, and he wanted to gag but stoically refused. With a *woosh* and a gust of refreshing air, Valla landed, and Lesh turned the nozzle of the spray bottle on her.

Victor watched the dark line of insects approaching. They were fast but not alarmingly so; he could easily leave them behind on Guapo. They were still coming out of the mound, and he figured there had to be thousands of them out on the sandy grass-covered plains, as Lesh had speculated. "I think they're slowing."

Lesh looked up, having finished dousing Valla in the awful stuff. "Aye, they slow." Victor turned Guapo so he could watch the insects more comfortably.

"This stuff is terrible," Valla said, and Victor could see she was fighting back a gag.

"Don't spit," Lesh said. "They may smell it."

Valla groaned, swallowing noisily and coughing into her elbow. "From there?"

"Aye. They've slowed because they lost our scent thanks to this concoction." He held the jar aloft. "Something gives them an uncanny ability to smell intruders. Likely a natural ability boosted by the Energy they harvest."

"You think they cultivate Energy?"

Lesh shook his head, grimacing as he swallowed, clearly as disgusted by the oily spray as Victor and Valla. "No. They're more like animals, passively gathering it, evolving, and advancing. Did the man who hired you say how long it had been since his last attempt at this artifact?"

Valla shook her head. "No."

"Perhaps they've advanced as a species. Hives are . . . amazing and terrible in an Energy-rich world. If their queen has made a breakthrough, her children will reflect it." Lesh pointed with Belagog. "Look, they turn back."

Victor nodded, watching the ivid slowly file back into the wide tunnel from which they'd emerged. "How much of that stuff do you have left?"

"I used a third to douse us." Lesh looked from Valla to Victor. "You each have a bottle, yes?"

"Right," Valla said. "So we must stay covered in it, or we'll be in trouble."

Victor nodded. "Yeah, but Erd said some of the insects will be hostile if they even see us. Do you think those were their 'warriors'? Or do you think worse things are waiting for us in there?"

"Those were warriors." Lesh nodded. "There will be worse things, however. If they're anything like the Kothids, they'll have more dangerous castes deeper in the hive."

"Well, if we meet 'em, we'll have to kill them quickly. I think as long as we stay covered in this shit, we shouldn't get swarmed." He frowned, thinking, then said, "You know, if things get really bad, I can probably get out alive. I have some cards I can play, but it wouldn't exactly be safe for you guys to be around." Victor was thinking of his new Volcanic Fury and Wake the Earth abilities. "Maybe you should, like, keep watch out here?"

"No." Valla laughed, shaking her head. "If things get that bad, I won't argue if you want to distract the creatures long enough for Lesh and me to use our recall tokens, but we should go in with you. It's better if we try to succeed without you trying to take on an entire hive with thousands . . ."

Lesh shook his head and interjected, "Millions."

Valla's eyes widened. "Millions! No, Victor! We must do this without you trying to do battle with the entire hive!" Her voice was strained and almost pleading, and Victor had to take a second, trying to understand why she thought he'd be so hard to convince. He wasn't an idiot; he knew he could kill a thousand or more of those things, but there was no way his Energy would last long enough to take on even ten times that many, let alone millions of them.

"Yeah. All right. Only a last resort, then, to buy you guys time to use those tokens." The tokens Erd had purchased for them were single-use and would transport them back to Sojourn's World Hall. According to him, they cost nearly twice as much as their travel tokens, which Victor could only assume was at least as much as what the System had charged them to travel from Fanwath. "Let's hope Erd was right, and these tokens will work in the hive."

Valla looked at him and frowned. "He said the magic keeping people from teleporting into the hive only guarded against entry . . ."

"Yeah, but how much does that dude even know? He said these damn bugs were only your size." Victor looked at Lesh. "Hop down, *hermano*. I'm going to cancel my rage, and Guapo's going to shrink. Might as well try to sneak in there at first." Victor looked back at the retreating horde of insects as Lesh dismounted. This job wouldn't be easy, but hopefully, it would be worth it. Hopefully, they'd earn some levels . . . "Hey, why didn't we get Energy for that big damn bug?"

Lesh followed Victor's gaze and said, "Perhaps the System is waiting for those hostile combatants to leave the field. It can be cruel, but it usually won't interfere with the affairs of the people and creatures it governs. It might consider sending Energy streaming toward us, exposing us to that horde, as interference."

"I hope that's true," Valla said, moving to a patch of short yellow grass and sitting down. "Those things are returning more slowly than they emerged."

Victor canceled his spells, and as Guapo shrank, he hopped down. "Yep. Let's chill here for a little while, then we'll try a sneaky, stinky approach."

21

LIMITS

When the last of the ivid had disappeared into the vast gaping hole in the side of the hill, Lesh said, "We should wait. If they're anything like the Kothids, the warriors will take time to settle and move back to their nooks and crannies." When Victor nodded, Lesh produced a leather-topped camp stool and sat down. Victor and Valla had their own camp furniture, hers an upholstered, fancy chair, his a sturdy wooden one. Soon, they were all three seated, sipping at canteens, looking through Far Scribe books, or in Victor's case, just staring at the weird yellow sky and the scattered wispy clouds.

"Valla," Lesh rumbled, breaking the quiet. "Tell me about your new class."

Valla looked up from her book, smiling. "I chose one that improves my mental attributes in hopes of offsetting my focus on martial ones for most of my life. The System said it was a class derived from the 'memories of my progenitors,' whatever that means."

"It means you've awakened enough of your bloodline for the System to delve into hidden memories, finding the secrets of their ancient bond with Energy." Lesh always sounded a little pissed off when he mentioned the System, and Victor knew why. The big scaly man felt he'd gotten a raw deal with the System's quest to hunt Victor down, but more, he felt his people had been borderline persecuted by the System and the favoritism it showed other species of "dragonkin," which seemed to be a pretty broad category of peoples. "What is it called, if I may ask?"

Victor almost answered for her, but Lesh's wording stopped him; he supposed it was possible that Valla didn't want everyone to know. His caution was needless—she replied almost immediately, "Storm Dancer."

Lesh made an approving sound deep in his chest that sounded almost like a purr. "Legendary?"

"Epic."

"I believe that was wise of you. Your sword skill is already quite masterful, and improving your casting ability will prove invaluable. I chose a different route; toughness and brute power have been the focus of my classes for many tiers, though I begin to wonder if I will ever see a proper pathway to the glory of my dragon ancestors."

Thinking of Tes, Victor said, "I'm not sure dragons ever submitted to the System. Aren't they still kind of doing things their own way?" He didn't want to mention that he'd tasted, even used, the elder magic of a dragon.

"Indeed, so the legends say. Ashenshoal saw its last true dragon four thousand years before I was born."

Victor made a vague gesture, trying to indicate the world or greater universe. "And you've never met one from another world?"

Lesh chuckled. "Nay, battle-brother. If one visited my world, I wasn't told. If one traversed the worlds I passed through, I was not made aware. No, when I saw that Death Caster's skeletal mount, it was the first time I had laid eyes upon one of my ancestors—well, her bones at least."

"It was a female?" Valla asked, raising an eyebrow.

"Certainly. Her hip bones and delicate crown of horns gave her away."

"Delicate?" Victor snorted. Lesh's reptilian eyes narrowed, and Victor held up his hand in surrender. "I'll take your word for it." He tried to move the subject back to elder magic because he selfishly wondered what Lesh knew. "If dragons don't use the System, do you worry about using System classes and System skills and spells? Do you think it will make it hard to evolve your species?"

"No. It will not stop me. If I can evolve my bloodline sufficiently and find the System's rules and guideposts are hindering me, I will learn what I must to break free."

"I guess a dragon, one who uses elder magic, might help you at that point, yeah?"

Lesh shrugged. "I have no idea. Our histories indicate that dragons are as varied as any other people—some might help me, while others may be just as happy to slay me."

Victor desperately wanted to mention Tes, explain what she was, and describe how helpful she was. He wanted to give Lesh some hope, but he also wanted to keep Tes's trust. He held his tongue. Instead, he asked, "Ever met any other elder race? Ever met anyone using elder magic?" His question got him a look from Valla; she knew about his run-in with the System when he'd used elder magic to modify his Spirit Totem spell.

"There are those on Ashenshoal who dabble with the old texts, attempting to develop their abilities outside the System. They are stunted and weak. What we know is too little. Perhaps if I ever meet a true practitioner, I can learn to throw off the System's shackles."

"You think the System limits us?" Victor found himself nodding. Before Lesh could answer, he elaborated, "I think the System gains something from us as we grow in power. So I think it helps us gain strength, but I also think it likes to do it *systematically*." He emphasized "systematically," grinning. "I think it wants us to grow stronger so we gather more Energy, but I think it also wants to control us and keep us on a certain path, or maybe more accurately, away from certain paths." He could still hear and feel the anger in the System's messages when he'd built his Wild Totem spell, coloring outside the lines with elder magic.

"Aye. I think you're getting to the truth of the matter. True dragons and others outside the System give it nothing. Hence, they are isolated, removed from the System's portal network . . ."

"They don't care, though." Victor laughed, interrupting him. "They can open their own gateways, and I think they even have a presence on System worlds, sometimes. I heard things when I was on Zaafor, stories from a powerful friend." Victor looked at Valla, wondering if he should just talk openly about Tes. He'd promised her to keep quiet about his true nature, but Lesh only wanted to befriend dragons, to become one, even. Surely, he wasn't a threat. Victor shook his head. A promise was a promise.

"Good! Perhaps when we return to Sojourn, I can do some looking around. I'd hoped to have more time in that city."

Valla stood up, brushing her hands together. "Speaking of returning to Sojourn, let's start walking. By the time we get to the tunnel, I'm sure they'll be settled, don't you think?"

Lesh stood also, nodding. "Yes. If we take our time."

"All right. No Guapo, then. Let's just walk." He stood, sending his chair into storage, and led the way. As Valla hurried to walk beside him, he turned to Lesh and asked another question he'd been wondering about. "Do you want to trade secrets about Breath Cores? Maybe we could give each other some pointers about cultivating and, well, breathing."

"I will share what I know, Victor. I would not pledge to follow you and then withhold knowledge that may aid you." His words made Victor feel all the more guilty for not telling him about Tes and what he knew of dragons, but no matter the loyalty he owed Lesh, he also owed Tes. He'd have to find another way to broach the subject, teach him what he knew of elder magic, and see if the two of them could expand Victor's current understanding. He might not need it now, might not even need it for another hundred levels or more, but someday, if he genuinely wanted to grasp the greatness of his ancestors, if he wanted to be his own man and a true power in the universe, he'd need to learn to go outside the System's guide rails.

"Darren Whitehorse, I am pleased that you've decided to undergo evaluation by the Genesis Order. I am K-eight, and I will be responsible for determining if you are a suitable candidate for the knowledge you seek."

"Thank you, K-eight." Darren smiled at the floating light. It looked identical to Y-seven, but this one had a voice that sounded more like it was coming from a flute than a human throat, and certainly neither male nor female. Y-seven had left him shortly after divining his affinities, saying that he wasn't of appropriate status to evaluate Darren's "character." He'd only waited an hour or so, but it had been long enough for Darren to wonder if he'd made a mistake. He was interested in the most powerful Core he could develop, certainly, but who were these lights with their rules and standards? Who were they to judge his character?

"Darren Whitehorse . . ."

"Just Darren is fine."

"Ah, yes. Thank you, Darren. I have the ability to see into your memories and to listen to your current, active thoughts. I would never do so without permission, and though you've asked to be evaluated by my order, I have yet to begin. I wanted to ensure that such an invasive inspection would not offend you."

Darren's palms had grown clammy at the mention of mind reading, and he felt himself bristling. "I, um, I don't think that sounds very good. Is there any way to evaluate me without you seeing all of my private memories?" He scrambled for some sort of justification for balking. "You see, in my culture, individual freedom is valued very highly, and having someone see our private thoughts and cherished personal experiences feels very invasive, very oppressive."

"I see. The Genesis Center is provided freely to the citizens of Sojourn. My order is funded by wealthy donors, and we provide basic knowledge to anyone without question of loyalty or morality. Some of our knowledge, however, is recognized as dangerous, and our services come with the responsibility of guarding it from those whose morality is antithetical to our order. I must, therefore, inform you that I am not at liberty to waive these restrictions. If you do not pass a thorough assessment, I am limited in what I can teach you."

"If you deem me unfit, what will happen?"

"If such should happen, then Y-seven will return and offer you what services we can approve. If you are unhappy with those offerings, you are free to leave and seek knowledge elsewhere."

"Well. All right, then. I suppose I've nothing to lose . . ." Darren's voice trailed off as K-eight began to glow with a soft yellow luminescence, and he felt a weird tingling sensation all over his scalp. Rainbow lights danced in his eyes, and unbidden, all sorts of memories came to mind. He watched himself showing his secondary school grade report to his father, watched his father have a meltdown and later bribe Professor Renfield to allow Darren to submit corrections on his term paper. He watched himself having a screaming match with his first wife and later log into her socials to post humiliating photos. Shame flared, hot and uncomfortable, and he said, pitifully, "We married young, and I was stupid . . ."

Another string of memories came into focus: memories of his time working at Charter Logistics, snippets of all the times he'd pretended to befriend colleagues only to undermine them later with management. The flood of memories was so dense that Darren felt himself reeling, dazed by the avalanche of backstabbing. Was he truly so bad? Before he could object or try to defend his actions, more memories streamed through his mind, horrible, uncomfortable recollections, and almost all of them had to do with being dishonest or disloyal. He was constantly looking to advance, and he'd never considered the fallout his words and actions might have on the people who trusted him.

When the memories became more current and relevant—his many political interactions in First Landing—things didn't improve. Looking in on those memories did nothing but deepen Darren's shame and self-loathing. When K-eight finished with him, he was on his knees, head drooping, hot shame flushing the back of his neck as his hands and armpits produced an uncomfortable sheen of cold sweat. "Darren Whitehorse, I apologize for the discomfort you've been through. Such memories can be painful when witnessed all together. At this time, I'm afraid the knowledge we are willing to impart will be limited. Please be patient, and Y-seven will be with you again soon."

Darren blinked slowly, trying to breathe deeply, trying to banish all of those shameful memories. He felt defeated, ruined. He hated himself; it was the feeling after Victor's demonstration all over again, only this time, he had nowhere to run. He was alone in the crystal pod-like room with no doors. His voice thick with emotion and the constriction of his throat, he spoke into the silence. "I am ready to leave. Please open the door or whatever." He wanted out. He wanted to flee. He wanted to forget what he'd been forced to remember. Darren stood, walked up to the smooth crystal wall, and began to pound on it. "Open up, please! I want to leave!"

Y-seven's voice sounded behind him, and he whirled to face the floating, glowing, misty orb. "Darren, you have my sympathies. I am unable to teach you that which you requested, but there are other options . . ."

"No. If I'm not good enough for your order, I'd like to leave." Darren's indignation slid on like a comfortable old glove, filling the void left by his demolished pride.

"It's not a matter of whether you are good enough, Darren. Rather, we want to ensure we don't give harmful knowledge to someone with the wrong temperament. This is not a permanent decision. If you can live your life well and build your character, we will reevaluate you—as many times as you'd like to try. Darren, K-eight informed me that you are relatively young. You have many years ahead of you in which to improve yourself. If you returned in ten years, after having . . ."

"Ten years?" Darren's question was more of an exclamation. "Please show me out, Y-seven."

"Would you not like help forming a Core? You have several affinities that K-eight deemed safe . . ."

"No. If you won't help me, I'll find the answer elsewhere."

"As you wish, Darren. Please be cautious." Y-seven didn't elaborate on the kind of caution he should have, but Darren could guess there were probably several meanings behind the words. Y-seven's glowing, misty form drifted past him into a tunnel that hadn't been there a moment before, and Darren sullenly followed him out. When they reached the vaulted crystal cavern that made up the entrance hall, Y-seven paused and spoke again. "Please return if you change your mind, Darren. If you allow us to help you form a Core, it will be for your growth, and it will be something we can build upon when you've proven yourself worthy."

Darren didn't reply. He was too angry—angry at himself and at Y-seven and K-eight and the stupid system they'd set up that would judge a person based on the hardships they'd faced in life. Who was K-eight to decide Darren's actions were immoral or "showed poor character?" He hadn't been in Darren's shoes. He hadn't had to deal with the demands of an overbearing father, of a society that expected so much! Was it Darren's fault he'd had the odds stacked against him most of his life? It wasn't easy getting where he was! It hadn't been easy gaining the support of nearly half the colony on Fanwath! Was it his fault he hadn't known the absurd truth of Energy, levels, and wild mythical races?

"Bah!" Darren growled as he shoved the door open and stepped outside. His thoughts and his guilty feelings were bouncing all over the place, and he tried to calm them by focusing on the gorgeous early-morning view of the city of Sojourn. He could see pale blues, yellows, and oranges to the east and knew the sun would be up soon. The crystal towers at the city center, not too far from where he stood, shimmered with the predawn light, and everything felt a little surreal and dreamlike. "So if they won't help me, then I'll help myself." Darren nodded, balling his fists up. "As usual."

He inhaled deeply through his nose and then turned, looking around for something he'd seen when he and Lesh had first arrived. Just as he'd remembered, a kiosk stood at the end of the sidewalk right before the steps leading up to the Genesis Center. He walked down the steps. Only a few people were out and about near the building, and he supposed that made sense; who would come for training before the sun was even up? He honestly had a hard time believing he'd been there all evening; to him, it only felt as if four or five hours had passed.

The kiosk was prominently labeled "Visitor Information" and despite the early hour was staffed by one of the now-familiar glowing beings of mist and light. "Hello," he said, stepping up to the window.

"Welcome, Darren Whitehorse. How may I help you?"

"I was hoping you had one of those interactive city maps for sale. I'm not sure how to get where I need to go."

"Of course. Please take this with Y-seven's compliments." One of the crystal tablet-like devices materialized on the counter.

"Y-seven? He told you to give me this?"

"Y-seven communicated the intention when you asked me for the map, yes."

"How much are they normally?" Darren produced a handful of Energy beads from his dimensional pouch.

"Twenty-five standard beads." The light pulsed, unfazed by his refusal to take the tablet gratis. Still, Darren counted out the beads and set them on the counter, taking the tablet with a frown.

"I'm not good enough for what you all have to offer." As he turned to walk away, Darren knew he was being petty, but it felt good, anyway. Who needed some charity organization to grow a Core? In fact, the more he thought about it, the more he was glad they'd refused to teach him a Core to utilize the chaos and lightning affinities. Maybe those weren't his best choices. Hadn't it felt like Y-seven was steering him toward those? Hadn't it felt like he hadn't wanted Darren to think about that mind affinity?

"No," Darren muttered, flipping through the map to a list of businesses in the city. "I think I need a second opinion, and if that doesn't work, maybe I need a third. I'm going to make the Core I want, and if no one will teach me, then I'll find a book and teach myself."

22

IN THE HIVE

The ivid tunnels didn't provide convenient hiding places. The best the three adventurers could hope for was to duck out of sight around the many corners and bends whenever they saw one of the giant insects coming their way. The magical perfume—Victor wondered if it was somehow mimicking pheromones—seemed to work very well, however, and as long as they didn't stand directly in the path of one of the lumbering worker ivid, they didn't get attacked or, worse, swarmed.

After they snuck into the opening, he, Valla, and Lesh had hidden behind some of the fallen dirt as a dozen workers arrived and began sealing the opening the warrior ivid had made as they'd streamed forth to defend the nest. The workers looked much like the warriors but were smaller, closer to orange than dark brown, and had long multi-jointed digits on their front legs rather than pincers. The trio had slipped away wholly unnoticed, and since then, something like an hour had passed, and they'd traversed endlessly descending tunnels with no sign that they were anywhere close to their goal.

Victor pulled his tiny Globe of Insight close, cupping his hands over the dim light and motioning for the others to come close. "I think I should send my coyotes out exploring," he whispered—they were afraid speaking aloud would alert the warriors who seemed to be lurking in omnipresent dugouts lining the tunnels every dozen feet or so. They were clearly in some kind of stasis with their eyes closed and completely motionless, but Lesh was sure the wrong smell or sound would have them up and swarming in a matter of seconds. Victor, obviously, wanted to avoid that.

"Can we mask their scent? Do they have a scent?" Lesh frowned, the expression very pronounced on his reptilian face, exposing half a dozen sharp teeth.

"I don't know," Victor sighed.

"I think we should avoid the risk while we can," Valla hissed. The tunnels were wide, easily ten yards across, and the soil they passed through was somehow hardened with a clear resin-like glaze. Valla had been leaning against the far wall, keeping to the shadow as much as she could, but now she leaned close, speaking quickly and softly. "While we can find a way down, we should be content. If we come to a blockage or some obstacle we can't find a way around, then we should consider other measures."

"All right." Victor nodded; she made sense. They knew they had to get to the bottom, and so far, they hadn't had trouble finding a downward-sloping tunnel. He started forward again, and when he came to one of the alcoves cut out for a sleeping warrior, he veritably tiptoed past the opening. A layer of transparent resin sealed off some of the warrior alcoves, but others, like this one, were partially open, as though the warrior had been out of his pod recently and hadn't been sealed in yet. Who closed them in? The workers? It made sense; the workers were currently closing up the exit tunnel the three of them had come through. Would they seal the repacked dirt with this resin? Was it some kind of excretion, or was it made from a natural use of Energy? Victor was strangely intrigued by the insects and their weird lives.

"I wonder if any of them think for themselves," he hissed to Valla, who was silently shadowing him.

"I hope not." She didn't elaborate, but Victor could catch the further meaning of her words. So far, they'd remained undetected thanks to the workers' lack of critical thinking. They might be in trouble if they came upon a different caste that operated on something other than instinct or hidden impulses from the queen.

"Something comes," Lesh hissed, and, as they'd done ten or more times already, they hurried back, ahead of the incoming ivid, until they reached a junction they'd recently passed. They ducked down one of the narrower side tunnels and waited, watching the intersection. Half a minute later, with a sweat-inducing clatter of claws on the hard tunnel surface, ten workers scurried through.

Valla let out a breath she'd been holding. "We're lucky they never seem to turn down these side tunnels."

"I believe these shafts lead to worker cells. There may be other tunnels accessible to other castes."

Victor thought about it, trying to imagine the layout of the enormous hive. "If that's true, if they don't use that big tunnel up there for anything other than, I don't know, like a highway, then maybe it doesn't access the heart of the hive. Maybe we need to check out one of the, uh, cells where the workers live to see if there are other tunnels."

Lesh nodded. "We haven't seen any downward-traveling workers. Where are those that hunt and gather? Surely, they must bring some sort of harvest into the hive . . ."

"Well, let's be honest: We don't know shit about these guys. Maybe they have openings to their hive a thousand miles from here. Maybe they grow their food underground. Let's check down this side tunnel, though, just to see if we get any ideas." When Valla silently nodded, Victor turned and walked further into the side tunnel, away from the junction. This tunnel was smaller but still plenty large enough for Lesh and Victor. The workers, while smaller than the soldiers, were the size of small automobiles, and the tunnel was wide enough to accommodate one traveling in any orientation. Victor shuddered, imagining a horde of the things swarming through the tunnel, some on the walls, some on the ceiling.

They'd only traversed a hundred yards or so when the tunnel took a very steep downward turn, so much so that Victor worried he might lose his footing and tumble. He turned, facing backward, and using his hands with his feet, began descending almost as if he was backing down a ladder. Lesh followed his example, but Valla seemed unbothered by the slope, partially spreading her wings and lightly hopping down, keeping pace with Victor's ponderous descent.

After another hundred yards, the slope smoothed out a bit, and Victor turned to continue creeping along as he had been up above. The tunnel wended left and right for quite a while, and Victor was beginning to worry he'd wasted a lot of time checking the side passage when he heard a strange, vibrating susurration in the air. He paused, straining his ears, and looked to Valla and Lesh with raised eyebrows. "I know not," Lesh hissed. Valla shrugged, and Victor continued. When they rounded the next prominent curve, he saw an opening ahead, and for the first time the glow of a light source other than his own.

He pointed, and Lesh and Valla nodded. They both held their weapons ready, and Victor reached over his shoulder, trusting his magical harness to push Lifedrinker into his hand. He pulled back the thread of Energy feeding his Globe of Insight, reducing it to a tiny spark that hovered near his head, and then he silently stalked forward, ready to see what lay beyond the dim opening. At the tunnel's edge, he leaned his head forward, peering around the strangely smooth corner.

A vast space greeted him, a hall that rose hundreds of feet in the air and stretched for such a distance that the far wall seemed tiny. Lining the long walls of the chamber were rows of cells just like those the warriors slept in, carved from the earth and stacked atop one another by the thousands. These were slightly smaller and lit with a faint amber glow. When Victor focused on one of the closer cells, he saw the source of the glow: The ivid within was slowly consuming a pile of yellow-orange luminescent sludge that looked very much like peach jam. Another difference he noted was that they were all open—not a single cell was closed off by the hard clear resin that coated the tunnel walls.

"There must be ten thousand in this chamber," Valla said, her voice just a faint breath beside Victor's ear. Victor nodded and pointed to the far wall, where he could just see a procession of much smaller insects winding out through a narrow tunnel. Valla leaned forward, close to him, peering where he pointed, and when she realized what she was looking at, she moved her mouth close to his ear and whispered, "Are those a different kind of worker?"

"Dunno," Victor said, trying to whisper as softly as she did and failing miserably. Still, he didn't seem to have alerted any of the ivid, so he turned and included Lesh in his following words. "Those insects at the far wall are different. Maybe they brought the food in here. Maybe that tunnel goes deeper."

Lesh nodded, pulling his magical perfume dispenser from a dimensional container and holding it up. The message was clear—he thought they should refresh their disguising scent. Victor nodded, producing his own bottle. Valla did the same, and soon they were all silently gagging amid a cloud of rank, eye-watering ammonia. Crouching low, eager to be out of the cloud, Victor started forward, trying to dart quickly past each occupied cell, hugging the short sections of wall between them. By the time they'd cleared half the chamber, the line of smaller insects had finished exiting, leaving Victor a clear tunnel opening to hurry toward.

None of the workers seemed to pay them any attention. It looked to Victor as though their eyes were closed as they doggedly nibbled at the glowing piles of jelly in their cells. Did they rest while they ate? Were they too simple of mind to do anything but one task at a time? He figured he'd never learn the answers to his constant questions about the strange species, but he was glad for whatever kept them calm in their cells, ignoring the three intruders hiding in their cloud of caustic odor. The smell of the perfume was strong to Victor and the others, but to the insects, it must have been a familiar, non-threatening odor, because they made it through the enormous dormitory without incident.

As Victor slipped into the new, much smaller opening, he had to duck to keep his head from scraping the hard resin-coated ceiling. He took a dozen steps, rounding a slight bend, and then turned to look at Lesh and Valla. "Good?"

"If uncomfortable," Lesh replied, grimacing as his hunched shoulders rubbed the ceiling.

"Let's hope this smaller tunnel opens into something bigger. C'mon, I wanna see where those bugs went." Victor turned and started forward again, and he heard the other two close behind. He had barely rounded the rest of the curve when he found himself face to face with an insect that wasn't only much smaller—person-sized, as Erd Van might put it—but also bipedal with two sets of arms ending in three-fingered, hook-like hands. The two-legged ivid's eyes, while definitely those of an insect, were far more expressive than those of the giant workers and warriors, and Victor swore he saw the carapace around them widen as its beak-like mouth opened and a warbling, clicking sound of obvious distress sounded from deep in its thorax.

Victor knew a cry for help when he heard it, and he reflexively cast Energy Charge and streaked through the ten feet between them in an eruption of hot rage-attuned Energy. He barely had time to lift Lifedrinker, but he did, and her blade cleaved sideways between the sharp razor-like ridges of the insect's mouth, carving off the top half of its head. The warbling alarm cut off as abruptly as it had begun, and Victor stood in the silence, Lifedrinker dripping yellow gore onto the fallen body of the ivid. He strained his ears, worried it was too late, that the cry had gone out and nearby warriors would be on top of them in seconds.

He stood that way, with Valla and Lesh similarly silent, their weapons ready, for thirty long seconds, and when they didn't hear anything more, Victor finally lowered his axe and turned to regard Valla and Lesh. "What the fuck is this thing?" He'd barely finished the question before a bunch of golden Energy motes gathered around the dead insect. Victor sighed with relief and pleasure as they all streamed into him.

"Ah, that must be nice." Valla shook her head, *tsking* her tongue at him. "Anyway, it seemed more intelligent, and it's alone . . ." She shrugged. "I don't know enough about insects to guess."

"Some sort of hive attendant, I would guess," Lesh whispered. "Performing rounds, checking the status of the workers, perhaps reporting to the queen what it sees." The big lizard-like warrior strode forward, spraying some of his alchemical mixture on the corpse. "If these things communicate with scents, then we have to assume a corpse would alert something or other. Best to delay that if we can."

"Yeah," Victor said, then he stooped and pulled the dead body and its dismembered head into one of his storage rings. "How's that?"

Lesh didn't laugh aloud, but something like amusement rumbled deep in his chest. "Good." Victor grinned and then turned back to the tunnel, advancing with Lifedrinker held ready. The passage continued, more or less straight, for another hundred paces before they came to a T junction. Victor peered left and right and settled on going right because it had a slightly downward slope. It wasn't long before they approached another intersection, this one more like a Y, and from the left-hand branch, Victor heard clicks that reminded him of the strange alarm the insect he'd killed made. However, these clicks were more varied and far quieter, and he wondered if it was the sound of the insects talking.

"Are they communicating?" Valla whispered, echoing his thoughts.

Victor shrugged. "Maybe. Maybe one of those hive attendants is down there giving instructions to some workers or something."

"This tunnel is too small for workers. We should investigate." Lesh's hunched dark form loomed close behind Victor, and his low rumbling whisper barely carried more than a few inches. Victor was torn—part of him knew Lesh was right and that they should learn what they could about the insects before going deeper, but another part wanted to avoid any possible interaction. Shouldn't they just turn right and skip whatever was making those clicks? In the end, Valla helped him with the decision.

"Yes, let's see what we can see."

Victor shrugged and stalked down the left passage, very carefully and slowly rounding the slight curve, aware of the faint glow of amber light from ahead. When an opening began to come into view, he froze, ever so slowly inching his head to the left, past the curve, so he could see what was there. The passage opened into a low but vast space, and in it were thousands of insects that looked to be halfway between the "attendant" they'd run into and one of the big workers upstairs. They were probably a match for Victor or Lesh en masse, but they walked on all six legs. Their forelegs ended in articulated joints but were only two-pronged, and their coloring was less yellow and more brown than that of the bipedal creature Victor had killed. Even so, they were clearly different from the workers up above.

Stranger than their appearance was their behavior. The smaller workers were arrayed in dozens of rows, fanning out from the center of the room. They all faced the middle, and there, on a raised dais of resin-coated dirt, stood one of the bipedal insects and before it kneeled, for there was no better way to describe their posture, five of the small workers. The kneeling insects faced the ground, heads low, and the attendant insect paced before them. It was from his beak-like mouth that the clicks emanated.

Victor felt Valla and Lesh press close behind him, peering down the short length of the tunnel to the large, strange gathering of insects, but his eyes were glued to the scene in the middle. The bipedal insect walked before the five workers, its four hands gesticulating as it clicked. After a minute, though, it bent before the kneeling insects, one by one, and while Victor watched in fascinated horror, it bit through the chitin atop their heads with a clear, echoing *snick*. With each bite, the victims spasmed, arms twitching, chitinous bodies shivering, but they didn't die.

First, the attendant bit the two on the left, then the two on the right, and when Victor thought it would bite the fifth one, the one at the center, he was proven wrong. Instead, it took its dexterous-looking fingers, pulled something wet and glistening from the incision it had made in the others, and held it in its palm for the fifth worker to consume. Victor felt his mouth go dry as a dizzying sense of nausea came over him. That thing was feeding parts of the four workers to the fifth while they still lived! Valla's hand tightened on his shoulder, and that was the first time Victor realized she'd gripped him.

He looked at her and saw her wide eyes and frantic gestures for him to turn around, so he followed her back toward the last intersection. Lesh was already there, waiting when they came around. The big dragonkin nodded when they approached and softly rumbled, "I know not what rite it was performing, but we should move while they are all in attendance. If it finishes and releases that horde, we'll be overrun."

"Yeah." Victor started down the other branch of the intersection and continued to whisper, "Pretty weird, though. Did you see it pull something out of their heads to feed the one?"

"Perhaps it's lifting one up." Lesh said the "lifting one up" as though it had a universal meaning. Victor looked at him quizzically.

"Huh?"

"Perhaps it can elevate one caste to the next with the sacrifice of its fellows."

"Is it replacing the one we killed? So quickly?" Valla asked.

"Perhaps. The Kothid were quick to replace the forces we slew during the war. Evolved hives are . . . disturbingly alien in their operation. We should consider that there's a greater awareness here, that there is a mind at work beyond each individual, even beyond the queen."

Victor nodded, looking back to reply, "Like a network."

"I wish we knew how deep we had to go and how deep we've come. I wish we knew what to expect." Valla sighed.

"Yeah . . ." Victor started to agree with her, but Lesh spoke too, and his words came more quickly, his thoughts fully formed.

"I expect death. This cannot end well. We've been descending for a mere hour, and already, tens of thousands of insects lurk above us. Already, we've learned that there's some intelligence at work. I'll be amazed if this stinking concoction works much longer." He wrinkled his short snout as he sniffed his forearm in illustration.

Neither Valla nor Victor responded to his sudden bout of negativity. Victor figured it was his memories of the war he'd fought back on his homeworld. It couldn't be easy sneaking into a massive hive like this—it was bound to dredge up all sorts of feelings. Still, he had to admit he was feeling a little less optimistic. They'd passed a hundred side passages. They'd descended through miles and miles of tunnel. What were the odds they were on the right track? What were the odds the magical egg artifact would be waiting for them when they'd gone down as far as they could? How many hordes of insects would be waiting? What other weird castes were there? One thing gave him a glimmer of relief in the darkness of doubt—they had the recall tokens Erd Van had given them.

"Let's just hope they work," he muttered, rounding yet another gentle curve and nearly stumbling into a black void. His light was dim, only allowing him to see a few feet ahead, but it was enough to show him that his next step would be into empty air. He braced an arm on the tunnel wall, then looked back at Lesh and Valla. "Do we want to risk a brighter light?"

Valla sighed and stepped forward. "Perhaps it's time I put my wings to use."

23

DEEPER

Wait," Lesh rumbled, nudging past Valla to better peer into the darkness. Victor felt a small surge of Energy, and then the giant warrior's reptilian eyes began to shine with mossy green luminescence. "I see a great chasm with tunnels branching off at the bottom. It's fifty times as deep as I am tall. There are shapes moving at the bottom—ivid, I'd wager. There's a narrow path cut into the face of this wall. If we're careful, we should be able to descend, though I'd brighten your globe a bit."

Victor nodded and willed his globe of light closer to the ground, brightening it slightly. Sure enough, a narrow path led downward to the left. "Too narrow for anything but the bipedal ivid," he whispered, stepping down and onto the path, hardly wide enough for his large, booted foot.

"Should I fly down?"

"If you do, you won't be alone." Lesh's reply, for some reason, made Victor chuckle. He supposed it had to do with his dry tone without any judgment. He wasn't saying Valla *shouldn't* fly down, but he wasn't saying she should, either.

"I'll stay with you." She didn't sound happy, and Victor could imagine why: being forced to trudge around through tunnels deep underground when you've tasted the freedom of flight in an open windy sky . . . He shook his head, pushing the thought aside; he needed to focus. The narrow path had come to a switchback, and there wasn't much room for maneuvering. He almost slipped as he turned back the opposite way, but the resin-coated dirt was hard, giving good traction, and his boot caught well enough for him to recover his balance.

"Victor," Lesh hoarsely whispered as they made the next turn.

"Yeah?"

"You should put your light out. Some of the insects have been glancing up at us. I'll warn you when the next switchback is coming."

"Great." Victor pulled his Energy back from his globe, reducing it to a tiny flickering mote of light that he kept close to his feet. It was barely enough to illuminate the tops of his boots, but his Quinametzin eyes used it to paint the path before him in monochromatic gray angles—sufficient to keep him from walking off into the abyss. They descended like that, painstakingly slowly, for nearly an hour before they came to the final stretch that would take them to the bottom of the underground crevasse. Victor couldn't quite make out the furtive, clicking shapes below, so he turned to Lesh, waiting for the big warrior to tell him when to move.

"The ground is ten feet below us," Lesh said, "and there's a tunnel straight across. I haven't seen any of the small workers going into it, so we should be safe to regroup there. Take hold of my belt, Valla, and Victor will hold your hand as we move. Straight down and across when I say. Ready?"

"Ready," Victor replied softly. Valla said the same, and then they waited for Lesh to choose the right moment. Seconds ticked into minutes, and then, just as Victor was beginning to daydream about things he wanted to search for in Sojourn, Lesh silently dropped off the ledge. Valla made a soft yip of surprise, and then she dropped after him, and Victor followed. When he landed beside her, surprisingly without stumbling, Valla fumbled for and grabbed his hand. Then Lesh darted forward, pulling her and Victor along. Victor could barely see the ground around them, but when they ran forward, he could feel the weight of the space above them, and his skin crawled with the sensation of being watched by a thousand sets of eyes.

He was almost surprised when they made it to the tunnel without some sort of clicking, hissing alarm being sounded. Lesh pulled them in, then turned back and rumbled, "You can make your light brighter here."

Victor did so, finding that they stood in a tunnel very much like the one they'd left up at the top of the chasm. "At least we're still going down."

Lesh nodded. "We are deep indeed by now."

"Let's keep moving," Valla said, and Victor thought he heard some strain in her voice. As Lesh turned, leading the way deeper, he moved his light closer to Valla to see her face better.

"You doing all right?" he asked, motioning for her to walk ahead of him.

"Not really. I think part of my racial evolution has made me more . . . claustrophobic, I suppose, is the right word. I'm not enjoying having miles of earth and insects above our heads. What if the recall tokens don't work?" She looked back at him, eyes wide with stress as she asked her question.

"Look, I'm not loving it down here, either, but I promise you, if I have to move the earth itself, I will get you out of this hive." Of course, Victor recognized his Quinametzin ego asserting itself, but it seemed to put Valla at ease, so he went with it. Was he really sure he could get them out of there? He supposed not, but he'd die trying, and that was good enough; there'd be time in the next life for regretting poorly made promises. Valla followed Lesh, and Victor followed Valla, and they made their way steadily downward.

They passed another great worker hall, this one housing tens of thousands of the smaller workers. In that hall, narrow catwalks made of dirt and resin ran between the dozens of upper tiers of insect cells. Constant traffic flowed over those high, strange bridgeways and at the ground level where Victor and the others walked. Still, the workers moved purposefully, heads down, and as long as they kept their distance, the bugs didn't seem to pay any mind to the three outsiders.

Lesh was good about keeping a retreat planned; every time a worker or one of the "attendants" approached them, he hastily moved back to a side tunnel or an empty cell, ducking to the side while the ivid went by. Another hour of descent became two hours, then three, and Victor lost count of the chambers full of cells and side passages they passed. Though they traversed mile after mile of tunnel, they constantly moved downward, and Victor began to wonder just how deep they were.

After a long period of silence, he asked, "There's no way we could have doubled back, right?"

"We're always going down . . ." Valla started to say, but Lesh shook his head and rumbled over her.

"No. I can feel the ground around us. It's different—we make progress."

"I know patience is important and that I don't want to fight the entire hive, but I'm starting to lose it here. You guys don't think I should summon my coyotes? They're pretty damn sneaky . . ."

"I can feel vast voids below us. I think we grow close to the heart of the hive." Lesh pointed downward in illustration. "Give me another hour before you call forth your spirit scouts." Victor nodded, and the dragonkin turned and started forward. Valla followed, and Victor, still gripping Lifedrinker, brought up the rear. He felt a tremendous buildup of tension in his neck and back and yearned to feel the sky above him. He was sure Valla was suffering even more, so with her as an exemplar, he kept himself under control, venting some pent-up energy by gripping Lifedrinker's haft tightly, twisting his hands back and forth.

True to his word, Lesh's downward path eventually took them into a vast tunnel that reminded Victor of the main thoroughfare of Greatbone Mine. It was illuminated by strange veins of yellow-white minerals, giving the whole place a kind of hazy sepia glow. The vaulted ceiling was a hundred feet overhead, and the sides of the tunnel were separated by a hundred paces of smooth resin-coated ground. The tunnel that led them to that great passage was high in the wall, and down below, Victor could see rows of orderly insects, some traveling inward at a slightly downward grade and some traveling up and presumably out. Between the high ceiling and the ground, suspended highways of dirt and resin crawled with the hunched, earthen-toned insects. The columns of ivid stretched farther than Victor could see.

"There must be tens of thousands of them marching along down there," Valla whispered from where she lay, peering over the lip of the tunnel.

"Do you see that side passage?" Lesh pointed, and Victor thought he saw what he meant. A wide oval opening about half a mile up the tunnel. "I believe that leads down to a great cavern that way." He pointed, indicating the side of the tunnel ahead of them. "It's a bigger space than any I've sensed."

"How do we get there? There are a thousand ivid between us and that tunnel." Victor frowned, contemplating the violence he'd have to unleash to fight his way into the tunnel. Then what?

"We must choose a time when none of the attendants are near. We'll refresh our odor, then jump down and shuffle along with the workers."

"Do you think they won't raise an alarm?" Valla asked. So far, they hadn't stood near one of the small workers long enough to determine whether they'd notice them.

"We are close. We cannot teleport or tunnel through this dirt. What option is there?" Lesh, for the first time, sounded a little on edge. Victor wondered if he was starting to lose it, being down in the belly of the hive for so long. While Lesh and Valla stared at the ground, contemplating what they had to do, Victor let his eyes drift over the many suspended walkways and the crazy architecture that allowed the ivid to take advantage of that third axis. As his eyes settled on something interesting, he nudged Lesh with his elbow.

"Look. That suspended walkway is empty." It was on the far side of the tunnel, only about fifty feet above and parallel to the ground. If they could get on it, it seemed as though it would take them right above the opening Lesh had pointed out.

Lesh must have been thinking similarly, because he said, "How do we get to it?"

"I can fly over there." Valla's tone was matter-of-fact.

"You could string us a line." Victor nodded as Lesh produced a thin silky rope rolled in a tight bundle.

"This is razzka silk; it will not break."

Valla took the loose end and said, "Feed it quickly; I don't want to get hung up."

"Wait," Victor said, bringing out his scent-dispensing bottle. "We should refresh this stuff before we go into that big tunnel."

Lesh and Valla nodded, and soon they were all breathing into their sleeves, eyes watering as the caustic chemical settled over them. Once the air had cleared enough to breathe without gagging, Valla climbed to her feet and stood at the tunnel's edge, knees bent, wings partially open, staring into the big open space, perhaps trying to choose a moment when none of the attendants were passing near. Victor wanted to tell her to be careful, but he knew it was stupid—of course she would be. Nevertheless, he was nervous for her, and his knuckles were white where they gripped Lifedrinker.

After several long seconds in which Victor and Lesh exchanged several looks, Valla abruptly dropped off the ledge, and her wings *whooshed* back, just once, propelling her like a silvery arrow straight through the gap between two of the suspended walkways, to land with perfect grace upon the empty target walkway. As she flew, the silky rope whistled softly as it rushed between Lesh's fingers. Victor watched her loop and tie her end around the walkway; it was only about three feet wide. She crouched low, utterly exposed out there, but so far, the insects had ignored her.

"You first," Lesh said, holding his end of the rope tight in his scaled fist.

"How are you gonna cross without anyone to hold your end?"

"I'll leap out, swinging from the rope, and climb up."

Victor looked the huge dragonkin up and down and snorted. "*Hermano*, you aren't built for that kind of shit. Let me hold it while you climb across, then I'll do the leaping, yeah?"

"I suppose." Lesh frowned. "You could reduce your size further?"

"Yeah, of course. If I fall, I can probably jump up to that walkway, too."

"Very well." Lesh handed him the rope, and then, as Victor pulled it tight, he tested his weight against it, pulling hard. Victor grunted and had to dig in his heels, but he knew he could support the dragonkin's weight. If he got worried, he could always cast Iron Berserk—he was already channeling his Sovereign Will into his strength and vitality.

"Go on!" he urged the dragonkin. Lesh gave him one more nod, then with surprising grace, he leaped out onto the silken line, pulling himself hand over hand toward Valla. Victor was surprised by the initial leap and had to jerk back on the rope, leaning backward with all his weight to keep from being pulled out of the tunnel, but after that, it was easy to keep the rope supported. Luck must have been with them, or the fresh dose of ivid scent must have been especially potent, because though Lesh passed between two other walkways, none of the ivid gave him a second glance as he passed over and under them.

When he was safely squatting beside Valla, Victor nodded, contemplating things. If he dropped off the ledge and hung from the rope, he'd be hanging across another walkway, and his line might touch one of them, or worse, knock one off as he descended. The only apparent way he could see himself getting to the walkway where Valla and Lesh waited was to jump past the other intervening span. Then he could let himself swing and climb his way up beside Valla. "Yep, gonna have to do it." He hung Lifedrinker back in her harness, then gathered up the feather-light rope and backed up for a running start.

He wrapped the rope around his right wrist several times and then switched his Sovereign Will boost from vitality to agility. "Here we go," he breathed, then took two long strides and leaped out of the tunnel, aiming to cross the walkway about twenty feet out and five feet below the ledge. He soared over it effortlessly and had enough momentum that he was afraid he'd hit the far wall on his way down, but then the silken rope snapped taut, pulling on his right arm, and he swung upward. Victor didn't wait to swing back the other way; he immediately started to climb the strand, easily pulling his weight up hand over hand. By the time he reached the end of his swing and started back the other way, he'd shortened his hanging distance from the walkway by half.

In seconds, he slapped a hand onto the smooth span and felt Lesh and Valla grab ahold of it. Once he'd scrambled onto the walkway, with their aid, Lesh untied his rope and gathered it up. "Very nimbly done," he rumbled as they hunkered down together.

"Let's go!" Victor didn't like being out in the open as they were. He took the lead, crouching low and hurrying along the walkway toward the distant tunnel opening Lesh had pointed out. Ivid moved along all around them. Some shuffled in the same direction, others in the opposite. They made strange sounds as they walked, like a constant susurration that filled the air, and Victor wondered if it was their breathing or just the sound of their chitin or fluid-filled joints. Whatever it was, it was nerve-wracking being amidst it, and he moved very quickly toward their goal, trusting that Lesh and Valla would speak up if he went too fast.

They reached the tunnel, and for the first time in the hive, Victor saw smooth stone walls and flooring. Either this tunnel had been there before the ivid, or they had another caste of workers that could shape stone. He looked back at Valla and Lesh. "Ready?" Lesh held up his rope, so Victor nodded. Could the big dragonkin really not drop fifty feet? Or was he worried he'd be too loud? Victor held the rope for him without arguing or questioning—time for that later. Lesh made short work of the climb down, and soon, he'd darted into the stone tunnel, peering up at Victor and Valla.

"I can hold the rope for you," she said.

"I can jump down . . ."

"Will that not be loud?"

Victor frowned, more annoyed that he'd been mentally judging Lesh for needing a rope than that she was right. "All right," he sighed, giving it a tug and grinning as Valla stumbled toward him. "Hold it tight. I'll put my weight on it slowly."

"You'd better!" She bared her teeth at him in a nervous smile, and he realized she was doing everything she could to keep it together. He quickly stepped toward her, trying to hug her, to offer some comfort, but she bristled, pushing him back. "Not now! I . . . I can't keep it together out here among them much longer!"

"Right. Sorry." Victor gripped the rope and slowly backed off the walkway, waiting for Valla to have his full weight before he rapidly descended. He set foot on the smooth stone only ten feet from a long column of workers, and he hurriedly turned and jogged into the tunnel to Lesh. When he glanced back, he was almost surprised to find that none of the bugs had chased him or raised an alarm. With a flutter of ammonia-laced air, Valla landed beside him and passed the silken rope to Lesh.

"Come on!" she hissed, moving farther into the tunnel away from the crowded ivid highway. Lesh and Victor followed her, and they'd only descended into the wide stone hall for a dozen paces before she pulled up short and slammed herself against the stone wall, trying to sink into the darkness there. Lesh followed her lead, and Victor slowed, crouching low, trying to see what had alerted her. He didn't have to look far—about a half mile down the smooth, straight tunnel was a massive arched opening backlit by what looked like daylight. On either side of the tremendous bright archway stood bipedal ivid with shiny silvery metallic carapaces and wielding enormous polearms.

"What the fu—" Victor started to say, but Valla slapped a hand to his mouth—one of the ivid guardians had turned toward them, though it seemed its eyesight couldn't peel Victor's shape from the shadows. After just a moment of scrutiny, it turned forward. Victor put his lips just a fraction of an inch from Valla's ear and whispered, "I can see why other groups failed this bullshit quest."

24

HIVE WORLD

They're certainly more intelligent *seeming* than those we've encountered thus far." Valla leaned past Victor, peering down the long gradual slope of the tunnel toward the two huge insectoid guards. Guards they clearly were—standing still, armored, holding weapons as their shiny carapace-covered heads swiveled left to right, ever alert. Victor had stared at them for a long while, using his excellent Quinametzin vision to discern details in their appearance. He'd convinced himself that the insects, with their four bulky arms and long scorpion-like stingers, were similar enough to the ivid that they must be the same species.

The similarities were most apparent in their faces and torsos, though the weird metallic nature of their chitin made it a little hard to see. It was the eyes that really made Victor sure; they were identical in shape and number—five slightly ovoid eyes on each side of the "nose," all of them narrower at one end and getting wider away from the cluster. More than the shape, their eyes had the same weird iridescent shimmer over the predominantly black color. "Do we try to talk to them?" He didn't see a way to sneak past them, so in his mind, it was either fight or talk. Or talk, then fight.

"If they raise an alarm . . ." Lesh grumbled, leaving the rest of his concern unspoken.

"So, we can try to murder them quickly or speak to them." Valla's choice in verbiage wasn't lost on Victor. Did her using the word "murder" mean she wanted to try a more peaceful tactic?

He wasn't one to play guessing games. "You think we should try talking?"

"Yes, but first use your scope."

Victor snapped his fingers, grateful she'd remembered the device that he constantly forgot. He pulled the little brass and glass device out of his storage ring and pointed it at the ivid guard on the left. Immediately, a soft yellow aura bloomed around the creature. Victor pointed it at the other one, and if he wasn't mistaken, the yellow aura on that one was a little darker. "Yellow." He hadn't used the scope since he'd been on Fanwath, and everyone there gave him green or blue responses. He turned the scope on Lesh, having never tested it on him, and found that he, too, had a yellow aura, though much paler than the two ivid. Victor handed the scope to the dragonkin. "You try."

Lesh held the little scope, comically small in his big clawed fingers, to his eye and peered down the ramp at the two ivid. "Orange and . . . dark orange, almost red." He handed the scope to Valla, and she held it to her eye.

She stared for a long while, then lowered the scope and said, "Deep red."

"Darker than me?"

"No." She pointed the scope at him, double-checking. "You're so red it's almost purple."

"Am I to believe this device has determined that those creatures are more powerful than I?" Lesh didn't sound happy.

"It's not really that exact. I don't know what it measures—maybe just total Energy or something simple like that. Still, we can bet these two *pendejos* are going to be a lot tougher than the bugs we've fought already."

Valla sighed, shaking her head. "We should try to reason with them. If they can communicate, we might save ourselves much trouble."

Victor nodded, twisting Lifedrinker in his fists while he thought aloud. "It's not really that I'm afraid to fight two tough guys, but I doubt we could kill them quickly, not before we made some noise, anyway. I'm sure they'd call for help. Could we take on another ten bugs that tough? What about a thousand? Who knows what's through that archway? Why does it look like daylight?"

"We've slain their kin. Will they even speak with us?"

"Good question." Victor shrugged. "Be ready to try to kill them as quickly as you can. Charge up your best offensive ability. Try to look intimidating." Victor looked at Valla and Lesh, nodding. "I'm going to take on my full size and cast Iron Berserk. Hopefully, they'll be more willing to talk if they think we could pose a threat. Ready?"

Valla's eyes began to shimmer with silvery-blue flashes deep in their depths, and a charged breeze picked up around them, ruffling her feathers. "I'm ready."

Lesh's chest expanded as he inhaled and stood up straight. Belagog, gripped firmly in both hands, began to smoke and drip caustic green liquid to the tunnel floor, each drop sizzling and sinking into the hard smooth stone. "I am ready."

Victor turned and started walking down the slope. "Okay, *chica*. Get ready." He channeled his Sovereign Will into strength and vitality. He cut his connection to his Alter Shape spell, expanded to his full, nearly ten-foot height, and cast Iron Berserk. His body surged with power and hot, potent, rage-attuned Energy. His vision tinted to crimson, and he swelled massively. His armor shivered and clanked as it grew with him, and his boots and pants strained against his bulging proportions, their resizing capabilities not quite as robust as his finer gear. The tunnel resounded with his further steps as he, faintly flickering with red rage-attuned Energy, stalked down the pathway toward the two ivid guards.

They noticed him almost immediately, and though something like half a mile of tunnel separated the insects from the trio, they stepped toward each other, crossing their long metallic polearms, clearly signaling their intent to stop anyone from passing through the archway. As Victor approached, despite the rage smoldering in his chest, held in check by his iron will, he felt heartened not to hear any outcry. It seemed the guardians would wait and see what sort of threat Victor and his companions posed.

As he descended and the ivid grew more prominent, he began to realize the perspective he and the others had enjoyed, looking down the long sloping tunnel, had been misleading. The tunnel grew gradually wider, and Victor realized the archway leading into the brightly lit area was much bigger than he'd thought. He was still a few hundred paces from the ivid, and he could tell the tunnel opening was something like a hundred feet high, making the ivid standing before it nearly his fully berserk size.

"They're huge," Valla whispered, walking behind and to the left of him. Lesh was on his right side, and he could feel the tension in the dragonkin's posture—if there were hundreds, thousands, or millions of ivid like these two, then the adventurers were in way over their heads. It was hard to see beyond the two guardians through the bright opening; some kind of haze hung in the air behind them, making the air translucent but blurry, obscuring whatever was in the brightly lit space. Victor thought it must be some kind of magical warding, something to keep prying eyes, mundane or magical, from seeing what the ivid were up to at the heart of their hive.

The guardians' posture became more and more threatening the closer they got. By the time Victor was a few dozen yards away from the giant insects, they were hunched forward, their polearms—long metallic bars with enormous triangular spear tips on one end—held menacingly high, ready to be swept down or thrust forward. Their many eyes were trained on Victor, and he could see a kind of Energy pulsing in them, a smoky gray shimmering aura that hinted at deep wells of power. Victor stopped thirty yards from the enormous bright archway and cleared his throat. "We seek an audience with your rulers."

He still held Lifedrinker in his hand, and he made a show of lifting her to his shoulder and allowing his harness to snatch her out of his hand so she sat snugly against his back. As soon as he did so, the two ivid noticeably relaxed, their posture straightening slightly, the angle of their weapons moving away from Victor. "Put your weapons away," he said. He heard Valla's sword slide into her sheath and the *clunk* of metal on stone as Lesh lowered Belagog. The two ivid straightened further and moved their weapons back together, forming an X before the archway but no longer threatening the trio. "Can you speak?"

His query was met with silence as the two insectoid guardians continued to stare. Lesh spoke, his voice rumbling softly in the enormous passageway. "Perhaps they simply respond to threats. Could we pass if we don't exhibit any hostility?"

"We could try . . ." Victor took a step forward, but then something happened behind the crossed polearms of the two guardians. The air shimmered, and with a soft *pop* like a large soap bubble bursting, a much smaller ivid stepped out of the archway. This one was similar to the "hive attendants" they'd seen on their way down through the endless tunnels. There were significant differences, however, starting with the fact that it was clothed in shimmering gray silky robes and carried a long rod of transparent rose-colored stone.

In a clicking, rasping voice that made the hairs on Victor's neck stand up, it addressed them. "Do you understand this one?"

The statement took Victor by surprise. He'd expected many things, hostility being the most likely in his mind, but this hadn't been on his list. "I understand you."

"This one was created to speak to you." It stopped speaking words and clicked and hissed oddly for several seconds. After staring at Victor through its ten eyes for several seconds afterward, it said, "You cannot understand our language, but it is far superior. Can you not learn?"

"Um ..." Victor glanced at Valla and Lesh, neither offering him any help. "Not easily. Can we keep using this language, please?"

"This one can speak this language. Why do you trespass?" The smaller ivid, about the size of Valla, stepped forward directly under the arch of the two giant guardians' polearms.

"We didn't know our presence wasn't allowed." Victor figured he wasn't exactly lying—they knew the ivid would attack intruders, but he hadn't known they were smart enough to understand trespassing. He thought it was just an automatically defensive posture.

"The hive is for ivid. Many hiveless have entered, only to be consumed and added to the record. From those memories, we have constructed this one to speak to you. Would you like to join the hive? Would you like your memories to live in the record?"

"No!" Valla said before Victor could wrap his head around the weird question.

"Then why do you come? It would benefit the hive to add you to the record."

"We seek an artifact and will trade in kind," Lesh rumbled, stepping forward.

"Knowledge, not artifacts, makes the hive stronger. We can take knowledge with your memories. Why will you not join the hive? There is no strength in the individual, no continuance."

"While your hive is glorious," Lesh said, "we owe our memories to others on a distant world. There is no threat to your hive here." He gestured to Victor and Valla, then to himself. "We will leave, and you will be stronger for our visit." Victor had to hand it to him; he seemed to have grasped the idea of how to talk to the hive emissary rather quickly.

"What artifact do you seek? Only recently have we begun to clothe and arm these ones."

Lesh looked at Victor, raising his scaled eye ridge in question. Victor shrugged and spoke up, his voice booming in the tunnel. "We want one of your eggs that never hatched, one of your dreamers." The insect didn't react but stood unmoving for several long moments. Victor was starting to wonder if he should say something more, but then it lifted its crystal rod, tracing a strange pattern in the air. A disc of shimmering light appeared, floating in the air before the ivid. It lifted one three-fingered hand to the disc, shifting it so its eyes could peer through it at Victor and the others. Was it examining them somehow?

"We will trade one of our sleeping children for one of the female's eggs and a sample of the males' seed."

Victor felt his rage flare, felt his fists clench, and he gathered his breath, ready to tell the damn bug-man off, but then Valla's cool fingers gripped his wrist, squeezing, reminding him that he wasn't there alone. Before he could speak or react further, she said, "May we discuss your proposal?"

"Yes. Hiveless must communicate with sounds or script. This we have learned."

Valla tugged Victor's wrist, leading him down the tunnel farther from the three ivid. When they'd put another fifty feet or so between them, she said, "We have to think about this rationally."

"I don't like the idea that these insects will have my seed to experiment with," Lesh growled.

"I mean, same here. But worse, how the hell will they take one of your eggs, Valla?" Victor hissed, trying to whisper but struggling to contain his emotions. He contemplated dropping his Iron Berserk to push the rage out of his pathways.

"Victor," Lesh said before Valla could answer, "use your scope on the speaking insect."

Grimacing with frustration, Victor did as he asked, summoning the scope from his ring and pointing it at the diminutive ivid between the two hulking metal-plated guardians. At first, he thought something was wrong, that the ivid wasn't showing up, but then he realized what it was—the hive representative had an aura so thick and dark that it looked like a shadow, a hole in space between the two guardians. Dread crept into his chest, pushing the rage back, summoning tendrils of fear-attuned Energy from his Core. He didn't have an instruction manual for the scope, but something deep in his gut told Victor all he needed to know—this thing was an order of magnitude more potent than he was.

He pushed the scope back into his storage container and, with a cold shiver threatening to cancel his Iron Berserk before he was ready, said, "That thing's a lot more powerful than the others."

"What color?"

"Black. Like a hole in the universe."

Lesh grunted. "So, we should eschew violence. It seems willing to bargain. Perhaps we can negotiate different terms."

"Any ideas?" Victor glanced back at the ivid as he waited for Valla and Lesh to think it through.

Lesh rubbed his chin, tapping a sharp claw against one of his hanging canines. "I have some treasures from my various conquests. I have a Kothid ravager pincer. Perhaps it would be interested in another insect species."

"I have some things, too." Victor's mind went to Dunstan's crown, still sitting in the hotel room back on Sojourn. He might have killed two birds with one stone if he'd brought that along. He reached to his chest where the key hung, the one with the silver globe that would expand into a room, its purpose unknown to him. It seemed stupid to bargain with things he didn't understand. "I have the hide from the lava king I was awarded. I think it's worth a lot. Also, the legendary magma-attunement gem."

"They may be interested in such things." Lesh nodded, then looked at Valla. Victor followed his gaze, looking into Valla's distant eyes. She realized they were looking at her, and she smiled, shrugging.

"I don't think they'll want objects. If it's an egg they're after, is that so much to ask? We want the same from them, after all. If it will save Edeya, I'll give one up." She pressed a hand to her abdomen, and Victor could only imagine what was going through her mind. The idea of some weird powerful insect hive wanting her genetic material, wanting to take an egg from her ovaries . . . He shook his head, hating the thought of it.

"Just a minute." Victor turned and stalked toward the ivid emissary. He knew Valla's bloodline was special; he knew Lesh, too, had potent ancestry. Victor was Quinametzin, though, and if the bugs had to pick one of them to sample, his pride wouldn't let him believe they'd choose either of his companions. He stopped a dozen paces from the ivid and, with a deep, firm voice, said, "We want one egg. You can choose one of us to sample."

"A moment." While the ivid stared into space, Victor felt Lesh and Valla step beside him. Valla took his thumb in her much smaller hand, holding it. Thanks to his constant inner heat, her skin always felt cool, and he felt his rage slipping further from his pathways at her touch. Some part of him knew he wasn't going to fight, and it was harder and harder to keep his Iron Berserk stoked. As he wrestled with the urge to let the spell slip away, the ivid began speaking again in its unsettling, clicking, hissing voice. "This one will guide you to the queen. Your companions will be fed and housed during your absence."

It didn't wait for a response. In perfect unison, the two guardians lifted their polearms and sidestepped away from the center of the bright shimmering passage. At the same time, the emissary turned and walked back through the hazy curtain of light. "*Chingado*," Victor hissed, looking down at Valla and then at Lesh. "Do we go in?"

Valla sighed, shaking her head. "We must. Thank you, Victor, for being protective of Lesh and me, but I hate that you're once again risking yourself for me." She didn't look happy as she let go of his finger and stepped into hazy air.

"My thanks are without caveat, Lord Victor," Lesh rumbled, stepping after Valla. Victor, frowning, annoyed that Valla was annoyed, followed them. The air felt normal. The haze didn't smell, wasn't moist, and didn't sting his eyes—it had to be some kind of magical screen. The bright flare of light forced him to shield his eyes as soon as he'd stepped through. As they adjusted to the brightness, he couldn't help the exclamation that slipped through his lips.

"What the fuck?" He stood atop a hillside with a long stretch of smooth glassy-brown roadway leading down toward a massive sprawling city of smooth stone towers. A yellow sky with a glowering orange sun hung overhead, and beneath it, as far as he could see, stretched roads and buildings. He could see thousands and thousands of the ivid moving around down there, traversing the streets, walking in and out of the buildings. Most of them were bipedal, though there were quite a few variants of the six-legged ivid they'd seen up in the hive.

The foliage was strange—everything was sharp and angular. The trees and shrubs beside the ivid roadway reminded him of desert plants—cacti and thorn bushes, with very little green. A weird rumbling buzzing sound overhead grabbed his attention, and Victor looked up to see a great bulbous insect with huge buzzing wings floating by lazily, a colossal platform hanging from its long black legs. He could just make out the tiny forms of bipedal ivid crowding the metallic railing of the platform. They were using another insect for transportation.

None of what he saw explained how a world, complete with sky and sun, could be twenty miles beneath the planet's surface. Had they gone through a portal? Were they in yet another different world? He couldn't contain the questions. "Where are we?"

"You are in the hive world. Follow me, individuals. You will not be harmed by the hive if you do not threaten these ones." The emissary gestured left and right with its crystal rod, indicating everything below the hill.

"How many?" Valla licked her lips and spoke a little louder. "How many of you are here?"

The ivid didn't answer right away as it started down the hill. Victor and the others followed, and after a short while, it turned to look at Valla. "This one cannot answer that question with words. Our memories of other outsiders indicate that the best way to reply is to ask you how many cells are in your body?"

"Cells . . ." Valla breathed, shaking her head. Victor had learned from his time on Fanwath that the people there were quite familiar with the world of microscopic things, from cells to bacteria to concepts very much like DNA. Valla knew what the insect was implying—it, or the hive speaking through it, didn't see its individual ivid as "people" but as parts of itself—tiny replaceable parts, too numerous to count. It was a frightening concept, considering the apparent power of the emissary.

25

TRANSPORT

The ivid emissary led them down the hill into the weird cityscape of towering smooth funnel-shaped buildings. Some of them were wider at the top and some at the bottom, and once they were among them, it felt as if they were underground again because it became impossible to see beyond one or two of the structures. Meanwhile, ivid walked everywhere, always moving with purpose, sometimes carrying things from rocks to plants to glittering gemstones.

Many of the ivid in the city were clothed in shimmering robes like those of the emissary, while others wore nothing but their chitin. Stationed at nearly every building, Victor saw the members of the guardian caste with their metallic carapaces. As they walked, Valla cleared her throat and asked, "Do you have a name?"

"This one does not," the emissary replied almost immediately.

"A title?" she pressed.

"No, but you may think of this one as a spokesperson or . . ."

"Emissary?" Victor provided, hoping to keep thinking of the strange insectoid as he had been.

"This term seems adequate." The emissary led them between identical-seeming buildings, walking in the center of the road between the lines of ivid traffic that marched in either direction. None of the insects looked at them, and certainly none spoke. Though they never uttered any words or even sounds, the air was filled with the steady background hum made up of tens of thousands of ivid breathing, clicking their mandibles, and tapping their hard feet against the resin-coated roadways. It was loud enough to make Victor feel as if he was in a machine shop. They walked for probably half an hour before the emissary directed them to the oval opening of one of the stone towers.

The arched entryway was large enough for one of the guardians to hunch within it while leaving room for Lesh and Victor to pass through behind their guide. The guardian didn't even look at them, and it made Victor wonder if the hive's awareness, the entity talking to them through the emissary, was able to control the insects on an individual level or if the emissary was emitting some kind of pheromone to keep the ivid around them placid.

The inside of the tower was much as Victor had imagined it—smooth walls, no furnishings, and round tunnels leading in every direction. The ivid emissary took them on a winding path, past many identical openings, and finally stopped in a round room with soft silken cushions lining the far wall. They looked as though they were made of the same material as the emissary's robes. The ivid turned and gestured with one of its four arms at Victor. "Please wait here, companions, while this one takes this individual to see our queen. He will be returned before the sun crosses the sky twice."

"Two days?" Valla's voice conveyed her alarm as she looked at Victor.

"The brooding center is quite distant."

Lesh frowned, looking around at the bare room. "We must stay within this chamber?"

Valla added her objection. "How will we gauge the time? We cannot see the sun!" Victor supposed she had a point—even if she took a clock or watch from her storage devices, they had no idea how long an ivid day was. How long would it take for the sun to "cross the sky"?

"This one can amend this." The emissary stepped past Valla over to the smooth wall and rested a hand against the stone. Victor felt a violent surge of Energy, pure and potent. Then the stone began to swirl like liquid, receding from the ivid's touch and forming a smooth four-foot-wide tunnel that stretched upward for nearly twenty feet until the pale yellow sky was exposed. "Will the individual companions require sustenance or waste receptacles?"

Victor spoke up on his companions' behalf. "A room to wash up and a toilet would be nice." The emissary didn't respond but touched its hand to the wall again, and Victor felt the familiar surge of potent Energy. A door-sized opening opposite the window appeared, and Victor watched as a tunnel expanded beyond it, rounding a gentle curve. He couldn't see what transpired after that, but he heard the weird liquid sound of shifting stone and, moments later, the faint trickle of water flowing into some sort of basin.

"Please inspect the accommodations and ensure there is nothing else required."

"Thank you, Emissary," Valla said. Then she took Victor's hand and tugged him toward the new exit. "Please allow me to speak to my companion privately as we inspect your work."

The emissary stared at her from its strange, faintly shimmering black eyes, and after a pregnant pause said, "Privacy is an interesting concept. We will endeavor not to hear your vocalizations."

"Thank you." Valla pulled Victor through the opening, and though she didn't say he couldn't come, Lesh sighed and sat down on one of the silky cushions. Once they'd rounded the corner, Victor saw that the emissary had created a spacious and practical bathroom. There were three fountains in an oval space—one shaped like a bath, one like a sink, and one obviously meant to serve as a toilet. The bath-like basin steamed faintly, making it clear that the water was warm. Valla sighed, looking around the room. "Whatever 'memories' it took from those the hive has slain seem to have provided it with the knowledge for making a restroom."

"Yeah, I guess so."

Valla faced Victor, taking his wrists in her cool fingers, concern digging a furrow between her eyes. "What will you do? Are you really going to give this hive your seed?"

"Can you think of another option? I guess we could ask to leave and try to find another way to help Edeya."

"What if it wants to . . . copulate with you?"

"With a giant insect?" Victor tried to keep his voice pitched low, but some incredulity entered his tone.

"It created that emissary to speak with us. What if it creates a . . . concubine for you?"

"Um, not happening, Valla." Victor couldn't imagine the insect hive mind creating anything he'd be willing to have sex with, but even if he could, it didn't feel right putting Valla through that. "Look, it's embarrassing enough trying to imagine giving these insects some of my 'seed,' you know."

"I could offer to come along. To . . . help." She grinned a little mischievously, and Victor chuckled.

"I'm glad you can find some humor in this."

Her smile faded and her eyes narrowed as she said, her tone deadly serious, "You understand what it might mean to give a hive like this your genetic material? It's evident that these ivid have gone through some massive changes since Erd Van last sent explorers here. What might they do with a sample of your Quinametzin heritage?"

"I don't know. It seems kind of far-fetched that they could even use it. There's no way insects and titans were meant to mate. I think they'll need to do a lot with my . . . sample before it's of any use to them. Maybe they just want to study it. Shit, I don't know, Valla. Can you imagine those giant guardians with titan blood? Maybe I should refuse just for the sake of the universe."

She sighed and shook her head. "As much as I want you to be careful, as much as I'd like to find a way around this situation, I'm reminded that the universe is vast. I can't imagine these ivid are the only hive species to reach this level of ascendancy. We know there are worlds where dragons reign. We know there are places where people like Tes are commonplace. You felt the powerful beings striding through the heights of Sojourn. I don't think a sample of your seed given to these insects will upset the balance of the universe." Her eyes narrowed further, and she grew quiet as her expression became decidedly pensive.

"What else?" Victor prodded.

"What if . . . what if it's not looking to do research but to create children? What if it's curious about individuality and wants to make offspring that can think for themselves? Do you want children sprung from your . . ."

"Valla!" Victor cried, then more softly, "Valla, Valla, Valla." He pulled her close, gripping her behind the shoulders and peering down into her eyes. He had half a mind to reduce his height further to more easily hold her close, but he didn't want to interrupt his train of thought. "Anything this hive creates will not be a child of mine. It might have some of my DNA, but come on! I can't imagine a more alien species. Nothing it grows will be anything like me and certainly won't need me to take a role in its life." He laughed, imagining a long-lost half-insect child coming to collect some overdue child support. Valla didn't say anything, so he pressed on. "I'll talk to this queen or, if she can't speak, the emissary, and try to get some reassurances."

"Promise? Promise you'll walk away if it doesn't sound tenable?"

"Promise."

"Well, let's get you going. The sooner you leave, the sooner you'll be back, and the sooner we can leave this strange place." She spoke softly, and though her words said she was ready to head back to the emissary, her face said otherwise. Victor stared at her eyes, the big silvery-teal irises, the soft feathery eyebrows, and all he wanted was to hold her close and get away from all this bullshit. It felt as though he was always going from one emergency to another, and he was fucking sick of it.

"I just want to do that—be done with this bullshit, so I can spend some time with you, doing what we fucking want to do without having to solve some goddamn crisis. If this is what it takes, me giving these asshole bugs some of my *pinché leche*, then I'm going to do it." His voice had grown hoarse with emotion, and when he heard the expletives flowing from his tongue like the old days, he chuckled and shook his head. "Sorry."

"Don't apologize for expressing how we *both* feel." She grabbed the sides of his head and pulled him down so she could kiss him squarely on the mouth. It was a hungry kiss, hot and full of carnal intent, and Victor almost lost it right there. She wouldn't allow that, though, laughing and pushing him off as he tried to push her back toward the bathing fountain. "Come on, now. Get going—time for this when we're done with this hive." Victor calmed himself, nodded, and as they turned to walk back to Lesh and the emissary, she snickered. "Really? Milk?"

Victor groaned. "It's slang . . . and it's Spanish in my head."

"Your language?" Victor had spoken to her about Spanish and English and how strange it was to have all of his words translated the same by the System.

"My dad's language." They'd also talked about their childhoods a few times, and she knew what he meant. She knew he'd never been fluent in his father's language and that it had been one of the many factors giving him a chip on his shoulder when he was younger. He couldn't get into it right then, anyway; they were already back to the "waiting" room. "Ready?" he asked the impassive insect man, still standing where he'd been when he and Valla had left.

"This one will guide you now." It started walking for the hallway they'd come through, but before he followed it, Victor looked at Lesh.

"You good?"

He nodded, rumbling, "I will take this opportunity to meditate, cultivate, and expand my breath Core. Valla and I will be well. Be wary and wise, Lord Victor."

"I will." Victor nodded, then squeezed Valla's hand again before letting go. Her jaw fairly trembled with her desire to say something, but she clamped her lips into a tight line and watched him, unblinking, as he turned and followed the insect into the oval tunnel. When he caught up to his ivid guide, he asked, "Well, Emissary, can I ask if you have a gender?"

It didn't hesitate to answer. "This one is non-gendered."

Victor followed it quietly until they exited the building and started meandering through the city again. Then he decided to try to get some of his many questions answered. "When you met us deep underground, and we walked through the misty opening, was that a portal? Are we very far from the world where we met?"

"We met at the aperture to the hive world. We are not far from the world where we met but within it."

"I don't understand. How can a sky and sun exist within a planet? Are those illusions to make your hive more comfortable?"

"The hive world exists within its own universe, young individual, a universe of our devising." That simple statement carried so many underlying messages that Victor found himself dumbstruck, pondering them all. This hive was creating a universe? Is that what it meant by "our devising"? If they could do that, if they could somehow manufacture worlds and suns . . . Victor couldn't wrap his head around it. It couldn't be that. How could any being create a sun? They were too damned massive. Even the System had called volcanos "sleeping gods." What would it label a sun? What would it label a species that could create a sun?

"Do you create all of the things in this universe? Did you create the sun?"

"We do not create these things; we find them and bridge our universe to the space where the things we covet exist, encapsulating them."

"You coveted the sun?"

"The hive world required heat and light. We found a sun to match our needs and brought it and its planets into our universe. Now we have heat and light and the resources of five planets."

"Did those planets have life?"

"Two, yes. Very plentiful resources."

Victor chewed on those words for a while, stunned by the idea that a species of insect could simply snatch a solar system out of its universe and bring it into its own. What was this universe? Was it a gigantic pocket dimension within the planet where the hive originated? Was it even really inside the planet, or was that simply where the "aperture" was? The train of thought brought another question to mind. "Why do you keep that aperture open? Why do you still have a hive on the planet where we met?"

"The answer to such a question is not easily explained to one not of the hive."

Victor tried a different approach, "What about the System? Are you part of it?"

"We know of the System from the memories of individuals who have joined the hive. This entity has no connection to us." Victor could have guessed as much; if the System were present in the hive, surely it would have translated the insects' native language.

They turned left, past one of the giant conical towers, and, for the first time in the ivid city, the horizon opened up ahead of them. Victor was looking down a long straight stretch of road toward an enormous open area shaped like a hexagon. At its center, on a platform the size of a city block, sat a gigantic beetle with two gas-filled membranes straining against cable-like tendons attached to its back. The membranes were shaped like oblong balloons and looked, from Victor's vantage, to be five or ten times the size of the hot air balloons he'd seen on TV. "What is that thing?"

"That will serve as this one's transport to the brooding planet."

"Brooding *planet?*"

"Yes, this one will guide you to the queen's residence within the hive world."

"That balloon beetle is going to take us to another planet? In less than a day?"

"In less than a day for this planet, yes."

Victor frowned, worried something had been lost in translation. He tried to think of a way to get the answer he wanted out of the emissary. "Can you search your memories for terms my kind use to describe time? For instance, everyone in the System-controlled part of the universe knows what a day or week means. There's a standard. Can you . . ."

"This one apologizes. We have accessed memories that make your meaning clear. Our journey to the brooding planet will take two of your months."

"Goddamn it. Can you somehow communicate to my companions how long this is going to take? It sounds like we'll be gone longer than they expected."

They were walking quickly, the emissary having no trouble setting a pace that had Victor striding with the entire length of his legs. As they descended the sloping road, the beetle's size became more and more impressive. It was roughly as big as one of the gigantic mine dump trucks Victor had seen on a school field trip. He could still remember how unbelievable it had seemed when he'd stood near one of the tires—taller than three adults standing on each other's shoulders. Nowadays, such scale wasn't as impressive, obviously, but the beetle was still something else. They'd closed half the distance before the emissary finally responded.

"We have altered another of our children for speech. It will relay your situation to your companions."

"Ah, shit. Is that what you did for this emissary?"

"This one was created when you were approaching the aperture."

"Then how did it get here? You said the 'brooding planet' was a month's journey."

"This one's Energy reserves and tolerances are much greater than our other children's. We sent it between space."

"Between . . ." Did it mean it teleported? "Can you not do the same for me? Do we really have to ride that beetle for two months?"

The emissary stopped walking for the first time and turned to regard Victor. "We do not believe you will survive such transport." It turned and once again continued toward the beetle. Victor hated the idea that he'd lose so much time and that Valla and Lesh were essentially in prison while they waited for him, but he couldn't think of a way around it. Realizing that, realizing he couldn't even grasp the concept of how it had transported its emissary "between space," he tried one more angle.

"You seem to have great knowledge about universes and worlds and space. Can you not think of a method to transport me that wouldn't be fatal? There are those far more fragile than I who can teleport great distances." Again, the emissary didn't answer immediately, and Victor watched the beetle as they continued toward it. It was black with rather beautiful curlicued orange patterns on its carapace. Its legs were probably fifty feet long, and the pincer-like mandibles jutting from its jaw looked as if they could slice a city bus in half. Now that they were closer, he could see the shimmering, iridescent quality of the air bladders and wondered what kind of gas was in them. Frowning, he studied the beetle for some sort of structure, wondering how they were supposed to ride it . . .

"We have considered your question. The primary difficulty lies in the density of Energy and space around the brooding planet. The forces required for instant traversal of that space would separate your molecules. We will, instead, transport you to a waiting transport beetle outside the dense space." The emissary stopped and turned to face him. "Are you prepared for the journey? This method will shorten transit duration by more than ninety-eight percent."

"Yes! Yes, let's do that." Victor nodded enthusiastically.

"Very well. Please grasp this one's appendage, and it will initiate the transfer." It held out one of its four three-fingered hands, and Victor reached down to grasp it. He'd expected it to be hard, but the chitin was strangely springy and tactile, and the three digits grasped the side of his much larger palm firmly. Then, with a surge of Energy so strong it took the wind out of his lungs and drained the blood from his brain, the world exploded into light, and Victor ceased to exist.

26

※

A SENSE OF SCALE

When Darren left the Genesis Center, he'd had the determined mindset he often felt when he knew he had to prove somebody wrong. If he had the self-awareness to look back on his life, he might have seen a pattern—failure leading to perceived judgment from others, leading to him trying to demonstrate how he'd been right by any means necessary. He'd tried other tactics; he'd tried doing things "their way" many times. In fact, hadn't he tried to put himself in Y-seven's hands? Was it his fault they wouldn't help him unlock his potential? How would he prove himself to Victor and everyone back home if he settled for a middling Core and the least of his affinities?

Part of him was angry Y-seven had ever told him about all of his potential, especially if he'd intended to deny him access to the knowledge he'd need to tap into it. Still, another part of him was grateful. Even if they wouldn't help him, they'd at least made him aware of the latent gifts waiting beneath the surface. He wasn't meant to be a failure; would a failure have so many potent affinities?

Those were the types of thoughts running through his mind as he made his way through the city, farther and farther from the great crystalline towers at its center, toward the glowing dot on his magical map—Rodar's Emporium of Esoteric Knowledge. The directory didn't list things as plainly as he would have liked; there were no entries for "Core Building Instruction," "Affinity Tutoring," or any of the other hundreds of ideas he'd searched for. What it boiled down to, he'd decided, was that he sought knowledge and, so he'd searched under the subheading for libraries and bookshops, and that's when he'd settled on Rodar's business. It just sounded right. At the very least, perhaps this Rodar person would be able to direct him to the right place.

The farther he wandered from the city center and the area where he and his traveling companions had secured lodging, the more diverse and strange the populace seemed. He saw clusters of beings who looked more like deep sea creatures than people—tentacles, sometimes floating, with eyestalks and clothing made of living moss. He saw a man—he assumed based on the beard—with nine-foot-long legs that seemed to be made of hardwood, a turtle's shell, and flesh as green as a Granny Smith apple. He passed a group of doglike ruffians who gave him menacing stares but either feared the laws of Sojourn or determined he wasn't worth their time.

At one street corner, he walked by a group of children with red beetle-like bodies and long black antennae. If he were describing them to a friend, he might say he'd seen some humanoid ladybugs. Along with the innumerable variations in people, the construction of the buildings grew less and less uniform as he meandered. He saw domes made of colored glass, a cylindrical tower with a dozen steam-venting chimneys, and an inverted silo-type building with an endless winding stairway leading down into depths too distant for his eyes to see. He stood against the wrought iron railing around that open pit and stared for a long while, wondering what sorts of people might live or work in such a strange place rather than above ground in the wonderous city.

Despite his many ogling pauses, eventually he came to his destination—a large two-story red-brick building decorated with a dozen elaborate murals. He stood before the wooden door with its inlaid polished stones, admiring the fanciful landscape painted around it. His eyes traced the green hills, the bright stars, and the young, very human-seeming woman leaning against a tree, reading a book, wonder on her face. The artwork reminded him of something he'd seen as a kid, something on a book cover, perhaps, but he couldn't put his finger on it. After a while, feeling good about his decision to visit that particular establishment, he opened the door and stepped into Rodar's Emporium.

Darren was struck by something like vertigo as he walked over the threshold. His brain reeled at the disparity between his expectation and the reality of the interior—shelves of books, equipped with rolling ladders, rose up to a ceiling that had to be a hundred feet above his head. The central row, into which the door opened, stretched so far into the distance that the counter and bookcases behind it seemed tiny from his perspective. The store's interior might well have been the single largest room he'd ever seen, and he'd been in some considerable auditoriums in his day. What boggled his mind, even more than the space that couldn't possibly fit inside the building he'd seen, was that it was utterly crammed with books.

If there were other patrons in the shop, he couldn't see them. Of course, a thousand bookcases were obscuring his view in every direction other than straight ahead, so there was no telling if he were alone. After he gathered himself, accepting that this was undoubtedly just a very advanced use of the same spatial and dimensional magic that made his storage pouches work, he started forward, aiming for the distant counter, hoping there was a proprietor to help him find the knowledge he sought.

He'd only traversed the first hundred yards before a deep voice cleared its throat and spoke up from off to his right, coming from behind the nearest towering bookcase. "Welcome in, stranger. Might I help you find something?"

Darren paused and looked at the case, peering between a shelf and the books below it, trying to spy the speaker. "Um, hello. I certainly hope so because I'm quite overwhelmed by the number of books I see!"

"Haha! Yes, old Rodar is quite the collector. He buys out libraries regularly." As he spoke, a figure emerged from behind the books, surprising Darren with his appearance. Despite his deep voice, he was quite diminutive, a three-foot-tall man who looked remarkably like a bipedal hedgehog wearing a green and brown pinstriped vest and pants. "I am Rodar's assistant, Ferl."

"Pleased to meet you. I'm Darren." He gestured around him at the cavernous space and its millions of books and asked, "Is there any sort of system to all of this?"

"Oh, of course! Rodar wrote the cataloging spells himself. We have sprites that gather and organize the books on a constant basis."

"Sprites?"

"You aren't familiar? Magical entities with a penchant for various things. The ones Rodar employs are knowledge sprites or book sprites. Hmm, I believe he has an ink sprite or two. In any case, they keep things well organized and maintain Rodar's catalog." He stepped closer, peering through beautifully crafted amber-tinted crystal spectacles up at Darren. "What can old Ferl help you find, youngster?"

Darren was slightly taken aback by the little furry man's choice of words, but he held his tongue, trying to remember some of the humility he'd been working so hard to display when near Victor and his companions. "I, well, you see, I come from a world where Energy is very new. I don't know much about it or Cores and whatnot. I was hoping to find some texts to learn from."

"Ah! I'm sure I can find quite a lot on that subject, but have you visited the Genesis . . ."

Darren held up a hand, cutting him off. "I've been there and learned a few things, but it's not for me. I prefer self-study."

"Well, this is the right place for that. Let's see here." Ferl held out his left palm, and a heavy black leather-bound book appeared. "My copy of the catalog," he said by way of explanation. He placed his pointer finger atop an inlaid silver rune and closed his eyes. When he opened them a moment later, the book flipped open, and the pages, thin and densely filled with text, fanned with a rustling whir. Several seconds later, the pages stopped moving, and Ferl peered at the page the book had settled on. "Row ninety-seven, stack fourteen, shelves one through eighty-four."

"That was quick. Can you point me in . . ."

"I'll lead you there. Not much else to do, if I'm honest. The sprites handle most of my job." Ferl turned and began waddling, for there wasn't a better way to describe his gait, up the central aisle. "Other sections might suit your needs, but I think this is the best one. It's categorized as 'Core Development by Affinity Type.' Have you purchased books from Rodar's before?"

"No, this is my first visit."

"In that case, I should explain the usage policy—Rodar doesn't run a charity. You may peruse the books at your leisure, but the enchantments of this emporium will prevent you from seeing anything beyond the first one percent of the pages."

"That's . . . fair. So if I want to read more, I'll need to purchase the books?"

"Exactly so."

"What if you have a book with only a single page?"

"Hah! I can't say I've seen any single-page books, but we do have many with fewer than a hundred. We also sell scrolls. You can rest assured, my good lad, the magic is clever. It will prevent you from reading more than a single percent of the content. My earlier explanation is generally enough for the youngsters we get in the emporium. I'm impressed by your curious wit!"

Darren couldn't ignore the continued references to his age, so he asked, "Excuse me, Ferl, but how old do you think I am?"

"Oh, I've no idea! We get all sorts of species in here, and they all have different ideas about what constitutes adulthood."

"But you keep calling me things like youngster. Why is that?"

"Well, you've barely a whiff of Energy about you! I assumed you were a child."

"No, I'm a grown man, sir. As I said, Energy is new to our world."

"Apologies, then, sir." Though his words said one thing, his tone said another—Ferl was patronizing him, Darren was sure. Regardless, he let the matter drop; he needed the little man's help, after all. "If you don't mind me asking, how did you come to visit Sojourn? Surely, if you've not even had a chance to cultivate a Core, you couldn't have built up a System Stone capable of transporting you here. Did a powerful Energy user visit your world? Did they open a portal for you?"

"Yes, sir, something along those lines." As they walked, turning down one long row of books after another, Darren plied the furry well-dressed little man for information. "How will I know the cost of a book? Will you stay with me while I peruse?"

"Each book is clearly marked with a price in Energy beads. Rodar has been known to consider other trades, but we'd prefer to keep our exchanges simple. As for whether I'll stay with you, that's entirely up to you. As I said, I've time to help, and so long as another customer doesn't require my service, I will be happy to attend you."

"Well, thank you. Are there books that are . . ." Darren tried to think of the best way to phrase his question. He'd been about to say "banned" but figured that might be a bit too severe a term. "Restricted to certain, um, castes?"

"Restricted? That's the case, though caste would be the wrong word. Rodar protects the innocent by placing dangerous books in a separate section."

"Dangerous? As in dangerous ideas, or do you mean something more literal?"

"Oh, quite literal! Some books would turn you or me to dust if we read them; their contents are meant for those of significant power."

"So, these books, the ones you're taking me to see, will they have information about all sorts of affinities and Cores or only those deemed appropriate by society?"

"Society? Why, this world is a crossroads. You realize this, yes? What one society deems acceptable, another might consider abhorrent. Rodar, wisely, does not take sides."

"Just what I wanted to hear, Ferl. Thank you." As he spoke, Ferl stopped walking and gestured to the towering stack of shelves on his left.

"Here we are, Darren. Now, I can help you sift through these if you'll just tell me the affinities you are interested in. I believe that's how the sprites sorted them . . ." He paused and ran his finger along the spines on a shelf at his nose level. "Yes, yes, that's it. Here we have a whole row about Cores for various nature affinities."

"That will be very helpful! Let's see, I'm most interested in learning about chaos and mind affinities. Do you think there are any books on those subjects?"

"Chaos and mind? My, my! I see why you were curious about Rodar's policies on restricted subject matter. No matter, no matter. Let's see here . . ." Ferl's words trailed off as he peered through his special glasses at the shelf, his odd button-like black nose twitching as he mumbled titles to himself.

Darren grinned, excitement filling his belly with butterflies, relief washing over him, banishing the unspoken worries he'd been battling the entire time they'd walked through the bookstore. Part of him had been sure the books he sought would be locked away or banned from sale in the city. He'd thought that if the Genesis Center was so concerned about the affinities, undoubtedly the city would have rules about them. He'd feared he'd have to find an illicit merchant, someone selling things on a black market of sorts. "I love a free market," he said, mostly to himself, but he thought he saw an answering gleam in Ferl's eyes.

Victor swore he felt his body coming apart, shredded, atom by atom. It was the most agonizing thing he'd ever experienced, and though it happened in an instant, it felt more like a thousand years. Time stretched and yawned, light bent and streamed around him, the individual waves of photons speckling his vision in cascades of brilliant dots. Not a single thought entered his mind while simultaneously he re-experienced every second of his lifetime. He thought he'd go mad; he thought he was mad, his consciousness dashed to bits by the potent, solar-system-moving power of the hive channeled through the emissary's hand into Victor.

Later, when he looked back at the experience, he'd never be able to truly recall the horror of that infinite-seeming instant, as that moment of time and space dilated to infinity and then snapped back, ripping him from one part of the universe and inserting him into another without care or concern for the rules of physics. One second, Victor was standing in the enormous square, looking at the giant beetle; the next, he was in an empty glass-walled room, looking down at the curve of a verdant green planet as whatever carried him descended through layers of swirling silver Energy. That time between, that eternity of horror, disappeared from his mind, and all he remembered was that instant, hurtling transition.

When he felt the glass beneath his feet and saw the madness of the view before him, Victor fell to his knees and heaved his guts out onto the smooth surface. As the contents of his stomach—his most recent meal and a large quantity of fluid—sloshed away from him toward the smooth curve where the glass wall met the glass floor, hot embarrassment flushed his neck and ears, and he looked up to see the emissary regarding him. "Are you unwell?" it asked.

"The . . . transition," Victor started to say, unable to find the words to explain what had made him ill. He felt something had happened during the teleportation, something that had bothered him, but it was like trying to remember a dream; all he could grasp was the vaguely disturbed sensation that something bad had occurred.

"Ah. The transport, while survivable, was difficult for you to tolerate. This one did not experience difficulty, but other members of the hive have suffered worse. It is good that you yet live."

"Was . . ." Victor coughed and stood up, his wooziness fading. "Was it in doubt? Were you not sure I'd live through that?"

"We were certain your flesh would tolerate the transport, but we failed to consider the fragility of your mind. We'll endeavor to modify our transport spell for your return, ensuring an easier transition for your consciousness."

"That would be nice." Victor coughed again, summoned a bottle of water from his ring, and drank it. He was starting to feel normal again; the sensation that something was wrong had nearly faded. Looking down, he wasn't surprised to see that his vomit was gone; somehow, the emissary, or perhaps whatever vehicle they were in, had cleaned it up. The "vehicle" passed through another swirling, shimmering layer of silvery Energy—Victor wasn't sure how he knew it was Energy, but somehow he did. As the sparkling flashes faded, he saw that they were much closer to the planet's surface, enough so that he could make out individual trees.

"Big trees," he noted.

"Vast and wonderful in their ability to house and channel Energy." The emissary didn't say more, but it didn't need to. Victor could feel the Energy in the air; not only were they passing through dense rings or layers of it, but the planet felt like a smoldering roiling ball of it to his inner eye, the one that saw and felt Energy in and around himself. In the past, he'd looked inward to his Core and been proud and impressed by the power there. Now, in the face of this planet and the power radiating from it, he felt like a speck of dust being tossed around in Jupiter's atmosphere. He was nothing to the power before him.

He blurted the thought that came to mind, unable to stop the words forming on his tongue. "You guys don't need my DNA."

"This one is not familiar with the term."

"My genetics. The information in my 'seed,' as you put it."

"Ah. The hive wishes to expand its universe. Thus, all knowledge has value. We will learn much of interest from your elder genetics."

"Expand? Are you going to take over other solar systems like this one?"

"We think not. We are on the verge of something monumental, something that will allow us to release our hold on our origin world. Soon, we will transcend the need for other-made matter and Energy. Soon, we will spark our first hive-made sun."

"Spark . . ." Victor swallowed, unable to think of a proper reply. Instead, he asked, "You always say 'we' or 'this one.' Am I ever going to meet you? Are you the queen speaking through this emissary?"

"We have met. This one contains part of me, as do all members of the hive. Still, when you meet the queen, you will meet one with individual thoughts. Brace yourself, for the transport will now rapidly descend. Behold and be honored—you are the first outside individual to visit the brooding palace." The emissary gestured to the clear glass wall, and Victor looked to see that the trees he'd thought enormous were, in fact, absurdly so.

He hadn't had anything to measure them against until now, but as he looked out, he saw a pyramid growing huge as the ship, or whatever it was, rapidly approached. It was a smooth-sided pale rust-colored structure, but the slopes were decorated with immense carvings of ivid faces, their eyes tiled with millions of glittering blue and black gemstones. He barely registered the pyramid, though, because he kept dragging his eyes back to the trees that towered over it, dozens of times larger. From the perspective as they approached, he guessed that the pyramid was several thousand feet tall at its apex, meaning the millions of trees they'd flown over were miles tall.

"Holy shit."

27

CRYSTAL

When the vehicle or insect carrying Victor and the emissary descended to the immense pyramid's base, depositing the glass carriage to the smooth sandstone ground, it settled with an almost delicate series of *clinks*. Then a dark shadow moved away, and Victor craned his neck, looking through the translucent ceiling to see a great shape rapidly climbing into the air, its precise form obscured by the streamers of bright sunlight filtering through thick white cumulus clouds. "Was that one of those giant beetles?"

"This is an accurate description." The emissary strode toward one of the glass walls, and with a *pop* and *tinkle,* their conveyance burst into billions of silvery motes of Energy. Victor stumbled briefly as he fell several inches to the sandstone, and when he straightened and looked around, he saw no sign of the vessel that had transported them to the planet's surface. From his current vantage, the trees surrounding the pyramid looked like skyscrapers, and if it weren't for the clearing around the structure, he was sure he wouldn't be able to see the sky through their thick canopy. He turned to the pyramid and saw that the emissary was several paces away already but had turned to regard him.

"I'm coming." Victor followed him toward an opening in the pyramid— a yawning passage that could easily allow a dozen passenger planes to fly through it at once. As they approached and its scale became apparent, and the pyramid's height grew too distant to see, he said, "Why is the pyramid so damn big? Do you have, um, children that need an opening that size?"

"This pyramid houses our young in their millions before they move off to other facilities. Every eleven of our days, a brood must pass through the nineteen stages of this structure." The emissary spoke almost offhandedly, but Victor's mind reeled at the idea, trying to imagine the hordes of ivid children as they hurried through their mysterious stages.

Of course, he voiced the most disturbing of his thoughts. "How can your queen lay so many damn eggs? Is she gigantic?"

"The queen is similar in size to your titanic form. Fear not for her health, for while her eggs are great in number, they are tiny, and their production does not overly tax her."

"Huh." Victor watched the streams of ivid moving down avenues lined with trees, into and out of the pyramid, and flying in endless streams from the heights. After they'd walked for a while and were still quite far from the great opening, he asked, "Why no wings for your emissary?"

"This one has wings, though you cannot currently see them. Our journey is short, however, traveler. The queen will see you in one of her gardens."

"The queen has gardens?" Victor's imagined idea of an insect queen laying eggs in a massive underground nest began to crumble.

"Please be patient, individual. This one will save explanations for the queen."

"All right." Victor grew quiet and let his eyes explore as they walked. To his surprise, they didn't enter the pyramid but took a side path that led toward the distant corner of the structure. As they progressed, he found many such side paths meandering up and down stairs, into walled-off sections of the grounds, and even down into steeply sloping tunnels. From the air, the grounds had seemed flat, covered in stone, and simply there to provide a clearing for the pyramid. "This is different than I'd imagined. It's . . . pretty."

"We appreciate your complimentary language. The queen has particular aesthetics." The emissary led him around a high sandstone wall, then through a red crystal gate that swung open noiselessly. Victor found himself standing in a garden of tall hedgerows bedecked in immense purple and red flowers. He couldn't see far in any direction because of the enormity of the hedges, but what he could see was something out of a fantasy, for it wasn't simply the flowers and perfect hedges, but the attendant ivid that drew his eyes.

They wore shimmering silvery robes, not unlike the emissary's, and carried delicate crystalline clippers, but more than that, they hardly looked insectoid. Unlike the emissary's robes, theirs were hooded and veiled, and their hands were covered in gloves of the same material. If Victor had seen those strange silent gardeners elsewhere, he'd have assumed they were just ordinary people under those garments, not members of a bizarre alien insect species. The emissary pointed to one of the clipper-bearing hooded ivid. "These are attendants to the queen. She will be nearby."

"Ah." Victor nodded, unsure what else to say. He followed the emissary through the maze of hedgerows until he stepped through into a wide clearing dominated by a crystal fountain with fluted spouts that delicately dropped clear water into a basin filled with floating purple and red flower buds. The ground at the center of the clearing wasn't tiled in sandstone like the rest of the area Victor had seen but covered in a well-manicured lawn. Reclining on that lawn was a being that had to be the ivid queen.

Her robes were made of silky material just like all the others Victor had seen, except for their color—rather than silver, they were golden. As the emissary had indicated, she was large, but not the gigantic building-sized insect with a bulbous egg-laying appendage that science fiction movies had told Victor to expect. No, she was shaped very much like the other bipedal ivid. She had a crystal device in front of her, sitting on a small delicate wooden table, and was busily shifting tiny levers and strings with her four delicate hands. Victor couldn't see her face through her golden diamond-studded veil, but he could see her eyes, and they were beautiful, if alien.

The ivid he'd met so far all had ten black eyes with an iridescent sheen. The queen's were fully iridescent, shimmering in rainbow hues, with a silvery backlight that shone forth. More, there were only two of them, angular and inset beneath a hairless brow that was absent on the other insects. The emissary stopped walking as soon as they rounded the corner into the clearing, and it held two of its hands out, indicating that Victor should stop as well. "Please wait for the queen's attention, individual."

Victor nodded and stood still, looking around the clearing, slowly becoming aware of all the other ivid in the area. They stood like statues near the hedges, robed attendants, guardians with metallic carapaces, and another sort of warrior ivid with twin crystalline blades crossed before their chests. Victor counted twenty-one altogether. When he turned his gaze inward, opening his inner eye, Victor saw that the ivid around him were all restraining prodigious auras. If he had to guess, he'd say the twenty-one attendants in that clearing were on par with the emissary in power. Still, when Victor tried to gaze at the queen with that inner eye, he found it akin to looking at the sun with his eyes, and he had to turn away quickly. The being before him was exceptional on a scale he couldn't quite wrap his head around.

The queen didn't look up, but a sharp melodic voice, clear and natural, sounded in Victor's head. "You may approach, outsider." Immediately, the emissary's hands dropped to its side, and it stepped away from Victor, clearing the path forward.

Victor nodded and started toward her. He was no longer altering his size, but he wasn't berserk, so he felt rather puny approaching the enormous insectoid monarch. Her size was an insignificant factor, though, for within her raged the power of a being on the scale of deities. This was a being capable of moving worlds, capable of, as the emissary had mentioned, sparking suns.

"Your thoughts are inaccurate, outsider. While I am the focal point of their efforts, those powers belong to the hive. I am but a vessel for all of us."

"You're an individual, though?"

"I am. In our evolution, we have seen the value of having some individuals in the hive. We see things from perspectives the hive could not fathom in its infancy." After a slight pause, the voice resumed. "Ah, you wonder how clearly your thoughts unfold before me. Quite clearly. No, Victor, I do not intend to force you to mate with me. I will take the promised payment, and the gift of a dreaming egg will be yours. You are made uncomfortable by my intrusion . . . apologies, Victor. I will withdraw from your mind."

Victor felt the weight of the alien mind pull away, and he sighed in relief, tension falling from his neck and spine. The queen had entered his thoughts so suddenly, and her presence had been so powerful, that he'd almost been struck dumb, struggling to keep up with her one-sided conversation as he fought to contain his emotions. His prideful outrage was a tiny voice beside his relief, so he simply muttered, "Thank you."

"Let us speak, Victor." This time, the queen's voice came from behind her veil, smooth and clear. "While listening to you and your companions, we endeavored to improve upon the vocal capabilities we granted our emissary. Does my voice please your ears?"

"Um, yes, it's very clear."

"If I hadn't learned your name from listening to your conversations, I would have learned it when I rudely invaded your mind. My apologies. You may call me Crystal."

"Crystal?"

"Yes. Until this moment, I did not have a name, but this one came to me during my brief exploration of your thoughts. You found our fountain to be beautiful, and that word stood out. Will it suit?"

Victor swallowed, nodding. "Yes, it's a nice name."

"I know our emissary told you that you're the first individual to visit this planet. We find you intriguing, but I'd like you to know that these circumstances only came about through happenstance. Earlier visitors to our origin hive were more violent in their intrusion, and our more autonomous defenses saw their demise. Additionally, we've made many strides in recent years, and our . . . understanding of alien nature has become more comprehensive."

"Is, um, have you always been the queen?"

"No, Victor. My life serves the hive, and so have the lives of the many queens before me. When the hive deems it necessary, I will be replaced. I believe I have much time to enjoy my gardens and my trivialities"—she gestured to the crystal device on the table before her—"before that happens."

She smiled and laughed, a soft delicate sound that didn't seem right coming from an eighteen-foot-tall insect lady. "I listened to your conversation with the emissary. You know we are on the verge of great things. We do not believe in deities, but we believe in fate and the bonds of spirits on the ethereal plane, ties that are difficult to see but hard to miss once they've been exposed. You were meant to come here, and it is fortuitous that it happened at this hour. Soon, we will sever our connection to our origin world and be gone from the universe we once called home. Contact with us will be impossible for most beings. I am pleased that we will have your bloodline to study as we separate."

"About that . . ." Victor cleared his throat and shuffled a little nervously. "What exactly are your intentions with my . . . bloodline?" He decided he was tired of talking about his "seed" and went with her choice of phrasing.

"You walk proudly with the blood of an elder race. There are those among the elder species who gained power enough to ascend beyond the mortal realms. While we toil to craft our own niche, our own pocket carved out of the void, we do so with the intent to continue our advancement, to move onto a higher plane. We hope that your bloodline will provide clues in that endeavor. It will be a millennia-long task, but one to which we are quite well attuned."

"So, you're not going to create a species of, um, titan-insects to take over the universe?"

Again, that trilling laugh sounded, and the queen shifted where she sat, lying down on her side in the grass, head propped up with one of her arms so she could more easily look Victor in the eyes. "Why would we trouble ourselves with your universe when we are creating our own? Our kind is not smitten with material things or the worship of lesser beings. We seek elevation and true enlightenment, which cannot be found in the subjugation or destruction of others."

"I hope that's true. I hope you're right, I mean. There are powerful people in the worlds I've visited who believe strength comes only through the conquering of others."

"For a time, that seems true; the theft of Energy from others and the gathering of resources far and wide serve to provide advancement, but we are beyond that. We generate more Energy each second than the consumption of a hundred heroes like yourself could provide. No, we have determined that growth at the cost of destruction is no longer a wise course. You can see it wasn't always so. Did you note the world of our origin hive? It shames me to say we killed it. Only our more instinctive children now live in its soil."

"But you stole this whole solar system, right?"

"Yes. Again, we have learned lessons from each stage of our development. Such theft is no longer necessary; we have learned many secrets in the study of this star. Victor, do you know about stars? That they aren't gods or fires but massive generators? I oversimplify—of course, they burn, so there is fire, but it's only a side effect. I was newly born when we annexed these planets and our sun, and the revelations in my lifetime from its study have moved us forward so . . ." The queen stopped speaking and cocked her head sideways as though listening to something.

Her hypnotic, beautiful eyes stared into space for several long seconds, and Victor looked around nervously. None of the other ivid had moved. "Is, um, Queen Crystal, is everything all right?"

"Apologies, Victor. A matter of some import will soon require my attention. Shall we conclude our business so our emissary might guide you back to your companions and thence on your way?"

Victor swallowed, looking around the garden, very aware of all the ivid standing around. It wasn't so much that he was embarrassed, but he wasn't exactly sure he could even perform with everyone looking at him. How was she going to get his . . . sample? "Um, yeah. I mean, sure. How, exactly . . ."

"If you will permit me, I have the means to painlessly retrieve a small sample of the seed that lies within your sexual organs. I will not harm you, Victor." She laughed softly, and Victor wished he could see her face behind the veil, wondering if she was smiling or if she could even smile. With that thought, he decided he was glad he couldn't see; he'd rather imagine she had a nice mouth with friendly lips and not mandibles or something worse. "I know from the memories we have of outside individuals that this might be rather mortifying. Think of this as a business transaction, Victor. Just as I'll soon have a sample of your material, you'll be walking away with one of my very own eggs, a dreaming ivid fetus that has been nourished and kept alive with great care."

"All right. You can collect it so long as you promise not to take one of my *cojones*." Victor snorted, amused by his absurd turn of phrase.

The queen took him seriously. "Nothing of the sort." She held out one of her golden-gloved hands, and suddenly a tiny crystal jar appeared on her palm. It was minuscule in her hand, but Victor could see it was small by any measure, not much larger than the sewing thimble his *abuela* used to wear on her thumb when she mended his torn jeans. "We are in agreement?"

"Yes."

"Excellent." Victor felt a pulse of Energy, experienced a slight sensation of warmth, and then the crystal jar flashed and disappeared. "That's your half of the bargain. Now, please carefully accept the dreaming egg from our emissary. Please never send it into one of your crude storage devices; it would be torture." As she spoke, Victor felt the emissary's presence as it stepped beside him, and when he turned to face it, he saw that it held a blue silk-wrapped bundle.

"Thank you," he said, accepting it. He could feel the egg within, round, pliable, and warm, about the size of a soccer ball. He could feel the Energy pulsing steadily from it.

"I am pleased by you, Victor," the queen said as he carefully cradled the egg in the crook of his elbow, tucking it against his chest. "May I give you a gift?"

Victor looked back at her and raised an eyebrow. "You've already been kind. I was very damn nervous about providing my, uh, sample. You made it painless."

"Are you refusing further gifts, then?"

"Hey, if there aren't any strings attached, I'm not going to turn down a gift."

The queen nodded and gestured to the emissary, and it hurried away. "The emissary will fetch my gift for you. I am doing something the hive doesn't understand—being impulsive. I have few individuals to interact with; the seven of us have important roles to fill, and our duties do not often allow for it. Impulsivity is something I've only recently begun to explore, but I must be cautious; worlds are at stake when it comes to my actions. This whim, the desire to gift you with something valuable, feels harmless, but I suppose there is some risk to you."

"Risk?"

"My gift is potent and, outside our hive, something that would be nigh impossible to acquire. I'm giving you a sample of the royal jelly my attendants fed to me in order to make me a queen. It's the same substance they will feed to my replacement. I do not feel it will threaten our hive at all to give you this small sample. You will take it away to your world, and soon, we will be separated from your universe. For this reason, I'm willing to risk the unknown effects it will have upon you. It will be up to you to decide if you are willing to take that same risk."

"Ah . . ." Victor didn't know how to respond. For once, his mouth, both the polite and impolite versions, was struck dumb.

"We have not fed this jelly to those not of the hive, but you have the constitution of an elder race, Victor. I believe you will survive and reap some benefits. Still, it would be wise to grow more powerful on your own first. Use this gift when you have encountered a ceiling with regard to your advancement."

"All right. Well, thank you. I'm, um, honored, Queen Crys—"

"Simply call me Crystal. No one else in my life would do so."

Victor looked into those weirdly alien, hypnotically beautiful eyes and smiled. She was a person, no matter how powerful and strange, and she was clearly very lonely. In a way, he wished he could spend more time with her, but in another way, he was ready to be away from that strange place. Still, his smile was genuine, and impulsively, he stepped forward, holding out his free hand. "Thank you, Crystal," he said as the alien insect queen took his hand in hers, and he felt the spark of her power lurking beneath the flesh, enough power to destroy worlds.

28

THE RETURN

The longest part of Victor's return trip was the slow ascent upward through the enormous brooding planet's atmosphere. First, he had to wait for what felt like half a day for the great beetle to return. He did so in the expansive courtyard of the pyramid, following the emissary from one garden to another, taking in the scenery and trying to build memories solid enough to last a lifetime; he kept reminding himself that he was in a different universe entirely and that the chances of him or anyone he knew ever returning to the ivid world were microscopically small. So he stared at the strange crystal fountains and the decorative mosaics of glittering gemstones—art from an alien mind—and tried to imprint them in his mind, images he could conjure up in times of reflection.

When the beetle came, and the emissary recreated the glass bubble for them to ride in, Victor sat on the floor and watched the great planet slowly recede as they rose into space. It was an experience he wanted to savor, a memory to add to the collection of his visit to these strange, powerful beings. It was evident to him that the ivid had somehow gone around the System, somehow found a way to advance their species to the level of transcendence; they wouldn't just be moving to their own universe, but they'd be progressing beyond this reality, moving on to the next stage, whatever that was. One thing he was sure of, though, was that he'd gained new perspectives on power, individuality, and the many roads and doorways that might seem closed but were waiting to be opened with the proper application of leverage.

The ivid queen had indicated that they were "generating" Energy, which created more questions for Victor, questions the emissary didn't seem capable of answering. He supposed that might not be the case; the emissary's silence might just as well indicate an unwillingness as much as an inability. The ivid had their secrets, and Victor would have to content himself with the clues he'd seen. As the mossy green orb of the ivid brooding planet fell away, becoming smaller and smaller, and flickers of dense Energy indicated the beetle's passage into deeper space, the emissary spoke, breaking an hours-long silence. "We will soon move between space again, individual. This passage will be more comfortable for you, as we've modified the technique to shield your mind."

"All right. Should I stand?"

"That will not be necessary. Are you ready?" The emissary stepped closer to him, holding out one of its three-fingered hands. Victor nodded, but his hands were full—he still cradled the dreaming egg, and clutched in his free hand was the warm, spherical crystal container of amber-colored royal jelly. It was about the size of a billiard ball, but Victor estimated its weight at something like fifty pounds. It was dense in more than one way—when he turned his inner eye toward it, it blazed like a miniature sun. He'd never seen an inert substance with such potency, and the idea of consuming it gave him serious pause.

"Ah, um, this is all right to put in a storage container?"

"Yes, though your spatial devices will degrade rapidly as they attempt to contain the royal jelly. We recommend . . ." The ivid trailed off as it reached up to its shoulder and, with the precision of a laser scalpel, severed its voluminous sleeve. It held the length of fabric out to Victor. "Use this as a sling. You can hang the orb of jelly from your belt until you've acquired a more durable storage device. This material will have the added benefit of shielding the jelly's potency from casual observation."

"Ah!" Victor gently set the egg down in his lap, then took the sleeve, pulling it over the heavy crystal globe. Once it was nestled in the tough magical silk, he tied the two ends together and then looped the extra length around his belt, tying it off. "Thank you." He picked up the egg, tucked it against his chest, and then reached up to take the emissary's hand. White light flooded his vision, and then he found himself sitting on a smooth, glazed roadway leading to the great aperture that led from the hive world back to the ivid's "origin world." Valla and Lesh sat nearby, facing each other, speaking quietly.

"We have returned," the emissary said, and Valla leaped to her feet in surprise. Lesh made a reptilian hiss, clearly also startled, and scrambled to his feet, reaching for Belagog.

"Victor!" Valla cried, rushing to him. Victor, meanwhile, was clambering to his feet, awkwardly cradling the priceless egg.

"Hey, beautiful." He smiled as she grasped his free hand, helping him up. "Mission successful!" He glanced at Lesh, nodded, and then jerked his head toward the enormous misty opening in the mountainside. "We ready to get out of here?"

Lesh strode forward, nodding. "We were surprised when the other emissary told us to await you here this morning. We thought you'd be gone longer."

"Yeah, I think the, uh, intelligence behind the emissary perfected their teleportation magic while I spoke to the queen."

"We made improvements." The emissary nodded its expressionless ten-eyed head. "This one will accompany you through the aperture and, once on the origin world, move you safely out of the hive."

Lesh frowned and rumbled, "Move us?"

"A trivial jump between space."

Victor laughed, shaking his head. "Don't worry, Lesh. It's painless." With his free hand, he took Valla's and started toward the opening. "Come on. Let's get back to Sojourn. I'm ready to be done with this weird quest." He heard Lesh's heavy footsteps behind him, then he stepped into the misty air hanging in the opening, and when he'd taken half a dozen steps, he found himself beneath the crossed blades of the guardians' polearms. He was, once again, deep in the ivid hive. The guardians didn't react to him; it almost seemed that they hadn't moved since their party had gone into the hive world, but Victor couldn't believe that was the case. They'd been in there for more than a day, maybe closer to two.

He turned, still holding Valla's hand, to watch Lesh and the emissary come through the opaque archway, and when their shadows resolved into their flesh and blood bodies, he nodded to the emissary. "Can you take us up from right here?"

"This one will do so. Please, each of you, take one of this one's hands." It held its four arms out to the sides, palms up, and Victor reached for one of them. Seeing his quick compliance, Valla followed suit, and then Lesh took one of the two free hands on the ivid's left side. Another flash of white light clouded Victor's mind, and then he was standing on the dead grass atop the hive beneath the hazy yellow sky of the ivid home world.

"That was sudden!" Lesh grunted, stumbling back in surprise, shielding his eyes from the glaring orange sun. Valla coughed, holding an elbow to her nose, as the weird chemical scent of the air began to make all of their eyes water.

"This one will leave you here, travelers. We bear a final word of caution: Do not return to this place, for its departure from this universe is imminent."

Victor nodded, and Valla said, a slight wheeze in her voice, "Thank you."

The insect nodded, and then, with a surge of potent Energy, it was gone, and they were standing alone, very near the spot where they'd first arrived. "Is that the egg?" Lesh asked, looking at Victor's cradled bundle of silk.

"Yep."

"And this?" Valla touched the sling of silver-gray silk hanging at his belt.

"A gift from the queen. Something too potent for any of us to contemplate consuming yet."

"Consuming?" Lesh rumbled, and Valla's eyebrow arched.

"A heart?" she guessed.

"No, but something just as good, I'm sure."

"Just as good . . ." Valla scoffed and shook her head.

Lesh had had enough dillydallying—he held up his coin-shaped token of recall and asked, "Shall we be gone from this place?"

Victor nodded, summoning his token from his ring. "Do we just channel Energy into it?"

"That's right." Lesh nodded and looked at Valla, ensuring she was ready.

"You guys first," Victor said, watching Valla delicately twirl the token between her long nimble fingers.

"As you say," Lesh said, then with a crackle of silvery Energy, the coin rippled with light and power, expanding with a bright slow-motion flash that vanished with a soft *pop*. Lesh was gone.

"He was ready to go!" Valla laughed.

"Yeah, this trip wasn't what he'd hoped. He hardly got to fight a single bug." Victor chuckled and shook his head, then nodded to Valla. "Your turn."

"Together." She held up her token, locking eyes with him.

"All right." Victor gripped his token in his fist and counted down. "Three, two, one . . ." Just as when they'd teleported via the System from world to world, he felt the transition as he hurtled through space back to Sojourn. It was a decidedly different experience now that he'd tasted the teleportation magic of the ivid. Somehow, he was aware of the enormity of the distance he traveled, and it wasn't instantaneous. Still, when he appeared in the World

Hall back on Sojourn, he barely stumbled as his feet caught up with his brain, and his senses were pounded with the sounds, sights, and smells of the vastly different location.

To his relief, Valla and Lesh were there, and she ran to him, hugging her arms around his waist. "I thought you were deceiving us somehow. I thought you'd made some damnable bargain and had to remain or go elsewhere."

"Why?" Victor laughed.

"Because you told us to go first!" She punched him in the shoulder.

Lesh rumbled a deep laugh. "I didn't fear any such thing."

"Because you don't know him well enough!" Valla cried.

"All right, all right. We're here, so just relax." He shifted the ivid egg from his left arm to the right and nodded toward it as he did so. "Let's go deliver this thing, 'cause I'm ready to see Edeya get some damn help. I'm ready to be done running from one fire to the next. 'Bout time we did something we want for a change, don't you think?"

"Mmhmm." Valla nodded and took his hand, walking with him as Victor moved off the metal teleportation disc toward one of the sunlit exits. Lesh followed behind, but as they exited the building into the shadows of tall dazzling sunlit crystal towers, the big dragonkin stepped up beside Victor and grasped his shoulder to get his attention.

"Lord Victor . . ."

"Victor's fine, man."

"Yes. I was wondering if you'd mind if I took my leave and returned to the inn. I've a mind to check in on my charge."

"Ah, yeah. I wonder how old Darren got along with his training. Yeah, sure, Lesh. Valla and I can deliver this egg."

"Thank you. I'll await word of your success at the inn, then." He nodded to Valla. "Lady . . ."

"Just Valla, Lesh." She giggled and winked, and Victor knew she was making fun of him.

Lesh rumbled his deep purr-like laugh, the one Victor was beginning to understand was reserved for things that genuinely amused him. He nodded his big flat angular head, and then he was gone, striding purposefully away from the city center. "He's a character when you get to know him," Valla said, squeezing Victor's fingers.

"Yeah. He's a good guy, but I'd hate to be Darren if he hasn't behaved himself." Victor laughed at the idea and started walking, falling in behind a large group of black-robed women, each with their long red hair coiled atop their heads and adorned with jewel-laden veils. It still rankled something in him to know that people the society of Sojourn found "greater than" were striding along the shimmering rainbow-laced walkways above his head, but something was different now that he'd tasted the power of the ivid. There were things in the universe that could humble the beings above him, so why should he be upset that they did so to him? All it meant was that he knew he had growing yet to do, and there was something worthy in that—having a goal to attain.

It didn't take them long to reach their destination. As the building where Erd Van kept his shop came into view, Victor paused and looked back, noting the distance they'd traveled. "There's some *pinché* magic going on here."

"Hmm?"

"I think the sidewalks make you move faster than normal. Look." Victor pointed to the distant crystal towers. "We've covered something like ten miles, but it only took us, what? Twenty minutes? We weren't exactly running."

I . . ." Valla looked back, then turned and looked at Erd Van's shop. "I think you're right!"

"Funny we didn't notice it before. Must have been too immersed in finding our way."

A passing woman, small and round, wearing a bright yellow cloak tied tightly beneath the wagging flesh of her extra chin, looked up at him with angular deep red eyes and said, "Pardon my intrusion, but I couldn't help hearing your conversation. These walkways will speed up your travel, but only if you know your destination and don't pay attention to your surroundings. The trick is to let your feet do the walking and allow your mind to wander!" She laughed, winked, and then hurried past.

"Interesting woman . . ." Valla watched her go, then she squeezed Victor's fingers and tugged his hand, pulling him toward their goal. "Come. As you said, it's time we were done with this quest." He followed along, pondering the idea that an entire city had enchanted sidewalks. Then he grew distracted as she pulled the door open and stepped inside, accompanied by the magical chimes Erd Van had hung from the entryway. Victor cast Alter Self almost automatically, reducing his size to fit through the doorway more easily, though he and Valla still had to duck beneath the lintel.

Inside, things were just as he remembered, though Erd wasn't in sight. Valla looked at him, shrugged, and then walked over to the couches, taking a seat to wait. Victor didn't feel so patient, however, and he walked over to the counter and rapped his heavy knuckles against the polished wood. "Erd!"

A distant voice came to him, muffled by the closed door in the far wall. "A moment, please!"

Victor sighed and walked over to Valla, sitting on the couch and depositing the silk-wrapped bundle between them. Valla shifted to look at the egg, gently resting one of her pale silver-blue hands atop it. She sighed softly as she felt its warmth and said, "It's . . . I think I can feel something! Almost like it's tugging at my consciousness."

"Careful." Victor took her wrist and lifted her hand away. "It didn't do that to me. It might be dangerous to someone without sufficient will. I have no idea."

Valla licked her lips, her eyes shifting back and forth from Victor's eyes to the egg. Then, almost reluctantly, she nodded and folded her hands in her lap. "I think you may be right." The sound of the door clicking open took their attention, and Victor looked up to see Erd leaning against his counter, looking at them with narrowed eyes.

"So, you've returned. You met with failure? Did the alchemical perfume not work?" He sighed and shook his head, waving a hand dismissively. "No matter. I'm sorry if you lost any comrades in the effort. I'm afraid my coffers cannot fund another expedition at this time."

"We didn't fail," Victor growled, something in him deeply annoyed by Erd's assumption.

"Oh?" Erd's eyes darted from Victor to Valla, then to the silk-wrapped bundle between them. "But I can't sense anything that could possibly be the object of my . . ." His eyes bulged, and he gasped, his hands falling to his knees to steady himself as Victor unwrapped the egg and lifted it in his bare hand. He'd only briefly touched the egg back in the hive world, wondering what it looked like under all that silk. He could feel it, the weight of the power in the thing. It was definitely spirit-attuned Energy, but not one of his affinities. Still, it was something else, that heavy, powerful spirit presence.

Valla's eyes opened wide, and she stared at the egg longingly, but her reaction was different from Erd's. He gasped and took a stumbling step toward them, faltering and falling to one knee. "W-wra . . ." He coughed and rubbed a hand over his face, slapping his cheek several times. "Wrap it! Please!"

Victor chuckled and wrapped the egg in the silken cloth, and Valla sighed longingly while Erd began to gasp deep breaths. When he'd recovered a little, he laughed like a madman. "Oh, by the ancient elder gods! You've done it! You've actually done it! Master Dar will be so pleased! So pleased! Heroes!" He scrambled to his feet and rushed forward, hands outstretched, but Victor pulled the egg close, snugly in the crook of his arm. "D-don't you intend to uphold our bargain?"

"Oh, I do. I just need to make sure we're clear on the terms."

"You bring me the egg, and I get you an audience with my mentor, Ranish Dar!" Erd's face had begun to flush with frustration and perceived insult.

"Relax, Erd. Listen, sit down." Victor nodded to the couch nearby. Erd scowled at him, but he complied, and Victor knew the guy was afraid of him. If it hadn't been obvious when he'd fallen to his knees before his Quinametzin anger, Victor would have figured it out when he sent them on what was basically a suicide mission. "Let's start being very honest with each other, yeah? You expected us to fail, right?"

Something in his eyes or voice must have cautioned Erd because he didn't try very hard to deny the statement. "I had high hopes for the alchemical perfume, but I've had so many failures over the years, I didn't think there was much chance you'd be able to retrieve the egg." He shrugged.

"You sent us to die?" Valla growled, the stupor brought on by the exposure of the egg rapidly fading.

"No!" Erd cried, then more quietly, "No, no, no. I gave you tokens of recall, did I not? I spent a great deal of money in that regard, ensuring you had a way out. I simply thought the task would prove too much. None of my earlier questors ever even laid eyes on the eggs."

"Okay, so as you felt, this thing's very damn powerful. I don't want to get an audience with this master of yours only to discover he has a laundry list of requirements before he helps us. If you want this egg, if you want what it promises, you need to impress upon him that we've earned his help."

"Ah." Erd held up a single finger and clicked his tongue, almost wincing as he continued, "Ah, I may have misled you slightly. The egg is, um, as you say, powerful and valuable, but it's beyond me. No, that egg is for my master. Still, I believe he will be very grateful for it. I'm not the only student who's been trying to get something of this caliber for him; I believe it's instrumental for his next breakthrough. Even so, I'm unsure that he'll grant me what I need in addition to helping you. The best I will promise is that I will ensure that he sees you and hears of your friend's plight."

Victor growled, but Valla put her hand on his wrist, gently squeezing, and he knew she was trying to remind him to be reasonable. He was just so damn tired of playing games. "I'm not fucking around, Erd. If this egg is for your master, then we'll go with you. I don't want you to take it to him and then get some line about how your master is busy and he'll see us in a month or a year or some other bullshit. Yeah. When are you going?"

"I . . ." He looked both panicked and excited. "I will go now! He'll surely see us if we have the egg, even before my assigned meeting time."

Victor nodded. "That's the spirit. Let's go pick up our friend, and we'll all go together. I told you I'd give you this egg, and I will, but I want to be standing in front of the guy who can help us before I hand it over. Fair?"

To his surprise, Valla spoke before Erd. "I think it sounds fair. Come, Erd. You can still claim credit for sending us after it."

"Well . . ." He stood up from the couch, his eyes darting around, clearly searching for a suitable response. Finally, he nodded and said, "Very well. It's enough." As though to reassure himself, he repeated, "It's enough. He'll be pleased. Yes." He continued nodding as he walked over to his front door and clicked the locks shut. "Yes, this will be fine. We'll take my coach. Come, it's in the back alley."

29

COSTS

Erd's "coach" was a rune-inscribed brass-colored globe the size of a small sedan that floated two feet off the ground. When he tapped a matching brass rod against a panel on its side, it rotated on hidden gears, sliding open like the aperture on a camera, revealing a spacious interior upholstered in soft red velvets. Victor and Valla had to struggle to get through the opening, but once inside, they had plenty of room to stretch out. All the while, Victor kept the egg held tight in the crook of his arm, shaking his head at Erd when he offered to hold it as he clambered through the doorway. Something about the man didn't inspire Victor's trust.

The coach surged forward, smoothly but quickly, and whatever magic guided it delivered them to the party's hotel in just a few minutes. During their brief transit, Erd was silent, though he looked occupied, and when the coach pulled to a stop, he said, "I've communed with Master Dar's assistant, and the master has agreed to see us. It's difficult to tell, but I believe he's excited! This means good things for us, Victor!"

"Yeah?" Victor scooted toward the door, ready to go into the hotel to fetch Lam and Edeya.

"Yes! I'd hoped the egg would be something he needed, but I wasn't entirely sure. Now that we've secured an audience, I don't mind telling you that my relief is monumental. I'd feared your wrath if he'd been uninterested in the artifact."

"Is that why you seemed so nervous?" Valla asked as she scooted forward in her seat, ready to follow Victor.

"Yes. I apologize for not being wholly forthright with you. I was reasonably sure the artifact would get his attention, earning me Dar's favor and his aid in my development, but I wasn't certain. Things seem to be working out, however." He nodded, grinning widely, and his relief was palpable.

Part of Victor wanted to cuss the guy out for sending them into the ivid hive on what was starting to feel like a hunch, but he simply grunted and said, "I'll be right back." He slipped through the doorway and reached up to take Valla's hand, helping her down. "You mind waiting here and keeping an eye on this guy? I'll go get Lam and Edeya."

"Of course." She pointed to the egg. "Want me to hold that?"

"Thanks, but no. If someone's going to try to steal this, they'll have to take it from me." When Valla nodded and leaned back against the coach, Victor turned and hurried into the hotel, up the magical stairs, and directly to the room where Lesh and Darren were staying. He only had to knock twice before the door opened wide, and Lesh's draconic countenance greeted him.

He looked down at the bundle in Victor's arm and said, "You ran into trouble?"

"Not exactly. We're going to meet that guy's master right now, but I want you to watch this." Victor reached down with his free hand and began unlooping the sling of ivid silk that held the globe of royal jelly. "I don't know how good this silk is at hiding what's inside it, but if this guy's as powerful as we think, he might sniff it out. I don't want to get mugged, you know?"

"Ah. Of course. I'll keep it safe here."

"Yeah, don't go wandering around with it. Just wait for me, all right? Keep it out of your storage containers unless you don't mind destroying them." Victor held the heavy bundle up, and Lesh nodded, taking it with a profoundly sober expression.

"I will guard it with my life."

Victor thought about telling him it wasn't worth his life and not to do anything crazy, but he decided that no matter what he said, Lesh wouldn't relax about the responsibility. It was just the way he was. "All right. Thanks, Lesh. Hopefully, we'll be back soon. Have you seen Lam yet?"

"No. I've been listening to the fosterling's report. He seems to have learned a great deal about his Core and has acquired some texts to aid his study. I'll give you the details after I hear it all."

"Uh, all right." Victor almost chuckled, but he held it in. He didn't really care all that much about what Darren was learning, but he had to give Lesh credit for taking his duty so seriously. Still, every time he called Darren a "fosterling," it made him smile. "Yeah, let's catch up when I get back." As Lesh nodded, Victor turned and walked to Lam's room. On the way, thinking about the jelly he'd just left with Lesh, he remembered the crown Lam was holding for him and wondered if he should give that to Lesh, too, or just carry it with him. He doubted it had a fraction of the value of the royal jelly, but he still didn't want to tempt thieves.

Lam opened her door immediately and surprised Victor by rushing to hug him. "I'm so relieved to see you! Is everyone well? Where's Valla?" Her response to his arrival surprised him at first, but then Victor put himself in her shoes—left behind, tending to her near-comatose friend, waiting in a strange city on a strange world in the hopes that the only people she knew wouldn't die trying to invade an alien insect hive. He gripped her shoulders as she released him, her cheeks reddening in sudden embarrassment.

"She's fine. Waiting downstairs. Fetch Edeya; we're going to see that guy about helping her now."

"Truly?" Moisture sprang into Lam's eyes, and she turned, hurrying toward a couch near the big floor-to-ceiling windows facing the park. Victor stepped inside the doorway and watched Lam use the control rod to get Edeya up and moving. "What about your crown?"

"Hide it here. I'll see to it when we're done with this business."

"It's already hidden. I was nervous with that thing around."

"You felt something?" Victor had, too, every time he held the crown, a kind of uneasiness like distant whispering and watching eyes.

"Yes. It made my skin crawl." Lam led Edeya to the door, and Victor stepped back out, holding it wide for them. As they all walked to the steps, Lam asked, "What was it like? The insect world?"

"Dead. Nothing lived except for the bugs. We got to the bottom of the hive and found out that the ivid had evolved, opening a . . . gateway, I guess, into a new universe they were creating. I gained a new perspective on power from them, Lam. Their queen . . ." Victor trailed off, unsure how to describe what he'd felt.

"That bad, huh? Did you have to fight?"

"Only at first, against the insect soldiers near the top of the hive. Then we snuck down, and the, um, evolved ivid dealt with us peacefully." He finished his sentence and stepped down the magical stairway, waiting for Lam and

Edeya to join him before continuing. "Keep that between us. I had to trade for the egg, but it wasn't nearly as hard to get as Erd Van thinks. I'll use that for bargaining."

"Understood."

While they walked, Victor looked at Edeya, noting the dimness of her wings, the wan, sallow look of her face, and the deep dark circles under her eyes. He knew she'd looked bad before they left, but she seemed worse, and he didn't think they could keep her like this much longer. They exited the hotel, and Victor pointed to the floating globe-shaped coach down the sidewalk. "That's our ride."

Lam started forward, but he stopped her and said, "Listen, Lam, if this guy won't or can't help, then I'm going to find a way to get to Dark Ember, and I'm going to kill my way to Victoria or Catalina, whatever that *bruja* calls herself, and I'm going to rip her apart bone by bone until she frees Edeya's spirit. Don't give up hope."

To his surprise, Lam smiled and nodded. She didn't try to protest or insist that she'd join him. She just said, "I know you will, Victor." He looked into her emerald eyes for several seconds, wondering at the pain, guilt, and loneliness he saw there. After a short, awkward silence, they walked the rest of the way to the coach, where Lam and Valla embraced before they all climbed inside, Victor bringing up the rear, still clutching the warm silk-wrapped bundle in his left arm. The coach didn't have windows, so they couldn't see exactly where they were going, but Victor could feel the coach lifting them and had the sensation of great speed as he was pulled down into the cushions.

"Where are we meeting your master?" Valla asked.

Erd smiled at her and made an expression that seemed almost smug. "He awaits us in a private tower of the Arcanum."

Lam came to everyone's rescue and asked, "The Arcanum?"

"Ah, yes. I keep forgetting you're all new to the city. The Arcanum of a Thousand Towers. It began as a library and research facility and has become something of a university over the centuries. People like me save our money and favors and spend them there, learning from people like Ranish Dar. Well, when they have the time and patience for those of us so far beneath them."

"Does it really have a thousand towers?" Valla asked.

"Oh, likely far more by now." Erd rubbed his chin, looking around the coach's interior, then added, "Apologies for the lack of a view. You'll get a good look at the Arcanum when we step out, though." His answer seemed to satisfy Lam and Valla, and Victor had enough on his mind, so the coach grew quiet as it silently conveyed them through the air.

After a few minutes, Valla said, "Edeya doesn't look well."

"She hasn't . . ." Lam started to say, frowning.

"I mean, she looks worse."

"Does she?" Lam leaned closer to Edeya, taking her limp hands and gently massaging her palms with her thumbs. "I've been ensuring she eats good food and gets sunlight, but something still fails within her.

"A body cannot exist long without a spirit. Her fragment will suffice for a time, but the flesh will fail." Erd looked at Victor and continued, "Forgive my unearned knowledge, but when I glimpsed your Core when you first came to my shop, I was surprised you were seeking help from me. I'm surprised by how little you know of spirits, considering . . ."

"Erd, I earned my power through combat and suffering. I've never found a very knowledgeable teacher, so, yeah, there's a lot I don't know."

"Of course. I don't mean to imply any willful ignorance . . ." He stumbled on his words, obviously aware of Victor's irritation, and then the coach rapidly slowed, sending everyone lurching forward in their seats. With a *thunk* and soft grinding sound, it came to a halt, and he announced, "We've arrived!" He practically flew out of the coach, and Victor had a feeling he saw their arrival as a lifeline, saving him from the awkward conversation.

Lam and Edeya followed Erd out, and before she stepped through the open doorway, Valla grabbed Victor's hand and said, "Be patient. We're out of our depth here, and I don't think your rage will serve you well."

"I don't plan to get angry, Valla; it just happens. Anyway, I'm out of patience where Edeya's concerned." He stared hard at her, unblinking, and eventually, she nodded and climbed out of the coach. Victor followed, and when he stepped out, he had to take a minute to regather his wits as they were blown out of his mind by the vista that awaited him.

The coach had come to rest on a dock of sorts, built from gold and pearl inlaid marble—a short span of solid stone that stretched out from the roof of a floating tower, which was, in turn, connected to ten other towers, also floating in the sky, and connected to hundreds more. The cluster of floating towers and the tunnels and bridges between them were, literally, hanging in the clouds, and Victor could see, distant and small, like a city seen from an airplane, the crystal buildings and streets of Sojourn down below. "Holy shit," he said, slowly turning in a circle, trying to guess how many towers hung there in the sky and losing count in the hundreds.

Some of the spires were marble, some were gray stone, and many were made of bricks of all sorts. Victor saw tile roofs, copper gables, and everything in between. The diversity of building materials might have seemed haphazard if not for the fact that every building was a tower, and they were all floating together high among the clouds. The sun was dim, approaching the western horizon, and the clouds and breeze turned the stiff wind chilly. Though it hardly bothered Victor, he could see the goosebumps standing out on Edeya's frail arms, and he nodded toward the doorway at the center of the roof. "We should get her out of the wind."

"Of course, of course!" Erd hurried to the door, resting his hand on the latch and muttering a few words that were indistinct and strange to Victor's ears. Lam pulled Edeya after him, and Victor and Valla followed. By the time they'd all gathered, Erd had the door open and pulled it wide for them all to go through. When he reached the door, Victor held it open with his free hand and nodded to Erd.

"I'll follow you."

Erd swallowed his reply, nodding and looking down, then hurried in. When Victor stepped through, he let the metal door clang shut behind him. Erd led them down several flights of stairs, past a few closed doors, and finally to the base of the narrow stairway where a single door opened into an arched, spacious gallery from which three doors and two other stairs led away. Erd approached the central door, a wide, darkly stained wooden one, and delicately knocked. "This is his usual study."

"Come!" barked a deep, scratchy voice, and Erd visibly flinched as he turned the brass knob and pushed the door open. "Ah, um, Master Dar, it is I, Erd Van, here to gift you with the ivid dreaming egg . . ."

The deep voice laughed and said, "Erd Van! It's been a decade at least, no? I'd nearly written you off as rusted."

Valla looked at Victor and mouthed, "Rusted?"

Victor shrugged and continued to listen, stepping forward to see through the doorway where Erd still stood. He couldn't make much out. Soft golden light, seeming to fall from an overhead fixture, illuminated stacks of books, built-in shelves, and clutter of every sort. Most prominent, obscuring most of his view, was a wrought iron rack formed to delicately hold dozens of shimmering crystal globes that looked very much like tiny planets to Victor.

"Um, no, Master, since my last session with you, I've advanced three levels and sit upon the cusp of Tier Eight. I hoped that, with this gift, I might earn a bit of guidance . . ."

"Yes, yes, I heard your message. Come in, boy, and bring your entourage. I'll have a look at you all."

Erd turned and furtively motioned for everyone to follow him, and then he stepped through. Lam moved to the side with Edeya, waiting for Victor and Valla to precede her into the room. Valla seemed hesitant to go in for some reason, and Victor was out of patience, ready to see the man behind the voice, so he moved past her. Clutching the egg close, he ducked under the lintel and entered the study. Once inside, he saw it was cluttered but large, with massive bay windows on the far wall providing a stunning view of the sunset and the golden, ochre, and rust-colored clouds laid out like a magical cotton candy landscape outside.

Amid the shelves, cases, tables, stacks of books, curios, and artifacts was an imposing desk with legs carved like dragon claws. Sitting behind it was a man who had to be Ranish Dar. Victor had expected an old cranky scholar type. He'd pictured a man with glasses and white hair with sharp eyes. What he saw was a giant made of black stone that moved like flesh. His eyes blazed like miniature golden suns, and bizarrely, he wore mint green silken pajamas. At least, they looked like pajamas to Victor.

"Ha!" rumbled the colossal man, easily a match for Victor's usual size. "What's this, then, Erd Van? Did you convince one of your betters to fetch the artifact? And is he willing to share the prize? What's your name, berserker?" Victor stepped forward, making room for his companions to follow him in. He didn't answer right away, and when Ranish Dar caught sight of Edeya, he made a sound that reminded Victor of a train whistling and said, "And a shattered spirit? Well, I'll hand it to you, Erd; this is the most interesting supplication I've had in a good many years."

"Um, thank you, Master Dar, I was hoping that . . ."

"Quiet now while I see what I've got before me. Well, berserker?" Ranish Dar leaned forward on his desk, the wood creaking under the pressure of his elbows.

"I'm Victor."

"And you hail from?"

Victor shrugged and said, "Tucson, I guess—by way of Fanwath."

"Yes, that's quite a Core you've been building for yourself, there. Well shielded, too. It's no wonder Erd's willing to lead you about, acting the prancing prince, unaware that he's got a dragon by the tail. Quite impressive, indeed."

Victor didn't betray any emotion or even flinch as Ranish Dar effortlessly saw through his Aura Veil. He thought the imagery of his idiom was apt and amusing, picturing Erd walking around with a dragon's tail, unaware of the monster on the other end. He wondered how accurate it was. Was he really so much stronger than the nearly Level Eighty spirit expert? Surprisingly, his Quinametzin pride wasn't the least ruffled, perhaps because something in him recognized the power of the man before him. Some instinct in him wanted to show respect. "Thank you." He decided no other words were yet necessary.

"So, an ivid dreaming egg, is it?" He nodded to Victor's bundle. "Bring it here. I'll have a look before I hear any more of your story."

Victor glanced at Erd and saw him looking down, clenching his jaw, clearly humiliated by Dar's earlier words. Deciding there wasn't much else he could do—he was reasonably sure Dar could take the egg if he wanted to—he stepped up to the desk, and as he walked, he canceled his Alter Self spell, rising to his full height. He didn't want to have to reach up to put something on a desk. As he smoothly stretched upward and outward, expanding in size and power, Ranish Dar chuckled and said, "A dragon, indeed!"

Victor couldn't contain the inner voice that insisted he correct the record, and he said, "Titan," as he placed the silk-wrapped egg on the desktop.

"Of course, of course. A figure of speech, young man." Dar pulled the bundle close and carefully unwrapped the silk. When the pale glittering flesh of the egg was exposed, and Victor felt its warm potent Energy wash over him, he heard the gasps behind him and saw the smile on Dar's stony face. "Lovely, lovely, lovely!" He rested two huge fingers on the egg and closed his blazing eyes. A moment later, he said, "Yes, this will do."

"Are you pleased, Master Dar?" Erd asked, his voice high and strained. Victor looked at him to see he'd fallen to his knees. His fists were clenched, and he was sweating bullets over his squeezed-shut eyes. Victor turned to see Lam and Valla leaning on each other, wan and gasping as they stood in the wash of power coming off the egg. Victor was a little surprised; he could definitely feel the egg's influence, feel the weight of it, but to him, it was like standing out on the pavement on an Arizona summer day. It was hot and uncomfortable, but nothing he couldn't handle.

"You're entirely too strong for an iron ranker, Victor," Dar said, ignoring Erd's question as he chuckled and slowly wrapped the egg, to the others' great relief. "Well? How will my blessings be bestowed upon this party? Erd Van would have me believe he is responsible for this great treasure. Is that the case?"

"I . . ." Erd started to say, but Ranish Dar held up a hand, silencing him.

"I'll hear from the only one of you capable of standing in its presence." He fixed those blazing eyes on Victor.

Something in Victor wouldn't let him take all the credit for the egg despite his significant role. He said, "Erd told us about the egg. He paid for our transport and gave us the means to sneak past many of the ivid. We"—Victor nodded to Valla—"fought and bargained for it."

"And what do you seek, Victor? I know what Erd wants."

"I wish to have my friend's spirit made whole. I hoped that you'd be able to pull it home. If you can't do that, I hoped you'd help me find a way to the world where it's being held, and I'll kill the one who's taken it."

"Gods," Ranish Dar said, surprising Victor. "Such conviction and power behind those words. Did you feel that, Erd? An oath of power made in our presence, one with binding karmic ties, and he did it with hardly a thought for the repercussions! That's the sort of spirit we need to cultivate, Erd. What a bloodline! What a Core! What a spirit! Erd, you need another few decades of hard, hard toil before you can hope to put such an edge to your words. I'll grant you your desired lessons, five of them, but then you'll need to put yourself through a crucible or two before I'll look upon you again. Go now. Await my summons." He made a shooing gesture at Erd, and the man stood and practically flew from the room, glancing at Victor on his way past with haunted eyes.

"And us?" Victor asked.

"I'll aid your friend, Victor, the titan from Tucson, but my help will come with a cost. A cost for your friend and a cost for you. Will you bear it?"

Victor didn't hesitate. He was ready to be done with this situation, ready to help his friend, and he wasn't afraid of any fee this man might charge. He opened his mouth to say yes, but Valla spoke first, filling the brief silence, "He will hear the cost before he decides."

Ranish Dar slammed his palm atop his massive desk with an ear-popping, thunderous *crack* and barked a short laugh. "Ha! A wise woman and a boon companion. Very well. First, we'll discuss what it will cost your friend. The mending of a shattered spirit and the trauma of my indelicate, mighty pull, dragging it through the fabric of the universe to be made whole in her body, will take a toll, paid for by the Energy she's gathered in her life. She will likely lose many levels. As for you, Victor, the cost I will demand of you will be years of service, for I need a protégé worthy of my knowledge."

30

WHOLE

After Ranish Dar spoke, the room grew quiet as everyone looked at Victor for a reaction. When he stood there for several seconds, clearly deep in thought, Lam broke the spell and asked, "How many levels will she lose?"

"Unknown." Ranish peered past Victor at Edeya for several seconds, then said, "She's just barely into the iron ranks. Just touching Tier Three, yes?"

"That's right."

"With so little to draw upon, she might find herself back in the stages of a neophyte, Classless and ready for the crucible." Victor heard him; part of his mind was listening to their conversation, but most of his concentration was dealing with his many half-formed reactions to Dar's demand. He'd hoped to have Edeya healed and to be done with obligations for a while. He'd hoped for some freedom to explore and live his life, enjoying some real quality time with Valla. What kinds of demands would Dar make of his "protégé"? Would Victor's entire life be co-opted? Could he refuse and risk Edeya's life in the hopes that he'd find another solution?

While he struggled with his concerns, another part of him began to weigh the demand in the light of an opportunity. He'd seen firsthand how badly some "iron rankers" desired the guidance of a man like Ranish Dar. Erd Van had spent a fortune and decades of his life to acquire the dreaming egg, and all it had gotten him was five lessons with Dar. Should Victor pass up the opportunity for regular tutelage from the master? As his brain spun through the implications, he felt Valla move beside him, entwining her fingers with his.

"So far to fall . . ." Lam said, her expression drooping into something like despair.

"It is far," Dar said, chuckling, "to you. To me, those first few dozen levels in the iron ranks are a blink of an eye, a drop in the ocean of my journey to this stage of my life. There's more I can tell you that might give you comfort. Would you believe that there are iron rankers who pay tremendous sums to Spirit Casters like myself to put them through such a process intention-ally? It's not without risk, either, as you well know. Still, there are those who would give anything to make another gamble with class selections, to focus their advancement differently. No, your friend will suffer some loss, but she's likely to come back stronger than ever. It's not as though she'll forget what she learned in her young life. Well, she shouldn't. Some memory loss is one of the many risks, however."

Lam nodded, and in the corner of his eye, Victor saw her put her arm around Edeya, pulling her close to her side. "Still, we cannot ask this of you, Victor."

"You're not asking. Edeya's not asking." Victor glared at Ranish Dar and asked, "What sort of service will you require of me?"

Dar's smoldering, fiery eyes flared, and Victor swore he felt some heat waft over the desk into his face. "Don't be too confident, young titan. I'm impressed by you, but I'll not be disrespected in my own study. I'll have your commitment, and then, after I've helped your friend, we'll discuss the details. I'll not say more on this matter, so either accept or take your broken friend and depart."

For the first time in the huge stone man's presence, Victor felt the pres-sure of his rage-attuned Energy seeping into his pathways. He felt his pride begin to bristle, but with a tremendous effort of will, he pushed it back and calmed his angry expression. He focused on Valla's cool fingers, lightly grip-ping his palm, and took a slow, even breath. "All right. I accept."

Darren closed the book and looked up, frowning, as his giant babysitter repeated the demand. "Explain to me again why you were not given a Core at this city's nursery." Darren sighed and closed the book, *Avera's Treatise on the Mind and its Elusive Affinity*, and looked into Lesh's green and yellow reptilian eyes.

"Well, they don't exactly give a person a Core there. They guide you in the process of creating one." Darren thought about lying. So far, all he'd said was that he didn't get the help he needed at the Genesis Center and that he'd found some books to figure things out on his own. Still, a lie was something he felt would be easy for Lesh to pick out; he was far shrewder than he looked. Instead, Darren decided to give him part of the truth. "They said my stronger affinities were too dangerous and offered to teach me to build a Core that didn't utilize them."

"So you took the initiative to find books on the subject and to teach yourself?" Lesh nodded. "I, too, would have balked at the idea of settling for a weaker Core than my potential would allow. Tell me, then, what are these affinities you are pursuing?"

Again, Darren knew better than to lie. "My strongest one is chaos, and I have a lesser affinity for mind-attuned Energy."

"Ah." Lesh sat on the hard marble floor opposite Darren, his back to the window behind him. "Both are rare in my homeworld, but a strong Mind Caster is someone to fear. I can see why a soft place like this would discourage it. I've never met a Chaos Caster, but I can imagine what might come of such an affinity. So this world found the prospect too daunting. Again, I cannot feign surprise. You had no other affinities that interested you?"

"I have a strong affinity for lightning, but it's hard to find a Core that will accommodate that and mind-attuned Energy. Chaos seems more malleable, able to be worked in with many different types of Energy."

Lesh grunted. "Lightning is a strong battle attunement. You're so set on mind-attuned Energy?"

"I just feel it will help me to achieve the goals I'm most interested in."

"There are many worlds where the rule of might is the only law of the land. There are other places, like this one, where many laws keep people civil. I visited several worlds on my way to find Victor, and some of them had strictly enforced laws regarding certain affinities; they were either seen as abhorrent and banned from existence, or they were tightly controlled by the powers that be. Mind Casters are often in that category."

When he didn't say anything more, Darren prompted him, "And, Elder?"

"And you should know that." He shrugged. "It's your choice."

"You're not going to try to talk me out of it? You won't forbid me to study it?"

"Why would I? Do you think I fear any affinity? If you try to toy with my mind, Belagog will mash you into a paste. I'd say Victor would likewise be willing to correct you. Knowing that, and also knowing that there are beings here who could just as easily smash me, I hope you will understand that caution and good judgment are more important than any affinity."

Darren was surprised and strangely grateful. For once, he wasn't being judged by his past or for what he might do. Before he could think about it, he said as much to Lesh. "Thank you, Elder. I'm glad to know that you don't assume I will do something terrible. I've made mistakes in my life, but it's nice to know you aren't judging me for them."

"You've yet to give me a reason to doubt you, fosterling. In my book, you've barely a page written. Let us see that you inspire tales of praise rather than condemnation." Lesh pointed to the book Darren was reading and asked, "Well? What sorts of Cores are you considering?"

Darren nodded. "Of the Core types I've found for mind affinities, only one meets the criteria I need. First, it has to be compatible with chaos-attuned Energy. Second, it must be something I could hope to create. Several require certain bloodlines—things I've never heard of." Darren flipped the pages so he could read aloud. "For instance, 'Tovekian Arkashi' or 'Sevenii Ash Progenitor.' Some require rare artifacts like a 'pearl of introspection.' Still others require a 'cadre' of Mind Casters to help focus the Energy into a specific aspect. The only one I think I can create is fairly generic sounding—Chaotic Mind Core. Still, the book describes it as 'robust with wide Energy pathways suitable for any caster whose primary sensory organ is visual.' What do you think?"

"Do you sense things with your eyes more than your nose or ears?"

"Yes. I believe so. Humans have evolved with sight as our predominant sense."

"Then I think you are a grown man with no Core, and you should quit dawdling and create something."

"This is a momentous decision, Elder. If I steer myself wrong, God knows what it'll take to correct my course."

Lesh scoffed and waved his hand, leaning back into the window, basking in the warm sunlight. As he closed his eyes and folded his arms over his prodigious chest, he rumbled, "Speak to me when you've decided on a course of action."

Darren sighed and looked back down at the book in his lap. He'd spent the last couple of days reading nearly nonstop, pausing only to use the bathroom, eat a quick meal, and when exhaustion truly set in, sleep a few hours. While Lesh and the others had been gone, Lam had hardly bothered him. He doubted she'd have even looked in on him if not for some obligation to Lesh. All in all, he'd been happy to be left alone. He'd spent most of his savings acquiring three books. The one in his lap, another about chaos Energy, and a third about air affinities—the closest he could find to a book relating to his lightning affinity.

He'd found a Core that would allow him to cultivate lightning and chaos Energy but set it aside because of his strange fascination with his mind affinity. After speaking to Lesh, though, he was beginning to wonder if he'd been acting out of some compulsion to defy rules or the expectations of people he didn't respect, namely those damn living lights at the Genesis Center, Y-seven and K-eight. Mind was a minor affinity for him, after all; shouldn't he focus on the lightning and chaos? Darren reached over and picked up the book about air affinities.

It was called *Borton's Electric Life* and was an autobiography of sorts, following the career and adventures of Borton as he rose in power from a novice to a master Wind Elementalist. It was only partially applicable to Darren—lightning was, as Y-seven had so smugly reported, a more specialized form of the elemental affinity. Still, in the small section at the beginning of the book, Borton mentioned some Core options he didn't pursue, and one was called a "Wildarc" Core, which Darren also found mentioned in his chaos-focused text. He read the small paragraph he'd annotated again:

On the subject of Cores, Maester Fulavius suggested a Wildarc, but Daenistra doesn't think I have the necessary minor affinities to make it worth the effort and slow cultivation. Fulavius, of course, argued. He was of the opinion that the slower cultivation meant greater gains in the long run, but I tend to side with Daenistra. My air affinity so outstrips my minors that the need to weave in something else would surely slow me down, and let's not forget that slow growth with high potential sounds wonderful, but quick growth might mean the difference between life and death in the Reekvah Trials, which I'm due to start in two short years.

Darren set the book aside and picked up the chaos tome, cryptically titled *Seeds of Infinity*. The first hundred pages or so were dedicated to the creation of a chaos-focused Core, and he had to flip through more than a dozen before he came to the section boldly titled "Wildarc: The Surge Lord Core." He'd only glanced at it before, being obsessed with mind-affinity-focused Cores, but now he gave it a careful read, pleased to see that each step of the process was explained and that he had everything he needed—affinities for lightning and chaos and an undeveloped Core. Suddenly, Darren was excited by the prospect, and he had to set the book down and take a hard look at himself.

Had he really been about to embrace a minor affinity out of spite? Had he wanted to build a Core around mind-attuned Energy because he wanted to influence people's minds or because of how taboo Y-seven had made it sound? What was that? Some sort of defiance? Some self-destructive need to rebuke authority? It would be one thing if the mind affinity were the best thing for him, but he didn't think it was. If he were honest, he could see how it might lead him into one troubling situation after another. When would he ever use it for good? He supposed that if he could influence people's minds, he could try to find bad people and get them to change their behavior, but that was a slippery slope, and Darren wasn't good at slippery slopes.

Once again, he felt grateful to Lesh. If he hadn't come over and asked about his studies, if he hadn't given him the benefit of the doubt, Darren might not have been introspective enough to see what a foolish decision he'd been about to make. "Elder Lesh, I've made a decision. I'm going to create something called a Wildarc Core, and it will allow me to cultivate and use lightning and chaos-attuned Energies."

"Good, Darren," Lesh mumbled, clearly dozing.

Darren nodded, for some reason feeling as if he'd shed a heavy weight. He sat up straighter and propped the book against the other two, tilting its open pages to make it easy to read. As illustrated in the book, he assumed a lotus position and squinted, reading the first instruction softly to himself: "Turn your inner eye toward your accumulated Energy and, while studying it, contemplate the chaotic nature of the many branches in a bolt of lightning."

Ranish Dar led the party out of his study and up one of the other stairways just outside. Despite his stone-like black flesh, his bare feet were silent on the steps, and he moved with the grace of a cat. He'd asked Lam and Edeya to follow him, and of course Victor and Valla accompanied them—he hadn't said they couldn't. They walked through high vaulted corridors brightly lit by an invisible source, past stained-glass windows, a dozen closed doors, and eventually into a large room with floor-to-ceiling cabinets lining every wall. The only other furnishings were two long tables lined with stools. Everything was made for a person of Dar's size, so it was a little amusing to see Edeya standing beside one of the tables, the top an inch higher than her head.

"Victor, place your companion here," Dar said as he shifted one of the stools from the side to the head of the table. "Place her head here." He gently tapped the smooth wooden surface in front of him. "I will conduct a Spirit Walk. Are you familiar, Victor?"

"Yes."

"Yes, I'm sure you are." Dar looked at Victor, then let his eyes drift to Lam and Valla. "Perhaps you think I'll be helpless while spirit walking, but please be aware that my Spirit Walk is at the legendary tier and that a fragment of my spirit will be standing guard over my physical form. I do not suspect you of duplicity, but for your safety, do not make any threatening actions toward me."

Victor lifted Edeya in his arms, disturbed by how light she was, and gently laid her on the table. Dar continued speaking. "I will need to channel a great amount of Energy, and depending on the distance between this world and the one where this young woman's spirit lies, I may need to refresh my stores." He held out his hand, and a softly glowing silvery-white potion appeared in his palm. He held it out to Victor.

Victor took the little bottle, amazed by the depths of Energy he felt within it. "What do I do with it?"

"Watch me with your inner eye. You'll see my spirit fragment standing guard. If it begins to fade, pour this into my mouth. Hopefully, I won't need it, for it was costly and time-consuming to produce." He looked at Victor and *tsked*, shaking his head. "A pity we don't have more time to prepare; I believe I could make use of that inspiration-attuned Energy in your Core. It's close to one of mine. You'll feel it." With that, he nodded and rested his fingertips on either side of Edeya's head. "One more thing before I begin. What is this woman's name?"

"Edeya," Lam said, breathless with anxiety.

"Fear not. Your loved one will be whole again soon." Ranish Dar closed his eyes and, with a soul-sucking vortex of Energy, he slipped into the spirit plane. Victor stumbled forward and caught himself on the table. Lam fell to her knees, and Valla slowly sank to the ground, gripping Victor's wrist to slow her descent. Victor shook his head, forcing himself to focus, and turned his gaze inward. When he saw his Core, he quickly traced his pathways out and looked at the room with his inner eye. Just as Dar had promised, Victor saw his spirit-self standing there, a great hulking shadow wielding a dark spear that bled waves of darkness like smoke from a torch. It regarded him with eyes like singularities, and Victor felt his blood grow cold.

If that thing was only a splinter of Ranish Dar, something like one of Victor's coyotes, then it only confirmed what he'd already known: He didn't want to make an enemy of that man. It also made him wonder what Dar had meant when he'd said Victor would feel his Energy, something close to his inspiration. That shadowy fragment felt a lot more like his fear affinity.

Just as the thought crossed his mind, though, he felt a surge of Energy erupt from the master Spirit Caster, so potent and brilliant that once again Victor had to fight for balance, gripping the edge of the table to the point where the wood creaked and groaned from the pressure of his fingers. He knew Lam and Valla were still down; they'd just begun to gather themselves when this new wave of power wracked the room.

As the initial shock of the Energy surge passed, Victor realized he was feeling something deep in his heart, something that sang to his spirit and made the Energy in his Core roil and churn. He felt endless possibilities and saw the shadowy gloom haunting the periphery of his thoughts fall away, only the brightest paths shining brightly before him. Everything would be all right, of that he was sure. Edeya would recover, he'd find a way to work with Ranish Dar that would still allow for some freedom, and the specters of distant enemies wouldn't find their way to him, not before he was ready. "Ha," Victor said as realization dawned on him. "It's hope. He's using hope-attuned Energy to pull Edeya home."

He glanced down to see both Lam and Valla openly weeping, great wracking sobs of relief and joy, and he knew the Energy was overwhelming them. He turned to the gloomy watcher, noting that despite the warm wonderful hope in the air, the specter was still dark, still balefully watching, his dark spear still held ready. It didn't look as though it was fading, but Victor held the potion ready; he wouldn't fail in his task. He never had to prove it, though—with a suddenness that left him gasping, the flow of hopeful Energy suddenly cut off, and Dar opened his blazing eyes, announcing, "Her spirit is whole."

31

APPRENTICE

Ranish Dar reached down and pulled the rune-inscribed circlet off Edeya's head, handing it to Lam. "This will only make it harder for her to wake." He took one of his thumbs, massive beside Edeya's much smaller form, and gently smoothed some hair away from her face. Standing close as he was, Victor could see the master's strange, stony flesh bend and compress just like normal skin. It made him wonder why it looked like stone to the eye while behaving like flesh. Would it feel hard if you touched it? Was it resistant to damage, or was it all just a visual artifact of Dar's exotic species, whatever that might be? While he speculated, Dar took the warm potion from his grip, and it disappeared into some hidden storage device. He said, "She will wake soon. I will give you some space."

"Thank you," Lam said, climbing atop one of the tall stools to lean close to Edeya's face, peering intently at her slightly twitching, fluttering eyes. Victor watched Dar move to the other table and take a seat. He still watched them, and when he caught Victor's eye, he nodded. Victor knew what the gesture meant—they'd talk after Edeya woke. Victor returned the gesture, then turned back to the others, taking one of Edeya's slender, limp hands. To his surprise, it was much warmer than the last time he'd held it. He could feel a change in the flesh, a vibrancy that had been absent before.

"She's in there," he said. Lam looked at him and nodded; she held Edeya's other hand. Valla took hold of Edeya's wrist, stroking it gently with her thumb.

"Edeya?" Lam said. "Wake up, sweet girl." Victor looked from Edeya to Lam, a little surprised by those words. He'd seen Lam show affection to Edeya, knew she was desperate to help her, but the depth of emotion in those words was a little surprising. Clearly, she loved her, but he wasn't sure if it was the love of a sister, a mother, or something altogether different. Of course, he wasn't stupid enough to ask. When Lam gasped, and new tears sprang from her eyes, dripping down her sharp cheekbones, Victor looked back to Edeya and saw that she'd opened her eyes. She blinked several times, and her brow creased in confusion.

In a raspy, scratchy whisper, she asked, "Where are we?"

"You're safe, Dey-Dey." Lam leaned forward and pressed herself against the young woman, resting her head on her chest. Valla sniffed, and Victor looked to see tears in her eyes, too. He put his arm over her shoulder and smiled when Edeya squinted his way.

"Victor?"

He squeezed her hand. "That's right, brat."

"Brat?" Her voice was hoarse, and she cleared it and swallowed, then added. "You're the brat!" She coughed again and peered down at the top of Lam's head. "What happened?"

Lam lifted her head to look with bloodshot, streaming eyes at Edeya's face. "What do you remember?"

"I feel . . ." She squeezed her eyes shut, shaking her head briefly. "I feel so weak. I remember floating in darkness. Was I lost at sea? I feel like I was surrounded by water and fog." Her eyes sprang open, and she said, "What happened with the fire? I remember we were in a keep. It's all so blurry. Victor was going to have them burn the forest. The undead . . ." As she spoke, her voice grew more and more hoarse, and she cut herself off, coughing so violently that Lam sat up, retaking her hand.

"Hush. I'll fill you in, but now you should rest."

"Excellent advice," Ranish Dar said, his voice loud and sharp like boulders scraping against each other. "Take her to your residence. Feed her. Give her a healing draught. She'll be fine, physically, in a day or two."

As her fit subsided, Edeya looked to the voice, and her eyes sprang wide. Her hand gripped Victor's as if she was about to fall off a cliff, and she looked at him. "Victor! Who . . ."

"Don't worry. He's a friend."

"I'll tell you everything," Lam said, reaching to scoop her arm under Edeya's knees, easily lifting her from the table.

"Do you have to carry me? I think I can walk . . ." Edeya's words trailed off as Victor released her, and she leaned into Lam's chest.

Lam kissed her forehead. "I'd carry you anywhere, sweet. You're not heavy."

"Victor." Ranish beckoned him over. "We'll have a talk now. Your companions can await you at their residence. I won't keep you long today."

"I'll stay—" Valla started to say, but Ranish cut her words off with a stern shake of his head.

"I'll speak to Victor alone. It was a pleasure to meet you all. Perhaps our paths will cross again." He snapped his fingers, and a shimmering, misty bird appeared, swooping and trilling delicate musical cries. "Guide these women to the lower dock and instruct Fregasius to convey them home." The little misty glowing bird trilled something that sounded almost like words and swooped over to Valla and Lam, circling them, trailing glowing mist that slowly faded into nothing.

"Go," Victor said, giving Valla a brief hug. "I'll be fine. See you soon." She looked into his eyes for a long moment, then nodded and turned, walking to the door where Lam, Edeya, and the swooping magical bird waited.

As they walked out, Victor heard Edeya's sleepy voice ask, "Who . . . is that Valla? But you have wings!"

Ranish interrupted his listening by saying, "Come over here, Victor. It is good news that your friend remembers you all."

"She's lost something, though. She should know Valla has wings, and more than a month passed between what she said she last remembered and her . . . injury."

"That will come. Be pleased that she can speak and knows your name. I've seen worse." He pointed to the stool beside his. "Sit here." Victor nodded and approached, climbing atop the large stool, just about perfectly sized for his nearly ten-foot frame. "We have much to speak about. You've agreed to enter my service as an apprentice, and I appreciate the consternation this has caused you. Would you like to give voice to your concerns?"

Victor wondered if the invitation was a trap. Would Dar use what he said against him? Was a cruel heart lurking in that chest? Was his affable nature with Valla and Lam a show? He'd certainly let his anger flare at least once in Victor's presence, and he hadn't exactly been kind to Erd Van. With those thoughts in mind, Victor decided to hold his cards close to his chest. He shrugged. "I was looking forward to some time when I wasn't running from one problem to the next."

"Much of your life has been a trial, hmm?" He watched Victor until he nodded. "If that weren't true, I wouldn't be interested in mentoring you. It's made you hard in ways that Erd Van will never understand. Looking at you, I can see that you've felt death's talons on your flesh, gripping so tightly that you nearly fell through the veil. Hmm?" Victor nodded, images of some of his close calls flashing through his mind—the "boss" of the dungeon near Greatbone, Rellia's lightning-fast rapier, the night brute prince, a horde of undead reavers, and the sharpest, most painful one, his time beneath Hector's veil star.

"Yeah, I guess that's true."

"And yet, you sacrifice much for a friend. I can assure you, Erd Van would never do such a thing." Victor didn't respond. He didn't know what Ranish was looking for; did he want Victor to trash-talk Erd? He didn't care enough about the guy to do so. Ranish didn't seem bothered by his reticence. "You have much to be proud of; I have the ability to see a great deal about you. Your Cores, for instance. Do you know how rare it is for a non-draconic species to have a breath Core in addition to their primary Energy Core? I can see you've done much to advance your bloodline, too. You've the blood of an elder race in your veins, and not just a hint of it. What's more, I can see that you have acquired a legendary Class. It's not unheard of for an iron ranker to do that, but it's usually the scion of an ancient family with resources that make even my wealth seem insignificant."

Victor shifted uncomfortably. It was one thing to dread what this guy would put him through, but having him heap praise upon him made him feel decidedly awkward. Was he supposed to say thank you? "I had plenty of help."

"Hah! Another thing those lapdogs who come crawling 'round here for scraps wouldn't say." Ranish sighed and stretched his neck, bringing forth loud cracks and pops that sounded like someone snapping pieces of slate in half. "I'm a very busy man, Victor. Think of the obligations you have around the worlds where you've traveled and multiply that by a hundred, nay, a thousand. Still, I find I must take time to myself now and then, or I begin to go mad. I begin to react to problems in ways that might seem . . . overzealous. I happen to be enjoying a time like that—some respite from the duties I've created for myself around the worlds, and one of my favorite places to come, when I'm using my time selfishly, is here, to Sojourn."

Victor contemplated his words, thinking about his friends back home, about Olivia and First Landing, about the Ridonne, and even about Zaafor

and the Warlord and the promises he'd made to the Degh. He tried to imagine a thousand times as many concerns and failed to wrap his head around
the idea. "I think I get it."

"Well, the reason I'm telling you this is twofold. One, you should know
that demands on your time will always exist, and you'll have to carve space
for yourself and your own desires. That problem doesn't go away. Two, you
should know that I'll be here, in Sojourn, for perhaps a decade before I get
back to my other obligations. When I take time, I take enough to savor it.
What that means for you is that I'll spend some of my recreational time
instructing and guiding you, but I'll also send you places to manage tasks that
I feel will challenge and instruct you."

Victor thought about his words, forcing himself not to react impulsively.
Part of him was glad to hear that Dar was going to be around Sojourn for
a while and that he was going to be giving Victor things to do on his own,
but another part was utterly freaking out at the mention of ten years and an
open-ended hint at "getting back to obligations" after that. Just how long
did this guy expect Victor to work for him? He'd already upset him once
that day when he'd asked. He'd taken it as a show of disrespect. With that
in mind, Victor spoke very evenly, trying to avoid lacing his words with any
emotion. "Can you give me some idea of how long you expect me to work
for you?"

Dar sighed heavily, but his eyes didn't flare, and he didn't smash his fist on
the table, so Victor felt he'd managed to avoid pissing him off again. "It's not
a matter of 'working' for me, Victor. It's a matter of learning from me. In the
process of which, you will certainly do some tasks that benefit me, but—and I
wish you could trust me here—they'll benefit you more." He looked at Victor
for a long measured minute, during which neither of them blinked.

Finally, satisfied with whatever he'd read in Victor's eyes, he nodded and
continued, "That said, I am ancient in comparison to you, and I move in a
timeframe that likely seems glacial to one so young. In these ten years that I
linger in Sojourn, I will relax, contemplate my recent gains, and take amusement in your progress. After that, I will become busy, and our interactions
will become less frequent. Decades may pass between our meetings, and during that time, I'll expect you to make progress, following the guidance I give
you. The length of this engagement between you and me will depend entirely
on your growth. With any luck, there will come a time when I can be proud
to name you as my protégé, and you will need to strike out on a path of your
own making."

"So, a long time." Victor tried not to sound glum or even to betray any emotion, but something must have shown on his face because Ranish Dar chuckled and reached over to grip his shoulder.

"Is it so bad to learn from a master? What is it that rankles you, Victor? I could list a thousand spirit cultivators who would be singing in the streets for this opportunity."

Victor tried to smile and nodded, then shook his head, his body unsure what his mind wanted. "I don't know. It's something in here." He thumped a fist to his chest. "Maybe my Quinametzin ancestry or maybe growing up wanting to carve out my own future, but something doesn't like the idea of such a long commitment. Then, there's the issue that I've already committed myself to other people for things . . ."

"Such as?"

"There are people back on Fanwath who depend on me, but, well, I guess I don't necessarily have to live there to help them. I could visit now and then?" When Dar graced him with a slight nod, he continued, "There's also this." He lifted his bracer and tapped the pink shard of the Degh Ancestor Stone. "I promised the Degh giants on Zaafor that I'd return and mend their Ancestor Stone, and"—he grinned fiercely—"I owe the Warlord there an ass kicking."

Dar let go of Victor's shoulder and pressed one of his thick stony fingers against the pink crystal. "Very, very interesting!" He laughed and shook his head. "You think I'd deny you such glory? No, lad, that would be a good lesson for you, if nothing else. As I said, I'll take some amusement from your progress these next ten years, and during that time, if you feel ready, I'll quite enjoy seeing you take on a warlord in a barbaric world."

"I'd also like to hunt down the *bruja* who stole Edeya's spirit. She's on a world filled with undead, and some of them are thousands of years old. I guess I'm not really ready to go there and start throwing shit around, but . . ."

"But you will be! Elder gods! It feels good to talk to someone with some *fucking* spirit!" Victor's eyes opened in startled amazement, and he answered Dar's smile with a fierce grin. The master nodded, narrowed his blazing eyes, and said, "Enough. I must learn more about you, so I'll give you your first . . . learning task, shall we call it?"

Victor nodded, still a little dumbstruck after hearing the ancient powerful being cuss. "Sure."

"Those like me who fancy themselves the lords of Sojourn often partake in competitions with one another. One such contest is a dungeon where we can send our iron-ranked students, children, or sponsored recruits to compete in a dangerous, randomly generated series of challenges. Does that sound interesting?"

"Sure, but how will that help you learn about . . ."

"We will see everything that happens in the dungeon. We designed it through the use of the System Stone, so we have some control over the things that happen there. While it's dangerous, there are safeguards built in. You'll be given a lifesaver—a magical device that will transport you to safety if you appear to be near death. It's not perfect; if someone were obliterated in an instant, the device would not save them, but for someone as sturdy as you, I don't see much risk of that."

"Will I have to fight other, uh, participants?"

"There are no rules in the dungeon, but you could just as easily ally with someone."

"What about Valla, or, I have another friend, a dragonkin . . ."

"No, no, Victor. I'll not sponsor another; it's quite costly, and your performance will affect my influence in Sojourn. I have confidence in you, but not so much your friends. I mean no offense, but you're on a different level than your sweet lady friend. As for your dragonkin friend, I can only offer caution—dragons are dangerous beings."

"How long do I have?"

"A new challenge begins on the seventeenth of each month. You have several days to relax." He pushed his stool back and stood. "Now, I'll give you two assignments to work on. One." He produced a closed leather-bound book. "Use this Far Scribe book to write to me about yourself. Your life, your greatest adventures, your abilities and spells." When Victor took the book, he nodded and said, "Two. Acquire a dwelling in Sojourn. I take it you're staying at an inn?" When Victor nodded, he continued, "I'll be helping you build a cultivation chamber, so you'll need your own place. It would be best if it had access to the actual soil of this small planet—don't purchase or rent an apartment."

"Okay." Victor felt a little numb, a little shell-shocked. How had things moved so quickly? He'd somehow agreed to spend many years helping and learning from this guy, and now he was getting signed up to compete in a free-for-all competition in a dungeon and being sent to buy a house. "Uh . . ."

"What is it? Any questions? I'll be in touch. If you see my spirit bird, allow it to chirp in your ear, and you'll hear its words."

"Um . . ." Victor's mind felt scattered, so he blurted the only question that came to his tongue. "I have some magical things to identify. Could you recommend . . ."

"Ha! No, boy. I have things to teach you, the first of which is to figure things out on your own when you can. You may leave. As I said, I'll be in touch with the details for your entry into the Vault of Valor."

"Vault of . . ."

"That's the name of the dungeon. Now, get going. I have an important meeting." He snapped his fingers, and the spirit bird reappeared. "Show him to Fregasius. He's to convey him home." The bird swooped around Victor, rushed to the door, and commenced flitting about, waiting for him. Victor turned to follow it, but Ranish Dar spoke again. "Victor, wait."

Victor turned back to him. "Yes?"

"Take this." He flicked something small that glinted like silver his way, and Victor snatched it out of the air. It was a signet ring—a broad silver band with a black gemstone inlaid with a flickering golden sun that seemed to burn in the depths of the facet. "Wear it. It will grant you certain privileges in this tower of the Arcanum, and should you run into trouble in Sojourn, people will know to alert me so that I might come to your aid. Do not use it to curry favor in my name, however." He stared hard at Victor until he nodded. "Good. Take some time to relax and live your life, Victor. You're going to be very busy soon."

32

⬥⬥⬥

SUCCESS

It turned out that Fregasius was some sort of being of magic and shadow, fully enveloped by dark robes and a hooded cloak. Victor could see two pale dim orbs in the depths of the hood that must have been his eyes, but he never spoke in the short time Victor spent with him. When the flitting magical bird chirped into his ear, Fregasius stepped onto a rune-inscribed silver disc about eight feet in diameter and beckoned for Victor to follow. As soon as he set foot upon it, the disc flared with blue Energy, and the next thing Victor knew, he was standing in front of the inn where he and his companions had rented rooms.

"Shit," he muttered, completely taken off guard. When he'd seen the disc, he thought it might be some kind of flying platform, not a teleportation platform! Outside the inn, pedestrian traffic was light, but plenty of people were going about their evening business, and they gave him a bit of a wide berth, likely due to his sudden appearance, not because of any threat they felt. Victor made a fist with his right hand and looked at Ranish Dar's signet ring. It was cool, he supposed, to have it, but it also rankled something in him, almost as if Dar was laying claim to his property. He shook his head and lowered his fist.

"No point crying about it now." He appreciated the comfort Lifedrinker's harness gave him, holding her out of the way on his back, but he also missed resting his hand on her silvery axe-head when he spoke to himself; it made it easier to shrug off any concern about how his muttered dialogue made him look to any casual observers. Sighing, he turned and made his way up to the room he shared with Valla. When he arrived, he found a note pinned to the door with a silver hairpin:

V,
We're in Lam's room. Come see us when you're back!
—V

Victor chuckled at the note from V to V, then turned and walked down the hall until he came to Lam's door. The handle was locked, but when he knocked on the wood, it opened in just a few seconds, revealing Valla's hopeful face. When she saw him, she pulled it wide and veritably jumped into his arms, squeezing him around the neck. "We were worried Ranish had duplicitous motives for sending us off without you."

"Nah. He's a serious guy, but I think he shoots pretty straight." When she let go of his neck, he handed her the hairpin he'd pulled from their door. "I'm saving that note. Might get it made into a tattoo," he said, pulling her a little closer to kiss her gently on the forehead. "Well?" he asked, pulling back. "How is she?"

Valla's smile fell away, and she whispered, "Inconsolable! She's only Level Seven now! Also, she broke into a sobbing fit when she found out you'd agreed to be Ranish Dar's apprentice in exchange for helping her. You should speak to her."

Victor groaned, shaking his head. He'd hoped Edeya would only lose a single tier at most, dropping down into the twenties from her recent acquisition of Level Thirty. "All right." He stepped into the room, and Valla closed the door with a solid *thunk*. He could hear women's voices from the bedroom and walked that way.

Valla didn't follow him. "I'll wait out here. Tell Lam I need something from her." When Victor looked at her with a raised eyebrow, she added, "You need to speak to her alone."

"Sheesh. Why do I feel like I'm going into an arena fight?"

She chuckled, squinting at him. "Be brave! You'll be fine."

Victor looked at her for a long second, savoring every detail, from her narrowed amused eyes to the gleam of reflected light on her wings. Then he nodded and went into the bedroom, where he found Lam sitting on the side of the bed beside a blanket-covered Edeya. They were speaking quietly, but he picked up a snippet of Edeya's last words, muttered in a bitter tone.

". . . forward to going back to the Blue Deep and hunting forest Yeksa trying to get my class again." When her eyes fell on Victor, though, they opened wide, and she threw her blanket off and tried to climb out of bed. Lam restrained her, pressing on her shoulder, apparently easily holding her down. In frustration, Edeya cried, "Let me up! I just want to hug him!" Lam relented, sighing and shaking her head.

"You need to rest . . ." Despite her words, she trailed off and smiled when she saw how furiously Edeya charged over the soft gray carpet to slam into Victor. He laughed and gently pressed her close, trying not to ruffle her delicate dragonfly wings. They flared brightly, shimmering with sparkling blue Energy, dripping motes that fell at their feet, forming a misty cloud around their ankles.

"Hey, hey," he said softly. "You're squeezing me like I'm going off to prison. I'm not going anywhere." She kept squeezing, and Victor laughed. "Jeez, you're going to break my ribs!" The truth was, he could hardly feel the pressure, but he could see her straining and didn't want to highlight her lack of strength. "Damn! Look at the Energy pouring out of those wings! Are they always like that?"

"It's enhanced by emotion," Lam answered for her.

Edeya finally spoke, loosening her hold on him. "Thank you, Victor. Thank you so much! Lam told me everything. I . . . I'm starting to remember that night. Just flashes of horrible things . . . that woman's evil laugh!" She shuddered against him; frustrated with his inability to look her in the face, Victor channeled some Energy into his Alter Self spell, reducing his size further, down to something like six feet so that he could hold her at arm's length and peer into her beautiful blue, faintly glowing eyes.

"Don't think about that shit, all right? Those assholes are dead or gone, and they'll never get anywhere near you again."

"She's still out there, Victor. I . . ." Again, she stammered, but she forced herself to soldier on, completing the thought with wide eyes, staring into Victor's soul. "I have faint memories, like glimpses of a dream. She spoke to me in my prison, whispered terrible promises . . ."

"Damn it! Stop giving that *bruja* power. She can't touch you now. She's a trillion miles away, and there's no one in her whole fucking world who can get to you here." He gently nudged her toward the bed and helped her back into her spot. Lam stood and pulled the blanket back over her, and then Victor said, "Um, Lam, Valla wanted to speak to you."

"Oh?" She narrowed her eyes at Victor, then glanced at Edeya and nodded. "I'll be right out there, sweet."

"I know." Edeya sniffed and offered her a smile. Victor sat down where Lam had been and took Edeya's small slender hand. "Roots, your hands are *rough*!" She laughed, and the genuine amusement in her eyes looked good on her.

"You're going to be fine," Victor said, as though he'd just come to that realization.

She groaned, and the amusement faded, replaced by fresh moisture as tears sprang into her eyes. "I'm so weak! I lost my class; I'm back to children's levels!"

"Eh, I wasn't much higher than that when we met. It doesn't take that long to get up to where you were . . ."

"Only my entire life!" She pulled her hand out of his, made a fist, and thumped him on the thigh. Her knuckles were light, and he barely registered the impact.

"That was the first time. Now you have resources and friends. You've got an advanced bloodline! This is good, Edeya. You're going to get different class options, and I bet they'll be a hell of a lot better than the first time through. Didn't Lam tell you? Ranish Dar said there are rich and powerful people who would pay good money for a second chance at class selection."

Edeya exhaled a big shuddering sigh and, to Victor's surprise, chuckled again. "She tried. I haven't been very reasonable. What about you, though? What about what you had to promise that giant . . . stone man?" She hesitated before she said "stone," and it was Victor's turn to chuckle.

"He's crazy looking, isn't he?"

Again, Edeya went from near tears to giggling, and she nodded. "He looked more like a monster than a man."

"That's just because you didn't hear him speak much. He's very, very powerful, Edeya. Don't worry about me, all right? Of course, I don't like being pushed into it, but learning from him will probably be good for me in the long run."

"I just feel so guilty. If I was stronger; if I could have fought her off . . . Lam said she almost killed her, too. If Kethelket hadn't—"

"Didn't I tell you to stop thinking about that shit?" Victor growled and took her hand again, squeezing it. "Think my hands got hard like this 'cause I sit around moping about the fights I lost?"

Edeya's eyes narrowed, and he couldn't tell if she was getting ready to laugh or yell. She settled for calling him out on his bullshit. "Lam said you moped around for about a month after the final battle."

Victor laughed. "Fair enough. You got me. Okay, so do you wanna compare screwups? You got caught by surprise by a Death Caster with thirty levels on you. I walked into a trap because I was too full of myself." He shrugged. "So, yeah, you can be mad, but not at yourself. Got it?"

She nodded. "I've got it."

Victor smiled and reached up to brush some lingering moisture off her cheek. "Now, let's talk about how you're going to get some levels quickly, huh?"

Darren gazed upon his newly formed Core and basked in the pride of his accomplishment. He could hardly believe he'd done it, could scarcely believe that the swirling ball of crackling red Energy was his. The process had been tedious, requiring some leaps of faith and deep contemplation, but in the end, he'd done it, pulling his Energy into the correct shape and infusing it with the *idea* of chaotic lightning. Where before he'd had an amorphous blob of golden placid Energy, he now had a swirling elliptical storm of wild red lightning in his Core. It seemed richer, deeper, and more potent despite the amount of reported Energy being the same on his status sheet. Before they faded or he accidentally sent them away, he looked at his System messages again:

Congratulations! You have learned a new skill: Wildarc Cultivation Drill, Basic.

Congratulations! You have formed a new Core: Wildarc Class, Base 1.

Congratulations! You have gained a new affinity: Lightning, 8.

Congratulations! You have gained a new affinity: Chaos, 7.4.

He felt an overwhelming sense of pride seeing those messages and wished he could save them somehow or share them with Lesh. As they began to fade, though, Darren sighed and pulled up his status sheet:

Status	
Name:	Darren Whitehorse
Race:	Human: Base 1
Class:	–
Level:	1
Core:	Wildarc Class: Base 1

Energy Affinity:	Lightning 8, Chaos 7.4, Unattuned 6.1		Energy:	97/97
Strength:	6	Vitality:	7	
Dexterity:	5	Agility:	5	
Intelligence:	9	Will:	3	
Points Available:	0			
Titles & Feats:	–			
Skills:				
System Language Integration		Not Upgradeable		
Wildarc Cultivation Drill		Basic		
Spells:				
–		–		

He didn't know how impressive it might look to anyone else, but to him, it was a damn sight better to see that he no longer had blanks where his Core was listed. It didn't hurt that the tome he'd been studying and the process of building his Core had granted him a "cultivation drill." If he hadn't listened to his colleagues back in First Landing going on and on about their levels and Energy, he wouldn't have a clue what that meant. Still, he *had* listened to them and knew he now had a way to build up his Energy reserves and hopefully level up his Core.

He was still sitting, legs crossed before him, in front of the big bay windows, and he looked out at the beautiful lights in the nighttime city of Sojourn. It was, literally, magical—a view that would rival a Manhattan penthouse for sheer impressiveness. The crystal towers of the city center looked like the fingers of gods sticking up from the glittering streets. Magical conveyances filled the night sky, all lit up with one magical light or another. Some glowed like faint neon roses; others flickered like rainbow bottle rockets as they zoomed hither and yon. "God, I'm glad I came with them," he muttered, feeling something like contentment for the first time in many, many years.

He was startled from his nightgazing when the hotel room door opened and shut with a thud. "Fosterling!" Lesh boomed. "How goes your toil?"

Darren sprang to his feet, his knees almost buckling from the sudden straightening after being crossed for hours. "Lesh! Er, *Elder* Lesh! I did it! I made a Core!" Darren stumbled forward, almost falling to the carpet, but gathered himself as he walked toward the door and the imposing dragonkin.

"I knew you would, fosterling. You're a member of my household now; failure was impossible."

"I . . ." Darren suddenly felt a wave of emotion he hadn't expected. It was something he couldn't quite explain, something like pride but different—softer, more . . . emotional. "Thank you, Elder."

"Well? Tell me about your Core."

"I successfully created a Wildarc Core, Elder. I also learned a cultivation drill in the process."

"Excellent! Not many can say the same. That's something to take pride in! You'll be gaining levels in no time. So? You have affinities for lightning and chaos, yes?"

"Yes! I think they're high, too. My lightning is . . ."

"Stop there, fosterling. I appreciate your trust, but you must know that the numbers the System puts on your affinities are things you should hold close to your chest. I will hear them if you trust me; you've already shared with me your affinities, so I know much that could harm you already. Still, keep such information well guarded. Only share them with people you fear no betrayal from, only with people who won't spread your secrets."

Darren stood only a few feet from the huge man, and he could feel something different about him, something like a palpable, heavy heat radiating from him. Was that his Energy? His aura? Darren wondered if he was more sensitive now that he had a Core of his own. He nodded and smiled, clasping his hands before himself nervously. He wanted to share! He was proud of what he'd done. Would Lesh think him stupid for doing so? Despite his fear, Darren nodded and said, "I trust you, Elder Lesh."

"Tell me, then."

"My lightning affinity is eight, and my chaos is seven point four."

Lesh coughed and then chuckled, shaking his big reptilian head. "Those are excellent numbers, Darren. Very high, by any world's standard. You're going to work great magics one day." Suddenly, a small cask was in Lesh's hand, and he moved across the room, sitting before the big windows on the ground near the spot Darren had previously occupied. "This calls for celebration. We'll drink to your success. Sit. I also have news for you."

Darren followed and sat beside him, accepting the mug of pungent, eye-watering alcohol Lesh poured for him. "News?"

"Lord Victor has succeeded in his quest to aid Edeya. She is awake and whole."

"Oh? That's great!" Darren looked out the window, and a wistful expression crossed his face. "Does that mean we're leaving soon?"

"I think not." Lesh reached over, clicked his mug against Darren's, and said, "A toast to your success! *Frakgrakshra!*" The last word sounded like Lesh was either choking or growling, and Darren winced at the volume of the word. Lesh laughed. "It's a toast from my home. It basically means that we enjoy the marrow of our enemies' bones."

Darren chuckled nervously, licked his lips, and said, "I'll drink to that." Of course, the liquor was potent and burned all the way down, sending him into a coughing fit until his face was beet red. Still, when it passed, he had a delightful buzz, and the view out the window looked even more beautiful. "We're not leaving?"

"No. The young Ghelli princess suffered a great loss of Energy in the process of her recovery. Victor and the others think this city offers too many opportunities for her to leave so soon. More than that, Lord Victor has new obligations to a great master here. We may be living in Sojourn for a while."

Despite himself, Darren took another drink of the harsh liquor. This time, it didn't choke him, and he noted some of the spices—he thought he tasted something like cinnamon and a weird floral aftertaste. As the warm euphoric buzz intensified, he stared out the window, watching a soaring silver and green bird that seemed to be made of living light. When it faded from view, he said, "I think I'm glad."

"As you should be. I never could have dreamed of gaining my first levels in a place so rich. I have bargained with Victor on your behalf. He's agreed to allow you to accompany Edeya into one of the many dimensional dungeons in this world."

"A dungeon?"

Lesh nodded, grinning and drinking his booze. Darren had, of course, heard of such things. He'd heard plenty of stories about Morgan Hall and his adventures prior to coming to First Landing. He'd had to sit through many speculative conversations and meetings about the System and its strange penchant for challenging the people who lived under its rule. Something was different now, however. For the first time, he was excited about the idea of leveling. He couldn't say he liked the thought of crawling through a dark maze filled with monsters, but there had to be a price for gaining levels, spells, skills, and Energy, right? Besides, if Victor sent Edeya into a dungeon, he'd ensure she was ready. Even if he didn't like Darren, he'd probably be safe with her, wouldn't he? "Did you say she's a princess?"

"Ah, nothing official. She just seems like one to me. Don't you think she's beautiful?"

"Um, sure. I mean, she seems kind of wan and sickly, but maybe if she weren't on death's door . . ."

"Ha!" Lesh clapped him on the back, and Darren sloshed some of his drink onto the carpet. "That's right! You've only ever seen her as a spiritless ghoul. You'll see what I mean." Lesh kicked his feet out and leaned back. "I'm pleased by your progress, Darren. I think your growth will be entertaining. I just need to convince Lord Victor to help me improve, too. I hope he shares some of the wealth of knowledge he gains from the great master he's now bound to."

Darren nodded, sipping his drink and mimicking Lesh's posture. "I'm sure he will, Elder Lesh. I'm sure he will."

33

THE VAULT

Three days after Ranish Dar healed Edeya's spirit, Victor woke early in the morning, and his mind wouldn't let him fall back asleep. He slipped from his bed, donned some comfortable clothes, and picked up the leather shoulder satchel where he'd stowed the dark stone crown and the globe of ivid royal jelly. He stared for a long moment at Valla's sleeping form, a stupid smile on his face. Despite her wings, she looked small and peaceful, and he savored the serene expression she bore as she lay curled under the fluffy white comforter, her head buried in an equally luxurious pillow. After several long seconds, soaking in the sight, he quietly slipped out of the bedroom and left a note for her on their suite's dining table.

> *Valla,*
> *Gone to do some shopping—back before lunch.*
> *—Victor*

He left the hotel unarmored, but Lifedrinker hung comfortably in her harness, and he wasn't really worried about a fight without his wyrm-scale vest; he'd grown much sturdier since Tes made it for him. It wasn't that he didn't think it helped. It was just that anything that couldn't cut through it wasn't likely to kill him very easily, especially if he berserked. Naturally, he'd rather not get cut or scraped or stabbed, but for a shopping trip, he felt comfort was worth the risk. He'd picked out a merchant from the map's guidebook the night before and hurriedly made his way toward the address, following the little line on the crystal tablet, chuckling at how much it reminded him of a GPS.

After ten minutes of his long strides through little to no traffic, he approached the building just as the sun began to rise, sending the distant crystal towers into a jaw-dropping spectacle of orange, yellow, and red shimmers. The Artificer's shop was a long narrow structure made of plain brown brick, but it looked well maintained, and the sign that hung over the black iron door looked like a piece of art—wood carved into the shape of a sleeping dragon painted turquoise and gold, and inscribed with the words *Slevensor's Fine Enchantments.*

When he pulled on the cold iron handle, the door didn't budge. "Of course," Victor sighed. Just because he couldn't sleep didn't mean the whole city would wake up for him. He stuffed his hands in his pockets and turned, looking up and down the street, wondering if any nearby businesses were open, hoping to find someplace to kill some time. He saw smoke rising from a chimney on the building at the corner and started walking that way, hoping he'd spy a bakery or restaurant. He'd only taken two steps, though, when a shutter clattered open above him, and a sharp feminine voice called out, "Who comes calling at this hour?"

Victor turned, looking up, and saw a human-sized bird looking out at him. Bird was the wrong term—she had a beak and downy yellow feathers, but he could also see her arms and hands on the windowsill. She wore a gauzy blue robe over her feather-covered but humanoid torso. "Oh, hello," he said, shielding his eyes from the rising sun as he peered at her.

"Well, are you here for business or something more sinister?" After she finished speaking, she made a funny cooing sound in her throat.

"Business."

"Come on, then. I'll open the door. Just finished my breakfast." Before he could reply, she slammed the shutters closed. Victor stepped back to the door and waited. A couple of minutes later, he heard the locks click, and then the same bird woman pushed the door open and beckoned him in. "Hurry now, don't let the morning chill in."

Victor had resized himself to a comfortable six and a half feet and easily slipped into the shop, allowing her to pull the door closed. The interior was a lot like he'd expected—lots of wooden shelves built into the walls and lots of curios, figurines, books, and knickknack-looking objects all over the place. The proprietress beckoned him to follow her to the counter, where she hopped atop a stool, trilled a pleased-sounding note, and asked, "What can I help you with?"

"A few things, I suppose. I'm Victor, by the way."

"Tria is what the beakless call me." Again, she chirped a funny, pleasant sound, bobbing her head, and Victor wondered if that was a thing avian species did because they couldn't express themselves with smiles and frowns.

"Nice to meet you. Um, first, I'd like you to have a look at an item. I think it has a spirit in it, or maybe it's just conscious, but I didn't want to bond with it until I knew more." He lifted the crown from his belt and set it on the wooden counter with a *thunk*. Tria immediately recoiled, waving her feather-bedecked arm back and forth in front of her.

"I'll not touch that, but I can see its auras and read its runes from here. You truly have no idea what it is?"

Victor shrugged. "I took it from the corpse of an undead son of a bitch." He frowned and added, "Actually, I killed him, then found his corpse in another place with this on his head."

"That makes sense. It has a wounded, mad spirit within. Moreover, the runes indicate that this is a lifeward relic—more precisely, an *undead* lifeward relic. It's a brutal, crude enchantment, too. Whoever created it was new to the concept, I'd wager. I can assure you that anyone whose undying life was preserved by this relic would have had a long, painful recovery. You say his body was dead, though, when you found him?"

"Yeah." Victor sighed and fidgeted for a minute, rubbing his chin. "I, uh, pulled his heart out before he could disappear. I also destroyed a piece of his spirit that was in the heart. Would that matter?"

The woman's large black and yellow eyes widened further, and she shrank back from him. "Elder gods! Such savagery!"

"He had it coming." Victor shrugged and put his hands in his pockets, trying not to look threatening. "I'm not a madman; you can relax."

"Whatever the circumstances, yes, I believe what you did to the being who wore this crown surely interrupted his reconstitution. Undoubtedly, it's his damaged spirit that dwells within it. Tell me, did you not find the crown's anchor?"

"Anchor?"

"A paired artifact where the crown would bring the wearer when it saved his life."

"Ah!" Victor pulled the heavy key still inside the marble-sized silver ball from around his neck and set it on the counter. "If I twist this key, that little ball of silver expands to make a round room. Inside that is where I found the corpse and the crown."

"Lovely!" Tria leaned forward, making tiny cooing sounds as she peered at the key. "This is something altogether different. Where the crown is crude and brutal in its function, this is elegant and powerful—it's Fae-forged silver and of a quality, I'm not ashamed to admit, I wouldn't be able to match. I have difficulty believing this is the anchor to that ghastly crown. Can we open it?"

Victor picked up the key and looked around the shop, frowning. "I don't think it'll fit in here."

"To my workshop, then—this way." She stepped through the curtain hanging behind her, and Victor followed, snatching the crown off the counter on his way. The room behind the shop was very spacious, with high ceilings and workbenches on three of the four walls. Tria pointed to some wooden tables near the center and said, "If we move those to the side, will there be enough room?"

"I think so. It filled the top of a stone tower when I found it, but it couldn't have been more than ten paces across." Victor measured the workshop with his strides, nodding when he reached fourteen before he could touch the back workbench. "Yeah, I think it's plenty big."

Tria lingered by the door. "Please proceed to open it, then. I'll watch from here." Victor nodded, stepped to the center of the room, and placed the little silver marble on the ground. Holding it in place with his finger and thumb, he twisted the key and stepped back. Brilliant silver light and hissing steam erupted from the little device as it rapidly expanded, filling the center of the workshop as it grew into the room-sized, silvery, rune-etched spherical vault. When it stopped growing and steaming, the door with the key protruding from it faced Victor and Tria. She began to make that cooing sound, rushing forward to run her delicate fingers over the surface of the rune-etched metal. "I wasn't wrong!"

"About?"

"This is Fae-craft—this metal, these wondrous designs! This is indeed a vault, Victor. A portable vault made for the storage of items most dear. I shudder to think of the power required to open this chamber without the key." She gestured to the key. "May I?" Victor nodded, his mind running away with her words. Was the "Fae-craft" vault capable of holding the ivid royal jelly? He wanted to ask her but worried about her reaction when she saw the treasure. What if she coveted it? What if she sold the information of his possession to someone more powerful who would want it? While he pondered the idea, Tria opened the door and stepped into the sphere.

Almost immediately, she cried, "I can see the crown's anchor." He followed her in and saw she was pointing at the hanging red crystal, squinting
at the baleful red light it cast. "This doesn't belong. Nor does that silver chair.
Look there, at the chair's feet; the silver clearly doesn't match the Fae-forged
silver. It's crudely designed, too, in comparison to the sphere's elegance."

Victor nodded. "Yeah, well, the guy's corpse was in the chair, under the
gem, so maybe he installed it for that purpose." He frowned, lifting the crown
from his belt again. "Is this thing valuable? Could it save me the way it tried
to save Dunstan?"

"Dunstan?"

"The name of the undead guy."

"Oh, I see. No, I'm afraid not." She chirped softly and shivered, ruffling
her feathers up and down her arms. "Not unless you wanted to become a
member of the unliving. As for its value, I'm sure you could find a Death
Caster or even one of the openly undead here in Sojourn who'd pay a tidy
sum for it and the anchor." She pointed at the glowing round jewel.

"I have a better idea." Victor reached up and pulled on the red crystal
globe, putting more and more pressure on the silvery chain it hung from,
smiling as the soft weld of molten silver separated from the harder metal
of the dome. When it came free, he set the strange glowing artifact atop
the throne, then placed the crown beside it. "Stand back." As Tria scurried
away, her dexterous taloned feet clicking on the metal, he cast Honor the
Spirits. A wild grin spread on his face as the white flames of his spirit
magic took the throne, the crown, and the red globe away to the spirit
plane.

"What did . . ." Tria rushed forward, little clicking chirps sounding from
her throat. "What did you do?"

"I gave them to my ancestors."

"What?" She looked at him with wide stunned eyes. "You destroyed
them? For superstition?"

Suddenly, Victor's rage-attuned Energy flared into his pathways, and
he felt his aura slipping from his control as his Quinametzin haughtiness
asserted itself. He seemed to swell with the power, and his eyes flared with
dangerous red Energy as he snapped, "My ancestors would not be pleased to
hear those words!"

Tria shrank back and ducked her head, waving her feathery arms over her
head. "Apologies, Lord! I spoke hastily, shocked at the loss of those materials,
that's all. I beg you, forget I said such a thoughtless thing." Her obvious fear

and obsequious behavior were like a splash of cold water to Victor. He hated that he'd scared her and was furious that he'd let his control slip. He yanked his rage back into his Core and clamped down on his aura like an iron vise.

"No, Tria, I'm the one who's sorry. I didn't mean to let your words upset me like that. It's my bloodline—sometimes I lose my grip on it."

She slowly straightened, dropping her arms to her side and squinting her big round eyes up at him. She was probably only about five feet tall, and clearly any levels she'd gained had come from crafting—he felt like a total asshole for frightening her. "May I ask you a question without enraging you?" Her voice was trepidatious, and he could hear the nervousness in the little clicking coos she made after speaking.

"Yeah, of course. I'm paying attention now; I won't lose it again."

"Are you young?"

"Yeah. I guess so. In years, anyway."

She nodded and took a hesitant step closer. "I think I understand then. My class allows me to see more about people and objects than the average person, and I can see you've advanced your bloodline greatly. That's always harder the younger you are. As one gains the power of a potent species without much time between ranks, it's sometimes difficult to come to grips with it. In that case, I commend you for the control you've thus far displayed."

"Thank you. By the way, I appreciate your help in identifying the crown and helping me understand this vault better. I'm happy to pay a fee for that help. I have another question, too, if you wouldn't mind."

"I've done nothing worthy of payment today, Victor. I happily share my knowledge with clients in the hopes of building a relationship. I only ask that you please think of my shop first if you need magical goods."

"Done." Victor gestured to the room, no longer tinged with the baleful red light of the crystal orb but instead seemingly lit from an invisible ambient source in a soft silvery glow. "Can this vault hold more powerful artifacts than my other storage devices? My rings, for example?" Victor held up his right hand, wriggling his fingers and the storage rings.

"Oh, yes! This vault is much, much, much sturdier! More than that, it's safe to put sentient beings within this vault and then reduce its size. Even a living person could sit in this room while you carried it about on that chain around your neck." She paused and made a strange, tremulous clicking coo. "Well, only until they ran out of air. This space would be quite tightly sealed when closed."

"Really?" Victor looked around the vault's interior at the softly illuminated silver walls utterly covered with strange engraved runes and patterns. "It can hold living creatures?"

"Yes! If you have the knowledge to understand them, I'll show you the enchantments that make it possible. Whoever earned or stole this vault from the Fae had a wondrous treasure on their hands. I can create something similar, but nothing this large or this sturdy."

Victor smiled. "I'm not an enchanter." He tried to think of a way to ask about the ivid royal jelly without putting himself or it at risk and decided it wasn't worth it. If she coveted what he had, she was likely too weak or fearful to take him on, but there was no telling what sort of powerful people she might know. Instead, he asked, "Is there any way to tell if something I put into this vault is harming it?"

She made a different sort of bubbling, cooing sound, clearly a laugh, and shook her head. "If you had something that could damage this vault, I'd be astonished. Nothing I've ever worked with could harm it, and I've assisted some of the masters deep into their lustrous veils, crafting special artifacts, one of which was so potent that I had to ward myself against it lest I turn to dust in its presence."

"Even so, is there any way to tell if I've damaged it?"

"Certainly. The walls of this sphere will begin to tarnish and then crack. If you see that happening, remove the item, and the vault will repair itself given enough time."

Victor sighed and nodded, delighted by the unexpected turn of events. He'd thought he'd have to begin a tedious search for a container capable of holding the royal jelly, only to find the thing he'd been carrying around his neck for weeks and weeks was exactly what he needed. That and being rid of the dark crown were like two weights off his shoulders. He gestured to the door. "Shall we? Before I leave, I'd like to look at some of the things you have for sale."

"Of course!" She preceded him out of the vault, and before he followed, Victor lowered the leather satchel containing the royal jelly to the floor, setting it just inside the doorway. Once outside, he swung the door closed with a heavy, satisfying *clang* and then turned the key all the way to the left, locking it and reducing the room back down to marble-sized. He put the chain over his head and let the priceless talisman hang beneath his shirt. Feeling much lighter without his earlier burdens, he followed Tria back into her storefront. She perched atop her stool and asked, "What sorts of things do you need?"

"I have a couple of very low-level friends who are going to have their first adventure in a dungeon soon. I thought I should buy them some supplies. A weapon for one, maybe some armor or magical clothing, some helpful trinkets, and maybe an expanding shelter." He chuckled and shook his head. "Nothing like my vault, but yeah, a sturdy tent or . . . "

"A cozy little cabin that's bigger on the inside than out? Something they might erect after a difficult battle?"

"Now you're speaking my language!" Victor leaned his elbow on the counter, grinning. "Truthfully, I'm only really concerned about one of them, but I can't very well bring her a bunch of equipment and leave the other guy empty-handed, right? I guess the better he does, the more help he'll be for her, so . . . " Victor let his words trail off and shrugged.

"I think we can come up with a wonderful beginner's kit for both of them, and it shouldn't cost you too much, either. Let's start by talking about armor—I've got some vests with shimmersteel rings you should take a look at, and then . . . "

34

A BRIEF RESPITE

The few days following his visit to Tria's shop were some of the best days Victor could ever remember. Reflecting on that time, he knew it was because he spent it with Valla, and they didn't feel there was anything they had to do, no emergency they had to handle. Nothing felt like life or death, and they took their time sleeping in, touring villas and townhomes for sale, eating at restaurants, and forgetting about everyone else's problems for a while. He'd purchased some low-tier dungeoneering gear, as Tria called it, for Darren and Edeya, and then he'd left them in Lam and Lesh's capable hands while he worked on his first quest for Ranish Dar—procuring property in Sojourn.

Even after buying a few excellent items for the two low-level members of his entourage, he still had roughly a million Energy beads, but Victor quickly learned that a million beads wouldn't go very far in Sojourn. He also learned that there were well-established money-lending institutions in the city and that he, being Tier Six and having an epic-tier racial status, would easily qualify for enormous loans—all he had to do was sign his soul away.

That's how he thought of it, at least, but even he'd admit he was being hyperbolic. The loans were structured in such a way that should he miss a payment, he'd start to notice a tiny draw on his Energy, a siphoning of his Core. If he continued to miss them, the draw would increase, and that process would repeat until he either became a living battery, feeding the bank a constant supply of Energy, or he paid the loan balance.

To Victor, the process sounded like glorified slavery, and he refused to consider it. Valla was in his corner, and so the property broker they'd found in the guidebook relented and began showing them homes that fit his budget—they weren't exactly palatial. In the end, on the third day of touring, Victor settled on a small villa in an older part of Sojourn about an hour's walk from the downtown crystal towers, and that was taking into account the sidewalks that sped a person's movement.

The villa was sandwiched between two others, and they all shared courtyard walls, but those walls were thick, made of sturdy stone, and twelve feet tall—once inside, it felt private. The villa was old but well made, built from whitewashed stone of some sort, and all the floors were tiled in a way that reminded Victor very much of Saltillo, so much so that he almost immediately agreed to the asking price of eight hundred thousand beads.

The home's layout was simple, with a kitchen, dining room, parlor, three bedrooms, and a communal bath. Victor's favorite part of the place was the basement, or cellar, which was spacious, cool, and fully lined with the same stone that made up the home. He figured it would be good enough for whatever Ranish Dar had planned with regard to a cultivation chamber.

Valla loved the courtyard and garden. It was clear that the previous owner had possessed a green thumb, and many of the mature plants bore fruit and flowers year round in the city's mild climate. A small fountain trickled musically amid a tiny hidden nook surrounded by high flowering shrubs, and it felt almost like a secret getaway from the rest of the city and even the home itself.

When Lam heard Victor had bought a property in Sojourn, she of course felt that she had to as well, but Victor talked her out of it. His home only had three bedrooms, but he reminded her about his travel home, saying he'd set it up in the courtyard. That opened a great deal more space for the group, and he reasoned it was silly for her to buy property when she had so much building and governing to get back to in the Free Marches.

Lam had agreed, and so that's where Victor and the others were, sitting outside in the garden on comfortable camp chairs with full bellies and glasses full of wine, when Ranish Dar's magical messenger bird flitted over the wall and swooped its way through the garden until it found him. When it fluttered near his ear, it chirped so that only he could discern its words, "Read the message in the master's Far Scribe book!" It didn't wait around for an answer. Rather, it streaked away into the night sky like a bottle rocket.

"What was it?" Valla asked, and everyone else stared at him with wide, expectant eyes, even Darren.

"I, uh, must have a message from Dar." Victor quickly scanned through his storage ring for the appropriate Far Scribe book and summoned it forth. He turned to the most recently filled page, just past the dense dissertation about his abilities and training that he'd written for Ranish Dar. On the new page, he found a short, elegantly scribed message:

Victor,
The time is nigh. Report to the World Hall at midnight.
—Ranish

"Huh. Short and sweet." He sighed, stretching his neck until it popped like an inch-thick branch being snapped. "Guess I have to report to that dungeon tonight."

"Dungeon?" Edeya asked, shooting to her feet. "I thought that was just me and Darren!" She'd grown quite comfortable with the idea over the last few days, and according to Lesh, she and Darren had been working hard on their basic combat abilities, though Edeya was miles ahead of the onetime politician.

"Nah, my new, uh, shit, what do I call that guy? Teacher? I'm *not* calling him master. Anyway, he wants me to go into this competition dungeon so he can watch my performance and, I guess, earn some clout in the city if I kick some ass."

Edeya looked from Lam to Lesh to Valla, scowling. "You knew about this?"

"Yes . . ." Lam started to say.

"Why didn't you tell me?" She looked incensed, and Victor couldn't quite figure out why, especially half-inebriated as he was. When Lam frowned and didn't reply immediately, she whirled on Victor. "Why didn't you tell me?"

"It didn't come up! You were busy with Lam or Lesh whenever we talked about it. What's the—"

"So you would have just slipped away tonight if I hadn't been here when that magic bird arrived?"

Victor felt his pulse quicken, felt the heat of indignation on his neck, and then he felt Valla's cool fingers gripping his wrist. He took a deep breath and said, "Hell no, Dey!" He and Valla had picked up on Lam's affectionate nickname for Edeya and had used variations of it frequently while she recovered. "I would've said goodbye. You don't need to be worried; Dar says this dungeon has training wheels."

the pursuit of power, so it will award some of that Energy to the others still lingering in the dungeon."

"I take it you don't mean the Energy in my Core."

Dar chuckled. "No, sadly, in your case, being Level Sixty, the System would drain you enough to take away six levels."

"And anyone still in the dungeon gets a share? Even if they had nothing to do with my, uh, life-threatening situation?"

"Correct. That being the case, if you last to the end, you will likely see great gains in the dungeon."

Victor squeezed his hands into fists until his knuckles popped satisfyingly. "All right. Sounds fair."

Dar's chuckle sounded again, like stones clacking together as they fell from a wheelbarrow. "I knew you had the right sort of spirit. We're going to work well together, Victor."

"Do we all start in the same spot?"

"No! The dungeon is structured like a tower, and you'll all start at the bottom, but it's vast and has dozens of starting positions. The level is designed in such a way that each starting position is equidistant from the stairway up." Dar paused, breaking his stride as he scratched his head. "If I recall, there's only one way up from the first level, so even if you start in a room by yourself, be prepared to encounter others as you ascend."

Victor nodded. "And you and the others will be watching? That reminds me—my friends were wondering if there's any way for them to watch. Are there public, uh, viewing screens or something?"

"Naturally! Many establishments in the city have access to the viewing stones. Ah! I should explain that. Each of you will have an egg-shaped stone following you, floating in the air behind and above you. People with the correct access can view you and your exploits through that stone."

"Huh. Like a drone, I guess."

"A drone? In a sense, I suppose the word makes sense, though these viewing stones are not controlled by anyone. Still, they aren't particularly intelligent, and you could compare them to an insect serving a hive."

"Uh . . . right." Victor didn't want to explain what he'd meant by the word. Dar walked a bit farther and stopped before large bronze doors held ajar by soldiers in dull red plate armor, their visors obscuring their features. Victor might have assumed they were human if not for their four arms and segmented, chitin-covered tails protruding from their lower backs. Inside the chamber beyond the door, a single transport pad sat on a big, marble floor in a domed chamber decorated with murals very much like those Victor had seen earlier.

More than a hundred people stood around in the chamber, though everyone clung to the stone walkway at the platform's edge—none stood on the metal. Dar gestured and said, "This is where you'll all teleport into the dungeon. It occupies a pocket dimension very close to Sojourn, as do all the dungeons purchased through the System Stone."

"Do you get to them all from the World Hall?"

"No, some are accessed through portals in parks, special buildings, or even in the limited real estate not occupied by the city." He and Victor had stepped to the side of the door and were standing apart from the other groups of people. Dar looked at Victor and nodded. "Your armor is good for an iron ranker. That helmet is nigh indestructible, and I can see the wyrm-scale was crafted by a master." He turned and slowly scanned the room, and Victor followed his gaze.

The people gathered in the hall were incredibly diverse. Most were bipedal or humanoid, as Victor thought of them, but he saw people with multiple sets of legs and others with none—serpent-like in their locomotion. Perhaps a third of the people gathered had wings of some sort, and they all varied in size from a single-eyed, brutish-looking man half again as tall as Victor to a tiny rabbit-like individual who couldn't have weighed more than twenty pounds.

Dar looked at Victor again, and his face didn't betray what he was thinking as he said, "There are some very dangerous foes in this room, but I don't see many with racial advancements on par with yours. That's an edge for you. Even those in the epic tier don't have such potent bloodlines. They'll underestimate you at their peril."

"Because of my level?"

"Exactly."

Victor folded his arms and continued to stare at the people around the room. It was hard to pick out which were contestants and which were there to send off their friends, their loved ones, or as in Dar's case, their students. Victor found the idea of calling himself a student sort of funny; he hadn't learned anything much from the man yet, but he supposed that would come. He'd only known him for a week. "Any rules?" he asked, figuring he should try to get more out of the master.

"Oh, excellent question! Once inside the dungeon, any dimensional containers on your person will become inaccessible."

"Shit. Seriously?"

"Aye. Too many folks carry too many artifacts in their storage rings. This rule keeps things a little fairer. Looking around, though, I can see many of the entrants have strapped all manner of containers on their bodies. Hmm. Do you have a satchel or pack you can fill with food? I'm not sure how long you'll be in there, but you may get hungry or thirsty."

"Jesus, Dar! Now, you tell me?"

"I don't require sustenance as you do." He frowned. "Not that you should require much with your bloodline so advanced. Have you never fasted?"

"Uh, yeah. Now that you mention it, I've gone quite a few days without food or water, and that was when my bloodline was only advanced or so."

"Aye. I imagine you mostly eat out of habit and pleasure these days. I wouldn't be concerned. I've never known this challenge to take longer than a week. You'll likely come across food and water in the tower anyway." He snapped his fingers and said, "Which reminds me: If you find a storage item in the dungeon, you'll be allowed to access it as much as you'd like."

"What about loot? I mean, if one of the others"—Victor jerked his chin at the crowded room—"dies. Can I take their stuff?"

"If the System fails to rescue them with the lifesaver, then yes, their corpses and all items upon them are fair game."

Victor opened his mouth, intent on grilling Ranish Dar until the last second, but then a gong sounded, and a bodiless voice announced, "Teleportation will commence in three minutes. All entrants must now step onto the circle."

Dar clapped him on the shoulder. "Good luck, Victor. Don't disappoint me." For the first time that day, he spoke without any levity in his voice, and Victor wondered what Dar would do if he got eliminated right away. He might lose six levels, but it also might be a quick way out of the master Spirit Caster's service. He almost laughed at the stupid thought—no way he'd throw a match even if there weren't any penalty. He nodded at Dar, gave him a thumbs-up, and strode onto the circle, watching the others as they, too, made their way onto it.

He saw that Dar was right; the people going into the dungeon were easy to pick out now that he knew to look for packs and satchels. Almost all of them had them, and one guy, who looked part snail, part lizard, part man, had no fewer than four packs and satchels hanging from his sizeable neck and shoulders, each bulging at the seams. Victor thought about digging out some healing potions and a few drinks and snacks and bundling them into an extra shirt or cloak—he was sure he had something—but decided against it. The main reason being that he didn't want to look like an idiot in front of all of his competition. Even he had to admit the sentiment was foolish, but he couldn't help it.

As he stood there, he noticed the weight of some of the competitors' auras. He'd been keeping his aura entirely in check, but he began to wonder if he should let it loose. Should he give them a taste of his power, or should he keep them guessing? The auras he felt weren't particularly potent, and he was sure his would drive them back and press far more heavily on the people around. What if he was wrong, though, and there were others standing on the pedestal who had more potent auras, only waiting to see who would give a hint of their strength?

He kept remembering when Tes had taught him how to control it, saying that people in civilized, high-Energy worlds would judge him harshly if he didn't have that control. He decided it was worse not knowing someone's strength than having a good measure, so he kept a firm grip on it. His decision was reinforced when he heard a tall man with ram's horns mutter to someone nearby, "Some weak wills on display."

Again, the gong sounded, and the weird bodiless voice announced, "Teleportation will commence in one minute." At the announcement, a circular aperture opened in the center of the ceiling, and with a faint humming sound, pale blue oval objects, almost exactly the size of a chicken's egg, floated down through the air, one for each person standing on the platform.

Thanks to Dar, Victor knew what they were, but one of the contestants nearby, someone behind him, asked in a deep scratchy voice, "What the scourge are these, then?"

A lisping feminine voice replied, "Them's how our exploits get displayed for all them folk in the city."

Victor stood far taller than most of the contestants, so when he looked around, turning in a slow circle, he could see everyone. Some wore armor, while others wore silky robes, and quite a few were dressed in very normal-looking clothes. One woman even had on an outfit that reminded him of the Legion uniform Valla used to wear. He saw weapons of all sorts, from quarterstaves to bows to hammers to a man who gripped the hilts of two short curved swords, each glowing faintly with magenta Energy. While no one looked exactly human, quite a few came close. Many such looked like human-animal hybrids, and he wondered if stories on Earth of werewolves or fox-people had their origins with such folk.

As he looked around, he immediately spotted at least one of the Tier Nine individuals. He wasn't sure how he knew other than the sense of danger he felt when he saw the flickering flames that seemed to sheathe the man's body, the dancing fires behind his cold blue eyes, and the mean, thin-lipped half-smile he wore as everyone near him tried to make space. As Victor stood there, wondering if he was right, if he was one of the "big competitors" as he'd subconsciously labeled the Tier Nines, he snapped his fingers and said, "Shit!" He'd almost forgotten about his little magical scope, and he barely located and dug it out of his storage ring before the gong chimed and the voice announced that they had ten seconds.

In a near panic, he dug around in his storage rings for a leather pouch, bag, or satchel that he could tie to his belt. He'd barely located a mundane belt pouch and tucked the scope into it as, with a flash of white light and nausea-inducing lurch, the portal hall faded away, and he found himself stumbling onto a slightly canted stone platform. The lighting had changed; bright daylight filtered down to him through the leaves of high trees, and wild animal calls sounded in the distance. Not far away, he heard the babbling of a stream or small river, and just to his left, the diminutive rabbit person he'd seen earlier squealed in surprise and leaped a dozen yards down a gravel-strewn flight of stone steps, taking flight into a stand of berry-covered saplings before Victor could so much as say hello.

Victor shrugged and tied the pouch with his scope onto his belt, then reached up and pulled Lifedrinker out of her harness. "All right, *chica*. Let's see what this place is all about. If this is a tower, it's gotta be big to have trees and sunlight in it, yeah?"

He descended the steps where the rabbit person had fled, switching his Sovereign Will boost to vitality and agility as he went. He figured he'd like to move quickly if someone got the jump on him, and failing that, he'd like to be as sturdy as possible. He'd only made it two steps, though, before a gong sounded, seemingly out of the sky, and several System announcements appeared in his vision.

All entrants are present; this competitive dungeon instance is now locked.

A Lifesaver Talisman will appear at your feet; wear it at your discretion. If you are saved by this device, you will be stripped of ten percent of your overall accumulated levels, and a portion of that Energy will be awarded to the remaining entrants.

The denizens of this dungeon have treasures that may be won through combat or subterfuge. Additionally, each entrant progressing to a new floor will be awarded a personal System-generated reward chest. The value of such rewards will be divided by the number of entrants in the dungeon.

Good luck, Victor.

Victor chuckled. He had to assume the final message was tailored to everyone. He doubted the System would single him out like that, especially to wish him luck. He noticed a little cloud of blue smoke at his feet, and when he bent down to wave it away, he found a golden chain affixed to a tiny dime-sized medallion with no markings. He shrugged and hung it over his head, tucking it under his vest. As he did so, he thought about how he'd arrived on the platform at the same time as the little rabbit person. What if he'd killed him? None of them had lifesavers at that point. It seemed kind of sloppy to him but not at all at odds with his view of the often callous System.

"So," he said, giving voice to his thoughts, using Lifedrinker as an excuse, "the more people in here, the shittier the rewards. Typical System BS." He hopped down the steps, noticed a faint dirt trail, and started down it, brushing aside the thin branches covered with juicy-looking red berries that grew close. They looked delicious, but he knew better than to start eating stuff he found in a dungeon.

True, this was only the third "pocket dimension" he'd ever been in, and only one of those others had been a "dungeon," but he'd learned not to trust things managed by the System. "Especially if we're in some kind of competition," he muttered. He pushed his way through the grove, and when he came out, he saw a long green slope below him. From that vantage, he could see a lot more of the landscape, confirming that he was indeed in some sort of structure despite the open-feeling air and magical sunlight.

Down the slope, he saw high white walls in disrepair, and past them, more and more walls and weird crumbling old structures that might once have been towers or buildings. In the great distance, through a haze that seemed almost like mist or fog, he could see walls rising to a firmament-like ceiling thousands of feet above. At the center of the distant, cloud-obscured stone ceiling, he saw a great spiral stairway descending. "Yeah, this place is nuts. Nobody could make a room this big." His distant gaze was interrupted by a flash of something bright and a squeal of pain or surprise.

Victor jerked his eyes toward the source of the flash and saw an eruption of bright yellow fire, and then, before he could decide to charge toward or away from it, a System message appeared.

Ekus Vi-dronip has been rescued from certain death and removed from the dungeon. Twenty-six entrants remain. Prepare for an Energy infusion.

Victor stepped back into the grove of berry trees and crouched down, watching the landscape between the narrow trunks. Sure enough, like a sun blooming to life near the top of the central stair, a ball of Energy appeared and then exploded, streaking down toward the ground in dozens of fragments, one of which came straight toward him.

He braced himself, but the infusion wasn't enough to make him lose himself in the euphoria. It was a lot, but nothing like he'd gotten from some of his battles back in the Free Marches. While he absorbed it, he tried to track some of the other Energy balls, and he was sure he saw two of them flash down at the foot of the grassy slope just a bit past the big crumbling wall.

"Two, huh? So those guys took out the rabbit? Or was the rabbit the one who took someone out?" He doubted it. If the rabbit person had been aggressive, why would he or she have run at the sight of Victor? He gripped Lifedrinker's haft, and with a grin that said a lot about how much fun he was already having, he started jogging down the slope. "Let's find out, eh, *chica*?"

36

HEAVY FEET

Victor loped down the grassy slope toward the tall crumbling wall, aiming for a gap near a thorny, nearly leafless hedge. The grass gave way to dirt and chips of stone that looked to be remnants of ancient mortar and fallen blocks. He slowed as he approached the wall, not wanting to sound like a bull let loose in a garden. He quietly padded to the gap in the wall and edged around it, slowly taking in the scene beyond, inch by inch.

Dust and gravel coated an ancient flagstone floor, surrounded by high stone walls, enclosing a space about fifteen yards across. He saw an opening in the wall to his right, and he darted over the stone floor to that archway, pausing to peer into the next room. Just like the roofless "room" he was standing in, the one beyond the archway was empty save for chunks of rubble and dusty debris on the ground.

Victor stepped into the space, aiming for another opening in the wall across the room and to his left, but he paused, peering more closely at the floor. "Are those tracks?" he whispered to Lifedrinker, crouching and creeping toward the scuff marks on the stone. They certainly looked like tracks to him, and he could see they led toward the opening he'd been aiming for. He hurried, nimbly stepping between chips of stone, to the wall and peered through.

The area revealed by the opening was larger than the two he'd just explored. It had grassy, overgrown floor sections and a slope that led down to a central depression where it looked as though the ground had caved in millennia ago. Down in that depression, Victor saw wisps of smoke rising off scorched grass and the slag of something that looked almost like molten stone. He immediately concluded that this was the site of Ekus Vi-dronip's demise.

He scanned the area and couldn't see any sign of the aggressors. Other than the one he lurked in, two exits led from the room: one through the far wall and another to the left. Still holding Lifedrinker ready, he moved in a stealthy crouch and approached the closer left-hand exit.

He'd just reached the opening when he heard voices. A feminine one, low and kind of smoky, said, "Agreed. We'll part, but the next time we meet, we shan't hold back."

A deep, masculine voice rumbled a chuckle and said, "You act as though you do me a favor. I show you this one mercy because you alerted me and stayed your hand when I slew the beastkin."

"You didn't slay him . . ."

"I would have if the System hadn't come to the rescue."

"A rescue we're all afforded in this place . . ."

The masculine voice scoffed in exasperation. "Are you trying to ignite hostilities?"

"No . . ."

At that point, Victor, unable to contain himself, itching for a confrontation, and feeling annoyed by the tone of the snippet of conversation he'd listened to, stepped through the opening and loudly proclaimed, "Well, you attacked that poor rabbit for no reason? Not very nice."

The woman he'd interrupted reminded him so much of Victoria (Catalina! He cursed the name in his mind) that he almost attacked her outright. She was pale to the point of near transparency, had long dark hair that hung behind her as though caught in a constant breeze, and wore layers of thin silky robes that were both revealing and obscuring at the same time. She bore a short twisted black staff that looked freshly cut from a dead tree, and when she saw Victor, she took two graceful steps back.

The man was another matter—Victor had seen him before. He was the one with the fiery blue eyes and the cloak of constant flames that wreathed his body. He looked human, for the most part, though he had a bearing that was hard to picture on someone from Earth, a kind of presence that screamed nobility and power, and when he turned his gaze to Victor, there wasn't an ounce of alarm in his eyes.

"Well," he said, smirking, as his flames grew brighter and danced more eagerly along his shoulders, "how nice of you to save me the chase." Without another word or even a flicker of movement to signal the danger, a column of fire, like a flame geyser, erupted from his body, crackled and ripped into the air, and then reversed course, dropping like an avalanche of liquid fire toward Victor.

Victor didn't hesitate; he squatted and jumped back, performing a rather impressive backflip. Even in his usual non-enraged state, he was resistant to heat and fire thanks to his racial advancements and his feats, namely Flame Touched and Mountain's Resilience. Nevertheless, despite his more than eighty percent resistance and his brilliant backward flip out of the center of the fire strike, he felt the heat of those flames, and for the first time in a while, he cried out in alarm and pain as his exposed flesh burned. It wasn't enough to kill him or even slow him down, but it was plenty to enrage him. Like floodgates opening, his Core poured out a torrent of rage-attuned Energy into his pathways, and he pushed it into the pattern for Iron Berserk.

He'd gotten out of the Fire Caster's line of sight, but even as he expanded in size and his rapid regeneration began to heal his burns, a sound like thunder combined with a tornado made him look to the sky, and there he saw half a dozen fiery projectiles streaking down toward him, growing larger and larger as they approached.

"Fucking hell!" he shouted in his deep basso titan voice. He dove for the far corner of the room, and hell was brought to life around him as something like a meteor shower pounded down in the ancient ruins. Fire, shattered stone, hot gasses, uprooted soil turned molten, and the roar of a cataclysm assailed Victor as he flopped and bounced through the stone walls. Eventually, he came to rest in a pile of rubble dozens of yards from where he'd first been struck.

He was bruised, battered, and singed, but more than anything, Victor felt fury. So, this fire-loving magician had decided to lead with some sort of alpha strike? He'd opened up the sky and called down the fury of a mountain upon him. On *him*? Did he not know who he was messing with? "I'll teach him," Victor growled, feeling his Spirit Core roil with rage, feeling the echoing growl deep in his magma-attuned Breath Core. "Burn me? Throw stones at me?" His voice was like thunder.

Victor clenched his fist around Lifedrinker's haft, still lying on the stone floor, face down, with piled rubble on his back, his pants all but burned to shreds, his skin blackened from soot but fully healed beneath it. He could hear distant words, the Pyromancer speaking, perhaps saying something to the other. Victor's mind was too thick with fury to make sense.

His magma-attuned Energy was seeping into his pathways, weaving with his rage, entwining it, dulling the clarifying effects of his Iron Berserk. He wanted to smash and rip, to show the world who he was. How could he be thrown aside like this? How could he let those faceless, nameless observers watch him be so humiliated?

As the rage mounted, his body began to glow with the heat of magma. He pumped his lungs like bellows, and his eyes sparked alight with the mountain's fiery heart; black smoke plumed out from beneath his bed of broken stone and rubble. Victor allowed the pattern for Volcanic Fury to build in his pathways, and then he channeled all that hot deadly rage and magma Energy into it, overwriting his Iron Berserk.

The world brightened in sepia tones, and Victor knew only hunger. Hunger for blood, for justice, for glory, and for destruction. Deep in his angry heart, he knew there was one nearby who deserved his ire. As his body began to burn, as his rage pulsed away from him like waves of radioactive fire, he surged to his feet, throwing thousands of pounds of stone off him like so much dust.

He towered over the ruins, his head and shoulders clearing the walls, affording him a view of nearby spaces enclosed by walls. He turned, looking at the trail of charred broken walls, and was dimly aware that he'd passed that way. He took a step, and a ball of fire streaked at him from an ancient half-crumbled archway.

Victor lifted a hand and let the fireball strike it, the flames washing over him like a warm breeze. He strode forward, and when he saw the red-robed, fire-sheathed man who'd thrown it, his fury took on a palpable presence, slamming out, assaulting the psyche of any who witnessed it. He leaned forward and screamed his wrath.

As his terrible fury roared forth, shaking stones loose from the walls, vibrating the dust and gravel as a passing train might, he opened his Breath Core and let loose a spray of white-hot magma that spattered a cone-shaped area in front of him, liberally coating the man twenty yards in front of him. Victor's breath Core wasn't high level, wasn't up to the challenge of a high-tier brawl, but his Volcanic Fury doubled its efficacy, and the splash of magma sent the Pyromancer reeling.

While the man did something to mitigate the horrible heat of the molten stone that had drenched him, Victor charged forward, lifted Lifedrinker in one hand, and brought her blazing hot, smoking edge down in an air-splitting chop. Somehow, the Pyromancer summoned a torrent of fiery

Energy, and with a pulse that rivaled Victor's fury, it burst out of him, scorching the world black in a hundred-yard radius.

The spell blasted the magma off the mage, and it had a palpable weight that caught Lifedrinker in its momentum, slowing her descent and pushing Victor back a handful of yards. Still, the fire didn't harm him, nor did it bother Lifedrinker. When it was over, the Pyromancer stood, a victorious expression on his face that crumbled when he saw Victor still looming over him, completely untouched by his cataclysmic flames.

The setback had done nothing but further infuriate Victor. His every muscle, every sinew, every inch of heavy dense bone, wanted to turn that man to paste. Again, he lifted Lifedrinker, and again, he stepped forward, bringing her down like a falling star. The Pyromancer lifted his arms, formed them into an X, and brilliant white fire erupted from them, creating a partial dome that covered the wizard.

The appearance of the fiery shield didn't daunt or give Victor pause; he smashed Lifedrinker into it with abandon, putting all his tremendous weight and strength behind the blow. A shockwave erupted from the impact like a bomb going off, ripping through ruins, knocking down walls, and throwing up a cloud of dust and debris that could be seen far and wide.

The concussive, thunderous sound caused by the strike would have been deafening to anyone nearby, but Victor hardly noticed it; he was too engrossed in his rage, too hungry for destruction. When the burst of white fire and light faded, he looked down with bloodthirsty dark thoughts of slaughter, only to find that Lifedrinker was buried in the earth beneath a split stone, and the only remnant of the Pyromancer was a dismembered arm.

Weird, annoying squiggles filled his vision, and he growled, ignoring them, looking around for something to kill. He stood amidst devastation—all around were blackened stones and piles of rubble. Everywhere he turned, his view was obscured by smoke.

When he saw nothing to fight, he straightened and started walking, intent on finding something to kill. As the immediacy of combat faded, as his rage was forced to cool slightly, he became aware of Lifedrinker, and though he had no room for worry or concern in his rage-filled magma heart, he felt bothered by her discomfort. Something was wrong with the axe. Still, Victor couldn't be bothered with sentimentality. He stalked the ruins, looking for a fight, until with a surprising burst of euphoria, he was transfixed by an infusion of Energy that lifted him off the ground, dispelling his fury and leaving him senseless for several long minutes.

Victor knew he was back to himself when he realized there were System messages in front of his eyes. He looked around, saw he was in a section of ruins indistinguishable from any others he'd passed through, and sat down on a huge fallen stone. He lifted Lifedrinker, saw the cracks in her living wood handle, and gently stroked her. "I'm sorry, *chica.*"

She vibrated in his hand, and he heard her thoughts: *I will heal, though my heart aches for the feast we were denied. Something pulled him away before I could take my fill! You were glorious, my brave, vengeful warrior! Promise me we'll find that one and take what's ours!*

"I'll . . . I don't know if we'll meet him in a place where we can fight again. We'll see." Victor turned to the System messages and ran through them.

Gyanna Rose has been rescued from certain death and removed from the dungeon. Twenty-five entrants remain. Prepare for an Energy infusion.

Arcus Volpuré has been rescued from certain death and removed from the dungeon. Twenty-four entrants remain. Prepare for an Energy infusion.

Congratulations! You have achieved Level 61 Herald of the Mountain's Wrath and gained 12 strength, 17 vitality, and 12 will.

Victor sat there, thinking about the messages and about what had happened with the Pyromancer—Arcus Volpuré, he was pretty sure. The other name seemed more feminine, and he figured it belonged to the woman he'd seen speaking with Volpuré. Of course, he could be wrong. Gyanna could be a masculine name, or whatever culture they came from could have completely different ideas about naming. Still, he felt that he was right. Arcus was the man who'd called down some kind of meteor strike on him, and if Victor hadn't been so nearly immune to fire, he might have been in serious trouble.

He thought about how he'd approached the two casters as they bickered. Had he been expecting them to banter with him? Why had he been surprised by that immediate attack? The obvious strategy for the most significant gains in this competition was to take out as many entrants as possible.

There were still twenty-three others in there with him, many of whom were possibly just as dangerous or more so than Arcus. Many might have affinities that Victor couldn't so easily shrug off. He needed to be more careful. Sure, his Volcanic Fury was a hell of a trump card, but he hadn't wanted to play it so soon. He also didn't want to rely on it; he'd almost broken Lifedrinker, and while he'd been mad with the volcano's wrath, he hadn't even cared.

Had he taken Gyanna Rose out, or had she just been collateral damage? Victor couldn't even remember. The whole battle, beyond the point where he'd been smashed by the meteor strike, was a blur of fragmented images in his mind.

He stood up and looked around. The dungeon seemed to have a day-and-night cycle, and the sky was noticeably dimmer above the walls surrounding him. "Where are all the monsters?" he muttered, finding it strange that he'd wandered for a while without encountering anything. Or had he? He was fairly sure but couldn't be certain, not with his spotty memory.

"I need to be smarter, beautiful," he said, once again caressing Lifedrinker's haft, watching as the cracks in the beautiful dark star-speckled wood slowly knitted back together. "I need to expect everyone to be hostile." Just as he said the words, System messages scrolled in front of his eyes:

Zandastre'va has been rescued from certain death and removed from the dungeon. Twenty-three entrants remain. Prepare for an Energy infusion.

Borna Hullstrava has been rescued from certain death and removed from the dungeon. Twenty-two entrants remain. Prepare for an Energy infusion.

Kim Jyster has been slain! Twenty-one entrants remain.

"Holy shit," Victor said, standing up and holding Lifedrinker close. He looked to the sky, watching the globe of Energy form and waiting for it to break apart, hoping to see if any portions were sent to other participants nearby. "So, one of them died, and it sounds like the System doesn't share that Energy with everyone. Whoever killed Kim Jyster is getting the full amount, I guess."

Lifedrinker throbbed in his grip, her only response eagerness. The globe of Energy in the center of the sky burst apart, and, to Victor's surprise and dismay, several of the balls of Energy shot upward toward the ceiling where the central stair led to the second floor. Many of the other globes streaked toward the center of the first floor, and, as far as Victor could tell, only one came his way, while others streaked to various far-flung corners of the level.

Seeing that so many participants were closer to the stairs than he, and several were already either on the stairs or the second level, Victor felt a deep, painful disappointment in himself. Was he really so far behind?

"I need to quit messing around and get serious," he muttered just as his ball of Energy hit him, and this time, he really felt it. It was so strong that he thought he might level, but he was still Level Sixty-One when the euphoria passed. "Close, though. All right, *chica*, let's get moving. Time to make up some ground."

Dar reclined in his usual booth, watching the view portal that filled the entire wall of Harbinger Row, his favorite drinking establishment in the upper spires. A section along the bottom of the wall displayed a small view of each of the remaining contestants, while the larger section was dedicated to those currently embroiled in the most action. At that moment, an avian woman with distinct griffin bloodline markings was battling a hydra on the second level. "Who's that?" he rumbled. "Yon's girl?"

His friend and sometime rival, Lo'ro the Grim, stirred from his reverie and looked at the screen. "Aye," he whispered in his scratchy undead voice. "She's closing in on her test of steel." He looked at Dar from the depths of his dark cowl and asked, "Are you disappointed? In your prodigy, I mean?"

"Hmm? No, I think not. He's still in, isn't he? A bit . . . heavy-footed so far, but I think he'll warm up to the contest. He's been at war for the last year, and before that, he might as well have been. What he lacks in nuance, he makes up for in determination and, well, sturdiness. You saw what happened when Arcus dumped his Energy pool on him. Elder gods! Crovius is going to be apoplectic. Can you imagine? His prime student was eliminated in the first few minutes! Not to mention Lady Rose! Her daughter ripped to safety as an *afterthought*. She simply got too close to the struggle!"

"Yes. Some heavy pockets will grow noticeably lighter thanks to your boy." When Lo'ro finished speaking, he took a breath as though to say more, but he seemed to hesitate.

"What is it?" Dar pressed.

"Did you give your apprentice a means of communicating?"

Dar was genuinely surprised by the question. "What? That would breach the code of conduct."

"Aye, but I've heard rumors. I hope I'm wrong, but I've heard whispers from an Artificer friend about unscrupulous members of his class providing high-end, quite easily hidden communication devices. Hopefully, word of your lad's ability to shrug off fire damage doesn't get around."

Dar shrugged and leaned back, reaching for his potent liquor. "You heard him talking to himself. He'll start being a bit more clever. I'm not worried."

"It is nice that he narrates his thoughts for the viewing public. Clea reports that he's one of the favorites amongst the public down in the city."

"Clea? One of your students?"

"Yes, that's right. My bloodline gift allows us to share thoughts."

"You've mentioned it. Can't say I'm keen on the idea. I'd rather it's just me up here." Dar chuckled and tapped his thick stony knuckle against his forehead.

"Something that takes getting used to, but I've grown quite fond of some of my disciples' minds."

Dar didn't respond; He just nodded and sipped his drink. He'd known Lo'ro for centuries, and he liked the man well enough, but there were things about the undead that he simply couldn't condone, one of which was the many ways they enthralled lesser undead, promising them power but feeding it to them on such a slow drip that they were paid a thousand times in service for what they gave in knowledge. Still, that was not a problem for Ranish Dar to solve, though Victor certainly seemed to have a vendetta against some of Lo'ro's kind. He chuckled at the thought. It might be an amusing venture to observe.

37

AMBUSH

Victor used the stairs, still visible in the twilight of the dungeon's night cycle, as a guide, hurrying toward the center of the first level as quickly as he could. The ruined walls seemed to extend all the way to that distant point, and it felt almost like traversing a maze, though an easy one—he never felt lost, and when he came to a dead end, he simply hopped the wall in the direction he wanted to travel. When he drew close enough to the central stairway to see the individual steps in the distance without any haze obscuring his view, he paused and summoned his coyotes.

"Okay, *hermanos*, spread out, have a look around, and let me know if you see any other *pendejos* lurking around." As his coyotes, yipping and calling to one another, slipped away through the gaps in the stone wall, Victor continued making his way toward the dungeon's center.

He was always sort of aware of his coyotes. He couldn't see what they saw but could tell if they found something or sensed danger. He was still a little surprised that he hadn't encountered any denizens of the dungeon, concluding that the people who'd designed the place, or at least chosen options from the System, had intended for the first level to serve as a staging ground. He had to assume there would be more to encounter if he could climb higher.

When he'd covered another few hundred yards toward the center, and the rooms surrounded by high crumbling walls grew ever smaller and closer together, one of his coyotes alerted on a presence. Victor mentally urged his other scouts to return and started stalking toward the excited pack member.

He knew roughly what direction to go and could sense how far away he was, but he still had to find his way through the broken walls. He could climb overtop, of course, shortening his path by making it more direct, but that close to the center of the level, he was afraid others would see him as his bulky body rose above the ruins.

So he prowled through the ruins, growing ever closer to his coyote as it, in turn, stalked the presence—Victor had the impression of more than one target. After a few minutes, his other coyotes came to him. They were empowered by inspiration-attuned Energy, and he constantly had to remind them to quit yipping. After a few minutes, he sent them home to the spirit plane; at least he felt he could be confident that the one who'd found some prey was being quiet as it hunted. "Next time," he whispered to Lifedrinker, "remind me to use fear Energy; those boys are always better at sneaking."

When he entered the ruined chamber where his coyote waited, he quietly thanked his little brother and sent him back home. Then Victor crept up to the gap in the wall and strained his ears, hoping for a clue as to what the scouting canine had found. It wasn't long before a feminine voice came to him. "I think we're close. Just another few rooms, and we'll be at the stair."

"And likely our doom as one of the needy brutes is sure to be waiting to strike us down." This voice was masculine, though very young, if Victor was guessing.

"Which young monster worries you? Arcus is out. Zandastre'va is out. I suppose we still have Arona to worry about."

"Whoever beat Arcus is sure to be a dangerous one to encounter . . ."

"Who's to say that wasn't Arona?"

The man, or boy, ignored the question. "I saw Valeska Thornrend in the chamber. She's known to have a cold heart . . ."

"Are we just going to list all the names?" The woman sounded exasperated, and Victor had a feeling she had more to say, but suddenly her tone changed, and she called out, "Who lurks yonder? We don't seek a fight!"

Victor froze, wondering if he was the target of her words, figuring he probably was because what did he know about sneaking? The people in the dungeon were all high tier, at least as far as he was concerned, and he honestly had no idea what sorts of skills and abilities such people might employ. There were probably some classes that gave people heightened awareness.

He contemplated retreating, leaping over a few walls, and putting some distance between the two others. They sounded like underdogs, though, and from what he'd overheard, they didn't seem to be spoiling for a fight, even if he didn't believe her direct declaration to that effect. He decided to try his luck; if they were afraid of Arcus, and Victor had beaten Arcus, it stood to reason that he shouldn't cower from this encounter. He cleared his throat and said, "I'll be willing to talk if you don't try anything."

Victor, on a sudden whim, cast Inspiration of the Quinametzin. As he swelled with positivity, the world looked brighter, and his problems seemed more distant. He stood tall, holding Lifedrinker on his shoulder with one hand, and stepped into the crumbled archway to look into the room where he'd heard the other two. They stood close together, one a wispy elven woman with wavy gray hair, angular silver eyes, and a fierce expression, the other a short boyish fellow with a bit too much pudge and soft dewy eyes. The woman held a bow, an arrow nocked but not drawn back, and the boy held a thick red wand made of smooth glass. Victor could see and feel the Energy built up in the wand, and he knew the kid was on the verge of unleashing a spell.

"Stop there!" the woman said in a sharp voice.

Victor smiled and leaned a shoulder against the wall, some ancient mortar crumbling with the pressure. "I'm not the kind of guy who attacks people for no reason."

"Ah, but we all have reason in this place, no?" the kid said, his voice surprisingly firm.

Victor shrugged. "Well, it takes more than a bit of Energy to provoke me into a fight. Let's put it that way."

"I don't know you, stranger," the woman said, stepping to the side and separating herself from her companion. "Are you new to Sojourn?"

"I guess so. I'm Victor."

The youth lifted his wand and, with a flourish, bowed elaborately. "I am Cam Lightly, and this fine lady is Sora Deval."

"You're a large fellow, and I can feel the aura you're creating. It's... lovely," Sora said, gently lifting the arrow from her bow.

"Ah, you feel the inspiration? That means I don't consider you an enemy." Victor grinned further and then straightened up. "Can I come a little closer?"

"Something tells me you'd do so even if we said no." Cam sounded a little petulant, but Victor could feel the Energy pull back from his wand as he began to relax. He stepped toward them, kicking some loose gravel to the side as he approached. Drawing near, he gestured to his pants, mostly tatters from mid-thigh down.

"Sorry for my appearance. I got a little scorched earlier." When he was just a few feet from the others and loomed over their much smaller frames, he gestured toward the stairway in the distance. "I heard you two talking as I approached. You think some of the others will be waiting to ambush people at the stairs?"

"I think so." Cam nodded, peering up at Victor and stepping back.

"Who burned you?" Sora asked, ignoring Cam's response.

"Oh, one of the other entrants. You guys didn't see the meteor shower over that way?" Victor jerked his thumb in the general direction of his earlier battle.

"Arcus!" Cam said, eyes widening. "You battled Arcus?"

Victor just grinned and shrugged. "Anyway, I figure if we all approach the stairs together, there's a better chance we might survive an ambush. How many do you think would do that? Lay a trap, I mean. Do you think the others get along well enough to help each other in that way?"

"Are you offering us your protection, good sir?" Sora lifted a sharp gray eyebrow, something like amusement in her tone.

"Um, not exactly, but I'd fight with you if we all got jumped. Look, I'm not trying to force the matter, and I've wasted enough time in this place, so I can go ahead alone if . . ."

"No, no!" Cam waved his wand frantically. "We'd love to accompany you with a gentleman's agreement."

"Gentlefolk," Sora corrected.

"Sure, right, whatever. What say you, Victor? We'll aid each other until such time that it's a hindrance on one or all of us, and then we'll part ways amicably."

"Sounds just right." Victor swapped Lifedrinker to his left hand, causing Cam and Sora to flinch, then reached out with his right hand, ready to shake on the deal. Cam looked at it for a heartbeat, apparently weighing the risk, then shot out his soft pale hand, grabbing a portion of Victor's palm. He smiled and backed away, and Victor held his hand out to Sora. She wore an odd expression, sort of puzzled and amused, then grabbed Victor's much larger hand in thin fingers that felt like iron bars.

She might be small, Victor realized, but she was damn sturdy. For the second time, he reminded himself that he couldn't judge people by appearances in this place—Cam might look like a pudgy kid, but according to Ranish Dar, everyone in there was Level Seventy or higher. Victor could only guess what that soft, almost cherubic face might be hiding.

"We're close," Sora said, gesturing with her bow toward a gap in the wall. "A few more wall segments, and we'll be there."

"My mentor, Duvius Black, will tan my hide for suggesting this," Cam said, wincing at some imagined punishment, "but I think I should go into the clearing first. If a trap there lies, surely they'll spring it on me, thus revealing their fangs for you two to pluck."

"And you?" Victor asked, frowning.

"I shall utilize my ability to slip free from harm."

"He has a chance affinity," Sora said as though it explained everything.

"Chance?" Victor tried to connect the dots. Was he talking about luck? Randomness? Both?

"Let's just say I have a few abilities that, while on lengthy timers, make harming me a rather confounding enterprise." He smiled and bowed again, his red glass wand flickering with faint sparkles. "Well? Is my plan suitable?"

Sora nodded firmly. "I have no arguments."

"Sure." Victor shrugged. If this guy wanted to spring the trap for them, he wouldn't argue. As they walked, Victor felt several soft pulses of Energy emanating from Sora, and when he looked at her, trying to spot a clue as to what she was doing, she caught his eyes and hurriedly explained.

"I'm not doing anything untoward! I'm scrying the area nearby; it's how I noticed you lurking earlier. For the record, it will also obscure our presence from others."

"Lurking?" Victor chuckled. "I guess I was. Anyway, your ability isn't perfect. I listened to you for a while before you noticed me."

"Likely your passive resistance . . ." she muttered but cut her words short, holding a finger to her lips. She looked from Cam's wide eyes to Victor's puzzled, questioning glance and mouthed, "Two," pointing past the next gap in the stone wall.

Victor nodded, pulling Lifedrinker off his shoulder and holding her ready. Cam, rather blithely, waved to the two of them and began to stroll for the opening, looking very much the part of a careless youth out for a stroll. Victor saw his red wand sparkle faintly and felt a surge of strange, almost pleasant Energy, and then the young-looking man practically skipped through the crumbled archway. When Sora darted forward, aiming for the side of the arch, Victor followed suit, taking up the other side, hoping to catch a glimpse of whatever happened. Peering from the shadows, hoping Sora's magic did the job of keeping them hidden, he watched as Cam entered an enormous rubble-strewn clearing.

Piles of stone blocks, clearly once part of the ruins, were scattered all over the clearing, but beyond them, beyond a hundred yards of crabgrass-covered rocky soil, the pristine white marble spiral staircase rose into the sky. Cal veritably skipped into the clearing, whistling a tune that wouldn't have sounded out of place at a Renaissance fair. He'd made it a quarter of the way into the clearing, edging to the left to skirt a high pile of rubble, when with a peal of thunder that rattled the wall where Victor leaned, a bolt of magenta lightning ripped the sky and exploded into the little fellow.

Victor blinked several times, trying to get the brilliant imprint out of his vision. When he finally focused on the spot where Cam had been, he saw only scorched grass and blackened stone. He looked left to right, and then he saw him, standing a dozen yards away from where the lightning had struck, tilting his head in confusion. In a singsong voice, the little guy called out, "Why would someone blast the soil in such a way? What'd that poor patch of grass do to hurt anyone?"

Stones clattered in the distance, and Victor squinted to see a metallic glint as a humanoid figure moved around the side of a nearby pile of rubble, trying, he supposed, to get Cam back in their sights. Victor felt a surge of Energy and looked to see Sora drawing her bow, taking aim with a shimmering, mirror-polished arrow.

Victor wanted to jump into action, but he held steady, waiting. Sora had said two people were lurking in the clearing, and he wanted to get his eyes on the second one before he made a move. Sora's bowstring *thrummed,* and he watched as the glittering arrow streaked toward the pile of rubble, not directly at the person Victor had glimpsed. Just before it looked as though it would smash into a large toppled block, it burst like a shattering mirror, and when the flashes of light settled, there were half a dozen copies of Sora standing on the pile of rubble. More impressive than the copies was that they all performed different actions.

Two drew their bows, aiming arrows at the shadow-obscured figure edging toward Cam. One of the mirror copies began picking up hunks of rubble, throwing them this way and that. Another began to howl strange words, summoning a storm of sparkling magic. Before he could continue staring, waiting to see what they'd do next, a new actor stepped onto the proverbial stage—fifty yards away, past where Cam currently stood, still shouting taunts in his singsong voice, a hulking green man with a leathery shell not unlike a turtle's, exploded out from behind a great toppled monolith. He bore a heavy-looking hammer in each hand and moved as if he'd used a charge ability. The soil churned under his feet, a cloud of debris in his wake, and Victor predicted he'd crash into Cam in less than a second.

"That's my cue," he grunted, launching himself out of the archway, bumping Sora as he passed, knocking her sprawling. Victor didn't notice his inadvertent rudeness; he was in the zone, focused on the big warrior, already visualizing how he'd deliver Lifedrinker's first blow. He didn't have eyes for it, but if he'd been watching, he'd have seen the shadowy attacker near the central pile of rubble blasting Sora's doubles into oblivion, one after the other, with metallic missiles that crackled through the air like lightning-charged rail gun rounds. As Victor ran, he cast Iron Berserk, and as his legs extended and his strength and speed increased, he turned the long-distance sprint into a short one.

Even so, the shelled-backed brute reached Cam first, his charge demolishing the ground between them. Victor watched, cringing, but just as before with the lightning strike, Cam was suddenly elsewhere, standing halfway between the dazed turtle-man and the battle the other unknown assailant was waging against Sora's doubles. Meanwhile, Victor closed the gap, and just as he was only four titan-sized strides away, he cast Energy Charge, fueling the ability with fear-attuned Energy. In a streak of smoky shadow, he blasted over the ground and collided with his opponent. The big shelled warrior wasn't a slouch—he saw Victor coming and somehow turned just in time, exposing his hard leathery armor to his charge.

Victor didn't care. He lowered his shoulder and swung Lifedrinker with abandon. He had no doubt she was up to the challenge, since she bore a shard of his spirit—he regularly kept her imbued with inspiration-attuned Energy. He exploded into the turtle-man, and Lifedrinker, screaming her excitement and fury, buried herself halfway to the haft in the thick material. The concussive release of Energy as he collided with his target echoed through the ruins like thunder. Victor felt a tremendous torrent of fear-attuned Energy drain from his Core as his ability shielded him from harm.

Meanwhile, his target exploded away from him, blasted by the force of his impact. Victor made the split-second decision to release Lifedrinker as the guy was pulled away—she'd screamed her hunger at him, and he knew she'd struck a vein, so he thought he'd let her do some draining while the turtle-man bounced and flopped over the stony ground.

He glanced at the other ambusher and saw him sprinting for the stairs, a rain of glittering arrows falling in his wake, exploding against the ground like mortars. A flicker in the corner of his vision alerted him to Cam casting a spell with his glass wand, and then, like an optical illusion, the youthful wizard flickered through the air until he'd closed the distance with the runner. He shouted something in his falsetto singsong, and then . . . the ambusher tripped, sliding through a patch of dirt and lying still just long enough for three of Sora's arrows to strike direct hits.

Victor turned back to his foe and saw the big leathery hairless green man struggling to his feet. Lifedrinker stood proudly from his shell as the hammer-wielding warrior started walking toward him, limping slightly. Victor was easily five feet taller than the bulky man and wasn't too worried about fighting him with his bare hands for a while. "That's right, *chica!*" he growled, "Drink up that ugly sucker's Energy." He jogged toward him, slapping his chest. "Come on!"

The man really did look like a turtle up close. He had no hair on his face, a smooth flat nose, and a mouth that looked almost like a beak. Still, the man scowled and grunted, "Big, huh? I've killed bigger!" Then, to Victor's shock and delight, he surged with a very familiar-feeling Energy. His eyes began to blaze with red fury, and his muscles seemed to double in mass, bulging as if they'd burst out of his skin. He lifted both his hammers and screamed, "Let's fight!"

38

COLLISION COURSE

Despite his obvious berserk nature, the shelled warrior didn't grow with his rage, aside from his bulging and swelling muscles. Still, his bruises and scuffs disappeared as his fury fueled his regeneration, and he moved with a sudden alacrity that put Victor momentarily on the defensive. He darted forward, whipping his sledge-like weapons through the air, aiming to shatter Victor's bones with each frenzied attack. Victor, for his part, began to laugh with the glee of good clean combat, darting back, slipping blows, and slapping the smaller warrior's arms aside as he ducked close.

While Victor enjoyed the contest, ducking, dodging, shoving, and grappling, he could see the green-skinned warrior was getting more and more enraged, his eyes blazing, his skin burning with palpable hate. He may have advanced his Berserk ability to a tier similar to Victor's, but he certainly hadn't unlocked Iron Berserk. Victor still felt rage when under the effects of his ability, but he was also rational and able to take joy in combat—his opponent was clearly feeling no joy.

After Victor ducked a wild overhand blow, sidestepping and shoving the back of the smaller warrior's shell, the turtle-like man stumbled forward and tried to perform a shoulder roll. Unfortunately, Lifedrinker interfered, using her impact with the stony ground to drive herself deeper into the leathery flesh where her razor-sharp smoldering blade had already begun to draw great torrents of hot red Energy into her hungry metal. The green warrior roared in pain and frustration, aborting his somersault to flop to his belly and drive himself up with a powerful thrust of his muscle-bound arms. He veritably dove at Victor, whipping his hammers like a whirlwind.

Victor stepped into the charge, lowered his center of gravity with a deep squat, gripped the green warrior behind his bulky, swollen thighs, and drove himself up and back, flinging him through the air with a tremendous roar. When Victor watched his opponent sail, arms flailing, feet kicking fruitlessly, he almost lost his rage in his amusement. He laughed and leaned forward to slap his knees as the hammer-wielding warrior smashed to the ground with a reverberating thud that jolted the ground enough to lift a cloud of dust all over the clearing. At nearly the same time, a System message flashed in front of Victor's eyes.

Vek Dydallion has been rescued from certain death and removed from the dungeon. Twenty entrants remain. Prepare for an Energy infusion.

At first, the message confused Victor because he could see the turtle-man already struggling to his feet. For a second, he thought the System had made a mistake, but then he glanced back toward the central stair and saw his two companions standing together with no sign of the combatant they'd been chasing.

The gray-haired woman, Sora, lifted her bow and started striding toward the downed berserker, but Victor waved her off and shouted, "No!" She and Cam exchanged looks, and the soft-looking wizard shrugged, immediately turning to jog toward the stairs leading up. Sora looked at Victor for a long moment, then waved a hand and hurried after him.

Victor turned back to his opponent, stoking the rage in his pathways with a fresh infusion from his Core. His companions were, apparently, willing to let him fight alone, but they weren't going to wait around. He was all right with that. The turtle warrior had regained his feet, and he was looking at Victor with murder in his eyes. He'd lowered himself to a squat, his legs spread wide, and Victor could feel the hot rage building in him, even from forty yards distant. Part of him knew he should try to interrupt whatever he was doing, but another part was eager to see what it would be. He'd never fought a berserker before, never seen someone using a rage affinity, at least not so purely as this man was.

He lowered himself into a fighting stance, slowly moving forward, watching with hungry eyes, waiting to see what the warrior would do. The turtle-man was beginning to shimmer with heat and power, and the air around him looked ready to explode as hot waves of Energy wafted away from him.

The ground began to tremble, pebbles danced on the ancient flagstones, and hairline cracks started propagating away from the warrior's feet, spreading outward like a spider's web. Whatever he was building up to was going to be awesome, and Victor peeled his eyes, eager to see it. "Come on!" he roared, "Show me!"

The turtle warrior screamed something inarticulate. His hammers suddenly blazed like twin molten stars, and the ground erupted under his feet. Victor, staring at the cloud of dust and broken stone, almost didn't see the warrior ripping toward him, tearing the earth in his passage, streaking like a comet, hammers held high, ready to crash into him on impact. He was moving very close to the extremity of Victor's perception, almost too fast for him to track, but not quite. If Victor hadn't been boosting his agility, and if he hadn't been further enhanced by Iron Berserk, he surely would have been devastated by the charge. He was boosted, though, and he had a fraction of a second to react.

Some warriors might have dodged to the side. Others might have jumped. Still others would have braced for the impact, hoping to use their opponent's momentum to slip the majority of the force. Victor's mind never contemplated those actions; he immediately channeled a torrent of glory-attuned Energy into his pathways and cast Energy Charge, answering the turtle-man's charge with one of his own. He ripped over the ground, a brilliant sparkling gold missile of meat and metal. He didn't wield a weapon but lowered his head and let his massively dense juggernaut helm lead the impact.

The green warrior was beyond fear or caution—he'd stoked his rage to apoplectic levels, and even if he'd been able to react in time, he likely wouldn't have turned aside or aborted his charge. They met in a full head-on collision that resulted in such an explosion of physical force and discharged Energy that the entire dungeon level shook. Victor felt his glory-attuned Energy drain like water down a whirlpool, the shielding portion of the spell valiantly trying to protect him from the destructive forces. The turtle-man must have had a similar function with his charge ability because the two of them hung together for a pregnant second as their Energies bled out, erupting in a nova-like mixture between them.

Victor grinned hungrily while his opponent snapped his beak and scowled. Then the turtle's red glowering Energy flickered out, and his flesh rippled with force as the explosion took him. He flew back as though he'd been hit full in the chest by a streaking comet. The concussion continued wracking Victor, and his glory-attuned Energy burned out a second after the turtle's.

He, too, was thrown back, hot gasses, burning Energies, and shockwaves of force flinging him head over heels. Victor bounced and tumbled, his bones cracking, his skin ripping, but only briefly—he had a surging store of rage-attuned Energy, and his Iron Berserk drew on it, healing him almost as quickly as he took each new injury. When he finally slid to a stop, dozens of yards from the impact point, he was quick to clamber to his feet.

As he'd suspected, his opponent either didn't have multiple affinities or couldn't use them while enraged, much like Victor under the effects of Volcanic Fury. The turtle-man lay crumpled at the end of a long deep furrow in the ground, heaps of upturned flagstones and churned-up soil piled along the track of his passage. Victor started toward him, noting the eager, hungry, keening song Lifedrinker was emitting, either directly into his head or into the sudden silence left in the wake of their collision—it wasn't clear to him which.

He walked into the trench, followed it to its end, and the battered broken man who lay there, his arms and legs bent and bloody, the leathery skin of his shell half peeled away, and his face a mass of scrapes and purple bruises. He was on his side, and Victor could see Lifedrinker pulsing with stolen red Energy, still digging and throbbing, trying to get something more out of the broken man. Even so, the shattered warrior lifted a bent, bloody arm, formed half a fist with his crooked fingers, and muttered, "Drobna," from a mouth full of blood and bits of broken beak.

Victor's rage was subsiding; he knew he could extend it by pulling more Energy out of his Core, but he let it fade, and as he rapidly contracted back to his normal size, he made a fist and pressed his knuckles against the sturdy, battered, nearly dead warrior's. "Victor." A soft silvery glow encompassed Drobna, and as he dissipated into a pearly fog, the System sent out another message:

Drobna Wyrm-Shell has been rescued from certain death and removed from the dungeon. Nineteen entrants remain. Prepare for an Energy infusion.

Victor stooped to snatch up Lifedrinker, noting her satisfied glow and the thick rivers of angry red Energy marking her silvery axe-head. "Nice work, beautiful." He had no doubt that Drobna would have had another round in him if not for her. The axe hummed in his hands, and as he slung her onto his shoulder, looking up at the sky to track the incoming Energy infusion, Victor could feel her pleasure; she'd enjoyed tormenting his foe while he wrestled around with him.

He watched the Energy ball form in the sky, watched it explode into nineteen different golden missiles, and braced himself to receive the one streaking straight toward him. Two others shot for the base of the stairs, several others went up the top, and quite a few streaked away to distant areas of the first level. When the Energy struck him, Victor was instantly lifted, poleaxed by the tremendous influx. He was glad the System had waited for him and Drobna to finish their fight before awarding the Energy from the guy Cam and Sora had taken out. Still, the combined award was a lot, enough that he fell to his knees after the infusion while the System informed him of another level gained.

Congratulations! You have achieved Level 62 Herald of the Mountain's Wrath and gained 12 strength, 17 vitality, and 12 will.

"That's fast," he grunted. He supposed it made sense; five entrants had been taken out of the contest since his last level. That meant all those awards were being split with fewer and fewer people. What would happen if everyone kept getting knocked out? What if he were the last one standing? It seemed certain he'd stand to gain quite a few more levels in this contest, and he was beginning to understand why so many people were willing to risk so much for a shot. Thanks to his gains, he'd already started to mitigate the risk of getting "rescued."

Victor stood, hopped out of the trench Drobna had created, and started toward the stairs, just fifty yards or so distant. He chuckled as he walked, noting the clean-blasted ground—his impact with the berserker had sent a shockwave out that had blown all the rubble and gravel to the edges of the clearing. He slowly turned in a circle and realized they'd done more than that. The impact had toppled many of the nearby walls. He craned his neck as he approached the smooth white marble stairway, trying to trace it to the second level but losing track as it faded into the misty clouds.

"Well fought, Victor," a youthful exuberant voice called from the stairs.

"Cam," Victor chuckled, lifting his hand to his eyes, shading them so he could squint into the shadows of the spiral steps. He spotted the youth's tousled blond hair peering over the rail about twenty yards up. "Thought you two would be up to Level Two by now."

"Nah," Sora said, stepping out from behind the stairs. She held her bow in a relaxed grip with no arrow in sight, putting Victor's thoughts of betrayal to rest. "We just wanted to get out of the way and, well, position ourselves to run if you lost."

"As if he would!" Cam laughed.

"Was it a struggle, Victor?" Sora lifted one of her silvery gray eyebrows.

"It was a good brawl—a good clean fight. Nothing against Drobna, but he wasn't ready for me." Victor shrugged and started up the steps.

"Is anyone?" Cam hopped down a few steps to get closer, awaiting an answer.

"In here?" Victor shrugged. "No idea. I'm new around town." He looked at Cam, then down to Sora, who still leaned against the railing at the bottom of the stairs. "So, what's this? We traveling together some more?"

Sora nodded. "We'd like our gentlefolk's agreement to stay in place if you're willing."

"Sure." Victor smiled, inhaling deeply through his nose and sighing, feeling far too relaxed and generally good—a side effect of the Energy infusion, he was sure. "Wonder how many are above us. I saw a few Energy balls go that way, but I figure if we stay together, maybe they'll think twice about jumping us. Let's clear some levels, yeah?"

"Yeah!" Cam cried, pumping his red glass wand in the air.

"God, he's a monster!" Darren cried, his eyes nearly bugging out of his head while the crowd around them erupted in similar shouts and cheers. Valla glanced sharply at him, initially thinking it was an insult but then realizing it was a sort of compliment. Lesh slapped his strange protégé's shoulder, laughing as he slammed down another pint of harsh fortified ale.

Valla turned back to the screen, looking over the heads of half a hundred other patrons who crowded the floor of the drinking establishment, sitting around low tables strewn with empty cups, pitchers of beer, and stacks of chips, dice, and other gambling implements. The "viewing house" was a wild, rough establishment, and Lesh had already proclaimed his love for it several times.

Lam seemed right at home, too, but Edeya was happy to be sandwiched between her and Valla, secure in the middle of the bench. Lesh had already drunk more than Valla had seen anyone drink in one sitting, and that included Victor when he was actively trying to get drunk. Darren was a bit red-faced, his words a little slurred, but he seemed to be having a great time watching the screen. Of course, it helped that Victor had been center stage a few times, his "view" filling the big screen while he got himself into fights. The latest one, with the shelled warrior named Drobna, had driven the crowd wild.

Valla had enjoyed it, but only because Victor had been laughing. She'd never seen him lose a fight when he was doing that. Well, she reconsidered, had she ever seen him lose? She supposed he had come close a few times—when he'd fought Rellia, back before she even knew him, she'd thought he was a dead man. Naturally, he'd surprised her and everyone else that night. Then there was the reaver army, the night brute prince, the Warlord, the Ridonne, his various arena battles, the ancient wyrm, his . . . Valla shook her head, refocusing on the present, content to admit that he'd been in a lot of close calls.

"He's not a monster," she said, finally deciding to correct the record.

"I didn't mean . . ."

"No, I know what you meant, but someone should speak for him. Victor has a big, good heart. It might prove his undoing, but he'll never be pleased to be considered a monster."

"Undershtood, Lady Valla," Darren slurred.

"Well, that charge . . ." Lam shook her head, snorting. "Those two nearly knocked the stairs out of the sky. Ha! I wonder what would have happened if they had broken them, cutting off the second level. Forfeit?"

Lesh cleared his throat, slamming his glass down and gesturing to a serving boy. "I'd pay all my wealth to see that! The System's in charge of that dungeon, after all."

"The, um, the dungeon Darren and I are going to . . ." Edeya shifted while she spoke, sitting up straighter between the two larger women. "It won't be competitive, right? I mean, other people won't be in at the same time, right?"

"No!" Lam smiled, leaning against the booth's rear wall so she could look more easily at Edeya's face. "That's why you had to sign up for a time slot—they only allow one party in each instance at a time, and you only get thirty-six hours in there."

"Some of them have much longer permit expirations," Darren said, slapping his hand on the guidebook on the table before him. "There's a tower dungeon for Tier Twos that has weeklong passes."

Edeya nodded and started to say something, but Valla heard Victor's voice coming from the viewscreen, and she hushed them, pointing. They all got quiet, listening as Victor spoke to his two new friends, agreeing to stay together for the time being. Then they started climbing the steps, and the proprietor switched the view to another entrant—a black-and-gold-feathered avian woman who was digging through the lair of a great multiheaded wyrm-like creature she'd slain.

"I'm glad he made some friends in there," Edeya said.

"I think he'll want to be friends with that berserker, too!" Lesh laughed.

Edeya nodded. "They touched fists! Victor loves that."

Valla sighed and stretched, wondering what sort of toilets she might find in the establishment. "I'm tired of watching and waiting while others do things," she said, surprising herself. "I'm eager for our dungeon, Lesh." She glanced at Lam. "You're still invited, Captain." Lam certainly held higher ranks than captain these days, but the old Legion title brought back many memories for the two of them, and Lam didn't seem to mind.

"Well, Captain," Lam said, returning the favor, "I might take you up on it. I was thinking I should stay out and wait in case Edeya and Darren needed something, but . . ." She trailed off for a second, looking into Edeya's eyes. "Watching Victor has brought back something of an old hunger."

"Good!" Edeya smiled. "You should go with them!" Valla had a hard time telling if she was being sincere or just brave, but Lam smiled, nodding.

"I'll think about it."

Lesh pounded his empty glass on the table, waving his huge thick arm in the air. "Come over here!" he said under his breath. "These folk are ignoring me!"

Valla, ironically, ignored him, still looking at Lam. "Don't think too long. Less than two days until our entry slot."

"No, I won't. I'll let you know tonight. Look!" Lam pointed to the screen. "They're back on Victor's party. Are they approaching some kind of lair?"

39

LAIR

The stairs worked with the same kind of magic Victor had seen in other places. Climbing a few steps seemed to activate it, and then, without any warning, he stumbled onto a landing. He lifted his axe, looking around, startled. His caution was unwarranted; he was in a small pale marble room with a single door on the far wall, closed and barred from the inside. Other than the stairs leading down, the only other object in the room was a marble chest the size of a shoebox sitting in the center. Victor turned, wondering where his companions were, but they didn't arrive, and he guessed the dungeon had used its transportation magic to separate them. "Hopefully, just so we can open our chests in peace," he muttered.

Speaking aloud reminded him that he was being observed, so he glanced up, looking for the floating stone egg recording his every move, but it wasn't there, further reinforcing the idea that the dungeon wanted them to have a private, safe moment in which to claim their rewards. Victor slung Lifedrinker into her harness and then walked over to the chest. He squatted before it and noted it was molded to the marble floor—he wouldn't be moving or taking this chest.

With a shrug, he lifted the lid. Motes of golden Energy sparkled out of the chest in a showy display, and when Victor blinked, clearing his eyes, he was left staring at two objects. One was a small black pouch that looked to be made of silk, and the other was a heavy leather left-handed glove with a wide wrist cuff.

"The hell is this?" Victor grunted, not exactly impressed. He picked up the pouch and confirmed that it felt like silk and also that it was empty. He'd been around long enough to guess there must be more to it, so he carefully trickled a tiny thread of inspiration-attuned Energy into it. Suddenly, his mind expanded with the knowledge of the pouch's contents—it was empty but contained a vast dimensional space. Victor nodded and tied the pouch to his belt. It seemed the dungeon was giving him a container since all of his were off-limits. With that mystery solved, he reached in and picked up the leather glove.

The leather was supple and fine, but the knuckles were stitched with an extra layer of much stiffer stuff. Still, it was just leather. Victor didn't even notice a particularly strong Energy aura coming off it. Frowning, he trickled some inspiration-attuned Energy into it, and a System description appeared in his vision.

Gauntlet of Sojourn: This is a set item. Collect five pieces of the set and bring them to the Sojourn City Stone to imbue them with curated set bonuses.

Victor turned the "gauntlet" in his hand a few times, wondering if he was missing something, but found nothing really notable about it. It didn't seem like anything special to him, but he supposed it might change drastically after you collected a set and had the items imbued. "Whatever that means." He stood up, put the glove into his new storage pouch, and walked over to the door. He paused long enough to pull Lifedrinker out of her harness, then he unbarred the exit and walked through. His vision flickered for an instant, the only clue that he'd been transported, then he stumbled into a gray stone chamber and almost bowled Cam over.

"Oof!" Cam said, stumbling back. He caught himself by reaching out to rest a hand on the stone wall.

"Sorry!" Victor grunted. "I just stepped through the door, and the dungeon dumped me on top of you."

"Not a problem. I, too, just arrived. Did you get a chest?"

Victor didn't see any point in lying. "Yeah. You?"

"Oh yes! Twenty-five thousand death-attuned Energy beads."

"Death? That useful to you?"

Cam shrugged, pursing his pouty pink lips. "Only as money. Covers half my entry fee, if nothing else."

"You paid fifty thousand beads to get in here?"

"A hundred, my friend. A hundred, unattuned. What, you didn't?"

Victor opened his mouth to reply, but then the air shimmered, and Sora appeared, stumbling toward him. Victor held out his hand, catching her. "Gods! That was careless! I almost fell atop you," she said, grasping his wrist with her slender fingers. He could feel the points of her nails, and she quickly let go. "I didn't scratch you, did I?"

Victor turned his wrist left and right, displaying his unmarred flesh. "Nah. I've got thick skin."

"Well?" Cam asked, his tone almost petulant. Victor turned to him with a scowl, but the young man's eyes were trained on Sora.

"Well, what?" she snapped.

"What did you get in your chest? I was made a touch richer."

Sora sighed and shrugged. "Just a bolt of something called evensong silk. It seems rather fine, but I'm not sure I'll find a use. I'll likely just sell it."

She looked at Victor, and so did Cam, and he knew they wanted him to say what the System had awarded him. Their hesitance to ask outright probably stemmed from the same reason he didn't really want to say—they hadn't built any trust for each other yet. So far, they'd gotten into one fight as partners, and it had been mutually beneficial to cooperate. So Victor shrugged and said, "Pretty much the same—some leather." He almost grinned at his duplicity; he wasn't technically lying.

Sora nodded and looked around the room. "More like a dungeon on this level, eh?"

Cam slapped the cold stone wall near the closed wooden door. "Seems so, based upon these dank stone walls." He reached for the rough iron latch on the door but paused, turning to look at Victor and Sora. "Since the stairs deposited us together, likely because the dungeon assumes we've teamed up, we can assume there are multiple entry points to this level. We may run into others, or we may not, but I'm certain there will be dungeon denizens starting on this floor. I'm not the first student Duvius Black has sponsored in this contest, and he told me as much."

Sora laughed, shaking her head. "This is what happens when you spend all of your time studying and playing Vongboard. Anyone who's watched previous competitions knows as much, Cam."

"Oh. Yes, I suppose that makes sense. Shall we?" He jiggled the door handle.

"You're going first?" Victor asked.

"Traps have a tendency to miss me." He flashed a bright smile, pulled the handle, and stepped through. Victor glanced at Sora, and she just shrugged, shaking her head so her long, nearly white hair bobbed back and forth.

"One day, he'll regret relying on whatever skill that is." She eyed Victor for a moment, then added, "Perhaps you should guard our rear flank." She held her bow in her left hand, and when she touched the string with her other hand, Victor was surprised to see a dark metal arrow appear under her fingers. Its razor-edged tip dripped something to the stone that sizzled.

"How do you do that? I thought dimensional containers were locked . . ."

"It's a function of my magical bow. I purchased an exemption so that I could pull the arrows from its storage."

"Purchased an exemption, huh?" Victor shook his head. It was starting to become evident to him that not every participant in the dungeon was on equal footing, even putting aside the level disparities. Sora winked and lithely followed Cam through the door. Victor brought up the rear, walking into a long marble passage dimly lit by regularly placed amber gemstones embedded in the ceiling. He could already count six branching passages in the long stretch before them.

Cam had walked ahead about twenty yards to the first intersection and was carefully peering around the corners. When Sora and Victor caught up to him, he sighed and whined, "How are we supposed to find our way through this maze? Do we even know what we're looking for?"

Victor answered, his voice more a growl than he'd intended, "Stairs. Something to kill."

"Suggestions?" Cam leaned against the wall, but not casually; it was more like he needed the support, as though his feet were killing him.

"I could scout . . ." Sora started to say, but Victor shook his head, channeling dark fear-attuned Energy into his pathways. He summoned his coyotes, and this time, when they appeared, crawling out of a pool of shadows by his feet, they were eerily silent, their smoky purple eyes peering beneath dark shadowy brows as they scrutinized Victor's companions.

Cam yelped and leaned back. Each of the five stalking canines was large enough to grab ahold of his leg and drag him off if they wanted to. Sora stepped back, too, but she seemed to recognize that Victor's companions weren't being hostile so much as curious. He could see she wanted to reach out a hand toward the closest one, but she resisted the temptation.

Before he said anything, Victor silently impressed his will upon his companions, and on nearly silent padding feet, they darted off, separating at the various junctions to explore the side corridors. Then he looked to Sora and explained, "I'll know if they find something interesting."

"Amazing!" Cam said. "Here I thought you were just a brute, a powerful one, but a brute, nonetheless." When Victor didn't speak but glowered at the man, he stammered, "I mean that with the utmost respect for raw, brute power . . ."

Sora chuckled and slapped Cam's shoulder. "Hush, Cam! You're making things worse." She looked at Victor. "Do we just wait here?"

"We can. Or we can go ahead and explore that passage on the left up there. I didn't have enough coyotes to cover every option."

"Coyotes?" Cam smiled. "What a lovely name for your hounds. They're a special breed, indeed!"

"Quit trying to put honey on a burn, Cam." Sora clicked her tongue and gave the youngster a shove, and he hurried ahead, bypassing another junction but stopping at the third. Victor watched him peering around the corners, but when he and Sora approached, he got a sensation from one of his coyotes—prey and danger.

"I think one of my companions found a monster." He paused, thought for a moment, and shrugged. "Or a person."

"Do we go to it?" Cam asked. "I see nothing but a long corridor down this way."

Sora nodded, looking at Victor. "Better to take the sure shot than pray for another hare."

"All right. Follow me." Victor turned and jogged back to the last junction. He could feel his coyote to the left, so he turned that way and hurried forward. He was reasonably sure he'd know if his companion had spotted or triggered any traps, so he didn't move too cautiously. They came to a four-way junction, and he could feel his coyote to the left, but still further ahead, so he wasn't sure if he should turn. He paused and willed the coyote to return. "Wait. He's coming to guide us."

"What a skill! Are they summoned beasts? How clever are they?"

"They're some sort of spirit . . ." Sora started to say, but Victor ignored them. His coyote was already there, silently darting out of the shadows on the left-hand passage.

"Good boy! Show me," he whispered, then, holding Lifedrinker ready, he jogged after the eager scout. He could hear Sora and Cam following. Victor wasn't reducing his size and had to lean forward to avoid hitting his head on the ceiling. For that reason, when he moved, he looked predatory and aggressive.

As he followed his companion, he channeled hot rage-attuned Energy into his arms and Lifedrinker, and he recast his Inspiration of the Quinametzin, washing himself and his companions in a warm encouraging light that pushed away the shadows. When his coyote came to a right-hand junction and stopped, pointing with his nose as only a canine can do, Victor slowed and glanced back.

He saw the egg-shaped spying stone dart back, having moved close to him as he was running. He scowled at it, something deep in his blood annoyed at being spied on. Farther back, he saw Cam and Sora. Cam gave him a thumbs-up when he saw him looking, and Sora nodded. Victor turned, stalked to the corner, and leaning forward like a tiger ready to pounce, he peered around it.

A short hallway opened into an immense cavern, and near its center was an enormous pink-skinned creature that looked like part elephant, part eel, and part octopus. It was shifting through piles of sludge-like refuse, and Victor could smell the rot and decay from where he stood despite a faint current of air tickling his ears as it wafted into the larger room. At that thought, Victor's eyes widened—could the thing smell him?

It didn't seem to. He watched its enormous body on its trunk-like legs shifting left and right while its great circular maw munched the piled sludge. The tentacle-like appendages surrounding its head reached out, pulling things into its mouth, where it squeezed shut, grinding the stuff into a paste that it could swallow. Victor felt bile roiling in his gut, threatening to rise up as he watched the process. He ducked back, looked over his shoulder, and waved the others forward. When they came to the corner, he held a finger to his lips and motioned for them to peek around the corner.

"Sludge gargantuopod," Cam hissed.

"Shit!" Sora softly cursed, earning a smile and a respectful nod from Victor.

"Do we kill it?" he whispered hoarsely.

"Can we?" Cam shook his head. "They regenerate very rapidly, and no offense, big man, but they're strong and huge and . . ."

"Let me rephrase," Victor interrupted. "Is it worth killing?"

"Oh, gods, yes." Cam nodded. "If we can, there's sure to be great loot . . ."

"So, it regenerates. Anything to combat that?"

Sora nodded. "I'll use fire arrows. That'll help."

"I can try to confuse it. If I can trick its mind into thinking it's uninjured . . ." Cam trailed off, shaking his head. "My mind affinity is my weakest. No promises."

"Do your best. I have a few tricks up my sleeve." Victor cut the Energy feeding his coyotes as he spoke, sending them back to the spirit plane. He had another companion he meant to call up for this battle.

"It's going to spew toxic gasses," Cam said, snapping his fingers as though he'd just remembered the fact.

"I'm pretty sturdy. I'll summon a banner that should help you two; hopefully, it'll push the gasses away."

Sora nodded. "I have some air affinity."

Victor couldn't help the grin stretching his face, and he knew he was baring his teeth at his two companions while they huddled there. He probably looked insane, but he couldn't help it—he loved fighting, and that thing in the next room looked as though it would put up a good brawl. More than that, he was eager to see what kind of treasure would prompt Cam to label it "great loot." He nodded, twisting his white-knuckled grip on Lifedrinker's haft. "So? Ready?"

Cam slapped his thick red glass wand against his palm. "Not in the least, but I'll do my best."

"I'm ready," Sora said, her brow narrowed fiercely.

"All right." Victor looked at Lifedrinker's shiny axe-head. The rivulets of rage Energy she'd siphoned away from Drobna Wyrm-Shell were all but gone, absorbed into her metal. "What about you, beautiful? Ready for another drink?" In response, her metal brightened and then burst into molten fire, black smoke billowing up to coalesce along the dungeon ceiling.

Cam recoiled; he'd been just inches from the axe while they hunkered together. Victor laughed, lifted her, and began stalking toward the giant monster, opening his Core to flood his pathways with hot rage-attuned Energy. "Let's kill this big *hijo de puta!*"

He broke into a jog, and as he ran, he cast Iron Berserk, then Banner of the Champion. He exploded with mass, taking advantage of the larger space. His banner blazed, pushing the gross hazy stagnant air away from him. Victor paused halfway between the tunnel opening and the giant monster grazing amid the piles of refuse and began to build his pattern for Wild Totem again. As he did so, the elephant-sized sludge gargantuopod whirled on him, taking note of his presence. Victor couldn't see any eyes on the thing's head, just a sphincter-like maw that twisted open and closed on rows and rows of stubby razor-sharp teeth, many of which were adorned with bits of rotting flesh and refuse.

As Victor completed his spell, the creature inhaled a massive torrent of air and exhaled it in a monstrous roar that rode the wind of an acrid green gas. The wave of caustic air billowed toward him, but Victor didn't flinch away. In fact, he stepped toward it, unable to resist roaring his own answer to the challenge.

His voice echoed off the chamber's stone walls, and his banner's light pushed back the bulk of the gas, but some of it touched him. It was acidic and smelled like chlorine, but Victor refused to shrink away. He was Quinametzin. He was the Herald of the Mountain's Wrath. Gasses couldn't bother him. Poison couldn't take root in his lungs or blood.

"Come on, *pendejo!*" He roared, "I'll burn your *pinché* gas up in my lungs!" To illustrate his lack of hyperbole, Victor opened his Breath Core, allowing some hot magma-attuned Energy to fill his lungs. As he laughed, black smoke and flames licked his lips. He lifted Lifedrinker high as a third roar rocked the chamber, and Victor's nightmare bear, nearly as large as the monster before him, exploded out of a pool of shadows on the far side of the chamber and leaped on the sludge gargantuopod's back.

"Let's go, *hermano!*" Victor cried, charging for the monster as it whirled to face the new threat posed by Victor's massive bear. As he closed the distance, a hail of fiery arrows streaked past him, punching into the thing's thick pink hide, and then the fight was on.

40

⚜

GARGANTUOPOD

In his titanic form, Victor figured he weighed close to a couple thousand pounds, especially with his helmet on, which added to his mass considerably. Even so, when he slammed Lifedrinker into the gargantuopod's rear left flank, despite her white-hot axe-head and the imbuement of his spirit, she barely penetrated its hide, and the great creature hardly flinched. When he'd first seen the monster alone in its lair, Victor had estimated it at about the size of an elephant. Standing behind it, Lifedrinker furiously trying to dig into its flesh, he altered that opinion; it had to be quite a lot larger because his head barely cleared its belly.

Sora's fiery arrows were sputtering, the flames failing to ignite the monster's calloused pink hide. As the behemoth shifted, trying to throw Victor's bear aside, its hip crashed into him, sending him sprawling. He felt as if a truck had just run into him. He came to rest against a pile of rubbish that stank of decomposition and shit and immediately struggled to his feet, eager to be away from the smell. The way the thing had rebuffed his attack was infuriating, and Victor could feel his Rage Core surge with renewed intensity, pumping more and more of the hot smoldering power into his pathways. Still, he couldn't help pausing to stare at the furious melee between his bear and the monstrosity.

The bear, much larger and more primordial than any bear to walk the Earth in Victor's lifetime, was drenched in blood, his thick dark coat torn in a dozen places by the gargantuopod's sucking, twisting maw. He roared savagely, his eyes ablaze with a fury akin to Victor's, and he swiped his great claws with terrible force against the monster's head, slicing through its groping tentacles and leaving long bleeding gashes in the more tender flesh of its open mouth.

Victor felt his heart surge with pride, and he almost started to cheer on his big furry brother, but then, almost as quickly as they'd appeared, the gashes closed up. The monster's tentacles wrapped around the bear's right forelimb and tugged it into its maw. It swirled shut like a tooth-lined sphincter, and with a horrible wrenching of its neck, left then right, it peeled the fur and flesh from the bear's limb.

"You *motherfucker!*" Victor screamed, horrified as he saw his brave companion stumble back, his mutilated leg flailing in the air as he fell to his side. Victor opened the floodgates on his Core, filling his pathways with fear-attuned Energy, and cast Energy Charge, aiming for the side of the monstrous creature, determined to knock it away from the bear. In a ripple of roiling shadows, he flew toward the gargantuopod, and his collision with its exposed flank was akin to charging a brick wall. Even so, Victor hadn't met a brick wall he couldn't do some damage to.

When he slammed into the mound of thick pink flesh, it rippled as a mud puddle might if you dropped a boulder into it. Moreover, the enormous stony ribs under the surface cracked like saplings in a landslide. As Victor's Core drained itself of fear-attuned Energy to protect him, the colossal monster slid a dozen feet from him, writhing and thrashing as its gore-filled maw yodeled out a weird undulating scream-roar of pain.

Victor had the wherewithal to release his bear, ending its suffering and sending it home to the spirit plane. Then he leaped at the monster, targeting its damaged side. He launched into a frenzy of attacks, hacking Lifedrinker in tremendous two-handed blows, left then right, almost as if he was trying to cut through a gargantuan fallen tree.

While he dug bloody furrows in the flesh, exposing splintered bones, the monster roared and thrashed, trying to get to its feet while simultaneously twisting to lash its hook-ended tentacles at Victor. He ignored them as they wrapped around his left leg and arm—they might as well have been clinging cobwebs; they were utterly unable to budge his rigid titanic frame as he lost himself in the furious frenzy of his assault. More fiery arrows punched into the monster's hide. There were fewer of them this time, but they seemed to burn more fiercely, and Victor was dimly aware that portions of the creature's thick pink hide were beginning to char and turn black.

Lifedrinker took two hits to penetrate the hide, and Victor was swinging in such a frenzy that she must have scored a half dozen bone-deep cuts, burning and charring the flesh on her way through, before the monster finally surged back to its feet and whirled so violently to face Victor that he had to thrust out a boot to keep it from snatching him up in its gaping mouth.

He slid back, driven by his foot on the edge of its sucking maw, and had a brief heart-fluttering panic as his foot started to slide into the orifice. As it came loose, he stomped into the ground and, still gripping her in two hands, hacked Lifedrinker with all his might into the lower rim of the monster's lunging, sputtering mouth.

She bit between the rows of daggerlike teeth, and her smoldering axe-head sank to the haft, fully buried. Victor roared his approval as Lifedrinker writhed and pulled, digging like a parasite into the folds of the softer flesh. He released her and leaped back, avoiding another lunge, and watched with sadistic pleasure as the monster's maw swirled shut on the axe.

Her haft stuck out of the puckered opening like a toothpick, but only for an instant as the creature opened wide again, coughing gouts of blood, saliva, and gore. Its remaining tentacles grabbed at the axe, wrapping around the haft, trying to draw it out, but Lifedrinker had dug deep, and the wormlike appendages didn't seem to have much leverage pulling away as opposed to pulling things in.

While it struggled, in a panic to get the hungry axe out, Victor noticed Cam darting around the edges of the chamber, planting thin metallic rods into the ground. He hoped the weird youthful caster had a trick up his sleeve to help finish the gargantuopod off. His rage was still high, simmering like recently boiled water in his veins, but he'd let off a lot of steam in his frenzied assault. Seeing Lifedrinker take root, driving the great monster mad as she dug into the softer flesh of its inner mouth, also served to cool his boiling blood. With his banner burning brightly, pushing away the toxic air, he turned to regard his other companion.

Sora stood atop a distant refuse pile, her bow held high, watching Victor, the monster, and Cam. He frowned at her, annoyed that all he'd seen her do thus far was release a few volleys of magical arrows. Was she up to something? Were she and Cam scheming to get him to wear himself out fighting the great monster? Did they intend to double-cross him?

Sora saw him looking her way and nodded. Then he saw the air around her begin to shimmer with blistering Energy. It coalesced like a fine orange mist and then streamed to the point of the arrow she held nocked to her bow. With the fluid grace of a master archer, she drew it back and released the string.

The arrow streaked through the air like a bolt of light, and Victor jerked his head around to watch its impact. The monstrous gargantuopod was on its hind legs, swaying back and forth, maw wide open as it struggled with all six of its tentacles to dig Lifedrinker out of its flesh. Sora's blazing arrow buried itself deep in the creature's goo-filled throat, flaring and smoking like a chemical fire. Green and black gas billowed from the monster's mouth as it howled and jerked its head left and right in a pain-filled frenzy.

Victor knew Lifedrinker was doing good work, draining away the thing's Energy, likely interrupting some of its abilities. Even so, he wished he had another weapon, something large enough to continue his punishment of the monster.

Rather than dig through the piles of refuse and debris in the lair, hoping to find something to pummel the monster with, he inhaled deeply, stoking the flames of his magma-attuned Breath Core. The gargantuopod had given up all pretense of an offensive and was rolling on the ground, shaking the cavern floor, throwing up mounds of rotting meat and slimy detritus as it struggled with Lifedrinker's deep bite and the flaming arrow still burning a pit in its insides.

As his Breath Core swelled and his lungs filled to bursting, Victor stomped forward. Risking a fate similar to his bear's, he reached out and snatched ahold of the monster's maw as it puckered open. He found grips on the round smooth sides of the sharp grinding teeth in fingers of steel, digging in, straining with every ounce of his prodigious strength. At the same time, he stepped on the bottom rim of the sphincter mouth, holding the great maw gaping wide around him.

When he felt himself losing, when the weird muscles that contracted that grinding orifice began to pull him in, Victor switched his Sovereign Will boost to strength and roared, pushing and stretching the maw wide. Then he emptied his Breath Core, blowing out every ounce of his magma-attuned Energy in a stream of liquid, fiery orange-glowing rock, dumping gallons and gallons of it into the thing's throat and down into its belly.

The horrible damage his magma did to the thing's insides was enough to send it into apoplectic convulsions, and even Victor's terrible grip wasn't able to keep hold. The monster bucked and flopped, and Victor was thrown head over heels backward as it rolled around on the ground, desperately seeking a release from its agony but unable to reach the fire destroying its insides.

Victor clambered back to his feet, and he was stunned to see a System message flash before his eyes.

Cam Lightly has been rescued from certain death and removed from the dungeon. Eighteen entrants remain. Prepare for an Energy infusion.

Blinking, Victor looked around the room but couldn't spot the young magician. When his gaze returned to the monster, still convulsing, spewing black and green gasses from an orifice that had to be its anus, Victor saw one of the silver rods Cam had planted jutting out of its rigid pink flesh. "Did the damn thing roll over him?"

To his surprise, Sora responded from just behind him, "No, I shot him." Victor whirled on her, hands up in a fighting stance, but she smiled and shook her head. "I didn't break the trust; he was trying to betray you. Those flags he was planting were meant to mesmerize you as you fought with the monster." She looked back to the giant creature and coughed, unable to easily breathe in the green and black fumes despite Victor's banner. "Is it going to die?"

Victor looked down at the woman, tiny to him in his titanic form, and contemplated grabbing her and flinging her toward the dying beast. The impulse came on the heels of a frustrated thought about how he couldn't trust anyone in that place. She could be lying. She could have seen an opportunity to eliminate a weaker opponent.

Scowling, growling faintly, some smoke drifting out of his nostrils, he stepped back to keep her in view while observing the monstrous creature. It was thrashing much more feebly now, lying on its side, exposed ribs heaving up and down as it struggled to breathe through its ruined throat and esophagus. "It'll die," he said with finality. "Lifedrinker won't let it recover."

"Lifedrinker?" Sora held a sleeve over her face, coughing again.

"My axe. She's deep in its maw."

"Ah!" Sora looked up from her sleeve, her eyes bloodshot from the fumes. When she saw Victor's scowling countenance, she took a step back, releasing her bow with one hand and letting it hang by her side. "I swear, Victor. Cam and I are friends in the city. He will be furious with me, but I told him not to try his scheme. He ignored me."

Victor kept one eye on the dying monster and shrugged. "So you shot him? I thought he was hard to surprise."

"Yes, but his talent doesn't help so much against people he deems friendly. If you doubt me, collect his flags after that thing dies. See what their purpose is."

Victor did doubt her, and he did intend to examine the silver rods, but no matter what they were, it wouldn't reinforce his trust in the archer; for all Victor knew, she could have encouraged Cam with the intent to betray him from the beginning. The cloud of noxious gas and smoke around the monster had grown so thick that he was having trouble seeing it. "Wait here if you want," he grunted, then strode into the caustic haze.

The gargantuopod was barely moving, its breaths shallow and rapid, and he could see Lifedrinker's haft jutting out of its open, smoking pit of a mouth. He wanted to be close as the axe finished her feast; he didn't feel good without her in his hand.

Standing beside the monster's head, the thing seemed pitiful, even though its gaping jaw was probably ten yards wide. "Come on, *hombre*," he said, wishing it had an eye he could look into. "Give it up. Time to move on." In a coincidence that sent shivers down his spine, the thing took a deep shuddering breath, wheezed it out in a cloud of black smoke, and fell still.

Before the System could blast him with a torrent of Energy, Victor grabbed Lifedrinker's haft and gave her a tug. She slipped free almost effortlessly. She throbbed in his hand, waves of satisfaction rolling into him as he noticed the thick veins of shimmering green Energy that stretched through her silvery metal and into her living wood haft. He wondered if she'd evolve again soon, perhaps after processing this latest feast.

A soft breeze tickled his neck, and when he turned, he saw Sora standing where he'd left her, eyes closed, hands outstretched, her hair whipping in a breeze she seemed to be creating. That's when a ball of golden Energy struck her in the chest—at nearly the same time, another hit Victor. The influx was significant, enough to lift him off the ground and fully replenish his Core. Euphoria washed over him, his anger melted away, and Victor dropped to his knees, panting as though he'd just sprinted a mile.

When he looked up, he saw Sora lying on her back in a similar state. As he clambered to his knees, then his feet, he turned to look at the dead gargantuopod and saw great balls of rainbow-hued Energy drifting up from the corpse, forming a big shimmering blob. "Shit, here we go again," he muttered.

He'd only seen the rainbow-tinted globes of Energy a time or two before, and he knew it would hit him like a runaway train. He was leery of being made insensate by the influx, still suspicious of Sora as he was, but he knew she'd be just as impacted. That said, he stood close to the monster's corpse, Lifedrinker in his hand. He figured that if he were closer, the Energy would hit him first, which meant he'd recover first.

Sora was still lying on her back when the shimmering cloud of Energy split into two streams, and one slammed into his back between his shoulder blades. Victor started to yell, not in anger but in victory, lifting his arms high, Lifedrinker in one fist as the enormous wave of power washed over him, lifting him into the air. He'd been hit with surges like this before—his greatest post-battle rush had to have been the reaver army he'd defeated single-handedly, but this was up there in the top five. Even as his conscious mind began to depart, drifting on waves of euphoria, he felt sure he'd gain another level.

When the Energy released him and he fell to the ground, he caught himself on the knuckles of his free hand before he tumbled to the filthy floor. Standing, he looked past the System message waiting for him until he caught sight of Sora sitting on the ground, her bow resting on her knees. She regarded him placidly and nodded at his instant scrutiny. "That was quite a reward you just received. Mine wasn't so large."

Victor sighed, stretching his neck until it popped. He should have guessed she'd recover more quickly if the System decided she'd contributed less to the kill. Remembering the battle, though, he frowned. "I thought that arrow you shot into its throat was pretty damn effective."

As she inhaled, gathering her words, he read the System message:

Congratulations! You have achieved Level 63 Herald of the Mountain's Wrath and gained 12 strength, 17 vitality, and 12 will.

He looked at his attribute panel on his status page, wondering how things were shaping up after three levels in his new Class:

Strength:	406	Vitality:	526 (579)
Dexterity:	190	Agility:	213
Intelligence:	172	Will:	589

While he stared at the numbers, inwardly amused by how much they'd changed since he'd first stepped foot into the Wagon Wheel and Yrella and Vullu had taught him how to look at his status, Sora said, "I'm sure I hurt it, and I got a lot of Energy, but that fiery kiss of death was what did the creature in. I don't know how it's possible for a giant to breathe fire like a dragon, but color me impressed." She rose to her feet with effortless grace and gestured with her bow to something behind him. "We received a chest."

"Titan," Victor grunted absently while he turned. Sure enough, resting on the filthy blood-and-gore-spattered stone floor was a large ornate silver-inlaid marble chest.

"Excuse me?" Sora stood beside him, no longer tiny but still quite a lot smaller than he was.

"I'm Quinametzin. Titan. Not a giant."

"There's a difference?"

Victor jerked his thumb at the crumpled corpse of the gargantuopod. "Titans can kill shit like that." He pointed to the chest. "How we doing this?"

Sora lithely hopped past the chest and mounted the corpse, like climbing a hill for her, to pull the silver rod from its side. "Do you want to inspect this? I'd prefer to think you believe me and that I needn't fear you will smite me down out of suspicion."

Victor shrugged. "I made a deal with you. A, uh, 'gentlefolk's agreement.' Remember? I'm not going to hurt you unless you betray me or unless we agree to split up. As for that thing, what's it going to matter? You could have tricked that little guy into placing them for all I know."

Sora frowned, and her brow narrowed. She was clearly angry at the impli-cation, but it seemed she couldn't formulate an argument that would counter Victor's logic. Instead, she tossed the "flag" to the ground with a *ping* and brushed her hands together, wiping off some unseen debris. "I hope I can earn your trust, Victor. I appreciate your honesty."

"You don't want that?" Victor pointed to the rod where it had rolled into a sticky mess of rotted flesh.

"They're useless to me. They require a mind affinity, and the set is incom-plete; he still had more to place." She walked to the chest and stood beside it. It was large enough that he figured she could get inside if she curled up. "As for the treasure, I'll defer the first choice of the loot to you. Then we can take turns. Maybe there's one item in here, or maybe there are twenty. I have no idea what to expect after slaying a monster of this caliber."

Victor realized he was still gripping Lifedrinker's haft in white knuck-les. He lifted her and looked at her blade; she was unusually quiet, and he wondered if it had something to do with the thick rivers of Energy she was processing. He held her over his shoulder, and his harness snatched her, pull-ing her close against his back.

He turned in a slow circle, looking around the great chamber. It was big enough to house a couple of full-court basketball games with room left over for the fans. The haze had cleared from the ground level, but near the high stone ceiling, a cloud of black and green vapors still clung. He saw the stone tunnel where they'd entered the chamber and, on the far wall, not too far from where the monster's corpse lay, was another exit.

Victor nodded, and as he stepped toward the chest, he called forth his coyotes, infusing them with inspiration-attuned Energy. Naturally, they came into the world yipping and whining, and Victor laughed. "Hey, *hermanos*, go watch those tunnels and make sure nobody surprises me and my friend here." They yipped and split up, darting through the refuse-strewn cavern. Victor looked at Sora, and when he grinned, she returned the smile. "All right, let's see what kind of loot that big boy had for us."

41

SKULLS AND DOPPELGANGERS

Lo'ro gestured to the doors, indicating a commotion, and Ranish Dar turned his gaze that way. He recognized the man coming through, Duvius Black, with his signature midnight robes and feline features covered with silken black hair, impossible to miss. Someone must have said something snide because the magician was hissing, his robes puffing up along his back as his hair stood on end. The man looked ready to fight to the death. "Something's got him quite ruffled." Lo'ro chuckled.

Dar nodded. "You saw what happened to his student. I'm sure one of those drunkards said something a touch too biting."

"You reckon he's here to confront you?" Lo'ro sipped his strange milk-white liquor, his pale features and dark eyes giving no hints of amusement to match his lighthearted tone.

"Confront me? It was my student who was nearly sabotaged. More likely, he's here to save face, to try to deny the elven girl's accusations." Dar looked at the viewing screen, watching as some students still on the first level traded blows. He was beginning to root for the young beastkin boy when, sure enough, Duvius Black stepped up to the table.

"Ranish!" he purred, his voice smooth and calm, as though he hadn't just been in a screaming match with those men near the door.

"Duvius. It's been a while, hasn't it? Why, more than a decade since we traded words, I'd think."

"Has it been so long? My, the years just slip away like sand through our fingers, do they not?" He shifted to the side, standing beside the bench on Lo'ro's side of the table. The undead Death Caster chuckled and slid further into the booth, nodding his hairless head at the seat.

"Please, sit down."

"Why thank you . . ." Duvius trailed off, clicking his tongue. "I'm so sorry, but I've misplaced your name, good sir."

Ranish had no doubt that Duvius knew exactly who Lo'ro was, but he humored him in his little power play: "Duvius, this is Lo'ro the Grim, an old friend of mine."

"A pleasure!" he said, sliding into the seat. As he settled, he compulsively ran his long pink tongue along his short-haired forearm. He quickly folded his hands on his lap beneath the table when he caught himself.

"The pleasure is mine, Mr. Black. I've heard much about you." Lo'ro's thin lips pulled back in a smile, revealing teeth that hinted at his ancestors' love of meat.

Duvius nodded, then focused his large feline eyes on Ranish's smoldering fiery ones. "That's quite a young monster you've thrown into the sandpit with our students."

"Pardon me? My young, under-leveled student is a monster? Need we rehash the words of that white-haired Fae-blood? She made it clear to all who watched what your boy was up to."

Duvius leaned forward, his black lips curling back, lifting his whiskers to reveal impressive canines. "Now, Ranish, that's exactly why I'm here! Cam is beside himself with grief; he's lost eight levels, and those were tough levels to come by. Still, even in his wallowing sorrow, he denies what the girl said. He has no reason to lie to me! We all know the stakes, and we're all reasonable enough to recognize a clever gambit, even if it didn't pay."

"Ah, let me guess," Lo'ro said, unconcerned about offending the man he'd just met. "She encouraged him, said she'd help, then when the moment was right, it was she who did the betraying?"

"Exactly!" Duvius slammed a furry fist on the table. Either he was too dense to register Lo'ro's teasing, or he chose to ignore it, giving the Death Caster a chance to back off. He glanced at the wall displaying the various images from the view stones. "How many remain? There were eighteen when I left my club."

Lo'ro was quick to answer. "Fifteen now. I reckon Ranish's boy must be about to gain another level."

"Did you see what he and that little bitch pulled from their chest?"

"No; the System blocked the feed from the view stones." Ranish pointed to the far end of the wall where two blacked-out rectangles hung near the edge. "They must still be in there."

"A gargantuopod!" Duvius *tsked*. "My student deserved a piece of that price. He will challenge that Fae girl after this. You watch!"

"That doesn't seem wise, considering what he's just lost. I suppose if she gets rescued, she might be an easier target." Ranish shrugged.

"Fah!" Duvius's eyes narrowed, and he jerked his head to the side, hissing as only a feline could. "It's infuriating!"

"Did you have a lot riding on your student?"

"You know how rare a chance affinity is! I'm still stunned she landed that shot."

"He must have been very focused on his flags—a complicated ritual to perform amid a battle betwixt titans." Lo'ro chuckled.

Dar held up a finger. "Only one titan and a behemoth."

Lo'ro shrugged. "Is it such an important distinction? Behemoth-type monsters are often on par with a titan's strength."

"Not that one." Dar smiled, enjoying his gloating a bit too much. He'd already made a fortune on Victor's showing.

"You're awfully smug, Dar." Duvius seemed to have tired of playing nice. "I'd be watchful, were I you." When Dar scowled, he held up his hands, palms out. "No, no. I make no threats. I simply say that your student isn't making friends there. I've already heard word that Arcus Volpuré will seek vengeance. Even after his early defeat, he's still nearly Tier Nine."

"You think my student needs to fear a man he soundly thrashed despite giving him the advantage of first strike?" Despite himself, Ranish Dar couldn't help closing his massive stony hands into fists atop the table. He didn't like threats, even indirect ones.

"Perhaps not, though Volpuré is a dastard; he might seek to hurt him in other ways. Tell me, does your student have a family?"

Dar leaned forward, and his eyes flared, heating the air around their booth. "He does not, so feel free to spread that word. Moreover, any who seek to battle or harm him in this city without the proper formalities will find themselves on the wrong end of my wrath."

"Dar!" Duvius held a hand to his chest, a look of dismay plastered on his face. "Do you think I would do any such thing? I'm no fool; I simply repeat the whispered rumors propagating the high streets."

Dar sat back, his frown like an upturned scythe blade on his stony countenance. "I'm weary of your warnings, Duvius. Leave me and my friend in peace, would you?"

"Oh." He cleared his throat and glanced from Dar to Lo'ro. "Of course. I simply wanted to congratulate you on your new protégé. Tell me, is he entertaining other offers? Surely you cannot devote too much of your precious attention to a single student . . ."

"He is not." Dar folded his arms over his chest, his brows angled inward, a dangerous gleam in his eyes.

"Very well," Duvius sighed, sliding out of the bench. "I'm sure we'll speak again soon." With those cryptic words, he turned and strode out of the club.

"What a strange visit," Lo'ro said, his humor bubbling into each word.

"I'm glad you're amused."

"Do you think there's any truth to . . ."

Dar waved a hand, dismissing the topic. He pointed to the wall where Victor's rectangular viewing portal once again projected an image of the large man. "We'll have plenty of time for speculation. I'm hungry, and Victor's spy has resumed coverage."

While Victor and Sora stood before the chest, preparing to open it, the System announced the rescue of three more entrants, bringing the remainder to fifteen. Again, they were struck by a massive Energy influx, but, to Victor's surprise, he didn't gain a level. When he mentioned as much, Sora chuckled and said she'd only gained one level since entering the place. "What level are you?" he asked bluntly as she reached for the chest's clasp.

She paused, her fingers just brushing the silvery latch, and looked at him with narrowed eyes. "I suppose it's not such a great secret. If we survive this place, you could find plenty in Sojourn who know I'm just a hair over Level Eighty." She resumed her movement and lifted the lid of the chest, releasing a cloud of sparkling golden mist. "And you, Victor?"

He shrugged. "Just a bit past Sixty." He figured it was only fair to answer, considering it had been his question. As she looked askance at him, obvious doubt in her eyes, Victor stepped forward and looked into the chest. "Man, your buddy wasn't lying. There's a lot of loot in here."

"My buddy? Oh, Cam. No, I'm sure he was right. The gargantuopod was a worthy challenge." She joined him, looking down into the box. There were quite a few different objects within—Victor saw something that looked like an empty crystal bottle, a dark, vaguely humanoid skull with two horns, a ring, a cloak, and a crystal that looked almost like a prism he'd seen in a teacher's classroom when he was younger. Half the space in the box was taken up by a bulging leather sack. "Shall we identify them before you make your first choice?"

"Yeah." Victor jostled the big sack, and the familiar sound of beads clinking against each other came to his ears. "Cash."

"Cash?" She frowned and then nodded. "Beads. Currency. I get it." She lifted out the bottle, and Victor saw her concentrate briefly while trickling some Energy into it. "The breath of a legendary master—one-time use. Inhale the contents to be inspired by a great master in a time of need." She set the bottle on the chest's lid. And Victor picked up the skull. He trickled some Energy into it and read the System-generated description.

Whispering Skull: This artifact is tied to the undying spirit of a once-great magic user. Ask it questions, but be prepared to deal with the spirit's cryptic language and penchant for trickery.

Victor immediately set the skull next to the bottle, not at all interested in it. He had enough trouble figuring out who was lying to him without adding an undead skull to the mix. Nevertheless, he described it to Sora, and she seemed intrigued. She lifted out the ring and a moment later said, "Voidstone Ring—once per day, this artifact will absorb and nullify any one spell cast toward the wearer."

Victor rubbed his chin. "Not bad." He watched her set it down, then picked up the prism, slowly turning it in his fingers so it caught the dim light and split it into rainbows against his palm. He could feel Sora staring at him, so he trickled some Energy into it.

Prism of the Doppelganger: If a single being carries this prism for a year, that being may use it to summon a temporary duplicate of themselves. This doppelganger will share their desires, thoughts, and abilities, but will disappear after one hour, not to be resummoned until another year has passed.

At first, Victor frowned. He didn't like the idea of an item he could only use once a year, but then he thought about how powerful it was, imagining how easy most of his previous battles would have been if he'd had a twin brother as strong as he was, who wanted exactly what he did. He carefully set the prism next to the skull as he described it to Sora.

"Quite an item. I can see why it requires so much time to charge." She stared longingly at the prism for several seconds, then reached in to pick up the cloak. A few seconds later, she said, "Mantle of Dreamweaving. It's a cloak that allows you to enter and manipulate the dreams of others, depending on the strength of their will."

Victor frowned, shaking his head. "Sounds kind of shitty. If I found out someone was messing with my dreams . . ." He trailed off, sighing and shaking his head. While he'd been imagining creative ways to pummel someone who'd interfered with his sleep, Sora had untied the bag of beads and plucked one out. "Dual attuned—fire and earth. I'd estimate ten thousand, but it could be more; that bag might have a dimensional enchantment."

"Right. So, we're taking turns?" When Sora nodded, Victor picked up the prism and slipped it into his new storage pouch.

She nodded. "I would've done the same." Victor watched her hand hesitate between the cloak and the bottle of "master's breath," but she settled on the cloak.

Victor rubbed his chin, contemplating. Had she been hovering between the cloak and the bottle to make him think the bottle was the next best item, or had she genuinely been tempted by it? Victor had no idea what a "legendary master's" inspiration would be like, but he supposed it might get him out of a jam someday. The voidstone ring was pretty great, too, though. Once per day, it could save him from a surprise magical attack. Once per day, it could mess up an opponent's first move. He knew he didn't want the skull. Sighing, unsure if he was making the right choice, he grabbed the ring and immediately sent some Energy into it, bonding with the item before slipping it onto his finger.

Sora smirked and picked up the bottle. "I'm surprised you didn't take this. It may prove invaluable when we reach the end of the iron ranks."

"Yeah. It might." Victor shrugged, then reached into the chest and lifted the sack of beads. "You can have that *pinché* skull." He tried to put the sack into his magical pouch, but it wouldn't go, which brought a wide grin to his face. Sending some Energy into the bag, his mind became aware of a sizeable dimensional space and a hefty mound of Energy beads within it. Sora didn't seem to notice; she was busy turning her new skull in her hands. She had thin lips on her angular face, and her frown of concentration was almost comical as she said, "Skull, tell us the best route to the stairs."

A voice as dry as dust began to emanate from the ancient blackened skull, "Ah, seeker of paths untrodden and stairs unseen, listen well: Where shadows dance at the edge of sight, and the echoes of footsteps are your guiding light, follow the gaze of the stone-lined throat, but heed this warning I do bring: The truest path often lies hidden beneath layers of deceit and sin. Seek not with eyes but with your mind's might, for only the wise can pierce the night."

"What the fu . . ." Victor started to say but broke off as laughter took over. "I knew that thing would be useless." Sora tried several more times to get a straight answer out of the skull, but Victor kept laughing as each subsequent response was more obscure than the one before. While she messed with it, he tied his sack of Energy beads to his belt and then walked over to the gigantic corpse of the gargantuopod. He reached over his shoulder to loosen Life-drinker from her harness and clambered atop the beast, using Lifedrinker as a climbing pick.

"What are you doing?" Sora called, her annoying skull hanging from a leather cord at her belt.

"I'm going to get its heart." With that, Victor began the long dirty process of hacking through the monster's ribs; unfortunately, they had collapsed on the side he'd already cut through. While he worked, building up a sweat, Sora walked closer and called up to him.

"Why?"

"I can use it for something," Victor grunted. Lucky for him, Lifedrinker was up to the task, and after a while, he'd chopped through several ribs and managed to dig around in the bloody hot meat until he found the thing's enormous heart. It resisted him; the arteries were tough and thick, and it didn't want to come out. The entire time he grunted and jerked on the thing, trying to pull it free, Victor wished he could go through his rings for a nice long sharp knife. Eventually, in a fit of frustration, he cast Iron Berserk again, and then, with surging strength and much larger fingers, he popped the recalcitrant organ out of the carcass and held it aloft in two hands, hoisting it over his head with a savage grin.

He had half a mind to eat it on the spot but managed to control his desire. There was no telling what would happen to him, and he didn't want to be left helpless while his body went through some kind of evolution. With a tremendous push of his will, he slipped the big organ into his storage pouch and pulled his rage-attuned Energy back into his Core, ending his Berserk. When he hopped down from the body, Sora was sitting on a relatively clean section of the ground, talking to the skull. "I'm afraid it's mad." She sighed, watching Victor try to rub the blood off his hands using the tatters of his leather pants. "I hope that heart was worth all that effort."

"Me too." Victor turned to the great corpse and cast Honor the Spirits, smiling as a ghostly bonfire burst into being, consuming the carcass in a matter of seconds.

Sora stumbled back, surprised, then glared at Victor. "What did you just do?"

"Sent my ancestors that big damn corpse." He shrugged. "Who knows what they can do with it." He pointed to the corridor leading away from the chamber, now clearly visible with the corpse out of the way. "Let's see where that goes."

Darren slammed his mug on the table and practically howled with excitement. "Did you see that? He breathed fire into its throat! He cooked it from the inside!" He wasn't the only one in hysterics. The entire bar was breaking into pandemonium. People were standing on benches, sloshing drinks in the air as they cheered, waving for bet-takers to come to their table, breaking into songs and chants, and generally acting as though they'd done the killing instead of Victor. Darren could see why; it had been an amazing spectacle, and when it started, most of the people in the bar thought Victor and his friends would lose.

Everything had changed when Victor doubled in size and slammed into the monster with such force that he'd sent it sliding. Who could do that? The thing had to weigh thousands of tons. Darren laughed, drinking more of his beer and remembering how he'd thought his little tanks would be able to stand up to people like him. He looked around the table and saw the pride in Valla's eyes, the joy on Edeya's face, and the solemn, knowing gaze Lesh gave him. Lam had excused herself to go to the restroom halfway through the fight, and Darren had a sneaking suspicion she'd been nervous for Victor.

"That's why I follow that man," Lesh said, his deep, rumbling voice having a little trouble with the consonants—he must have drunk two gallons of liquor by now.

"Were you worried?" Edeya asked, looking earnestly up at Valla.

"Me? I was only worried that he'd be betrayed by those two companions of his. It seems the woman may be too clever to tempt Victor's wrath." She looked at the wall and frowned as the image shifted to show another pair of adventurers bickering about which path to take. "Why do they change it? Wouldn't seeing their rewards be more interesting than this?"

"The view window turned black when they looked at the chest," Lesh said. "The System may be granting them privacy." He leaned back in his seat and reached down to pull a pocket watch out of his belt. He peered blearily at it, then looked from Darren to Edeya. "You two should rest. It may be hours before Victor sees more action, and the night grows old."

"We have a whole day before our dungeon shlot, Lesh," Edeya said, folding her arms over her chest. She'd had plenty to drink.

"Do as you please, but Darren will retire." He looked at Darren and raised a scaly eyebrow.

"Um, right. Yes, Elder Lesh." Darren sighed and began to slide to the end of his bench.

"Oh, fine!" Edeya groused. "I'll go back with you."

Suddenly, Lam was there, leaning on the table beside Valla. "I'll walk with them. You and Lesh can stay and keep watching. Use the Far Scribe book if something happens. Otherwise, I'll come back in the morning."

"Thank you, Lam. I will. Did you see the battle?"

"Oh, yes. I was returning from the privy and saw him finish that thing off." She shook her head, grinning wryly. "Remind me to buy that man some soothing tea for his throat." She looked at Darren and Edeya. "Ready?"

Darren nodded, and Edeya smiled brightly with red cheeks. "Yesh!"

He followed the two women out of the bar; Lam was a good deal taller than he, so she cut through the crowds, looking over the patrons' heads for the best route. Once they were outside in the chilly evening air, he took a deep breath and sighed happily. "What a fun time!"

Lam laughed and led the way past the many groups of loitering patrons. "That's because you were rooting for Victor. If you'd been friends with one of those others, you might not have had so much fun."

"Well, most of these people don't know any of them," Edeya said, waving her arm in an arc, indicating all the various strangers lingering around, talking and carousing. "And they had plenty of fun!"

"Good point!" Lam put her arm over the smaller woman's shoulders, and to Darren's surprise and immense joy, paused for him to catch up so she could drape her other arm over his shoulders. "I'll keep you close, or Lesh'll have my hide."

"Ah, ahem, yes." Darren nodded, his cheeks flushing. "Wouldn't want Elder Lesh angry."

"Oh my!" Edeya laughed. "Is he mocking his mentor? I'm telling Lesh!"

"No!" Darren cried. "No, I wasn't mocking . . ."

"Hush," Lam laughed. "She's teasing."

Darren tried to regulate his breathing, allowing himself to relax as Lam guided them along. They'd only cleared a building or two and were approaching a corner when a smooth masculine voice called out from behind them. "Excuse me! I say, excuse me, but did I hear correctly? Are you three friends with that gigantic warrior in the challenge dungeon?"

42

TENSION

Victor glanced at Sora, and she nodded, closing the door behind them. They'd just found what they believed to be a set of stairs leading up to the third dungeon level and were preparing to climb them when the message appeared. It was the second one since they'd left the gargantuopod's lair, and Victor was sure it would level him. He could feel the tension in his body and Core; it felt like even a hint of Energy would push him over the edge. They were in a round stone chamber with one exit and a spiral staircase leading up to shadowy heights.

Sora sat down with her back to the door, her bow in her lap. "It might be a few minutes; it seems the System tries to wait for battles to halt before throwing the Energy at us."

"Yeah." Victor sat down on the steps facing her. "You think we'll get another chest when we go up?"

"That's my understanding. Each level awards a chest, and the value of the prizes is supposed to increase as the number of participants dwindles." She smiled, shrugging. "Should be quite a bit better than the last one. A few people have been knocked out since."

"Mmhmm." Victor nodded absently as he stroked Lifedrinker's haft. She'd been very quiet since the gargantuopod, and he could still see the faint lines of shimmering green Energy in her silvery metal. He didn't know exactly how it worked, but it seemed like she was slowly digesting what she'd taken.

"Your axe is made of Heart Silver?" Sora's intonation made a question out of the statement.

"Yeah. Well, she started with just a Heart Silver core, but it's expanded as she's . . . evolved is the word for it, I guess."

"A wonderful weapon, to be sure. She must have drained much from the gargantuopod. I'm sure it helped our fire to slay it." When Victor didn't respond, not wanting to chatter about his axe or her secrets, Sora tried another topic. "You called yourself a titan, yes? Are there many of your kind on your homeworld?"

Victor looked at her with narrowed eyes. He'd grown leery of strangers trying to dig information out of him. So many unscrupulous people had tried to use knowledge of his abilities against him that he was mistrustful. The problem with his thinking, though, was that the questions felt innocent enough; she could simply be trying to make conversation, perhaps trying to bolster their tenuous alliance.

Rather than answer her, he decided to turn the tables to see how she handled some personal probing. "Hmm, how about you tell me about yourself? On my homeworld, people who look like you are often called elves. Is that right?" He didn't mention that he'd only seen them in fiction.

"Elves? Well, I have a Fae bloodline and as a result have devoured many a text on the subject of the Fae. They have subgroups of people, and yes, I've read the terms 'elf,' 'elfin,' and even 'elvish.' However, my people are called the Ramash, and most don't share my pointy ears, strange coloring, and large eyes. I hail from a world somewhat distant from Sojourn; I had to traverse another hub to reach this place."

Victor nodded, more interested than he'd expected to be in her answer. He'd made a lot of assumptions about her—about most of the people in the dungeon. For some reason, he'd held himself apart as though he weren't benefiting from a wealthy patron like most of the other entrants.

He was starting to see that he often gave himself more credit than he deserved, that he considered his efforts to get where he was somehow out of the norm. In his mind, the other dungeon goers were akin to spoiled rich kids, pampered on an easy world and handed opportunities that he'd had to work for. Had he, though? It sounded as if he'd had an easier time getting to Sojourn than Sora. He decided to be more open-minded and to try to learn more about the people he encountered. "How'd you get to know Cam?"

"In another dungeon. We were both signed up for the same time slot, and the coordinators put us together. I still consider him a friend, and I'm dreading the outcome of my betrayal." She looked down, and Victor saw real emotion in her eyes, real hurt. He'd been so suspicious of her earlier that he hadn't considered the weight of her actions if she were telling the truth; she'd gone against a friend to keep from betraying Victor's trust. As he completed the thought, another voice in his head scoffed—she'd betrayed a friend to keep from getting smashed by him. Just because she wasn't stupid didn't mean she was loyal to him.

"I don't know exactly what Cam was going to do, but you made the right choice. I don't tolerate betrayal well. At least in here, your friend had the Lifesaver, and your attack wasn't enough to kill him outright. I couldn't make promises to that effect if I lost myself in rage."

"So you don't always have control?"

Again, Sora's question rubbed Victor the wrong way, as if she was fishing. He glanced up to the air at the center of the spiral stair and saw the two spy stones floating around up there. There was no telling who was listening to their conversation. He was about to change the subject again when, out of nowhere, glittering balls of bright golden Energy slammed into each of their chests. Victor grunted as the euphoria swept over him, and when he came back to his senses, he had a System message waiting for him:

Congratulations! You have achieved Level 64 Herald of the Mountain's Wrath and gained 12 strength, 17 vitality, and 12 will.

He waved the message away and looked at Sora. She was staring into space, her eyes moving left to right as though reading something. She did it for a long while, and Victor figured she'd gotten more notifications than a simple level; maybe she'd gained a new skill or spell or some other kind of upgrade. With a grunt, he stood up and slung Lifedrinker back over his shoulder. "Ready to head up?"

Sora shook her head and blinked rapidly, hopping gracefully to her feet. "Aye. If we're separated again, I'll wait outside the award chamber."

"Yep, same here." Victor turned and started up the stairs. Sure enough, after just a few steps, he found himself stepping into a room almost identical to the one at the end of the first level. The only difference he could perceive was that the chest was made of wood and inlaid with dark metallic runes. He stepped toward it, looking over his shoulder to ensure he was alone, that the floating spy stone was gone, and that Sora hadn't been sent to the same award room. The stair leading down was empty and quiet, so he turned back to the chest.

It was about the same size as the last one, only about twenty inches by twelve and something like ten inches deep. When he reached down to lift the clasp, it made a kind of ringing sound as it rubbed against the metal of the latch, and when Victor lifted the lid, sparkling golden fog billowed out, accompanied by a distinct chime. "Fancy," he chuckled, waving the haze away so he could see the contents.

When his eyes found his award, Victor frowned and reached in to lift out a pair of sturdy-looking dark leather boots. As soon as he saw them, he knew they were part of the same set as the gauntlet he'd gotten in the first chest. "Two boots. Does that count as two parts of the set?" To answer his question, Victor channeled a little Energy into the left boot to read what the System had to tell him.

Boots of Sojourn: These boots count as one item in a set. Collect five pieces of the set and bring them to the Sojourn City Stone to imbue them with curated set bonuses.

Victor's scowl deepened as he set the boot down and peered inside the chest again. It was utterly empty. "Seems like bullshit," he grumbled and sent the pair into his storage bag. He stood up, ready to head out, but then he felt Lifedrinker begin to vibrate on his back, and with a nerve-grating, elongated crackling sound, he felt a sudden increase in her weight pulling against his harness.

Victor's mind flew down panic-laced pathways: Had the Energy Lifedrinker absorbed harmed her somehow? Was she trying to tell him something? Had some invisible fiend tried to pull her off his back? With his thoughts whirling, he reached up to grab her haft and found it much more of a handful than before.

Sudden understanding dawned on him, and Victor's worry turned to excitement as he lifted her free of her harness and pulled her around to grasp in both hands. He lifted her high before his face, staring at her beautiful shape. Lifedrinker's star-dappled, living wood haft had grown by more than a foot, and her brilliant silver axe-head had to have increased its mass by fifty percent. The blade was larger and heavier, with wicked swoops at the ends of the crescent. She glinted with her own inner light, and when Victor held her close to inspect the shimmering glow, he saw that her edge was so fine as to be nearly transparent. "*Qué rico*, beautiful!"

Pride and satisfaction emanated through her haft into his hands, and Lifedrinker veritably hummed with excitement. *Let us hunt!* she cried, filling his mind with images of wolves chasing down prey. Victor chuckled and slung her back over his shoulder. Her new size felt right, a good deal more substantial and a more proper fit for his own growth. As he stepped forward to open the door, his disappointing treasure was forgotten in the warm pride he felt for Lifedrinker's advancement.

Darren felt Lam stiffen as the stranger called out his question. When she turned, he stepped back as she slowly lifted her arm from around his shoulders, nudging him and Edeya behind her. "What's that, stranger? Were you speaking to me?" Lam's voice was crisp and sharp, her earlier slurring utterly banished by either adrenaline or the strength of her will. Darren peeked around her faintly fluttering dragonfly wings, peering through the cascades of golden Energy motes at the man who'd stopped them.

He was tall and had that palpable vibrancy that spoke of many racial advancements. It was a feeling Darren often felt when near Valla and Victor and, to a lesser extent, Lam and Lesh. Even Edeya felt similar, though the depth of her power was clearly much shallower.

Before he got too sidetracked, wondering about racial advancements, Darren continued his inspection of the man. His skin looked almost golden, and half-extended behind him were broad powerful wings adorned with crimson feathers. The wings tilted forward and hugged his shoulders like a great cloak. He was terribly handsome, with big golden almond-shaped eyes, full pleasant lips that spread in a gentle smile, and feathery red hair that matched his wings.

While Darren felt comforted by the pleasant aspect of the man, he saw Lam bristle, and suddenly a shimmering, silvery war hammer was in her hand. "Ridonne," she said, veritably spitting the word.

"Ah! I wasn't mistaken, then! I thought sure those were Ghelli wings, but I wasn't aware of any Ghelli in Sojourn. Have they changed the access policy in Tharcray?"

"Not likely. We came by other means." Lam didn't lower her hammer, and the enormous sledge-like head began to hum, vibrating the air in discernable waves of force.

"Dear me! I'm not sure what fills you with such angst, dear Ghelli, but I offer no threat. I was simply intrigued by the sight of you and your companion there, and when I walked near, I heard you mention the giant warrior. Curiosity is the only motive for my approach!"

When Lam didn't respond immediately, and her hammer remained in her hand, he cleared his throat and folded his arms, cocking his head at her. "You're aware of the laws in Sojourn, yes? I'd hate for us both to get into some trouble if you start swinging that thing. Tell me, why the hostility? I haven't been home in decades and was hoping for a bit of news."

His mention of Sojourn's laws seemed to get through whatever was clouding Lam's mind, and she slowly inhaled, lowering the hammer but keeping it in her hand. Darren had a good idea why she'd reacted the way she had. He'd heard plenty about the Ridonne, and of course had heard all about how they'd attacked Victor's army before he reached the Untamed Marches. If this particular Ridonne had been in Sojourn for decades, though, then surely, she couldn't hold that against him.

Before Lam could prove Darren right or wrong, Edeya stepped out from behind her and snarled, "We've seen what kind of honor to expect from the Ridonne."

"My, my! I'd hate to bear the brunt of that anger. What makes such a lovely lass spit such venom?" The Ridonne stepped closer, lowering his arms but clasping his hands before him in an unthreatening posture. "My dear, I've never seen a Ghelli with your coloring! Such striking shades of azure! Whatever my kin did to you back home, please don't hold me accountable. Who was it? Ravasha? Trenia? Mordo-dak? I've so many ill-mannered kin that I could probably list names all night. Is there aught that I can do to make amends? I've so wanted to speak to someone from home without the tedium of checking in with my family! Couldn't I entice you to a dinner or . . . Oh! I have it! Won't you come to Warin-dak's victory ball?"

That took some of the steam out of Edeya, and she looked up at Lam in confusion, waiting to see if she'd made more sense of the tall stranger's words. "Warin Dak?" Lam asked, obviously trying to dredge through her memory for the name. Darren could see why—the man before them spoke it as though everyone should be acquainted with his meaning.

"Oh, ancestors!" The Ridonne chuckled, shaking his head. "I'm so out of practice. My name is Chal-dak, and Warin is my cousin. He'll likely win in the challenge dungeon, and I'm sure he'll throw quite a feast."

"What?" Lam's eyes opened wide. "There's a Ridonne in there?" She looked at Edeya, then down at Darren. "I didn't see one on any of the spy windows . . ."

"Ah! I see the confusion! Warin-dak didn't awaken the, um, more pleasant side of the bloodline. He's more bedecked with horns, and his coloring leans more toward crimson and less toward golden. Moreover, he fancies himself a wizard and wears heavy robes with a hooded cowl . . ."

"Oh! The one who killed the three others while they battled those troll things," Edeya said. Darren knew precisely who she was talking about; they'd watched the battle on the big "viewing window" just before Victor and his two friends began exploring the second level. Three adventurers had been fighting a pack of brutish horned giants with green pox-ridden flesh when a fourth had arrived, blasting them all with terrible bolts of red Energy. It looked like something out of a science fiction movie to Darren—death beams that melted through flesh and stone alike.

"They didn't die . . ." Chal-dak began to say, but Lam spoke at the same time.

"Eliminated . . ." She shook her head as they both stopped short, not wanting to speak over each other. When Chal-dak remained silent, she said, "I wouldn't plan a victory party just yet."

"Aha! Our conversation comes full circle! Might I inquire again? You know the giant warrior?"

It was Lam's turn to fold her arms over her chest and smile knowingly at the Ridonne. "I do know him, and though he'd be angry if I spoke much about him to a stranger, I would say he has no love for the Ridonne."

"Ah! Such a shame. I don't suppose you'll expand on the source of his—and your—animosity?"

Again, it was Edeya who spoke up, her voice fierce, her brow narrowed in a scowl. "Should we start with how you and your kind have kept the rest of Fanwath ignorant and subservient, locking away the world travel options for you and yours?"

"Oh? I suppose I can't be surprised that you don't know the System's mandate, handed down when Fanwath was new. As far as I know, it's not something they teach outside our academy."

Lam frowned. "Mandate? Academy?"

"You see! There are things for us to talk about! There's much I could explain. Won't you come to our party after the challenge dungeon?"

Lam sighed, clearly ready to end the conversation. "I won't commit to anything, and, as I said, you shouldn't invest too much in a victory party. In any case, we have other obligations in the near future."

"Well. I do hope you manage to find the time. Even if Warin-dak fails to secure the top position, we'll celebrate his homecoming. Here." He flicked his fingers out, and a glittering golden card appeared between his pointer and middle finger. He extended it to Lam. "My calling card. Simply feed it a touch of Energy, and you can send me a message. Conversely, I can leave a message for you. I'll send you the address of our estate in Sojourn and any forthcoming details about the victory—or not—gala." Darren knew he shouldn't, but he found himself liking the man. He was smooth and charming despite the hostility Lam and Edeya had been showing him.

Lam took the card, sent it into one of her dimensional containers, and nodded. "We must be moving on. Obligations."

"It was my pleasure, Lady . . ." He lifted an eyebrow expectantly, obviously hoping to learn Lam's name.

"Lam."

"Ah!" He smiled, his eyes glittering with pleasure. "No surname? Well, Lam the Ghelli from Fanwath—I'll have to be content with that. I do hope to hear from you soon." With that, he bowed with a flourish, spun on his heel, and strode confidently away, back toward the drinking establishment.

"What a cocky asshole!" Edeya growled.

Lam groaned. "Roots, Edeya! You've been around Victor too much."

43

FOR GLORY

"So? Get anything you want to talk about?" Sora was waiting for Victor when he stepped out of the award room onto a vine-covered stone platform that appeared to be in the middle of a jungle. He looked at her and noted she was wearing a silky dark-gray cloak with a luxurious-looking rust-colored lining. Rather than answering her, he shrugged and pointed at her new garment.

"Got yourself a new cloak?"

"Aye. It's not doing anything for me at the moment, but it's one of those new Sojourn set pieces." She shrugged and smiled, pulling the cloak's sides close over her chest. "It's comfortable!"

Victor seized the opportunity to fish for some information. "Set pieces? You say they're new?"

She nodded, rubbing the silky fabric of her hood against her cheek. "Yes. The lords of the city recently unlocked the option in the System Stone. Supposedly, these items are rare drops in any of the city dungeons. They all have different potential—you can't enchant the ones from the low-tier dungeons as much as ones like this." She gestured around her, indicating the dungeon. "When they announced it, they listed off a bunch of features I can't remember, but I think you can upgrade them with rare materials and add all sorts of enchantments at the city stone. Some of the artisans in town were up in arms about the whole thing."

Victor frowned as he considered the statement. "They think the sets will take business away?"

"Mmhmm." Sora turned to face the narrow path into the jungle. "Of course, the lords said the drops were too rare to have much of an impact. It's not like they care what some iron-ranked crafters think; they all have powerful artisan friends who are above the likes of us." She pointed down the trail. "I heard roaring a minute before you came out, but it seemed distant. Shall we explore?"

"Sure." Victor unslung Lifedrinker and started after her. While she crept forward, presumably using her abilities to sense for presences and traps, Victor followed quietly, boosting his agility and dexterity with Sovereign Will. He wanted to cast Inspiration of the Quinametzin but wasn't sure if the aura, which would negatively impact "enemies," might give them away to lurking beasts or other dungeon entrants. As that thought crossed his mind, he quietly asked, "Is there a time limit on this dungeon? I think my mentor mentioned something like that, but I've forgotten. This whole thing kind of came up suddenly for me."

Sora paused and turned to speak softly over her shoulder. "No set time limit. We'll be in here until only one person is standing or someone clears the boss of the top level."

"And how many levels are there?"

She shrugged. "Between five and ten. I think it's random, or the Lords of Sojourn select the number in secret." Victor contemplated her words while he followed her farther into the jungle. Other than the two of them, only nine others were still in the dungeon, and he had no idea how many were ahead, beyond the third floor. He'd already picked up a few levels and gained a couple of pieces of, apparently, rare loot. Wouldn't it be wise to ride things out, kill some monsters on this floor, maybe go up another, and avoid people until one of the high-ranking local heroes finished the dungeon? After that, they could all make it out with their gains. Something about the idea of coasting, lurking on the sidelines, while someone else took the glory of victory didn't sit well with him.

Victor paused, concentrated, and then summoned his fear-attuned coyotes again. As they sprang out of pools of shadow, slinking silently along the sides of the path, he said, "Okay, *hermanos*. Find the stairs up. *Pronto!*" The five mastiff-sized coyotes darted away without a sound, one bolting past Sora on the path, the others charging into the jungle. Sora turned to look at him quizzically.

"A new plan?"

"Yeah. We'll quit messing around and start climbing this sucker like we mean it." He glanced over his shoulder at the thin line of hazy "sky" through the trees. Sure enough, amid the nearby branches, the spy stones floated, ever watching. "Let's give 'em something to watch."

"Shouldn't we be cautious? I know some Tier Nines made it up to the second level long before we did."

"Couldn't have been that long before." Victor frowned at her. "You can be cautious, but I'm about to start moving. Stay with me if you want." As he spoke, Victor cast Inspiration of the Quinametzin, then Iron Berserk, relaxing his hold on his aura. If people were lying in wait, he'd let them feel what they had coming.

At first, as he surged in size and began to radiate heat and fury, Sora stepped away but kept her face neutral, having seen his titan form before. Then, when he cast his inspiration spell, her brow uncreased, a slight smile played over her lips, and she leaned toward him. That's when Victor unleashed his aura, and though she didn't stumble or fall, she certainly stepped back again, and her eyes opened with alarm.

"Dead Gods!" she hissed. "Are war and conquest all you've known? I've never felt such an aura from an iron ranker, even from the blowhards down at the martial yard!" Victor ignored the question, inhaling deeply, tasting the Energy in the air, and sucking it into his lungs. He tried to pull some magma-related Energy out, but all he tasted was verdant and thick with life. He exhaled and nodded.

"As soon as one of my brothers finds a hint, I'll start running. Stay close if you're coming."

"Of course. I'm coming!" Sora was more than small to Victor now, her voice tiny with the rage roaring in his ears. He'd turned his attention outward, listening and feeling through his coyotes, but the determination in her words caught his attention, and he looked down at her with red glowering eyes.

"Good. Glory awaits." He'd just uttered the words when one of his scouts alerted him; something was happening off to his left through the jungle—a battle!

"A fight!" he roared, dashing into the clinging, thick undergrowth, bowling over saplings and snapping branches as he shouldered through. Life-drinker began to buzz and hum in his hands. Her silvery head shone with Energy that deepened from white-hot to smoldering orange as she began to trail a plume of black smoke over Victor's shoulder.

He leaped thornbushes, smashed through thick ferns, and as some of the trees actively tried to ensnare him, ripped vines and branches from trunks as he exploded through the jungle, leaving a broad, easy-to-navigate wake for Sora. He was breathing heavily, his lungs pumping like a steam engine, his Breath Core flaring with smoldering magma as the excitement of battle spun his glory-seeking Quinametzin pride into a frenzy. At some point, he switched his Sovereign Will boost to strength and vitality, readying himself for anything.

He could feel his coyote approaching and sense flares of Energy tickling his widespread aura. He was determined to smash any resistance he met, but he was inspired and a clever fighter—Victor knew enough to slow his rampaging headlong rush as he drew near to his scout. He slid to a halt before a thick stand of wide-boled trees and their hanging vines, crouching next to his coyote. He rested a hand on his shoulders, his fingers and thumb on either side of the animal's rib cage. He felt the warmth of pride seep out of the canine into him, and Victor grinned as he followed the animal's dark-eyed stare with his smoldering furious one.

A clearing opened up beyond the trees, and three figures battled on its grassy ground. Victor saw an avian woman—tall and lanky, with black and gold feathers, a sharp beak, and predatory, hawkish golden eyes. She wore layered leather armor, wielded an enormously long whip, and seemed to be defending against the other two.

One was a man who had to be twelve feet tall, wearing shining silver and red-enameled full-plate armor and wielding a tremendous two-handed sword. The other was a woman who looked as if she might have been a relative of Sora's. She was slight, wore green tights and a gleaming silver breastplate, and carried a deadly-looking crossbow. She tucked it close as she rolled and leaped, avoiding the avian woman's whip.

A tiny whisper came to him, and Victor glanced down to see Sora crouched near his coyote. "The bird woman is Strista Kono. She's ninth tier. The man is Dovalion Boarheart, also Tier Nine, and the Fae blood is Lyla Rose—his wife."

Victor nodded as he touched his dimensional belt pouch, summoning the spy scope he'd stowed away in there. The thing was tiny in his hand, but he held it between his thumb and finger and peered through it, noting the auras of the three in the clearing. The avian woman, Strista, was yellow, deepening toward orange. The giant man in his thick head-to-toe armor was yellow, and the woman with the crossbow was dark blue.

Victor grinned, tucked his scope away, then looked at Sora. "Thanks. Stay hidden. Don't let anyone sneak up on me," he rumbled, then stood up and pushed through the trees. Part of his brain asked him what he was doing, but he pushed it down. He'd decided to act, to try to win this stupid dungeon challenge, which meant he needed to crack some skulls.

As soon as he stepped into the clearing, toppling one of the trees with a creaking, popping crash, the three stopped fighting. Facing each other warily, they all regarded him with hostility. "You intrude, stranger," the hawk-faced woman screeched.

Victor's Iron Berserk let him keep his mind clear enough to contemplate the statement. He thought about a response, about making an offer to these three, but a large part of him wanted to leap into battle, uncaring about sides or numbers. He had to fight his urges for a heartbeat, and, in that time, he took a few steps forward, and he saw the reaction as his aura fell upon the three. Each one flinched, though the Fae woman with the crossbow nearly fell. He knew they weren't exactly friends, so he decided to see how deep their animosity ran. "I'll take you all one by one or three together. What will you prefer?"

Lyla and her husband stood to Victor's left and Strista to his right. Victor saw the giant warrior, Dovalion, tilt his metal-covered face to the hawk woman, and they both nodded almost imperceptibly. "I say die, then, fool!" the huge warrior cried, lifting his sword. It burst into flame, white-hot but clean-burning—not a shred of smoke rose from the flaring metal.

Victor felt his cheeks rise as his smile widened, and he began to laugh with the joy of impending combat. Then, a whirlwind erupted at his feet, and a tremendous cyclone-force wind lifted him off his feet, hoisting him into the air. As he spun, he saw Strista lifting her arms, crackling blue Energy dancing along her dark feathers, and he knew she'd summoned the wind. Pain lanced through his left thigh, glute, and lower back as he was hammered with powerful crossbow bolts.

Victor arched his back, trying to find some sort of control over his movements, straining as he reached back to yank one of the thick bolts from his leg. As he did so, he caught a glimpse of Lyla reloading her crossbow and a gleaming streak as Dovalion charged him, his burning great sword held high.

Victor dropped the bolt, noting how green fluid pumped from its tip, sizzling on the grass. He wondered if it was poison, which made his mad laugh all the louder. Just then, Dovalion crashed into him, his great burning sword cleaving into his unarmored thigh and sending him careening through the air to crash and tumble into the underbrush at the clearing's edge.

Victor didn't like being controlled and made helpless. His pathways were so full of frustrated rage that he veritably burned with it. More than frustration, he was in pain; Dovalion's sword had bitten deeply, grinding against his bone. He wondered if he'd been more solidly braced, not floating in the air, if the great sword would have cut through his leg entirely.

When his tumbling fall came to a stop, he pressed his hand to the wound, watching great torrents of hot blood spewing through his fingers. Still, it slowed almost immediately, his immense vitality and the healing nature of his berserk already working to stitch the wound closed. He yanked the other bolts out with soft grunts, dropped them to the ground, and stood.

Victor had been in enough fights to know he'd bitten off a massive mouthful, maybe more than he could chew, but he couldn't help the joy in his chest at the prospect of finally being challenged. How long had it been since he'd bled like that? He could feel the pressure against his aura as Dovalion gave chase, stomping over the clearing toward the wrecked foliage where Victor had fallen. With a grunt, he leaped to his feet and, surprisingly adroitly, darted around the edge of the clearing, putting some distance between himself and the metal-clad warrior. As he crouched low, stalking around the edge, he called his companions to him.

He could hear the hawk woman screeching at the others, telling them he was moving. He heard cracks of thunder and saw trees and branches explode into flaming, smoking splinters not far from him, but the noise and wreckage gave him further cover as he continued to flank the winged, whip-wielding caster. When he felt his coyotes growing close, he'd nearly circled the entire clearing and could still hear Dovalion grunting, crashing around, hacking his sword in wide, burning arcs, slicing through trees and undergrowth. The jungle didn't love the destruction; acrid black smoke rose from the burning plants, and Victor's feral grin widened as he heard the enormous armored warrior coughing.

Victor was big, and if he hadn't been in a dungeon filled with giant magical trees, it might have been harder to sneak around, but he wasn't so sure. It felt natural for him, darting through the vines, broad-leafed plants, and ferns. The ground was spongy and somehow familiar to his feet, and he was almost surprised by how quickly he left Dovalion and Strista's lightning bolts behind.

Couldn't they feel his aura? Couldn't they track his Energy? On the heels of the idea, another followed—his aura was overwhelming them. They felt it, but it was confounding them, dulling their senses and wearing down their wills. That was the price of fighting inside a stronger enemy's aura. As he lurked behind a massive tree, peering around at the clearing, his smile gleamed in the shadows.

He saw the Fae, Lyla, crouching near the center of the clearing, turning in a slow circle, eyes narrowed. Her back was to him, but he knew her sharp senses would feel him if he kept watching. Rather than hide again and wait, he urged his coyotes to attack her, and then he bolted forward, scanning for Strista.

His dark shadow-clad brothers burst out of the jungle, streaking toward the archer. One exploded in a blast of blue lightning, and Lyla pumped another with three rapid-fire crossbow bolts, sending it back to the spirit plane as it melted into a pool of shadow. Then, the other three were on her, and she had to dart and weave, using her impressively graceful movements to avoid being mauled and ripped to shreds by the three savage canines.

Meanwhile, Victor burst into the clearing and saw Strista to his left, near the edge where Dovalion still lumbered about, hacking through trees. She was facing Lyla, lifting her hands, ready to blast another coyote, when Victor cast a fear-fueled Energy Charge, streaking through the clearing in a ball of roiling shadow. She saw him at the last second and pumped her huge black wings, but it was too late; Victor collided with her right flank, and she wasn't built to take a charge from a titan. In an explosion of black feathers, Victor sent her flying, tumbling out of control into the jungle, where she smashed through half a dozen trees. The air rained feathers.

Strista Kono has been rescued from certain death and removed from the dungeon. Ten entrants remain. Prepare for an Energy infusion.

Victor lifted his head, arched his back, and screamed his triumph to the dungeon. He could hear Dovalion crashing through the burning undergrowth toward him, but Victor whirled on Lyla and saw she'd put down two more of his coyotes, but the last one had her by the ankle, pulling her over the grass. She had bleeding wounds on her shoulders and arms and had dropped her crossbow. Victor's heart swelled with pride when he saw how dearly his companions had made her pay for their lives. He stomped over to her bow and lifted Lifedrinker to hack it. "No!" she cried, giving up her struggle against his coyote. "She lives!"

Victor frowned, stooped to pick up the bow, then stalked toward her. He wasn't exactly feeling merciful, but he knew how he'd feel if someone destroyed Lifedrinker. He wasn't that kind of asshole. His coyote had stopped dragging her but had her bloody ankle in a death grip, growling and snarling. He heard Dovalion's stomping steps as he broke back into the clearing. Victor was right beside the bloodied, desperate woman, though, and, lifting Lifedrinker high, he stepped around behind her so he could see Dovalion, too.

The warrior's armor was smeared with soot, but his sword still burned, and his posture said he was ready to charge Victor at any second. "Wait," Victor growled. He clicked his tongue, and the coyote released Lyla's foot. As she gasped in relief, he dropped her bow onto her lap and said, "Use the lifesaver. You're done."

Lyla looked from Victor to Dovalion, her face streaked in bloody smudges, her eyes filling with frustrated tears, but she reached into her leather vest and pulled the medallion out. She and the helmeted warrior stared at each other for several long silent seconds. Then Lyla sent Energy into the lifesaver, and, in a cloud of hazy blue smoke, she disappeared.

Lyla Rose has been rescued from certain death and removed from the dungeon. Nine entrants remain. Prepare for an Energy infusion.

"Thank you for your small mercy," Dovalion said, bowing at the waist. Victor saw a gray shadow flitting around the edge of the clearing behind the knight. Sora? He regarded the man for several seconds. He was easily as large and bulky as the Degh back on Zaafor. He had to have some kind of giant bloodline.

"Sora, stay out of it. Make sure no one else sneaks up," he shouted. Then he gathered up his rage-attuned Energy, sending it into his Core and canceling his Iron Berserk. As he fell back to his usual size, Victor called forth his glory-attuned Energy and summoned his Banner of the Champion. Golden light flared behind him, shadows fell away, and Victor felt the glorious pride of a spectacle, of being the center of everyone's rapt attention. He looked up at the sky, saw the floating spy stones, and lifted Lifedrinker. "Ancestors!" he roared. "Witness me!"

"What is that young fool doing?" Lo'ro asked, scooting further toward the edge of the booth, his dark, undead eyes staring at the view window. "Why would he cancel his berserking titan form? Is he out of Energy?"

Ranish Dar sighed, shaking his head. "No, my friend. I'm sure he's not. He's putting on a show in some misguided attempt to earn favor or honor or . . . glory. Ah, that's it. He has a glory affinity, and I'm afraid, coupled with his titan ancestry, this is something I should have probably anticipated."

"Do you think the Fae girl will betray him? What others are still on the third floor?" Lo'ro and Dar both scanned the other windows. Three showed the same scene—Victor's, Sora's, and Dovalion's. Of the other six, none showed any jungle scenery. "It seems he might be lucky this time."

"Luck? Was it luck that sent Strista home with a single blow? Was it luck that made Lyla Rose, the Black Thorn, surrender?" Dar frowned and shrugged. "Perhaps there's some luck involved, but Victor is as pure a warrior as I've ever seen. Even Dovalion there has spent decades crafting, meditating, and raising a family. How many entrants do you think have a skill set so purely focused on conquest? Victor's Core, his Class choices, his bloodline, and his life experiences are all focused on battle. Few of the other entrants understand what that means. Few could imagine what kind of spirit is forged from the constant exposure to death's cold embrace. He may have dropped his berserk form, but, my friend, he did so because he saw no glory in the utter domination of another warrior."

44

※彩※

DUNGEON FRIENDS

Dovalion straightened from his bow and stepped forward, his white-hot flaming great sword held up and tilted slightly back in a high guard. His voice came out of his fully enclosed helmet, echoing strangely, like a man speaking from inside a well. "So, you have a hidden ally?"

Victor ignored him, grinning, Lifedrinker held loosely before him. She was eager, tugging toward the giant warrior, hungry to test her edge against his thick plate armor. Victor often fought Lesh without Iron Berserk, so he wasn't daunted by the man's size. The armor-clad man wasn't much larger than Victor, after all, and Victor was stronger than he looked, which said a lot. He quietly circled the tall warrior, his posture more like a wrestler's than a proper duelist's. He kept his center of gravity low, his shoulders and arms loose, leaning slightly forward in a hungry, predatory posture.

"I see you've dropped your rage. I salute your control. A test of skill, then?" Dovalion did something quick with his hands, and the great sword whipped through the air before him, arcing in a circle, the white flames flaring as he spun it. It was a quick movement, one meant to showcase his talent, and when his sword stopped moving, it was once again in a high guard, ready to strike or react to Victor.

For his part, Victor felt he'd been patient enough. He darted forward, thrusting out Lifedrinker, feinting a crushing blow toward the giant's face. Dovalion tilted his blade to parry, but Victor yanked the axe back at the last second, darted past the warrior's flank, and performed a quick lightning hack at his torso. Dovalion was fast and nimble, but he was hampered by his thick armor, at least enough so that he failed to dodge the blow. Lifedrinker sparked and flared as she tried to dig through the heavy plate on his stomach and side, but, as far as Victor could tell, she only bit about halfway through.

"A fine axe, sir, but my armor is a relic from an ancient world, crafted from the ore of a fallen—*ungh*!" He choked off his impromptu lesson regarding his family heirloom as Victor launched himself into an attack, swinging Lifedrinker in a series of swooping lightning hacks, driving the giant back, scraping and denting the armor in a shower of molten sparks. Lifedrinker's frustration was palpable as she flared and glowed, using every bit of the edge Victor's inspiration-attuned spirit fragment gave her.

Dovalion turned one of his heavy shoulder plates into the attack and swung his blazing sword in a great circular cleave. Victor was loath to let up the pressure of his assault, and he decided to keep swinging, moving with the cleave, hoping to mitigate the damage. The blazing great sword struck him in the ribs, sparking against his wyrm-scale, the edge finding purchase as it slid between two scales, ripping through the heavy wyrm-hide backing, then splitting Victor's skin and sliding along his ribs. Dovalion channeled some Energy, whipping the sword through the arc of his cleave faster than should have been possible and transitioning into an overhead chop that Victor barely avoided by diving to the side and rolling. When he bounded to his feet, he was grinning like a madman.

"First blood, sirrah!" Dovalion's hollow voice announced as he spun his flaming sword in another flourish, tracking Victor's predatory circling movements. Victor grunted in response, his wound already forgotten, despite the sheeting blood running down his side beneath his armor to dribble onto the grass. He may not have been berserk, but his vitality was high, his body was strong, and he wasn't worried about a cut on his flank. Grunting in frustration, annoyed that Lifedrinker couldn't pierce the man's formidable armor without his berserk strength behind her, Victor determined to continue the dance, to find a gap in that armor or, failing that, to beat on it long enough that it started to affect the man beneath.

So he darted forward again, his great thighs bulging with the force of his dash. He wove his axe, his partner, through a series of hacks, feints, frenetic combinations, and parries. For every two or three swings of Lifedrinker, Dovalion only answered with one with his great sword, choosing to use his bracers, pauldrons, and even helmet to deflect many of the blows. He was skilled with that mighty sword, but he fought a very different style of combat than Victor or, if he were honest, anyone he'd ever sparred with. He was like a juggernaut, wading through Victor's mighty blows, trusting his armor and sturdy frame to absorb the damage while he waited to deliver decisive hacks and thrusts with that deadly burning sword.

Victor began to amass cuts on his arms that smoked as the sword boiled his blood but failed to ignite his flesh. His wyrm-scale armor deflected indirect hits but parted beneath cleaves or stabs. Still, it held well enough for Victor to roll away from those hits, taking only minor wounds. Part of Victor grew increasingly irritated, yearning to unleash more of his abilities. His mind was distracted, debating with itself. If he didn't want to cast Iron Berserk, fine, then why not unleash his Aspect of Terror? If not that, then how would Dovalion fare against the Inevitable Huntsman? Why not some Energy Charges? Dovalion was burning Energy to speed his movements; wouldn't that, at least, be fair? Perhaps some coyotes or his bear would enjoy mixing things up with the giant warrior.

Victor gritted his teeth and growled through his internal debate, trying to focus on his axe work. He wanted to give his ancestors a show. He wanted to keep his other darker aspects a secret for now. More than any of that, though, he wanted to enjoy a good hard fight, one where he didn't have to pull any punches. As Dovalion surged with golden Energy and some of the crumpled dents in his armor popped out and smoothed over, Victor frowned and gave in just a little, casting Inspiration of the Quinametzin. As the white-gold light of inspiration merged with the golden sparkling glory of his banner, Victor smiled and laughed.

As he ducked, weaved, parried, and hacked, he began to see patterns in Dovalion's movements. He was skilled, sure, but he was just a man, and he relied on his armor a great deal. Victor knew he would have won the fight a dozen times over if not for that man's skilled use of his nigh-indestructible metal shell. He wondered if he could call forth the Paragon of the Axe. Would that give his hacks enough bite to cleave that metal? He was reasonably sure it would, but the problem was that Dovalion didn't use his weapon like a master. He didn't push Victor's axe work to the limits.

As he dodged back, avoiding another cleave, Victor shook his head. That was an excuse. Hadn't he seen glimpses of the ghostly Paragon edge when he'd fought the reaver army? He'd been pushed to his limits, but not because those reavers were exceptionally skilled with their weapons. No, Victor had let his mind relax, he'd stopped worrying about nonsense, and he'd embraced the battle. With that thought, Victor endeavored to cease all further thinking.

He inhaled deeply and felt the magma in his chest surge, but savored the warmth rather than thinking about using it. As he exhaled with a clear mind, he went to work.

"Bah!" Lesh growled, thumping his massive fist on the thick wooden table, jostling the empty cups and mugs. "Why does he toy with that man?"

Valla looked away from the battle depicted through the magical window and offered him a pained smile. "He . . . I don't know, Lesh. He gets strange ideas in his head. You saw him fight the reavers. You saw . . ."

"Aye. I've seen enough. Some point of pride won't let him use his berserking rage." Lesh clenched and unclenched his fist. "If he doesn't, though, he might lose. Look at the wounds he's amassed. He has the wrong weapon to fight a man with armor like that!"

"Look closer." Valla nodded toward the view window. "His wounds are all but closed, and he's not taken one in a while. Can't you see a difference? Perhaps he'd been distracted, or perhaps he was getting a feel for this armored warrior, but don't you see how he dances around him?"

Lesh narrowed his eyes and stared for a while, watching the fight. Valla saw understanding start to dawn as the dragonkin watched. She knew she was right. She could see the metal-clad giant burning Energy more and more frequently, trying to speed his great sword's cleaves, repairing his armor as it more and more rapidly amassed dents and blackened score marks from Lifedrinker's hungry burning edge. Even as his burning great sword moved in nearly invisible blurs, Victor was never there to feel its fiery edge. Was he reacting too fast? Was he thinking ahead, aware of what the warrior would do before he did it? Valla didn't know, but she felt her heart swelling with pride. The crowd hadn't realized it yet, but Victor was making a fool of the giant.

"He doesn't burn Energy," Lesh said after staring for a long while. His tone had gone from frustrated to amused, or perhaps amazed. "He'll wear the giant down? How long can they battle like this?"

Valla didn't answer as she watched Victor glide around the warrior's flank, hack Lifedrinker against his side and back in three lightning chops, then roll away as the great sword split the air where he'd been standing like a thunderbolt. The spy stones projected sound as well as images, and the grunts and heavy breaths of the metal-bound warrior were starting to grow loud and strained. Conversely, Victor looked fresh and hadn't stopped smiling in a long while.

"Old gods!" a stooped, white-haired, bear-like man hissed at a nearby table. "They've been fighting for nigh on twenty minutes!" He thumped a younger black-haired individual on the back. "You'll learn about this in your training, Goja! Even a couple of minutes is exhausting!" Valla smiled, looking around the public house. The tables had grown silent as they watched the deadly dance playing out.

Earlier, when Victor had dropped his rage and reduced his size, the bet-takers had gone wild, crying out new odds, and there'd been a frenzy of noise and activity as money changed hands and people speculated about there being something wrong with Victor: Was he out of Energy? Was Dovalion working some magic to cancel his Berserk? Would he run? Then, as the fight drew out, with both men trading blows, things had begun to get quiet, and now she was confident she could hear a whisper in the place. Everyone's eyes were glued to the contest. Valla almost chuckled at the irony of her thoughts when several people gasped, and a loud, strident voice cried out, "Look!"

She followed the man's pointing claw and saw what had gotten the crowd talking again—a ghostly extra edge had begun to flicker in the air around Lifedrinker. Valla took a breath and held it while she watched Victor swing his axe, watched as that shimmering glass-like edge moved with the smolder-ing metal one, and split Dovalion's armor with a terrible ringing eruption of gasses and flaring Energy.

Victor knew it when the Paragon of the Axe appeared; he could feel it. His movements took on a new level of perfection. It was the difference between a student who knows the keys of the piano and how to read music and put the notes together and a master playing from inspiration and intuition. He'd stopped diving and rolling around, and now he shifted just a hair, this way and that, letting Dovalion's blade carve the air inches from his flesh and armor. He moved with the giant, Lifedrinker like a rudder in a storm, guiding Victor away from the monstrous swings with a tap against the fiery blade.

When Victor felt the Paragon, when he felt the ghostly specter of the perfect axe, he stepped back, parried, and when Dovalion was extended, he hacked Lifedrinker against the hard magical armor of the giant's right arm. The ghostly edge wreathing Lifedrinker's fiery axe-head split that metal like a steel chisel through a soda can. As a can might spew its carbonated con-tents, the armor vented gas, heat, and Energy as though it had been under pressure. Dovalion cried out, stumbling forward as his right arm fell to the bloody grass. He fought to hold on to his swinging sword with his left hand, but the momentum and weight of it were too much, and its fiery tip sank into the soil. He kept his hand on the hilt, but he slumped as steam and blood spewed from the truncated armor of his right arm.

All his life, Victor had trained to finish. He'd never been taught to stop when his opponent was on his heels. It didn't even cross his mind to stop; this wasn't wrestling, but Victor aimed for the equivalent of a pin, not a draw. He was on Dovalion in an instant, gliding like a leopard over the grass. He held Lifedrinker high, her blade wreathed with the ghostly edge of the Paragon, as he swung her like a falling star at the spot where Dovalion's neck met his shoulder. She bit into the metal, and he heard that awful splitting sound again. Then Dovalion was gone; there was nothing but a cloud of blue smoke where he'd stood.

Dovalion Boarheart has been rescued from certain death and removed from the dungeon. Eight entrants remain. Prepare for an Energy infusion.

Victor grunted in frustration as Lifedrinker hacked through the smoke. He'd won, and he'd done it cleanly, but the victory felt hollow. He felt robbed. He stood there, letting the smoke of Dovalion's rescue drift into nothing, contemplating the battle and his win. He lifted Lifedrinker and looked at her smoldering blade, seeing no sign of the Paragon. He'd lost the battle trance that had summoned it. Footsteps alerted him to Sora's approach, and he turned to regard her.

"An amazing battle, Victor. I can't believe you took all three of them." She held her bow loosely in one hand by her side. Victor nodded, offering her a half smile. His frustration was fading, and he knew they'd be hit with some Energy at any moment.

"Thanks for watching my back." He had no idea if she'd done so. For all he knew, she'd been training her arrows on him, waiting for the perfect moment to betray him. He supposed he could probably count on her loyalty now; she'd have to be stupid to want to earn him as an enemy, and she seemed bright enough.

"It was nothing. Honestly, I was dumbstruck while you faced Strista and the other two; I couldn't believe you walked out there like that."

Victor chuckled and started to respond, but then swirling, potent balls of Energy streaked through the jungle canopy and struck both of them in the chest. It was a massive infusion, enough to blast all thought from Victor's mind as weird rainbows and strange alien vistas passed before his mind's eye. He saw purple plains, heaving, swelling red-frothed seas, and bizarre gigantic naked fur-covered people. Some had two eyes, and some had one, and more than a few wore great racks of horns like crowns. They toiled to climb a steep rocky mountainside.

Victor tried to make sense of the vision, but then the euphoric rush of Energy faded, and he saw his surroundings again. Sora was sprawled out on the grass before him, and a System message obscured his view:

Congratulations! You have achieved Level 65 Herald of the Mountain's Wrath and gained 12 strength, 17 vitality, and 12 will.

Congratulations! You have earned a Class spell: Roots of the Mountain, Basic.

Roots of the Mountain, Basic: A mountain weathers all storms. A mountain isn't moved. The mountain moves the earth. With this spell active, only the force of a true cataclysm can uproot or shift you. Energy Cost: 100 per second of active use. Cooldown: Minimal.

Congratulations! Your Imbue Spirit, Basic has become Imbue Spirit, Improved.

Imbue Spirit, Improved: You are able to imbue an object or individual with a shard of your own spirit, granting some of your own power and will to the recipient. At the improved level, the granted boons are larger. This effect will last until you recall your spirit shard. Energy Cost: Variable. Cooldown: Long

"Badass," Victor said softly, sitting up in the grass.

Sora blinked rapidly and looked at him. "That was quite a lot of Energy. There are some very unhappy iron rankers sitting around Sojourn watching us right now."

"Yep." Victor stood up, grunting as he did so. He hung Lifedrinker in her harness, then stood there, rubbing the soot and blood on his arms as though he had any chance of getting clean without a bath. The Energy had fully healed him; not even a scab remained of the many cuts Dovalion had given him. While Sora scanned the edges of the clearing, Victor summoned his coyotes, this time using inspiration-attuned Energy. They yapped, yipped, and whined as they circled him, and Victor laughed. "Go find the stairs going up, *hermanos*."

"Why are they sometimes evil and dark and sometimes bright and full of exuberance?"

Victor looked at her and narrowed his eyes. She was ever asking questions. When she looked back at him without a touch of animosity, he shrugged, relenting. "Sometimes I want them to be quiet hunters, and sometimes I want them to be clever scouts."

"I'm sorry to ask so much. I know how it feels when strangers want to know your business. May I ask you one more, though?"

Victor's lips curled into a smile as he tried out the annoying line he'd heard from so many coaches over the years. "You just did."

She groaned and apparently decided just to forge ahead. "Why didn't you keep your giant size when you fought Dovalion? I mean, I know you're quite large as you are, but you were . . . much larger before."

"I don't know. I wanted a good fight, and I knew my ancestors would have more fun watching a battle like that."

"They're watching?" Sora looked around, squinting with suspicion.

"Not always. If I want them to watch, I have to give them something worthwhile to see." Victor could feel his coyotes covering ground, could feel their excitement as they hunted for the goal he'd given them. So far, they hadn't run into anything to worry about, so he sat down in the grass.

"But—" Sora winced, shrugging as if to apologize for asking yet another question. "Why do you want them to watch?"

"How will I earn their favor if they don't see the glory I achieve? I have to earn my place among them, you know. I don't want to show up like a weakling with no great story to tell, begging to carry water. I want to show up and be celebrated. I want to earn a good place among them, and I want other titans to cry my name when they go into battle."

"Ah!" Sora sat down in front of him, leaning closer. "So, you have a clan to make proud? Titans who follow you? Children?"

Victor sighed and leaned back, waiting for word from one of his scouts. He closed his eyes and let the heat from the incongruous dungeon jungle bring a sheen of sweat to his golden-brown skin. It felt good—right. Somehow, he missed the jungle even though he'd never visited one in his life. "Enough questions, Sora. We're dungeon friends; if we stay friends afterward, we can learn more about each other."

45

ALLIANCES

After only fifteen or twenty minutes of waiting, one of Victor's coyotes alerted on something, and to Victor, it felt like the triumphant pride of success—it had found the object of their hunt. So he charged through the jungle, Sora hot on his heels, and on the way, he stumbled into a clearing filled with weird half-flower, half-leopard creatures.

They launched themselves at him with wild abandon, biting, clawing, and grasping with thorn-tipped vines. The dungeon animals were tenacious and numerous but fell quickly to Lifedrinker's smoldering cleaves and Sora's fiery arrows. Once they'd received some Energy for their quick victory, the two allies resumed their charge through the jungle.

Victor savored the heat and moisture. He loved how his feet seemed to know exactly where to step, how he slipped through vines, snagging thorns, and clinging undergrowth almost effortlessly. This was the environment of his ancestors. The sweltering sun, the damp air, and the rich green foliage all combined into something oddly familiar and comforting. When he passed between the boles of two large, moss-covered trees and saw a vine-shrouded stone opening in a cliff face, he almost felt disappointed; if his coyote was right, the end of the jungle level was just ahead.

Tyra Vexmore has been rescued from certain death and removed from the dungeon. Seven entrants remain. Prepare for an Energy infusion.

"Another!" Sora panted, leaning to rest her hands on her knees. She was drenched in sweat, and her silver-gray hair looked wild from the rough, fast passage through the jungle.

"You know that one?"

"Only by reputation. Very stealthy—a Shadow Caster."

"Huh." Victor nodded. "Yet someone spotted her."

Warin-dak has been rescued from certain death and removed from the dungeon. Six entrants remain. Prepare for an Energy infusion.

"What the fu . . ." Victor trailed off, staring at the announcement. It sounded like a Shadeni name. "Or Ridonne," he breathed softly, his mind racing with the implications. He shouldn't be surprised, he supposed—the Ridonne had had access to Sojourn for nearly four centuries. Wouldn't it make sense for some of them to be there? Even so, it was a wake-up call. Sojourn might be a big city, but that didn't mean he wouldn't run into some enemies. The idea brought to mind Valla and the others, especially Edeya and Darren, who were so fragile in their current state.

It was Sora's turn to ask. "You know him?"

"The name rings a bell. Have you seen him?"

"I've watched him perform in other spectacles—arena fights and sanctioned duels. He's popular in the city. I'm surprised he was knocked out. I'm quite sure he was Tier Nine before entering."

"Can you describe him?"

"Huge. Well, to me. He's about your size, with crimson flesh, spikes on his shoulders, elbows, and around his crown . . ."

"Golden eyes?"

"Um, some gold, perhaps, but mostly crimson. He's brutish but wields terrible Energy beams. It's some kind of specialized fire affinity, but not fire . . ." She trailed off, staring at the sky, searching her memory. "Something to do with an infernal plane." She shrugged and looked back at Victor. "I'm sorry, I can't remember."

"It's all right. More than I knew a minute ago." Victor pointed to the stone tunnel opening. "My coyote is just in there. I think it's the stairs."

Sora jogged toward it. "Then let us climb before the Energy hits." Victor nodded, following her. The tunnel was too low for him to enter without stooping, but after only a few yards, it opened up into a spiral shaft lined with steps, not much different from the last staircase they'd found. Victor's coyote was sitting on his haunches by the steps and started whining with excitement when Victor and Sora stepped out of the tunnel. Victor patted his head, scratching around his ears.

"Good job, *hermano*." He was about to send him home to the spirit plane, but that's when orbs of golden Energy slammed into Sora and him, blinding him and sending his mind reeling through a kaleidoscopic series of images and colors, none of which made much sense to him. Part of him, still cognizant, hoped for another glimpse of the strange hirsute giants climbing the mountain, but it didn't come. When the rush of Energy was over, he didn't have any System messages, but he felt fully refreshed and restored. Sora was sitting on the steps, petting his coyote, which made Victor wonder why she'd recovered before he did. Hadn't they both gotten the same share of Energy from the System's award?

"That one really took you," she remarked, looking up from his traitorous coyote. "I think your friend likes me."

"Oh, he likes the attention." Victor almost joked about the coyote being a fragment of his spirit and how they both loved that sort of thing. He cut himself off, though, deciding Sora and everyone listening to their conversation had learned enough about him. "Shall we go up?"

"Yes! Let's see if the awards are better this time!" She hopped to her feet and, with a final glance over her shoulder, ran up the stairs. After her fourth step, she shimmered briefly and faded from Victor's view.

"Okay, brother. Head on home. I'll call you again soon." Victor dismissed his companion and then followed Sora.

For the third time, after just a few steps, he walked into a small stone room with a chest at the center and a closed door opposite the stairs. The chest was similar to the last one, but the material was different; it looked almost like sandstone with inlaid copper glyphs. "Maybe a little bigger," he muttered as he knelt before it, lifting the rough, delicate-seeming lid on its polished copper hinges. It swung wide, and, just as before, golden mist spewed forth. After waving it away, he saw two items: a thick leather belt and a piece of fruit that looked like an apple-sized blueberry.

Victor picked up the fruit. It had a bright green stem with a label attached to it by a short length of silken string. The flesh under the taut blue skin felt soft, spongy, and strangely warm in his palm as he turned it to regard the words on the thin slip of pale yellow paper. Before reading it, he inhaled the scent of the fruit, savoring the odors that reminded him of orange blossoms and honey as they tickled his nose. With a salivating mouth, he read, "Urd

Berry of the Windswept Moon. Eat when nearing a difficult breakthrough." Before he lost control and took a bite, he quickly slipped it into his storage pouch.

Victor lifted out the belt, already guessing it was part of the same set as his gauntlet and boots. When he trickled some Energy into it, his guess was confirmed:

Belt of Sojourn: This is a set item. Collect five pieces of the set and bring them to the Sojourn City Stone to imbue them with curated set bonuses.

"Too easy," he muttered, slipping his third set piece into his pouch. He stood and pulled Lifedrinker out of her harness, striding toward the door. He tried to open it, but it wouldn't budge, and Victor turned, annoyed, wondering if he'd missed something in the award room. He didn't see anything; even the stairway was gone, just a stone wall where it once had been. The chest had crumbled to sand, and the individual grains burst into golden steam as he watched. The room was utterly empty.

Victor slowly walked around the wall, dragging his fingertips over the stone, but he found nothing out of the ordinary when he'd made a complete circuit. The delay was annoying; Victor was tired of the dungeon and wanted to end it. Besides Sora and himself, there were only four others still in action; he figured if he and the slight elven woman hurried, they'd either get to the end or run into whoever was ahead of them, hopefully on the next level.

He stared at the door, contemplating hacking at it with Lifedrinker, but wondering if that would be stupid; it was part of the dungeon, controlled by the System. Would it really expect people to have to break through a door to leave an award room? He stood there for several long seconds, staring at it, working himself up to the action, but he heard a click just as he started to lift his axe.

"Finally," he grumbled, pulling it open. He wanted to get out there, gather up Sora and haul ass for the next stairs. He figured he'd summon his coyotes again to find them. Of course, plans were one thing, but reality was another.

When he stepped out of the award room into an enormous natural-looking cavern with gigantic redwood-sized stalagmites and stalactites stretching from the floor and ceiling and a far wall so distant as to be shrouded in misty shadows, he found himself side by side with Sora, facing four other people. Victor sighed, looking at the threatening crew. He'd wanted to chase down whoever was ahead, but he didn't think it would be four of them working together and a step ahead, waiting for him instead.

They didn't look like slouches; each was primed with Energy, glaring at him in varying degrees of hostility, weapons ready. Still, they hadn't immediately attacked, and in fact, Victor had heard a choked-off utterance from the tall armored woman at their center as though she'd been mid-conversation with Sora. Mid-conversation or mid-threat? As he examined them each, he smiled grimly and twisted his fists on Lifedrinker's haft, getting ready to prime some spells in his pathways.

The man in the center was the biggest, but he didn't feel the most dangerous. That honor went to the dark-robed woman on Victor's left. He could feel the bite of her aura, thick with killing intent, cold with the chill of the grave, and slippery as it sought to glide around his own heavy aura. She held a staff that looked like a polished two-meter bone, and her black eyes glared at him from beneath a silken cowl.

The man beside her was close to Victor's size. Seeing that, Victor's mind went off on a tangent about how he was starting to realize that the bipedal people of at least this part of the universe came in roughly three categories when it came to size—human-sized; "giant-sized," which was around ten feet; and titan-sized, which was more like fifteen to twenty. Of course, Victor was technically a titan, but he hadn't grown into his full size, not unless he berserked. The weird side thought only took an instant as he regarded the giant in his fur-covered leather clothes. He wielded a club that reminded Victor of the giant axe he'd used to smash Darren's tanks. It wasn't a fine weapon—more like a petrified tree branch, both enormous and heavy looking.

To the giant's right was another woman. She was lithe but tall, something between Valla's height and Victor's—maybe eight feet. She wore fine silvery mail and a winged visored helmet, and held two hatchet-like axes. Finally, to her right was another magician type. This man was cloaked in soft green robes, wielded a staff that looked like a living sapling, and wore a crown of fall leaves. He smiled rather pleasantly when Victor's eyes passed over him.

"They can't attack us," Sora said.

"Tut, little elf," the tall hatchet-wielding woman said, pouting her full red-stained lips beneath her silvery visor.

"Not until we step off this stone platform." Sora tapped her foot, and Victor looked down, nodding. It made sense that the dungeon wouldn't allow someone to camp the entrances to each level, at least not without giving the people coming up a chance to react.

"So? What is it? You *pendejos* want to fuck around?" Victor stepped toward the platform's edge—one more step, and he'd be off it.

"Gods, you are a cocky one, aren't you?" the armored woman spoke again. Victor ignored her—he could tell she wasn't the strongest. His instinct was to focus on the giant man, but he knew better. He felt strong, but Victor knew he'd crumble if the two of them went toe to toe. He turned his gaze to the pale Death Caster and smiled.

"Well, *bruja*? What's it gonna be?"

She looked at him, smiled her black-painted lips, revealing teeth that would make a vampire proud, and turned to Sora. "Well, elf? Did you make a decision?" Those words opened Victor's rage-attuned Core, sending hot red Energy into his pathways. So, that was what they'd been talking about when he'd abruptly appeared—they'd offered Sora a spot on their team.

Victor turned to his right, looking down into almost too-large angular silver-blue eyes. "Well?" he repeated.

She frowned, scowled at the dark-cloaked woman, then shrugged. "It's a competition, Victor. You're strong, but Arona is in the ninth tier, Brontes has never lost a martial battle, and Valeska is sought as a master axe instructor by people from a dozen worlds." She jerked her chin at the man in green with the living staff. "Never mind that they have Elandor here to work his nature magic." She tentatively reached out her slender fingers to grasp his wrist. "Will you hold it against me?"

For some reason, Victor felt that what he said mattered to her. He had a feeling she might tie her fate to his if he asked her to. The thought brought a smile to his lips and lowered the heat of the rage in his pathways down to a simmer. He didn't need this woman's mercy. He didn't need her to sacrifice for him. He took a long slow breath, then nodded as though to confirm his words were true, saying, "To be honest, Sora, I'll fight better knowing I've nobody to protect. I won't promise you'll survive if you join the four of them, but I won't hold it against you if we all make it out of here. At least you had the guts to betray me to my face."

"Dead gods, this one has a pair of balls," the big man said, his voice like a mudslide, loud and rumbling but indistinct and poorly enunciated.

Victor stretched his neck, released a few staccato *pops*, and then looked over the four again. "How long is your deal with Sora going to last? If you beat me, she gets to work with you all the way to the end? You all like each other that much?"

"Do not concern yourself with our arrangements, big man," the Death Caster, Arona, said. Her voice was cold and sharp, like her fangs and death-attuned Energy. "Come, little Fae, join us." Victor watched as Sora, her gaze averted, refusing to meet his eyes again, walked off the platform to stand beside the green-clad man. As she stopped beside him, he reached out his left hand to gently squeeze her shoulder, offering her a commiserating smile.

Victor sighed and slowly turned in a circle. He was backed up to the cavern's wall, and his four—five now—enemies were arrayed in a loose semi-circle facing him. They were each about ten yards from the edge of the platform, giving them room to maneuver or react if he did something.

They stared at him, each full of Energy, their pathways charged, their weapons throwing off auras from cold frost on Valeska's hatchets to something like toxic gas seeping out of Brontes's club. The Nature Caster, Elandor, still wore that enigmatic smile, but Victor could feel the potent, verdant Energy pouring out of him. These were five high-level, dangerous people, and their skill sets were very diverse. He figured he might stand a decent chance of eliminating one of them with a burst attack, but he could be wrong. Any one of them could have some sort of skill that would let them avoid his attack or escape with their life. If he berserked, they might have a way to snare him up, confuse him, or lead him on a chase, forcing him to waste his Energy.

What he needed was a way to separate them or get out from under their focus. They couldn't attack him while he was on the stone, and he had a feeling that protection would disappear if he initiated hostilities. He gazed over their heads at the forest of giant stalagmites. If he could get out there among those stony protrusions, he might be able to use them for cover. He might be able to pare down his enemies one by one or two by two.

He had to consider that they were expecting that. He had to consider that they'd heard rumors of his rage or even talked to Sora about his abilities before he'd interrupted. Had the damn dungeon kept him locked away so they could talk behind his back? Even if not, any of them might have witnessed one of his earlier fights, especially on the first level.

No, rage might not be the answer yet, though his Volcanic Fury was always a nice Hail Mary. How would they fare if he brought the cavern down? He must have chuckled or grinned at the thought because Arona hissed, "Something funny? Are you going to stand there all day? Take your medicine! If you're afraid, just use your lifesaver now and save us the trouble!"

Victor chuckled and gently twisted his hands on Lifedrinker's haft, forming the pattern to summon his coyotes. He had to assume that his protection would fade as soon as he cast it, so he knew he had to be ready. Still, he wanted to catch them off guard, so he began pacing back and forth, carefully avoiding the platform's edge.

"Sora, I feel sorry for you a little bit, and I feel like I'd be bummed if you died, so let me just say, if you start to hear something that scares the living shit out of you, that literally starts to make your bowels turn to water, do me a favor and use your lifesaver. I don't want to kill you." Victor had heard plenty of accounts of what people in his own army had thought of the sounds he'd made during some of the battles they'd waged.

"I . . ." she started to say, but Victor cut her off, not done planting his seeds of doubt.

"Actually, that goes for all of you. I don't know any of you enough to hate you yet. I can't promise the System will be able to pull you away fast enough if I get my hooks into you. Honestly, if you all back down now, I might just walk past and finish the dungeon, and you can escape this whole thing without any losses. I won't even make you use your lifesavers. What do you say?" As he posed the question, Victor had three spell patterns ready to go, the most he'd ever prepared all at once. He was surprised by how easy it had been.

"I think you're a fool who knows far too little about the world," the hatchet-wielding woman said.

Arona lifted a hand. "Don't feed his ego with an answer, Valeska . . ." Her words were cut short as harsh growls erupted behind her. Victor's rage-attuned coyotes sprang out of red pools of Energy, leaping at his urgent instructions to attack his foes, one for each. Meanwhile, he cast Energy Charge using glory-attuned Energy, streaking in a shower of golden sparks at the man in green. He wasn't sure why he'd chosen him as his first target, but something about him being attuned to nature made Victor think of grasping vines, thorn patches, and other things that might slow him. So even before his coyote could leap at the man, Victor crashed into him.

The impact was tremendous, and his glory-attuned Energy rapidly depleted as it protected him from the damage. Elandor, too, used some sort of defensive spell; a brilliant green shell erupted around him, and the force of Victor's impact washed over it, throwing up dust, shattering a nearby stalagmite, and sending Sora reeling. Victor didn't wait to see or experience any of that. As soon as he impacted the man's shield, he bunched his legs and fired off Titanic Leap, angling into the forest of enormous stalagmites. While he soared through the air, he cast his third prepared spell: Aspect of Terror.

46

TERROR

Sora tumbled over the hard dusty ground, channeling wind Energy into her Gusts of Balance spell so she gracefully rolled to her feet. She lifted her bow, and one of her crystalline mesmer arrows appeared under her fingertips as she drew the string back, but Victor wasn't where she'd last seen him.

She saw Elandor there, down on one knee, his hands grasping his staff as though it kept him from sinking into the earth, pumping torrents of green Energy into a shell as two massive, frothing, red-eyed wolf-like creatures tore at his barrier. Looking around, seeing the others all dealing with similar canine antagonists, she had to wonder if one of the two on Elandor had been meant for her.

With a thought, she sent her arrow back into her bow and began firing simple moonsteel arrows into the wolves attacking Elandor; the others were managing fine. As she landed mortal shots, they disappeared in gusts of red-tinged smoke, and she wondered where they went. From what world had Victor summoned them? She tried to think of the word he'd used to describe them. Cotees? The thought was shoved aside as a firm armor-clad hand grasped her shoulder, and Valeska growled, "You didn't tell us he could fly!"

Sora looked up, peering toward the massive stalactites hanging down and the dense pockets of shadow between them all. "He flew?" She'd missed that part as she'd tumbled in the force wave of Victor's charge. Before Valeska could say more, a terrible keening howl echoed through the cavern; the mists and reverberations made it impossible to discern its exact source, which made it all the more disturbing. Victor's words came back to her, his warning about fleeing if she heard something that "turned her bowels to water." That wasn't happening, but perhaps it was only the distance that lessened the wail's impact.

"Is he a man or a beast? Does he shift?" Brontes asked, lifting his club to his shoulder. None of the wolves remained.

Sora was quick to reply, "I never saw him change shape; I saw him grow, as I told you, but that's all. I knew he could charge but never saw him fly."

"He didn't fly," Arona rasped. Though her words were more a whisper than a shout, everyone flinched. "He leaped into the shadows up there. An impossibly high leap, but a leap, not flight. I'm sure he came down behind one of those protrusions."

"Stalagmites," Elandor said, straightening from his kneeling position. He looked wan and exhausted. "I'll need time to recover my Energy; my shield burned much, defending me from his charge."

Sora watched Arona as Elandor spoke. The cowled woman smirked and shook her head. Elandor had a Core that utilized life and nature-attuned Energies, and Arona was ever looking for a reason to mock him. The Death Caster lifted a necklace of bones from around her head and said, "You can wait here then." The consideration surprised Sora, but she supposed the stakes were rather high; they were the last ones in the dungeon, and none of them had finished a challenge like this. The previous champion was already working on his test of steel.

Arona broke the string of her necklace and scattered the bones around the rocky cavern floor. Sora knew what was coming; she'd adventured with her before. She backed up a few steps and watched as the Death Caster began to glow with misty blue Energy, and then the bones started rattling and jumping about.

A surge of grave-scented wind rushed out from Arona, and then the bones exploded with growth, stretching and multiplying until the clearing around the platform was crowded—dozens of skeletal horrors had sprung up from Arona's scattered bones. No two were alike; some were the size of people with two legs and two arms, but others looked like giant canines and others like demonic predators. The only commonality was the eerie blue light in their eye sockets as they stared at Arona, waiting for their master's instruction.

"We should have lain in wait further afield and surprised them both well away from the platform!" Valeska growled, her hand still gripping Sora's shoulder.

"She's with us now," Brontes rumbled, stepping up behind the two women and nudging Valeska's hand away with his enormous fur-wrapped arm.

"Indeed, but was her loyalty worth giving up the surprise?" Valeska flicked her right hand, sending both of her hatchets twirling in an arc before her, then snatched them again, one in each hand. She didn't wait for a response, turning away from the giant savage and Sora, gazing at Arona through her thick silvery visor. "What's the plan, then, boss?"

The black-cloaked woman let loose a surge of cold Energy, and the small army of skeletons turned in unison and *click-clacked* into the forest of stalagmites. "My bones will fish him out." As she spoke, another unnerving cry echoed through the cavern. Sora fought to keep her face neutral, and even Arona flinched.

Valeska hissed, "Dead gods! What is he?"

"I . . ." Elandor started to say, but another cry cut him off, and when Sora turned to him, she saw his face had grown even more pale. His eyes were wide, and he licked his lips, clearly feeling stressed in his depleted state. "I can feel fear biting at me, permeating the air. Is that from him? I thought he was a berserker!"

Arona waved a hand. "Many Spirit Casters have more than one affinity. Get a grip on yourself, nature boy. If this bothers you, you're lucky you haven't glimpsed the things I've seen through the veil." She turned to Valeska. "You and I will search in that direction." She waved vaguely northwest. Then she pointed to the southeast. "Brontes and his little girlfriend can go that way. Elandor, recover yourself here."

"Alone?"

"He's clearly not here. If he returns this way, we'll see him—he's not small." She shrugged and gestured toward the backs of some of her bony minions. "My bones will likely flush him out shortly, in any case." Turning back to Sora, she added, "Fire something bright into the heights if you find him. I'll do similar."

The Aspect of Terror hung high above the cavern floor, clinging to the rough stone of a stalactite, fully shrouded in shadow. The cavern was dark, but darkness didn't exist for him. Everything was cast in shades of gray save the bright spirits of those he wished to feed upon. They sat clustered down there, brilliant sparks flaring in the monochrome world. He wanted to leap upon them and feast until he burst, but a vestige of his former self, that one called Victor, still clung to his mind, curbing his enthusiasm. No, these were powerful spirits, and the feast would be short-lived if he tried to enjoy them all at once.

So he lurked hundreds of yards overhead. Now and again, losing himself in his hunger, he'd cry out, sharing his fear and burning need with the world. A lesser predator might have been cautious of making such noise, but Terror knew better. His instincts were crafted over millennia, and he knew his cry would echo strangely in the cavern. Hadn't his kind hunted in the depths of the earth for thousands of years? His screams would echo, and his prey would begin to taste his fear, and when they felt his claws, they'd be all the more ready to succumb.

His great shadow-clad, black-feathered wings hugged the stone, his talons bit into it, and there he perched, just another shadow among many as he watched the pale blue spirit burst, sending tiny motes of herself into nearly thirty smaller ones. Even so, her spirit still flared brighter than any other, and those tiny motes were hardly tempting. While he puzzled over the strange phenomenon, he heard snatches of voices drifting up to him, tickling his ears and fanning the flames of his hunger. Why did he wait? What could these morsels offer to him in terms of a threat? He started to loosen his hold, preparing to dive, but then a thought came to him from that *other*, a command that bristled the feathers along his spine: *WAIT!*

So, Terror hung there, his shadows, steeped in fear, pooling around him like a comfortable bath. He watched as the tiny spirits drifted away from the five brighter ones, spreading out through the enormous cavern, several passing directly beneath his perch. A few more words drifted up to him, meaningless in the face of his hunger, and then, to his delight, the five spirits separated. Two moved off to his left, two to his right, and one, the dimmest, frailest, lingered. Terror's hunger surged, saliva dripped over his grinding teeth, down to his razored beak, to slide along the surface of the stalactite.

Still, the *other* urged him to bide his time, to wait until the four had well and truly separated from the lone straggler. He glanced around the gray monochrome environment. He saw the distant fall of a frigid waterfall and the tunnel behind its sheeting water. Some instinct or sense he couldn't understand told him a draft moved up through that tunnel.

He saw other spirits, too, bright in their sluggish movements. There were denizens of this world that he could feast upon when he finished with the five who'd troubled his alter ego. Fantasies of ripping flesh, drawing fear-tinged Energy into himself, and gorging on the cries of his prey filled his mind for several minutes before he came back to himself and took stock of the wandering spirits. They'd moved a long way from the lone straggler, which had, in turn, begun to grow brighter.

Terror couldn't restrain himself longer. He released his hold on the hard stone and fell, his dark shadow-clad feathers rippling in the wind as he plummeted, streaking for his prey, talons extended. As Terror fell, he saw his prey sitting on the stone, his soft gray form awash with the light of his spirit.

Something must have given the pale green spirit a hint that he was in danger—halfway there, feathers hissing in the wind, the spirit leaped to his feet, and a bright green orb of Energy surrounded him. Terror didn't care. He screeched his hunger, his fear, and his frustration, sharing it with the world. His bright silvery talons began to glow, soft orange, then bright yellow-white as they gained more and more heat. Black smoke trailed from them, joining the shadowy tendrils streaming from his wings. Then he hit the spirit with another horrible screaming cry of hunger.

He could feel the Energy of the orb surrounding his prey, trying to fling him off, but with crackling sizzles and drips of smoldering Energy, his talons pierced it, grasping hold, refusing to be dislodged. Terror flapped his wings, using them for leverage as he dug and dug at the obstacle.

The spirit was bright, but he could see it fading; he could feel the barrier growing more and more fragile as his talons sank deeper and began to rend it. With a final, savage cry, he drove his beak into the shield, and it shattered. He was much larger than the little spirit and bore down on it, hooking his burning knifelike talons into its flesh. He put his horrible maw before the spirit's eyes and opened it wide, screaming, projecting his fear-attuned Energy like a geyser.

His terrible grasp, horrible aura, and projected Energy twisted the spirit's Energy into something he could feast upon. Terror clung to his prey, drinking deeply of the radiating fear. The spirit had gone entirely limp, lying on the stone, hot juices pouring from the deep, burning holes Terror had put in it. The feast was rich; despite this spirit being dimmer than the others, it was something incredible—satisfying on a level he couldn't remember.

The satisfaction was brief; his hunger, after all, was insatiable. Worse, before he could even drink the last dregs from the limp vessel, the flow of Energy was suddenly cut off, and the System announced it had cheated him. Terror screamed.

Sora moved closer to Brontes as yet another scream echoed through the cavern. "Was that from behind us?"

"How can anyone tell?" he grumbled, his consonants, as ever, indistinct. "These stone columns echo and distort the sound."

"It felt louder."

"Aye," he rumbled.

"We shouldn't have separated. Even if I launch a fire arrow, who's to say Arona will see it? These stalactites hanging above might block it from view."

"Hush, little bird. Your arrow will shed light in the dark, making itself seen, even around these rocks." Sora blushed at his words; she'd known Brontes for a while, one of the first people she'd met when she'd come to the city. He doted on her, but she'd never been wholly comfortable with his pet names. Another shriek sounded, and this time, she felt the hairs on her neck stand on end and some moisture gather on her palms. Was the thing wearing her down? Was she losing control? Was her overactive imagination making things worse?

"Gods, that sound grates," Brontes rumbled. "Why doesn't he flee? He could move on or hide. Hells, he could use the lifesaver. Why risk"—he gestured at himself and vaguely back toward Arona and the others—"this?"

Sora shook her head. "You didn't see him fight. He's . . . well, he's like you—fearless, powerful, shrugging off anything thrown at him. I would have stayed by his side if you weren't here, despite my earlier arrangement with Arona."

"Don't let that witch hear you say . . ." His words were cut off by a shriek far louder and more frenzied than before. It also sounded as if its source was moving. One cry after another split the air, echoing sharply off the stone walls, each one driving a knife of fear just a little deeper into Sora's chest. It sounded like Victor, or whatever he'd become, was going mad or . . . "He kills something!" Brontes growled, hefting his club and turning in a slow circle. Was he right? Sora thought it made sense; it reminded her of when she'd been a child watching her father hunt—the sounds his hawk made when it fought a fox.

"A creature?" she asked, knowing full well there had to be dungeon monsters in the cavern with them. Before Brontes could ask, the shrieks rose into a crescendo of outrage, and a message appeared in her vision:

Elandor Wildspeak has been rescued from certain death and removed from the dungeon. Five entrants remain. Prepare for an Energy infusion.

"Bastard!" Brontes roared, turning to jog back the way they'd come. Sora trailed after him, her heart cold, her eyes wide, looking up into the shadows of the cavern.

Her voice was small as she gripped her bow. "We shouldn't have separated."

When his feast was interrupted, the Aspect of Terror launched himself up, soaring to the heights of the cavern. Something crackled and ripped the air behind it, but too slow, dispersing in a cascade of ghostly blue flames that fell downward, effectively blinding anyone trying to track his movement into the shadows of the stalactites. Once he rounded a large cluster of them, he banked to the right, cracking his wings to launch himself farther afield. His fear-attuned Core was pulsing, thick and swollen with Energy—time was on his side. Once he'd maneuvered to the point where he could see the bright spirits of his pursuers, confirming that they'd lost sight of him, he dug his talons into a stone stalactite and hugged it close, watching their movements.

The blue and orange spirits had stopped, lingering near where he'd feasted, and the enormous golden spirit ran through the stalagmite forest, aiming for the same spot. They were reuniting. Still, the more diminutive silvery spirit was lagging, hardly moving. Had it become wounded? Was it time to strike again so soon? He eyed their movements for several seconds, trying to time things in his mind. Something in him growled, the *other*. It was angry that he waited. A thought came to him: *Momentum*. Terror's hunger surged as it let go of the stone and drifted down, gliding toward the small but very bright spirit.

He desperately wanted to scream his hunger and frustration, wanted to project his fear into the world, but he was on the hunt, and this time, he had to be stealthy as he struck. So, gliding on palpable waves of darkness, he descended like an eagle toward a rabbit. The spirit was strong with Energy, and she must have sensed him. Bright streaks of light and biting metal filled the air between them, punching holes in his wings and slamming into his fur, feathers, and scale-clad ribs. They ground furrows in his shadowy flesh, but the darkness streamed out of him, filling the holes, patching his bones, and wriggling the lodged missiles out, dropping them to the cavern floor as his talons slammed into his target.

Terror didn't stop his glide. He latched onto the spirit, pumping his wings and dragging her over the stone as he worked to turn his descent into a climb. He pulled the bright silvery spirit into the air, trailing rivulets of Energy-tinged blood through the air. It splashed against the stone as it fell, a bloody, glowing trail. He felt his quarry writhing, struggling to do something, and he squeezed his talons, driving the knifelike hooks through her body, punching them through her chest and back. He'd just gained the heights again, swerving left and right to avoid collisions with the many stone protrusions, when he suddenly lurched up to crash into the ceiling; his burden was gone.

Sora Deval has been rescued from certain death and removed from the dungeon. Four entrants remain. Prepare for an Energy infusion.

The Aspect of Terror screamed his bloody frustration, and a new but familiar sensation came over him. Hot rage was seeping out of his Core, crowding the dark fear-attuned Energy, and something stirred deep in his mind. The *other* was starting to assert himself again.

"What in the name of the ancient Dead Gods have you unleashed on our students?" The man was livid, red-faced, spittle flecking his pale green lips. Ranish regarded him; he was Fonroy Boloviture, the master of Elandor Wildspeak. He was a well-regarded man known for his impressive healing abilities. Still, he was apparently unwilling to accept that his "student," a grown man well into his sixth decade, had started something he couldn't finish.

Ranish would have shrugged, but his physique didn't lend itself to the gesture. Instead, he turned his thick black palms up and rumbled, "I did not tell your student to join four others to attempt the assassination of mine." Fonroy had appeared at his table not five minutes after Elandor's elimination. Either he'd been in the building or had teleported; both options were equally plausible. Still, Ranish didn't know why he was accosting him. "Is there aught I can do? He escaped with his life; count yourself blessed. Kim Jyster's loved ones mourn today, thanks to the efforts of your student's team."

"He is a shell of himself! Something in his wounds, unhealed by the System and its lifesaver, taints his soul! He appeared on the ground, curled into himself, unable to speak coherently, fear alive in his eyes."

"Ah! I knew my boy had a fear affinity, but I wasn't quite aware of how strong it was. A pity, but I'm sure we can help to mend Elandor's spirit; time and the right meditations will do wonders. Perhaps I'll give the task to Victor; he has much to learn in the areas of finesse." He paused and rubbed his chin in contemplation. "What of the Fae girl? Is she similarly stricken?"

Fonroy's pale green flesh was still hot, and he scowled deeply, but he knew better than to press the matter further with a man like Ranish Dar. He frowned and glanced from Dar to Lo'ro, who watched the exchange with an amused grin. "I don't know. She funded herself; does she even have a mentor?"

"Ah," Lo'ro clicked his tongue. "Shall I send someone to find out, Dar? I'm sure your boy will feel poorly if something terrible happens to her."

Dar nodded. "That would be well received, old friend." He looked back to Fonroy, and his heavy stony brow shifted lower in a scowl of concentration. "Tell me, Fonroy, do you think those other three have communication with the outside?" He knew they likely did. If anyone in the contest were cheating, he'd lay a bet that it would be Arona and her master.

Once again, the man's cheeks bloomed with a scarlet flush of blood. "How would I know? Are you making an accusation?"

Ranish Dar chuckled, a sound like axe blades on a whetstone, and shook his head. "No, no. I was simply going to say that if those other three were my students and I had the means of contacting them, I'd probably encourage the immediate use of their lifesavers."

47

A BRUTAL BRAWL

As Victor's rage grew and he pushed his conscious mind into control of his body, he felt his Aspect of Terror begin to fade. He knew he could fight the change and maintain the aspect, but he never felt good when he came back to himself after running amok as an incarnation of fear. He wanted out of it. Flexing his wings and angling downward to swoop around a massive stalagmite, he fought to push away the stomach-churning waves of guilt and paranoia that came to him the same way they might a drunk after a blackout binge. No, he was done with fear for now; he was ready to embrace some good clean hot-burning rage.

So as he scraped his talons on the stone, coming to rest behind the giant stalagmite, he pushed the fear out of his pathways, flooding them with rage instead. The shadows swirled around him, taking with them the strange fur, scales, and feathers of his terror form. The hot fury boiling his blood straightened his limbs, pushed his muscles to the point of bursting, and tinted his gray monochrome vision into shades of blood. Victor cast Iron Berserk and tilted his head back to roar into the echoing cavern.

It was then that he noticed a System message lurking in the corner of his vision:

Congratulations! Your Impart Nightmare, Basic has become Impart Nightmare, Improved.

***Impart Nightmare, Improved: While wearing your Aspect of Terror, using gathered fear-attuned Energy, you can corrupt the spirit of another

being with a seed of fear, sending it to dwell in their Core where it will grow and fester. This ability will fail upon those whose will can resist your intention. As you improve your mastery of this spell, it will become harder to resist and spread its roots more rapidly. Energy Cost: Minimum 100, scalable. Cooldown: Dependent on harvested fear.***

Victor brushed the message away; he didn't have time to contemplate the repercussions. He was aware of what the Aspect of Terror had done while he'd taken a back seat. He knew only three enemies were left in the dungeon, and, with the simmering heat of his rage stoking the fire in his chest, he didn't have the emotional bandwidth to feel sorry for Sora or the pitiful Nature Caster he'd feasted upon.

He could feel his swollen, fear-attuned Core and knew he'd taken much from them both, even with the interference of the Lifesaver charms. He gripped Lifedrinker, comfortable and eager in her proper axe-shaped form, no longer the talons on his nightmare alter ego. "Let's slay," he rumbled, lifting her in one titanic fist, his smoldering gaze scanning the darkness.

Arona crept through the shadows, following behind Brontes and Valeska, pondering the sound of that great roar as it echoed through the cavern. It was of a decidedly different timbre than the screeches and shrieks that had pounded on everyone's psyche for the last several minutes. Had the stranger changed again? This new sound was that of a great beast—a predator staking a claim, a primal challenge for territory.

She'd anticipated losing some of her team in the confrontation, but not two, not before they'd managed to harm their adversary in the slightest. For all she knew, he was fresh and whole, undamaged by Sora or Elandor. She couldn't stop the doubt from creeping into her mind—could he handle them all at once? Was it wise to throw her lot in with these "friends"?

That last thought stung, but she couldn't help herself. What would Master Vesavo say? He'd mock her for any sentimentality. He'd remind her that the universe is cruel and friendship mere currency, meant to be spent for the greatest profit. Wouldn't it be wise to hedge her bets? As the so-called titan bellowed again, much closer, and Brontes began to surge with hot, golden glory, she rasped, "I will try to flank." Then, she cloaked herself in cold dark mists and drifted away to the northwest, where they'd earlier mapped out the exit to the fifth floor. Let these brutes thrash about, distracting each other; she would finish the dungeon.

* * *

"Thash right," Lesh slurred, slamming his sack of arcanite billets on the table. "Pure arcanite. I'll wager it on Victor winnin' tha' fight." The bet-taker, a man who likely shared some common ancestry with Lesh's people, ran a thick pink tongue along the lip of his crocodilian snout.

"May I weigh it?"

"Yesh." Lesh peered at him through a bleary eye while still trying to focus on the viewing window at the center of the big wall. Through one of the smaller magical windows, he'd seen the Death Caster slink away, abandoning her companions, and he had confidence that Victor was about to lay out a titan-sized thrashing.

"Lesh," Valla said, reaching across the table to grip his wrist. "You've had much to drink . . ."

Lesh waved her hand away, snorting. A fine mist of acid escaped his nostrils, spotting the table and sizzling as it sank into the dense, heavily stained wood. "Am fine!" he grunted, working hard to enunciate each word. "Weight it!" he growled. "But be quick before my bet is too late!"

The man's scaled, clawed fingers hefted the bag, and he grinned. "Very well. On condition that it's proven to be pure arcanite, I'll value this sack at two hundred thousand beads." He turned to glance at the various viewing windows. "Seeing as your boy is now only facing two enemies, and considering his earlier victories, I'm only willing to give one-point-three to one odds. That work for you?"

Lesh nodded, waving him away. "Yesh." The bet-taker scribbled something in his notebook, hefted the sack, and wandered over to another table where patrons shouted for his attention. Meanwhile, Lesh turned a bleary eye on Valla. "Should've bet earlier. Don-shu think he'll win?"

Valla sighed and shifted on the hard wooden bench. He knew how she felt; his arse felt sore, too. "I have to believe he will. Still, Lesh, those are powerful people, and they don't seem to be the soft, untested sort. The only thing keeping me sane right now is that I don't believe anyone in there can kill Victor so quickly that the lifesaver won't function."

Lesh shook his head. "He'll be pished if he gets reshcued." He narrowed his eyes at the woman. He'd never considered that Victor might die in that dungeon, but, for the first time, he let his mind wander down that path, wondering what Valla would do. Putting that aside, he wondered what he'd do. Seek vengeance against whoever killed him? Yes, he supposed that was the only honorable thing. He couldn't progress, couldn't move on with his life, with Victor's unavenged specter haunting him.

Would Valla return to Fanwath? Would the others? Not Darren. No, Lesh would keep him close and train him properly. He was making progress, changing his outlook, turning away from his old habits of blame. When the youngster had built his own Core, Lesh had been surprised and proud, but he knew better than to offer too much praise too soon.

"Where did you go?" Valla asked, chuckling. She pointed to the viewing window. "Look. The two fighters close with Victor."

Victor didn't hide or stalk. He was ready for a brawl. He pumped his Sovereign Will boost into strength and vitality, summoned his Banner of the Champion, and stood waiting. He held Lifedrinker loose but ready; he and she both were limned with a red halo of rage, and Victor's eyes smoldered balefully under the golden light of his banner. Of course, his aura was enormous in his titanic form, and so, too, was the area affected by his banner's glow. Not a wisp of shadow surrounded him as the bloody sun sparkled in the air behind him. He breathed deeply, with purpose, stoking his Breath Core, fanning the flames of his magma, priming it for the fight to come.

When the giant fur-and-leather-clad warrior stepped around a stalagmite into his banner's light, Victor's grin widened, his white teeth glinting as his keen eyes tracked the challenger. He recognized the answering gleam of golden Energy in the aura of the giant; here was another Spirit Caster, another glory hound. Something deep in Victor rejoiced—had he, at last, found a worthy opponent? Victor lifted Lifedrinker and roared a challenge. By way of answer, the burly giant smashed his club onto the stone floor, shaking the ground and cracking a nearby stalagmite. Victor's furious Core surged at the challenge, and he cast Energy Charge, fueling it with glory-attuned Energy.

Iron Berserk allowed Victor to control himself and think with a rational mind while driven to the brink of frenzy by his rage, but it only worked that way if he consciously exercised his will and made an effort. When his titanic pride and hunger for the glory of battle goaded his furious temper, there wasn't much thinking taking place in his head. It seemed the big mumbling giant didn't suffer similarly. He'd been ready for Victor's charge, and, using some movement skill of his own, he flickered, almost like a ghost, and shifted behind an enormous stalagmite.

Victor was moving too fast to correct his course, so he propelled himself into darkness, bathing the new space in light as he moved, revealing the tall, hatchet-wielding warrior woman. She stood to the side of his streaking path, hacking those deadly crescent blades deep into Victor's side and hip as he passed by.

Victor roared in fury, sliding to a halt, spinning with Lifedrinker arcing out, cleaving the space behind him, anticipating a follow-up attack. No one was there, but he saw the woman to his left and the giant to his right. Victor's instinct was to charge again, but he forced himself to breathe and think, giving his rage a moment to heal the deep cuts the woman had imparted. Had his wyrm-scale helped at all?

The woman, Valeska, was half his size, made larger by some magic of her own, but the giant had swollen further still, probably two-thirds as tall as Victor but significantly bulkier. As Victor glowered at them, his mind going through a dozen attack scenarios, Valeska laughed, a sound full of confidence and genuine mirth. "He struggles to think, Brontes."

"Rage ca' make tha' har'." Brontes chuckled, his voice rumbling, his words flowing together, muddled by his lazy tongue.

Victor had been goaded before. He'd experienced a lifetime of trash talk long before he was ever summoned to Fanwath. It didn't further enrage him. In fact, it had the opposite effect, convincing him that these two were afraid. He let go of Lifedrinker with his left hand, reached to smear the blood off his side, and drew it across his face, grinning madly as he did so. If they thought he was enraged, they hadn't seen anything yet.

Valeska stood beside a stalagmite, and Brontes leaned on another. Two dozen yards separated them, and Victor knew they aimed to bait him, get him to charge again. They wanted to set him up for another sneaky attack, but he had other ideas.

The fact was, he'd expected something more; he'd expected something from the Death Caster, but he'd gotten a good feel for her aura, and there wasn't any sign of it. Was she lying in wait, hiding herself, looking for the perfect opportunity to strike? He figured that was the case. Still, he couldn't find it in himself to care all that much. He wanted to hit one of these two fighters, wanted to make up for that charge into nothing. As far as he was concerned, he'd deal with the Death Caster when she showed her face.

So, grinning, face bloody, Victor reached into his Core, pulled forth a torrent of inspiration-attuned Energy, and summoned his great bear, willing him to appear behind Valeska. He chose inspiration because he had plenty of it and because the bear would coalesce out of a cloud of white-gold Energy; it wouldn't be obvious in the light of his banner.

Stalling momentarily, giving his bear time to appear, Victor slapped Life-drinker's haft into his left palm and growled, "So? Two at once, then?" He kept his posture neutral and relaxed, almost lazily looking from Valeska to Brontes and back again. They both had eyes only for him, so neither saw the cloud of Energy behind the woman.

"He just cast something," Valeska said, staring hard at Victor. "Maneuver two . . ." Her words were cut off by a bone-rattling roar as Victor's bear burst into being—tawny, almost golden fur covering a mountain of bone and mus-cle, bright yellow-gold eyes, and teeth like gleaming sabers spread wide as it emptied its lungs directly behind the woman. Just as he'd hoped, even Bron-tes couldn't resist looking to see the source of the roar. In that split second of distraction, he filled his pathways with fear-attuned Energy and charged again, rippling over the cavern floor in a cloak of purple-black shadows.

Valeska rolled to the side, avoiding a double swipe of the bear's saber-like claws. Brontes turned back to Victor, but only in time to register the streak of shadows flying his way. His eyes opened wide, and he jerked his club before himself and channeled his Energy, blazing with brilliant golden light, as Vic-tor smashed into him. Victor had timed an overhead chop with Lifedrinker, aiming to split the giant's sternum, but the great gnarled club got in the way. Lifedrinker flared with molten fury, and her razor edge cut into the trunk-sized bludgeon, biting deep. Meanwhile, the force wave of Victor's charge washed over them both.

Victor's pool of fear-attuned Energy rapidly poured into the effort of shielding him. At the same time, Brontes flared with golden, sparkling light, his entire body rigid with the strain of holding his club up and weathering the storm of the collision. As they stood, two juggernauts in a whirling tem-pest of destructive forces, the shockwave propagated, shattering stalagmites, sending fragments of rock, showers of dust, and palpable roiling waves of Energy outward. Valeska and the bear tore into each other, slashing, hacking, gnashing, ducking, weaving, and stumbling in the force blast from Victor's charge.

As the collision resolved and Victor's fear-attuned Energy stopped pour-ing out to protect him, he jerked Lifedrinker, pulling her from the club, and began hacking in earnest, working to get past Brontes's guard. The stout war-rior was surprisingly nimble and skilled with his bludgeon. Moreover, he used his glory-attuned Energy in weird showy maneuvers that erupted with blazing sparks or false images—flickering copies of the club, the giant, or both that served to distract Victor or even draw strikes away from the real target. If they weren't both moving with lightning speed, Victor was sure the dazzling echoes of reality wouldn't be so effective, but when a tiny fraction of a second meant the difference between landing a blow and striking nothing but air, they took a toll.

Brontes was strong, his girth giving him what it took to absorb Lifedrinker's hacks, soaking them up as she bit into his enormous cudgel. The weapon was sturdier still; each deep, smoking groove Lifedrinker tore into the wood closed before Victor's eyes as he pulled her out. Even so, Victor maintained the offensive, pushing Brontes around and forcing him to expend his Energy abilities just to keep from being dismembered. He grunted and groaned, great gouts of golden Energy surging through him, bolstering his movements, distracting Victor, and drawing things out.

Of course, the constant rebuttals to his masterful strokes began to wear on Victor's state of mind. More and more rage seeped into his pathways, turning his vision darker and darker shades of crimson. He'd forgotten Valeska and his bear, their contest nothing but a token afterthought in the focus he devoted to breaking through the giant's resolute defenses. Just because he'd set her aside mentally, though, didn't mean the axe woman had forgotten him.

If Victor were paying attention, he would have known his bear had been vanquished. He would have probably backed off on his furious assault and tried to get eyes on the woman. He didn't, though, and she caught him mid-attack, using a charge of her own to streak through the air and bury her two hatchets into the meaty spaces beside his upper spine. They snipped through his armor as if it wasn't there, and he knew they'd buried themselves to the wooden hafts. To a man Victor's size, the wounds were an inconvenience, but he'd taken much worse.

Roaring in fury, he backed off his attack on Brontes, bunched his legs, and launched himself into the air using Titanic Leap. Valeska was still clinging to her axe hafts, hanging from his back, and Victor aimed to impale her on a stalactite. He was so committed that he fully expected to do the same thing to himself in the process, but he was banking on being able to recover faster than she could. Valeska was no slouch; she grunted with surprise as they exploded into the air but braced her shoulder against Victor's back, holding onto one of her hatchets for purchase. At the same time, she somehow created a silvery shield of Energy with her free arm.

The glowing shield shattered the stalactite, sending a rain of rubble down toward Brontes. Victor careened sideways from the impact, tumbling in slow motion as he fell toward the ground. At the last minute, he jerked his shoulder, rolling, trying to smash Valeska into the stone floor beneath him. She, too, jerked, pulling on the hatchet she still held, sliding it out of Victor's flesh and rolling over his side, bouncing off as he hit the ground. Victor roared in pain and fury as the remaining hatchet was driven further into his back, and he bounced with a cavern-shaking crash.

He'd barely managed to get up to a knee before Valeska was on him, hacking her single hatchet like a madwoman, left and right, then downward, and reversing the blade to hack it up toward his chin. Victor bobbed and weaved, got an arm in the way, and then, as he bled from three or four deep gashes, finally brought Lifedrinker around in a terrible chop that caught the woman on the side of her helmet, sending her much smaller frame tumbling and bouncing over the stony ground. Victor couldn't savor the perfect hit— Brontes smashed into him. The fur-covered giant had bounded across the cavern on floating discs of sparkling golden Energy, building momentum each time he pushed off.

Victor grunted as thousands of pounds of meat, bone, and enormous club barreled into him, driving him back into another stalagmite, shattering it. The two giants tumbled through the stone fragments, acquiring cuts in their flesh wherever they weren't armored. Victor was nearly blind with rage by then; everything was crimson, and he moved by touch, grabbing Brontes under one arm, then over his neck with the other. He arched his back and pulled with all his might, flinging the gigantic man over him, sending him flying over the rubble-strewn cavern floor. Grunting with fury, Victor lurched to his feet, dimly aware that Lifedrinker had slipped from his grasp.

He turned, scanning the floor, trying to spot her gleaming burning axe-head in the crumbled stone. Struggling to focus with the rage clouding his sight, he just caught a glimpse of flickering silvery light coming toward him. Knowing it was Valeska charging him again, Victor growled, lowered his helm-covered head toward her incoming form, and cast Roots of the Mountain.

Maybe it was clever, or maybe it was stupid; he didn't know yet, but he was pleased by his quick reaction, regardless. Valeska's single hatchet led her charge, much like Lifedrinker usually led Victor's. The blade hit him square on the crown of his Kethian Juggernaut helmet, and Victor's head and body didn't even flinch. His spell had made him unmovable. Instead, a hundred percent of the impact was absorbed by Valeska's hatchet, Victor's helmet, and Valeska's body as she crumpled against him.

With a terrible screeching explosion, the magic that bound the incredibly dense metal of Victor's helmet failed, and he felt it loosen on his skull as it split. The hatchet must have been made of amazing stuff because its bright blade survived the destructive forces, but the handle turned to splinters and dust in Valeska's hand. Her fingers twisted and snapped as they hit Victor between the eyes. Then, as her body crumpled against him, he heard several more sickening wet *snap*s as larger bones broke. The entire collision lasted a split second, and then Victor was left reeling, blood dripping into his eyes, his ears ringing. Valeska writhed in agony at his feet.

Growling, Victor reached up and pulled off his damaged helmet, shaking his head, trying to get his ears to work properly again. The mighty helmet was split from the noseguard to the crown where the axe had hit. Worse, it didn't feel as heavy as it once did. Victor frowned and sent it into his storage pouch. Then, blinking and swiping at the blood in his eyes, he canceled the Roots of the Mountain spell before it drained his Core of Energy. He saw a glimmer in the dust to his left and stomped toward it, hoping it was Lifedrinker.

His foot touched something soft, and he remembered Valeska. She was still alive, grunting and gasping, struggling to turn from her twisted back onto her side, away from him. Her broken arm was pitiful, curled up and bleeding with fragments of bone sticking out of the flesh. Victor couldn't find the rage in him to stomp on her, to break her neck, or shatter her skull—whatever it might take for the System to recognize she was done and activate her Lifesaver. Instead, he growled, "You have until I pick up my axe to use your charm."

As he stalked over to the shiny glint of metal, he was well aware that he'd lost sight of Brontes. His ears still rang, but he glanced left and right, thankful for his banner's light, as he glared through the blood in his eyes. The giant didn't make an appearance before he stooped to pick up Lifedrinker, but as soon as his fingers closed on her haft, the System announced Valeska's removal:

Valeska Thornrend has been rescued from certain death and removed from the dungeon. Three entrants remain. Prepare for an Energy infusion.

The message was a splash of cold water on Victor's muddled thoughts—he'd yet to see the Death Caster, and several of his Energy pools were running perilously low. Thanks to the System's strange, hidden rules, he couldn't count on that Energy infusion until the fighting was done. Tumbling stones and rubble got his attention, and he turned in time to see Brontes lifting himself from the broken rubble of a stalagmite; he'd, apparently, tumbled into another when Victor had thrown him.

The giant lifted his great gnarled club, and then, surprising Victor but sparking something like respect in his heart, the giant began to flicker with a strange, hazy, yellow-green aura as he strode toward him. He felt that weird spirit Energy immediately; it was something that pulled at him, digging up haunting moments of failure and secret regret—his inability to return to his *abuela*, his rejection of Chandri and her simple peaceful life, and, most damning, his choice to be with Valla rather than wait and see if he could ever measure up to Tes. A dozen more shame-inducing thoughts fought for attention in his mind, and Victor felt his grip on Lifedrinker loosening.

"I didna' wan' ta use this," the stout bloody dust-covered giant rumbled as he drew near. "Makes things too easy." He lifted his massive club and, with a belly-shaking grunt, jerked it down toward Victor's unprotected head.

Now, Victor might have been troubled, shamed, and even dazed from the onslaught of the giant's unpleasant spirit Energy—Shame? Regret?—but his will was like a mountain fortress, and he saw the giant coming his way, saw him lift his club, and fully recognized the threat. As the massive cudgel fell toward his head, he lifted his left hand and caught it, the fury in his eyes flickering red like twin torches in the face of that sickly yellow-green aura.

Brontes grunted, jerking with his two arms, but Victor didn't let go; he squeezed his iron fingers into that hard uncaring wood and felt it give. He felt his mighty grip find purchase, and his mad grin returned as he stoked the fires of rage in his pathways with something extra—the furious fire of his magma heart. Flames began to flicker between his teeth, licking upward, as black smoke drifted out of his nostrils. He didn't speak. He simply continued to squeeze that cudgel, looking down at the enormous fighter as the magma spread through his pathways, and he activated Volcanic Fury.

48

THE MOUNTAIN'S FURY

Ranish Dar watched Fonroy as he stiffly retreated, walking through the crowded club to the elevator that would take him up to the more private viewing chambers—no doubt on his way to report every word of their conversation to some of the other masters who were too proud to show their faces. Across from him, Lo'ro chuckled as his privacy spell fell back into place with an audible *pop*, dampening their words. "A little hysterical, wasn't he? Has he never watched a death match in the colosseum?"

Ranish sighed and shook his head, idly watching Victor embrace his berserk titanic form, openly waiting for the last three challengers to find him. Gods, but he had a hell of a spirit! He turned to Lo'ro. "Not involving their students. Well, let me rephrase that: not unless they were certain their students would win. That's the problem with Sojourn. Thousands of years of placidity have led to a generation of soft, untested souls. Consider this, Lo'ro: That man's student, what's his name? Elandor? How old is he? Seventy-odd years?"

"Something like that. Not more than a hundred, certainly."

Dar slapped his hand on the table. "Exactly my point! Thank you. You consider him young, yes?"

"Naturally . . ."

"In the world where Victor was born, Elandor would be considered a senior citizen. Think of that! Elandor has had a life of study, mentorship, and dungeon delving. A truly safe, tranquil existence."

Lo'ro's eyes narrowed. "Dungeons carry with them quite a risk . . ."

"Fah!" Dar waved his hand dismissively. "In Sojourn? Where every dungeon is mapped and cataloged, and where they're all curated and offered only to appropriately leveled entrants? You could read a dozen encyclopedias on any one of the dungeons available to the citizens of this city. Do you think a pampered nature student like Elandor would go into a dungeon if there were any chance he couldn't escape? This is likely the first contest he's entered where there was a true risk of death, however small; you've seen how effective the lifesavers have been." Lo'ro started to say something, but Dar wasn't finished. "Let's not forget he went in with an alliance of rather absurd strength."

"I begin to see your point. So, you're saying this is why your boy is different?"

"Exactly. Just this morning, I was reading through the journal I tasked him with writing. That young man has been on the brink of death more times than he wasn't. He's been enslaved, tortured, had his Core shattered, and recovered while under the threat of constant death and brutal beatings. He has regularly battled enemies stronger than himself, and each time that he's felt death's breath on his neck, he's fought his way back. I had no doubt he would thrash any one of the entrants in this dungeon, given a face-to-face challenge. The surprise of some of the other masters is telling."

"So, you think he'll win?"

"He'll win this fight, aye, but look." He pointed at Arona's viewing window. "The young death caster has more wisdom than her friends, though some might call her cleverness cowardice. I won't be surprised if she wins the dungeon, but Victor won't be eliminated, especially as his biggest threat slinks away."

Lo'ro shifted, smiling. "I know I'm biased in my agreement, but tell me: Why do you consider her the biggest threat?"

"I worked with her master on a project. I'm sure you know him—Vesavo Bonewhisper?"

"Oh, aye. I know him quite well, quite well, indeed. I'm also well acquainted with the young lady pictured there." Lo'ro gestured to the viewing window where, even now, Arona was slipping away behind the curtain of the waterfall.

"Well, then you know that, unlike other Death Casters, his practice specializes in harnessing and cultivating champion spirits, bringing them forth in constructs of bone and flesh. I'm certain that young woman has some powerful summons she can employ, and, with an enormous Energy pool, she might have been able to wear Victor down. Especially with her two brawny allies."

"We may never know." Again, Lo'ro pointed to the viewing window. Arona had slipped into a short stone tunnel and now approached a set of stairs.

"Perhaps not in today's contest." Dar smiled, leaning back, interlocking his stout, black fingers on the tabletop.

"Yet you seem smug, even in the face of Arona's impending victory."

"Victor's showing has already confirmed my hopes and won me enough money in the gambling halls to fund a decade of projects. I am not displeased. Moreover, is it not lovely to know a few of the more passionate, active members of the Sojourn political scene have been taken down a notch or three?"

"Aye." Lo'ro smiled, his corpse-like skin stretching tight along his facial bones. Just a second later, though, his eyes unfocused, and the smile faded from his expression. "My follower has set eyes upon the Fae girl, Sora Deval. She suffers greatly."

"Is she alone, then?"

"Aye. She lies in the recovery room of the World Hall, unattended."

"Will your follower convey her to my estate?"

"Which?"

"The lake house."

Again, Lo'ro's eyes unfocused, and then he nodded. "Shevelia is taking her now."

"Good. I'll teach Victor how to remove his curse upon her, and then I'll let him decide whether he'll help Elandor or not."

"Is he the only one who can . . ."

"Ha!" Dar chuckled. "Not in the least. A hundred Spirit Casters in this city are qualified, but do you think those pompous fools know that?" Dar pointed one of his thick fingers toward the ceiling, indicating the club's private viewing parlors. He sighed and shrugged. "Given a little research and the right expenditure, I'm sure Elandor will find the care he needs, but it would be good for Victor to put Fonroy Boloviture in his debt."

"Ah! A two-fold lesson for your prodigy, then."

Again, Dar folded his hands, and his grin reappeared. Softly, he rumbled, "Exactly. Exactly right, my old friend."

As the potent mix of magma and rage began to propagate his pathways, flooding into Victor's body, his vision shifted into pale shades of yellowish sepia. His banner flickered and faded in motes of sparkling golden Energy, and Victor's need for destruction outweighed every other thought in his mind. He still gripped Brontes's club, and smoke began to rise from the dense, stone-like wood as his fingers burned into it.

For his part, Brontes seemed to have overcome his stunned surprise at Victor's ability to shrug off his mental attack and was once again channeling his glory-attuned Energy. Grunting with the effort, he wrapped both hands around the narrow end of his club and pulled, jerking his stout body backward, driving a foot against Victor's hip. Victor was preoccupied with his fury, only idly gripping the weapon by now, and the giant's gambit worked; he freed his cudgel and flung himself back, losing his footing in the process.

Victor saw the over-large man stumble away, collapsing onto his butt and scrambling to stand, but something else was distracting him. Something stung at the center of his back, and he could hear a weird keening, wailing sound almost on the edge of his range of hearing. He still held Lifedrinker in his right hand, but he took his now empty left hand and reached back over his shoulder, probing for the source of his discomfort. Prodding around, he felt it—something hard jutting from his flesh. Growling in annoyance, he gripped it with his viselike fingers and tugged. It slid free, and when he held the object before him, a dim, distant part of his mind recognized Valeska's hatchet.

The metal was white-hot, the wood charred black, and his ears told him it was the source of the wailing sound. If he'd had the capacity to care, he might have wondered if the axe had been suffering from the molten heat of his blood. He didn't, though; he only knew he was angry at the man before him, and he didn't want to hold the little weapon, so he threw it at him. It ripped through the air like a missile, smashing into the fur-covered chest of the stout giant, and, as if it were designed for throwing—it was—the smoldering blade sank deeply into his flesh. Brontes grunted in pain, stumbling back further, and then Victor lifted Lifedrinker and did the only thing he had the presence of mind for: He tried to kill the man before him.

Brontes had defended against Victor's berserking axe attacks before. He'd stood toe to toe with him, using that massive club to intervene in Victor's hatchet attacks. Earlier, he'd been able to use glory-attuned spells and abilities to distract, daze, and misdirect, but none of that worked for him now. Victor had no eyes for distractions, no mind to be dazed—he saw only a target for the endless waves of hatred and fury boiling in his blood. Perhaps it said something about his Iron Berserk upgrade: It took away the purity of his rage, allowing his other emotions and thoughts to dull its edge. His Volcanic Fury had no such problem.

Lifedrinker answered his molten violence with her own, her blade blazing like a white-hot scythe as she cut the air, ripping massive smoking gouges in Brontes's club, making wounds that were slow to close, carving off chunks that might be too much for the club's ability to self-repair. Just being close to Victor was taking a toll on Brontes; the heat rolling off him was difficult for the giant to bear, and desperate sweat sheened his red, strained face as he struggled to avoid the terrible, powerful, skillful cleaves of that axe. To his credit, Brontes stood up to Victor for more than two dozen seconds before he started looking around, fervently hoping for some sort of intervention.

If Victor could read his mind, he would have heard Brontes vehemently cursing Arona. He would have seen images replaying Valeska's impotent charge. He would have heard him cursing himself for aligning against Victor rather than listening to Sora when she'd whispered her doubts, suggesting he try to join her and Victor instead. Victor couldn't hear them, though, nor did he have any desire for it. He was lost in the heat of his rage, in the undeniable urge to deliver punishment to any who stood before him. With each resounding, deadly impact of Lifedrinker on the giant's club, he bared his teeth in a cruel grimace of pleasure.

His brutal punishment was cathartic, feeding his fury, encouraging his rage, driving him to more and more violence. Everyone who watched the fight could see the writing on the wall: Victor was too much for Brontes to handle. He'd been too much before, even with Valeska's aid, but now, in this state, seemingly burning with an endless supply of furious fire, he was utterly dominating him.

The fur-covered giant was more than on the defensive; he was in full retreat, seeking an egress, a way to escape Victor's fiery frenzy. He tried to dash away more than once, but even using the ability to run on glittering glory-infused steps of light, Victor was too fast, and Brontes couldn't risk showing him his flank. Finally, the frustrated despair was apparent on his face: He'd realized he had no way out other than to embrace the painful penalty of the lifesaver.

Victor's breath was short and ragged as he panted his lustful fury, hacking Lifedrinker in precise deadly strokes. His eyes smoldered, burning like white-hot coals. Smoke and flames licked his lips with each exhalation, and if he hadn't been reveling in the destructive smashes of his axe against that club, he might have sought to end things faster with a burst of magma-infused breath.

His opponent stumbled back, and his face took on a new expression, one Victor couldn't read in his current state. After a deep inhalation, Brontes straightened and braced himself, blazing with golden glittering glory-attuned Energy as he dug his left hand into his neckline, pulling on a cord from which a tiny charm dangled.

Victor saw the charm, and a corner of his mind knew he didn't want the giant to activate it. With desperate, frustrated strength, he lifted Lifedrinker high. He hacked her down, seizing the moment to strike when the giant's cudgel swayed to the side, unable to guard effectively with only one hand guiding it. Lifedrinker, trailing black smoke, screaming through the air, descended toward the side of Brontes's neck, and Victor's maddened eyes widened with the anticipation of the blow, eager to see his enemy's blood flow. Just as her edge sliced the first layer of the giant's flesh, though, he burst into golden smoke and was gone.

Victor's eyes flared with fire as he stared at the dissipating smoke. Lifedrinker hung at his side, his hand gripping her handle with enough force to shatter stone. His veins bulged with boiling blood. The wreathing aura of fire that encased his body flared, lifting toward the cavern ceiling like a torch doused with kerosene. His mind was driven blank by the apoplectic agony of his righteous fury. He had been denied, and the world would feel his wrath! Victor arched his back and opened his mouth in a scream of outrage that carried no sound other than the freight train roar of a torrent of fire as he emptied his magma Core in a fountain of streaming white-hot lava.

Simultaneously, he stomped his foot and cast Wake the Earth. As a Herald of the Mountain's Wrath, Volcanic Fury and Wake the Earth walked hand in hand in his subconscious, instinctive brothers of destruction. It was instinctual, automatic, and there was not a single thought behind it. He poured everything he had into the spell, his wrath having removed any temperance. The ground shook, a ripple of force rolling out from him at the epicenter, and like a spider's web, hundreds of cracks tore open on the stone cavern floor, widening as they spread away from him. Stalagmites burst as the cracks went through them. Stalactites fell as the world shook. Stones the size of buildings crashed down in a deafening cacophony of destruction.

Through it all, Victor howled. His initial burst of magma had done much to paint the world in hues of orange and red. The fire of his breath Core was hot enough to melt stone and had a liquid quality that clung to the surfaces it touched, continuing to burn as the world came apart around him. He screamed and frothed, and the world exploded and fell, and through it all, Victor's ire burned, his mind utterly gone in the face of it.

Arona watched as Shol-pan, the first spirit she'd ever harnessed, finished killing the bridge trolls. She could see the stairs to the sixth level on the other side, and she hadn't minded the opportunity to let some frustration out. Valeska was out. That meant Brontes was left to stop or slow the stranger. "Victor, I suppose," she muttered, facing the fact that everyone would know his name soon enough. And if Brontes failed? How quickly would Victor catch her? She'd hoped the fifth level would be the final one, that she could wrap things up quickly before he had a chance to pursue. It didn't seem likely, however. Not with the speed with which Valeska had fallen.

Shol-pan glided back to her, trailing lines of blood from his long spectral claws—a trail of gore leading to the two dead trolls. "Mistress." He bowed, staring at her through his weird ice-blue eyes, waiting for praise, dismissal, or a new task.

"Well done, Shol-pan. You grow ever stronger; I am pleased." She stood and started over the bridge, pondering the bodies, contemplating the removal of a bone or three for later use. "No time, I suppose." Was she being overcautious? It could take Victor hours to find the stairs in that great cavern, assuming he beat Brontes . . .

Brontes Ironhide has been rescued from certain death and removed from the dungeon. Two entrants remain. Prepare for an Energy infusion.

"Damn it!" she hissed, breaking into a jog toward the distant stair. She'd just cleared the stone span when the ground lurched, and the dungeon's diffuse pale light flickered and winked out. Arona stumbled, falling to her hands and knees, scuffing her palms on the rough stone. Her eyes flared with cold Energy, turning the darkness to twilight, and she looked around, mouth partially open, wondering what could have caused the dungeon to react in such a way. Another faint tremor vibrated the stone under her hands, and, to her shock, the bridge split with a thunderous *crack*, and the near side slipped into the chasm. Arona scrambled forward, putting more distance between herself and the abyss.

"Mistress . . ." Shol-pan hissed, his semi-corporeal blue form glowing in the dark as he swooped near.

"Hush!" she hissed, scrambling to her feet and stooping to pick up Balefrost where she'd dropped him. The polished bone in her hand comforted her as her brain scrambled for an explanation. Leaning on the staff, its hard end pressed against the stone, she felt the vibrations continuing, and her grasping mind couldn't fathom what it could mean. Suddenly, the sourceless, simulated daylight flickered on again, nearly dazzling her Ghost Sight–enhanced eyes.

Attention: This dungeon's dimensional bonds are being strained, requiring an ongoing Energy infusion to maintain. All entrants will be removed to allow the owners an opportunity to provide Energy, facilitating repairs. The remaining entrants will be awarded a chest as though they have cleared their current level. No penalty will be applied to the entrants removed due to this emergency. No outstanding Energy infusions will be awarded.

Arona frowned, studying the words to ensure she understood. There wouldn't be an award for the elimination of Brontes, Valeska, Sora, or Elandor. The city of Sojourn would be on the hook for the repairs, and she would get a chest for this level. "And no penalty, Shol-pan. I'll take that. Again, I am pleased."

"Your pleasure brings me joy, Mistress."

Arona started to make a quip about him being incapable of joy when the world flared with white light. The ground seemed to shift under her feet, and as her vision recovered, she found herself stumbling onto the teleportation platform in the World Hall annex, where they'd all gathered to enter the dungeon. Three gray-robed attendants rushed forward, but two of them stopped beside the enormous, steaming, dust-and-blood-covered form in front of her—Victor.

49

CONSEQUENCES

Victor was stunned by the sudden violent shift in his circumstances. One moment, he'd been a passenger to his rage and magma-fueled alter ego, half participating and half observing as he unleashed his frustrated wrath upon the world. The next, he'd been stripped of his Volcanic Fury, ripped from the dungeon, and deposited on the metal teleportation platform back in Sojourn.

As the world reeled, he dropped to one knee, cradling his spinning head with his dirty bloodstained hands. He squeezed his eyes shut, trying to remember the System message text he'd glimpsed before furiously swiping it away. "What the hell did it say?" he grumbled.

Several gray-robed attendants rushed onto the platform, two of them stopping next to him. Even with him kneeling, they had to look up slightly to make eye contact. "Do you require healing?" the man on the left asked, reaching to scratch at his smooth pink-skinned head nervously.

"Nah. I just wish I had read what the System said. Why am I here?" Victor stood, grunting with the effort, and started dusting his tattered, singed, utterly ruined pants.

"You didn't read it?" a raspy emotionless feminine voice behind him asked. Victor recognized Arona's affect, so when he turned, he found his hand reaching for Lifedrinker's haft, which made him wonder when he'd put her back in her harness. Had the System done it? "Peace, angry one!" the woman said, stepping back. She held her hands out in the universal sign of "I'm not looking for a fight."

Victor lowered his hand. His rage was gone, spent on his Volcanic Fury and then ripped away by the System. The only emotion he could muster at that moment was something a lot more like apathy than anger. "I . . . was preoccupied." He shrugged, narrowing his eyes, suddenly wondering why this woman hadn't helped her friends. "Where the hell did you go, anyway?"

Before she could answer, the attendant who'd spoken earlier said, "Please vacate this teleportation annex. We'll close it now that everyone's out of the dungeon."

Victor scowled and then walked to the door, which was currently held open by another attendant. Arona followed, saying, "I was trying to win the dungeon while you and the others were occupying each other." There wasn't a hint of shame in her voice. "The System, or at least the part of it in charge of the dungeon, threw us out. The message said something about the 'dimensional bonds' being strained. Whatever that means."

"And the Energy?" Victor asked, turning to face her once he stood in the hall.

"You mean our pending infusion? The System greedily claimed it, no doubt justifying the theft by using the Energy to maintain the dungeon's integrity."

"That's some bullshit," Victor growled.

Arona shrugged her broad bony shoulders, her black-painted lips curving into a wry smile. "Well, at least we weren't penalized for our removal. We're supposed to get a chest, too, but I don't know where to claim it."

Victor stretched his neck, and several loud *pops* erupted from the maneuver. He looked up the hallway and saw figures approaching. One of them was Ranish Dar. "Here come some answers, I hope."

Arona leaned on her polished bone staff, facing the approaching group. Victor saw four others besides Dar, all humanoid, some even appearing human, though Victor doubted that was the case. He glanced at Arona again, realizing she, too, looked human—vampiric but human, nonetheless.

"What's your species?" he bluntly asked, seizing the moment to gather some information before the group arrived.

"Hmm? I'm a Faeling," she replied. When Victor wrinkled his brow in confusion, she sighed and explained, "On my homeworld, the Fae have lain with the natives for centuries, resulting in people like me."

It was strange, he decided, how relaxed he was speaking to a woman who'd been intent on killing him not long ago. Hadn't he been just as murderous, though? Hadn't he been eager to fight? Coming down from the enormous wave of rage he'd been riding, he found himself oddly introspective. The truth was, he hadn't been treating the dungeon like real life; the lifesavers and the competitive nature of the setting had made him reckless and a lot less concerned about individuals and the lives of everyone involved, his own included. He shook his head, forcing his mind to focus on present circumstances. He gestured toward the people walking with Dar. "Are they? Faeling?"

"Oh, something similar, no doubt." She narrowed her eyes, a gleam of amusement brightening her dark irises. "Surely you know about the elder races? Many were similar in appearance; you could be descended from the Fae based on your features if not for your great size. Some elder giant race, no doubt?"

Victor couldn't help but grunt, "Titan." After a pause to think, he asked, "So, the elder races wandered around the universe screwing everything they came across until we all started looking like long-lost cousins?"

"Well, not *everything*. Surely, you've seen the many unique species in this city. What an unexpected conversation! I thought you'd be spewing threats and glowering with murderous . . ."

"Victor!" Dar bellowed, interrupting Arona.

Victor glanced back down the hallway and saw the group had drawn close, only a dozen strides away. "Yeah?" Dar's tone and the scowls he saw on everyone's faces began to drive home the idea that everything wasn't exactly rosy.

Two men in ornate robes, one silver and one black, flanked Dar, and behind them were two large individuals wearing black metallic armor, their heavy helms hiding their faces. They carried long wicked-looking polearms, and their posture was decidedly aggressive. The auras vying for dominance were palpable and heavy, and Victor had to brace himself in their presence as the group continued closer. Dar didn't answer Victor, and he soon realized why, listening to their ongoing conversation.

". . . should be held until the trial."

"There will be no gods damned trial!" Dar roared, whirling on the much smaller man. He wore a cape made of some kind of shimmering, almost metallic fiber. It was crimson with a high collar that gave Dar's already imposing stature an even more regal bearing. The fabric snapped as he turned dramatically, causing the smaller silver-robed man to step back nervously.

"Inquest, then! Peace, Ranish, peace!" The fellow, a gray-skinned man with curly white hair, opened his deep purple eyes wide, making a sort of soothing expression with his mouth as he tried to placate Victor's new mentor.

Dar flexed his stony hands into anvil-sized fists, and something very much like rage began to emanate from his towering form. "How can you think to hold him responsible for . . ."

"Peace!" the second robed individual snapped, his voice like the hiss of a green log in a fire. Victor felt a wave of power behind it that made his knees threaten to buckle. It was enough to stop Dar's words in their tracks, and that was something Victor had never expected to see. He couldn't see the speaker's face; it seemed to be shrouded in black smoke within the cowl of his robes, quickly banishing Victor's notion that he was humanlike. Victor looked for his hands, hoping to catch a glimpse of his flesh, but they were obscured by the robe's long voluminous sleeves. "Save your arguments for the inquest." He turned to Dar, adding, "Yes, Ranish Dar, there will be one. It is decided."

The other man, the one in the silver robe with the much more pleasant demeanor, said, "Arona Moonshadow and Victor Sandoval. You are both hereby ordered to attend an inquest by order of the ruling council of Sojourn. Report to the Council Spire at noon tomorrow. Am I understood?"

Arona immediately bowed and mumbled, "Yes, Lord."

Despite himself and his Quinametzin pride, Victor found he had no will to argue or refuse. He nodded his head and said, "Yes." He was heartened to see Dar nod along with him.

The cowled, smoke-bound individual turned while simultaneously saying, "Very good." Then he, the two armored halberd-wielding guards, and the other silver-robed fellow departed just as quickly as they'd arrived.

"Moonshadow, you should find your master," Dar rumbled after waiting several seconds for the clanking footsteps of the guards to retreat.

Arona, still bowing, asked, "What's this about, Lord Dar?"

"Don't fret. I believe Victor will bear the brunt of the council's wrath. He broke the dungeon."

She whirled on Victor, straightening, her black eyes widening with the first emotion he'd seen out of her. "What? Is that why we were ejected? What did you do?"

"I . . ."

"Not now, Moonshadow. Begone." Dar's voice had taken on a particular edge Victor recognized; he'd spoken that way to him back when he'd tried to argue about the cost of Edeya's healing. Arona pressed her palms together, bowed low to Dar, and then scurried away, walking quickly down the hallway. "Making friends of your enemies so quickly?"

"Not friends." Victor shrugged. "Just talking."

"You shared a challenging experience. It's only natural to find some camaraderie, so long as you can look past the cutthroat behavior so many of you displayed in there."

"I didn't betray anyone." Victor found his brows drawing together in a new scowl. Was his Rage Core recovering so quickly?

"Don't quibble, pup. You fought like the monster you are, and sore feelings abound in this city." He glanced at the distant figures of the two robed individuals. "Even the current consuls are eager to see you pay. The System's demanding a financial penalty to put the challenge dungeon back in order." He shrugged. "I won't rescue you with a gift, but there have been worse debts. I'm sure we'll sort things out at their little inquest." He reached out to rest a heavy hand on Victor's shoulder, and, for the first time since his arrival, Dar showed a pleasant expression, not quite a smile, but certainly not a scowl. "I think we can afford to celebrate a bit. First, let's go and get your chest. I hear it spawned near the city's System Stone."

Victor's eyes widened. "What if someone grabs it?"

"Impossible. It's your reward; no one can take it, just as you couldn't take the one awaiting that young Death Caster." He turned and started striding purposefully toward the main World Hall. Victor hurried to keep pace, and Dar kept speaking while they walked. "Tell me, your friends, those who traveled here with you to find aid for the young insect girl . . ."

"Edeya's not an insect!" Victor laughed.

"What? She has gossamer wings and tiny antennae on her head. Are you certain?"

"Uh, well, shit." Victor shrugged. "I never thought of Ghelli as insects. They make me think of fairies more than they do bugs."

"Fairies, hmm? I suppose I could see some Fae in her appearance. This is beside the point, whelp! Tell me, are they still in Sojourn?"

"Yeah. They should be. How long was I in the dungeon? It only felt like half a day to me."

"Closer to a day and a half! Time flies when you're bludgeoning half the city's most promising iron rankers." Dar chuckled. Then his brows narrowed, and he growled, "You distracted me again! I'm trying to warn you! As I said earlier, you ruffled many feathers with your brutal dispatching of so many of Sojourn's finest. Most were Tier Eight or Nine and have likely lost close to a decade's progress from the lifesaver's Energy tax. I wouldn't be surprised if some sought retribution."

Victor wasn't stupid. He growled and increased his pace. "If anyone hurts one of my friends . . ."

"Calm down, Victor." Ranish reached out and grabbed his shoulder again, effortlessly slowing his pace. "I have spies out and about. I don't believe anyone's taken action yet, but it's something we should be wary of. Your friends should always travel in pairs, and the one I healed, being so low level, should be escorted by two or more of your stronger friends wherever they go."

"She and another very low-level friend are planning to go into a dungeon, um, later today, I think. Maybe tomorrow. I've lost track. Should I have them cancel?"

"No! If they are partners, the Tier Zero dungeons are perfect for them. No one of any strength can enter, so they'll be on at least even footing with any would-be assassins or kidnappers." As Dar answered, they stepped out of the World Hall into the morning sun, and Victor sighed, pausing to soak it in as he breathed deeply of Sojourn's fresh air.

"God, that feels good." He saw Dar watching him with his smoldering coal-like eyes and shrugged. "So, you're saying they should spend as much time in dungeons as possible for now. Yeah?"

"Ha! Aye, though I warn you, you trounced some of those so-called champions in the challenge dungeon because they gained most of their levels in these dungeons. They don't know real war or the desperation of a true life-and-death battle. Well, they do now!" Dar laughed and clapped Victor's shoulder again. "At the least, encourage your friends to take on dungeons a tier higher than themselves. This advice pertains to their careers after they've gotten their classes. The Tier Zero dungeons are fitting for their current situation."

"And Valla? She and another Tier Six friend are planning to enter a dungeon. Should they, too, take on a higher-tier dungeon?"

"As a team? Definitely." Dar pointed down a nearby street. "Come, the System Stone is in the Council Spire, this way. It'll be good for you to see where we'll meet for tomorrow's sham of an inquest."

Victor frowned as he followed him. "Can you explain that? I think I get the meaning of an inquest, but, like, am I on trial?"

Dar sighed, shaking his head. "Nine consuls sit on the Sojourn ruling council at any given time. They're voted for by those few thousand of us with voting privileges and serve an eleven-year term. I've served a time or ten over the years. Their word is law, so no, it's not a trial like you might be thinking.

Still, they must consider the political fallout of their actions and they'll want to avoid offending me and my allies too much.

"Your detractors will start off clamoring for your head, then they'll suggest enslavement, and finally, they'll look to levy a fine. We'll find a creative way to settle the debt; don't worry. I'll bring an advocate for you and also stand by your side. Nothing much will come of this other than people rightly learning to show you a bit more respect than your level would usually warrant."

"I still don't see why the hell I'm in trouble. Was it my earthquake spell? How was I supposed to know the dungeon was so fragile? You'd think it should be designed to handle any sort of Energy ability!"

"Aye. Your quake brought the entirety of the fourth level crashing down. I'm glad you weren't squashed before the System pulled you out." Dar started up the steps of the largest building Victor had ever laid eyes on, save maybe the Warlord's citadel in Coloss. It was certainly much, much taller than that great structure, but the citadel had a larger footprint. Regardless, Victor's complaints and objections were thrown from his mind by the wonder invading his thoughts as he craned his neck, looking toward the distant shimmering heights of the spire; he couldn't see the top from where he stood.

"I wonder if this is what skyscrapers look like up close." Tucson had a few tall buildings downtown, but they were nothing like this or, he supposed, the great buildings in cities like New York.

"Skyscrapers? A poetic moniker for a great building. I think I'll add that to my vernacular. Come now, Victor. You may gawk on your own time. I'll see you to your chest, watch to see your award, and then be off; I have a lovely friend waiting to grace me with her company."

"Oh yeah?" Victor smiled, wondering if he knew Dar well enough to rib him a little. He decided he didn't. Perhaps he would have risked it if he weren't so exhausted, filthy, and ready for rest. He was ready to hurry, too; Dar's talk of people seeking vengeance had him more than a little worried about Valla and the others. As he followed Dar through the lobby, past floating platforms adorned with silken cushions, crystal fountains, and plants that looked to be a cross between gemstones and succulents, he had a sudden thought. "Do people know I'm alive? What did it look like when the System shut things down?"

Dar walked through a massive archway into a great domed cathedral-like central hall. The ceiling was hundreds of feet above them, supported by enormous gold-inlaid white marble archways. At the center of the space was the towering System Stone of Sojourn. It looked a lot like the one Victor had planted in the Free Marches, only about five times the size—a black obelisk that rose more than a hundred feet into the air, pulsing with shifting Energy-rich glyphs and runes that seemed to float beneath the surface. Dar paused and turned to answer him, "The viewing windows went blank, but then the council announced what the System did and proclaimed you and Arona victorious. If your friends were watching, they know you're alive."

Victor nodded, his question almost forgotten as he looked at the monolithic stone. Nine separate sets of stairs approached the stone, allowing for multiple queues, but, for whatever reason, there wasn't much of a crowd at that hour. Only a few people stood near the stone—hands resting on its surface—and the stairs were clear. Dar pointed, and Victor saw a faintly glittering golden chest near the platform's edge. Of course, not five feet from that unattended chest stood Arona with a skeletally thin man who had to be eight or nine feet tall. He wore a black capelet over a fine black velour suit, and atop his bone-white skull sat a wide-brimmed black hat.

Dar shoved him. "Climb those steps and claim your chest. Let's see what you receive."

Victor started moving, but he turned back to his mentor. "Who's that with Arona?"

"Her master, Vesavo Bonewhisper. Do not offend that man."

Victor sighed, shaking his head. Why did everyone expect him to pick a fight with everyone he met? He made short work of the steps and moved to stand by his chest, sort of hoping he could open it without having to talk to Arona again. His hopes were dashed when the scarecrow of a man beside her said, in a voice like dry tinder, "Ah, Ranish Dar! I'm pleased I'll have the opportunity to meet your young champion. What a thorn in my Arona's side he was!"

"Master . . ." Arona started to say, but when the man turned his weird crystalline diamond-colored eyes her way, she snapped her mouth shut and looked down.

Dar moved very slightly between Victor and the other two and, staring at the tall, strangely dressed man, said, "Victor Sandoval, greet Vesavo Bonewhisper, one of Sojourn's great Death Casters."

Victor cleared his throat and nodded, trying to banish any aggression from his features. "Pleased to meet you, sir." He could feel the cold Energy of the man's aura seeping out, and if he looked closely, he was sure he saw frost riming the marble platform near the man's feet. He kept his head ducked for three or four seconds, then looked up to see those weird diamond eyes staring at him. The man's skull-like face, with flesh so thin and pale as to be nearly transparent, regarded him for another two or three long silent seconds, and then he nodded and turned to regard Dar.

"A good showing. We gave the lickboots and flower sniffers something to talk about, eh? Well, in three weeks' time, I'll be hosting a dinner. You'll both attend, yes?"

Dar's answer was immediate. "With pleasure."

"Excellent! One of mine will deliver the invitation." He turned to Arona, who was still staring at the ground. "Come." With that, he turned and strode away. He didn't use the steps; rather, he gently glided down from the platform as if floating on an invisible cloud. Arona hurried after him, scurrying down the nearest stairway. Dar watched her and the strange floating man depart through the nearby archway, then turned to Victor.

"That's one of the most dangerous people in Sojourn. I don't fear him, but I certainly respect him." As Victor nodded, his eyes glazing over as he stared after the two Death Casters, wondering what the man with the diamond eyes was capable of, Dar jostled him. "Come now. Open the chest."

"Right!" Victor turned and reached down, lifting the lid and watching as a torrent of glittering golden steam burst forth. He waved away the steam, wondering if the award could possibly make up for all that he'd lost by ruining the dungeon and getting kicked out.

50

WELCOME HOME

Victor leaned over the chest and peered within, immediately amused by the System's sense of justice. His trusty old Kethian Juggernaut helm had been broken in the dungeon, so now he was being awarded a new one. Was that the case? Had the System tailored the reward for him, or was this just random chance? He supposed he'd never know. He reached into the chest and lifted out the rather plain steel-colored helmet. It looked as if it would cover his head, his brow, and the sides of his head. The inside was lined with supple padded leather and looked quite comfortable, but he couldn't help being disappointed; his old helmet had been a lot more unique and stylistically intimidating. "Bleh," he grunted, holding it up for Dar to see.

"You sound disappointed. Isn't that one of the new set pieces?"

"Probably." Victor trickled some Energy into the helmet and was awarded with a System-generated description:

Helm of Sojourn: This is a set item. Collect five pieces of the set and bring them to the Sojourn City Stone to imbue them with curated set bonuses.

"Yeah, it is." Still holding the helm aloft, Victor peered into the chest, ensuring he hadn't missed anything. As he looked, though, the chest began to break apart, turning into Energy mist and fading out of existence, going wherever the System drew it.

Dar took the helm, turning it in his hands, studying the angles. "These aren't common awards. Did you receive any other pieces in the dungeon?"

"Yeah, I did." Victor looked around, surprised they hadn't drawn any sort of crowd. Was it due to Dar's presence? Was he intimidating the "lower" Sojourn denizens? He supposed it wasn't an everyday occurrence for someone of his stature to be standing around with the simple folk.

"I believe these sets will change in appearance when fully enchanted, based on the imbuements you select or provide. It's quite a robust system; the council spent a fortune on it." He handed the helmet back to Victor, who slipped it into the pouch with the rest of the pieces he had gotten.

"I need another piece before I can 'imbue' them."

"Visit the auction house. The drop rates are high in the Vault of Valor, much higher than in the other city dungeons. Few people would have the patience to gather a full set on their own, so there are likely to be some for sale." Dar turned to the archway leading from the vaulted hall. "I'm off. I'll send transport for you tomorrow. I'd like you here early so my advocate can prepare you."

He gave Victor a long look, making a sound like softly grinding stones in his chest. Victor realized he was chuckling as he took in Victor's shredded, burned pants. "Dress appropriately." He didn't wait for a response; rather, he seemed to shimmer for a few seconds, and then he was gone. Victor had to jerk his head toward the entrance to see that Dar had either moved impossibly fast or teleported down from the platform. He just caught a glimpse of his flowing red cape as he departed the hall.

"All right, then." Victor took a deep breath and started down the steps, glancing around nervously as he realized more and more people were stopping to look at him. It confirmed his earlier theory; no one had wanted to be caught daring to stare while Dar was around. He suddenly wished he could step into a bathroom or something to change his pants, but with no idea where to begin looking for one, he decided a hasty exit was more in order. He hurried down the steps and through the spacious, magically appointed lobby. The sun had risen further, and its light sparkled on the crystal towers, forcing him to squint as he looked around and inhaled the fresh air.

Traffic had picked up, and throngs of people walked to and fro on the sidewalk. He saw a man wearing a short black cape flag down a passing vehicle—something that brought to mind a cross between a carriage and a steam train. Victor noticed an emblem on the side like a fanciful P, and when he looked at the traffic, he saw several other strange vehicles, all different in design, with a similar emblem. He supposed he could summon Guapo and see what it was like riding around in the traffic, but he was tired and eager to be out of the public scrutiny, so he tried his luck flagging one of the cars down.

He chose a large one, about the size of a panel van from Earth. It was brass with tall, thin, spoked metal wheels. Something clung to the rims, moving around them like steam, and he figured it had to be some sort of Energy enchantment to provide padding and traction. The driver sat on the top, controlling the big vehicle with brass levers. He was a small fellow wearing a high brimmed hat, and when he saw Victor wave, he nodded eagerly, steering the steam-belching conveyance over to the side of the street. "Need a lift?" Victor nodded, giving him his address.

The driver nodded. "I know it! It's down in the old River View neighborhood, right?"

Victor nodded, remembering the realtor mentioning a riverwalk a few blocks from his house. The driver pulled a lever, and the door opened with a hiss, revealing a spacious interior with headroom even for a man Victor's size once he'd sat down. The seats were plush leather, and the air inside was scented with coffee and vanilla, making Victor's stomach rumble. He wondered about the scent's origin but found nothing other than more leather seats when he looked around the interior. The door hissed closed, and the vehicle started moving. Surprised by its speed and smooth ride, he watched out the window as the buildings rushed by.

They were forced to stop for traffic a few times, but Victor hardly noticed. He was close to drifting off to sleep, his mind replaying the weird jumbled events from his time in the challenge dungeon, especially his final encounter with Arona and her team. Had she really slipped away to try to finish the dungeon? He could only imagine how irritated those she'd left behind were.

He hardly remembered what he'd done as the Aspect of Terror, but it couldn't have been pleasant for Sora and that nature guy. And Arona had left them to that! Thinking of the aspect, he didn't feel much lingering guilt after using the spell. That felt like a first. Was it because he knew he hadn't killed anyone? He thought it was probably more likely a result of them starting the fight five versus one. How could he feel bad about anything he did in that situation?

When the taxi—as Victor thought of it—pulled up in front of his house, he was pleased to have solidified his outlook. He shouldn't feel guilty about any of that business, least of all damaging the dungeon. How was he supposed to know how fragile it was? For all he knew, the System and any environment it governed were indestructible. He found himself almost looking forward to the so-called inquest. In his mind, there was no way the council's accusations would stand up to logic.

The driver asked for five Energy beads, and Victor handed him ten, amazed that anyone could make a living on so little. He'd barely reached the gate leading to his little courtyard when Valla slammed into him, wrapping her arms around his waist in a viselike squeeze. "Oof!" Victor laughed.

"I'm so glad you're home. Rumors at the public house were wild! Some people thought you'd be imprisoned!"

"What the hell? Why?"

Valla looked up at him, squinting in the sunlight. "As I said, rumors—drunken ones, at that. People seemed to think the council would hold you responsible for the dungeon's damage. Lesh wanted to find the council building, but he was drunk, and I hoped you or Ranish Dar would send word to us. Well, more, I hoped you'd come home. And here you are!" She laughed and squeezed him again.

"Well, whatever rumors you heard were only half right." Victor sighed, returning her hug, pressing her against him, gently stroking her back, and running his fingers along the soft ridges of her feathers.

"Half right?" She looked up at him, and Victor grew weary of stretching his neck down, so he cast Alter Self, bringing himself closer to her height.

"Yeah, I guess the System's going to charge them an arm and a leg to fix the dungeon, so they're mad at me." He shrugged, draping an arm over her shoulders and guiding her toward the house. "Dar says not to worry, so I'm not going to. Anyway, I have to go to some stupid hearing tomorrow to argue about it."

Valla stiffened under his arm. "Tomorrow? But we're meant to head into Desperation Gap tomorrow! Lesh really hoped you'd come along!"

"Lesh did?" Victor cocked an eyebrow as he pulled the door open for her.

"Well, of course, I did too!"

"Look, Valla, I want to go too, but I can't miss this hearing—inquest. I also think Dar has plans for me. If I'm honest, I'm fucking tired, too; that challenge dungeon took a lot out . . ."

"It's okay." She cut him off, lifting his arm off her shoulders, and despite her smile, he could see the strain behind it. Victor almost said to forget what he'd said, that he'd find a way to join them, but he wasn't only being selfish. He wanted Valla and Lesh to get stronger, and how would they do that if he came along and steamrolled everything? Was he being a little full of himself with that thought? He supposed so, but he knew how much stronger he was than Valla, and he had a good idea that he could toss Lesh around, too; they only had draws while sparring because Victor never used his strongest abilities; he never berserked.

Rather than try to placate her, he shifted the topic. "Is Lam coming with you?"

Valla sighed, shaking her head as they walked into the little kitchen. Victor sat down with his back to the table, stretching his legs out while she chose her words. "She's determined to escort and wait for Darren and Edeya. I know it's for Edeya's benefit, really, but she keeps pointing out how Darren has yet to gain a single level: 'He's like a newborn,' etcetera. Lesh scoffs, tells her his 'fosterling' needs to stumble on his own, but she insists that, at least for this dungeon outing, she wants to be near at hand."

Victor grew curious as she mentioned the others. "Where are they all?"

"In the travel home, sleeping the night off. Everyone had a bit too much, but you should have seen Lesh! It was both funny and frightening. He made a lot of money betting on you, by the way."

"Really? Ha!" Victor slapped his hand on the table, watching Valla doing something by the sink. He thought he saw something red in her hand, and as he craned his neck, trying to see, she smiled and held up a bright red fruit; it looked almost like a tomato.

"From the garden." She put it on the butcher block counter and started slicing it into segments. "You're going to love it. It's sweet but a little tart. Lesh puts salt on them, but I like sugar." She looked at him, the question plain on her face.

"I'll try both." He chuckled, his stomach telling him he needed to eat a hell of a lot more than a fruit. Of course, that made him think of meat, which reminded him of the gargantuopod he'd harvested. Should he eat that heart? Should he wait? He supposed he'd ask Dar about it.

"Are you very hungry?" Valla set the plate before him, and Victor picked up the fruit, smelling it. It reminded him of citrus, and when he put the piece in his mouth—salty—he grinned.

"I'm starved, and this reminds me of an orange, but, as you said, a little sour. I'd say half orange and half lemon."

Valla smiled, watching him eat more slices, then asked, "Which is better?"

"Oh, the sugar is great, but the salt brings out the flavors; I dunno which one I like more." He laughed as she snorted, shaking her head.

"Won't pick a side, hmm?"

"Just telling the truth!" He finished off the fruit, and he had half a mind to start pulling some of his favorite foods out of his storage rings, but he wanted to see if Valla had something planned first. She'd resumed shuffling around in the kitchen, pulling things from the cold cabinet and pantry. "What are you doing?"

"I'm going to make you some food!"

"So you're not mad?"

"About?" When she didn't look at him, he knew darn well she knew what he was talking about.

"The dungeon?"

"No. How could I be mad at you for being honest? I was foolish to expect you to want to run straight into another dungeon after all you went through in that challenge."

Victor groaned and folded his arms on his chest, kicking his feet out further and pushing the table legs to the edge of their endurance as he leaned into it. "I wish the stupid thing wasn't televised."

"Televised?"

"Those dumb spy stones, projecting the whole thing for you guys to watch. It seems to me that couldn't have been fun for you."

"It was nerve-racking, but watching Lesh cheer and listening as you quickly became a crowd favorite was fun, too. Naturally, knowing about the lifesavers helped, but I heard one of the entrants died. Is that true?"

"Yeah, early on, I saw that message." Victor rubbed a hand through his hair, sighing as he felt the grit sticking between his fingers. "I didn't meet the person, and I'm not sure who eliminated them. You didn't see it on the screen?"

Valla began chopping some vegetables and turned on the sink; it all looked so much like a scene out of a modern Earth kitchen that Victor felt a weird wave of something like déjà vu, so strong that it started up some butterflies in his stomach. She turned and answered, "No. When you weren't on the central viewing window, I watched your smaller window most of the time. I missed it."

Victor nodded and stood, jerking a thumb toward the hallway leading to the bedrooms. "You care if I go clean up? I could use a soak in the bath if there's time."

"Of course! I should have suggested it." She put down the knife and came over to him. "I'd join you, but I'm enjoying the idea of cooking something good. I invited the others, too. Do you mind? We'll spend a lot of time alone tonight, yes?"

"Yeah. Yeah, that's perfect. Thank you, Valla." He looked over to the counter at the start of her preparations and added, "If you're tired, we could take a nap. I've got tons of prepared food in my storage rings . . ."

"No! We'll have something fresh. There's much to celebrate and even more to discuss; Lam met someone you'll find interesting, and Darren and Edeya will enjoy some advice about their first dungeon."

"Oh yeah? Well, now you've piqued my interest." Victor leaned down and, intending to give her a quick kiss, found himself wrapped up in something far more amorous. Valla's mouth tasted like the fruit he'd just eaten, and she must have liked something about his because neither broke it off quickly. After several long, feverish moments while both of them did some exploring with their hands, she finally pushed him off.

"Tonight!" she panted, breathless.

"Right," he chuckled, wiping his mouth with a grin.

"Did you just wipe my kiss off?"

"Uh . . ."

Valla laughed and pushed him again. "I'm teasing! Go get cleaned up; you stink."

"I stink?" Victor grinned, then he stepped forward, squatted, stretched his arms around Valla's hips, hooking them just below her butt, and hoisted her over his shoulder. "I think that dinner can wait a few minutes. I'm kidnapping you!" As she howled in protest, slapping his butt with her palms as she dangled behind him, Victor carried her back to the bedroom and their private bath.

Arcus Volpuré leaned against the high limewashed brick wall, gazing down the street at the little villa gate the giant and his winged woman had just stepped through. So, this was his home. He'd expected something grander, but size and prowess didn't necessarily translate to class. Still, it stung a bit more knowing a peasant had gotten the better of him. Strista shifted beside him, pulling her cowl forward, further sinking her visage into shadow. "Nervous?" he asked, his thin lips curling into a smile.

"Of course. I said I was interested in vengeance, not suicide."

"Relax. Didn't you see how they fell all over each other when she came to the gate? He won't be back out soon. Even if he was, it's not like we're doing anything untoward; we're just out for a stroll."

"As if he'd buy that. Two people he just vanquished happen to stroll into this old slum?" She turned and gestured toward the city. "Come. You've seen his home. It's enough for now."

"A fearful little bird, aren't you?"

Strista turned a huge golden eye his way, and Arcus had to hand it to the avians; they could certainly scowl. Her dark feathers and golden beak only made it more severe. "I'm afraid of him, yes, but I'm not a little bird, and I'm not weak. Don't mock me, Pyromancer!" He noticed her hand resting on the coiled whip at her side and held up an open palm.

"Peace, Lady. I agree; I've seen enough for now. We must tread lightly with this matter—his master is influential." He *had* seen enough; now that he knew the house, setting up a watchful familiar would be simple. He'd learn the man's routines, learn more about his acquaintances, especially that lovely celestial being who'd just met him at the gate, and find a way to extract some payment, be it material or symbolic. "I will have justice," he whispered harshly, turning to his coach parked at the corner. "Come, I'll deliver you to Balefor Estates. You still live there, yes?"

"That's right. Can your coach fly, then? It's rather distant."

"Oh, aye. On wings of flame, no less. I'm happy for the ride; we can discuss who else might enjoy our little alliance. The giant made no small list of enemies yesterday. With a few good minds coming together, I'm sure we can think of a way to extract our due."

Strista nodded and took his proffered hand, careful not to hook his tender flesh with her needlelike talons. They'd known each other most of their lives and had, once upon a time, been lovers. Now, though, Arcus had little time for romantic distractions; he was close to truly understanding the nature of fire, to becoming one with it. Well, he'd been closer two days ago. Now that he'd fallen back into the eighth tier, he had years of hard work ahead of him to regain what he'd lost.

As the thought passed through his mind, his body began to steam, and flames lit up behind his eyes. Strista tried to pull her hand away, but Arcus tamped down the fire and persisted with his grip—something in him yearned for the closeness despite his bravado. Something in him still stung from the punishment that bastard giant had doled out.

51

INQUEST

Darren clutched the smooth hardwood quarterstaff Victor had bought for him. It was sturdy and supposedly enchanted to do extra bludgeoning damage, and he found it very comforting as he looked toward the glowing portal on the dais down in the little walled-off cave. He, Edeya, and Lam stood outside in one of Sojourn's many parks, waiting for the dungeon attendants to call them forward. Their entry slot was in just a few minutes.

Edeya stood near, also clutching her weapon—a fine ivory-colored spear with a gleaming silvery blade. Victor had given it to her, and when Darren's eyes had betrayed his jealousy, the giant man had shrugged and said, "Edeya's been training to use weapons for years. That staff will suit you well for now." Darren had immediately put aside his jealousy; Victor had gone out of his way to ensure he had something solid to swing around and defend with, which was more than he could ask for. Besides, it wasn't his only gift.

Both he and Edeya wore armored vests made from rings of impossibly light metal. If Darren were back on Earth, he might guess it was aluminum if not for the odd blue tint. The rings were sewn to supple pale leather, and the garments were enchanted to repair and clean themselves. Moreover, the rings were incredibly sturdy. Victor had demonstrated by tasking Edeya with trying to stab a knife through one while he held it in his palm. "Shimmersteel," he whispered, remembering the name of the material.

Edeya heard him and smiled. "Comfortable, huh?" Darren couldn't deny that she looked especially good in her vest. It hugged her narrow frame, and the blue in the metal was highlighted by the cobalt Energy motes that constantly drifted down from her dragonfly wings.

"Yeah. It's great." Darren smiled, amazed at how different she looked from the pale, deathly figure she'd been when they first met. Her cheeks were flushed, her blue eyes bright with excitement, and her red-gold hair hung in curly ringlets from the silver half-helm Victor had given her. She'd gone to a lot of trouble to look nice for their first dungeon dive, which Darren found both amusing and endearing. It was like dressing up to work in the sewers. Or was it? He had no idea, truthfully.

According to the guidebook Edeya had been reading, the "Grotto" was a cave system, but that didn't mean there would be rank or disgusting water in it. In fact, she'd pointed out that some of the deeper sections were blocked off by clear cold water they'd have to swim through, assuming they went that far in. Darren wasn't too sure.

Lam interrupted his thoughts. "Show me again," she said, nudging his shoulder. He knew what she meant; she and Edeya had spent quite a lot of time teaching him to channel his Energy into his first spell. He'd even gained some Energy from the System when he learned it: Arclight Wisp. It was the name of his version of the very basic "light" spell that most new Energy users learned.

Darren held out his palm and built the spell pattern in his pathway, sending some of his lightning-attuned Energy into it. A tiny buzzing, crackling mote of red light appeared above his palm, flickering then growing steadier and brighter, almost like an old incandescent light bulb warming up. It hovered in the air, moving to and fro as it waited for him to direct it with his will.

"Nice!" Edeya laughed and snatched at the wisp, but it flickered through her fingers. "I think it's getting brighter."

Lam nodded and squeezed Darren's shoulder. "I hope you gain a level quickly and learn a useful spell right away. Whatever the case, even if you don't, you'll gain some attribute points and more Energy, and we'll find a way to teach you some things when you get out." She reached out with her other hand and pulled Edeya close, grasping her neck in the crook of her arm. "Stick close to Edeya and follow her lead. She knows how to cast a lot of spells."

"Most require more Energy than I have now," Edeya pouted. "But not all!"

"You'll both be fine. You're sure you have every—"

"Thing. Yes, Lam! You've asked us ten times." Edeya laughed and quickly stretched her neck up to kiss Lam on the cheek in a surprising show of sweetness and affection. "We'll be fine. This dungeon is for babies."

"Well . . ." Lam smiled, eyeing Darren meaningfully.

"All right, I get it!" Darren sighed, shaking his head. "Lesh has made it abundantly clear that I'm basically a newborn. Don't worry, I won't get in Edeya's way."

Suddenly, in a strident, clarion voice, one of the attendants called out, "Edeya! Darren! Your time slot begins now!"

When they were finally invited into one of the council's conference chambers, Victor wasn't surprised to find a table ornately carved from what looked to him like a single enormous slab of ivory. Nor was he surprised to find chairs suitably large for himself and Ranish Dar. They sat on one side, Victor in the middle, Ranish to his right, and the advocate Ranish had hired on his left.

The advocate was a strange individual, ostensibly a male, but not exhibiting any such mammalian characteristics. His flesh and body were entirely composed of an odd orange gelid substance that jiggled and flowed bonelessly in a close approximation of a bipedal humanoid figure. His eyes were like softly glowing red candies, and Victor couldn't help thinking of him as a Jell-O man. Even more strange, he refused to be named, insisting that Victor and Ranish address him as Advocate. Nonetheless, Ranish said he was highly regarded, so Victor went with it.

Great stained glass windows lined the wall behind the council members who were arrayed opposite the trio. The windows depicted scenes from nature—birds with bright plumage, colorful flowers, and other little animals like red-furred foxes bearing more than one tail alongside perfectly ordinary white rabbits. Victor found the artistry hard to look away from, though the light in his eyes certainly put him at a disadvantage. He thought about that for a moment, how those windows would brightly light his face while the council members' faces were dim in the glare of the midday sunlight. Surely it was by design.

Speaking of the council members, only five were in attendance, but Victor supposed that made sense; it was a big, busy city, and he doubted they could all be bothered by a problem with a single dungeon caused by a relatively insignificant new citizen. Of course, the man with the smoke-obscured face, deep in his dark gray cowl, was in attendance, sitting in the center. Victor had learned his name was Lord Roil and that he and Dar shared a centuries-old grudge. To his right was an avian man with the features of a blackbird. He looked so much like a giant bipedal crow that Victor struggled not to stare; the man's wide, startled-looking yellow bird eyes were almost comical as he turned his head left and right, his beak hanging slightly agape.

The advocate had earlier told Victor who to expect, so he knew who the avian was—Yon, the master of Strista Kono, whom Victor had rather summarily vanquished from the dungeon. Lord Roil looked to his left, where a grandmotherly figure sat, and a sound like hissing steam issued forth. Was it some sort of whisper? Victor ignored it and looked more closely at the woman. She could have been human—she had pale flesh, deep wrinkles, and pudgy cheeks beneath curly gray hair held in a bun by long wooden pins. She could have been if not for her unsettling black eyes gleaming with a hidden inner light.

To her left was a person who looked very much like a bright green praying mantis wearing yellow silken robes. On the other end, to the right of the bird man, sat an elf-like fellow—tall, handsome, with a chiseled jawline, glistening golden hair, and ears that stood out from his head and pointed upward in a far more pronounced manner than the Fae girl, Sora's. Victor had forgotten the names of those last three; he'd only heard them once from the advocate and had been more preoccupied with his defense than memorizing the names of then faceless lords and ladies. He'd just taken in the scene and gotten a good look at the consuls when the door clicked open and Arona stepped in.

"Apologies, Lord Consuls," she said in her whispery, scratchy voice, bowing low.

"Sit," Lord Roil hissed, and the word was laced with power so absolute that Victor found himself trying to sit even though he already was. He heard Arona hurry to comply, rushing to the seat to his advocate's left. "You have no representation, Arona Moonshadow?" the hissing, smoky voice demanded.

Arona ducked her head, her forehead nearly touching the table, and said, "No, Lord Consul. I throw myself upon your mercy." Victor's eyebrows shot up at that. Was she being smart or stupid? Perhaps she and her master had realized that Victor was the one really in trouble that day, and she was trying to earn favor by appearing compliant.

Some mutters and several nodding heads on the consuls' side of the table confirmed his theory; they were pleased with her submission. "Then we shall begin. If it pleases the committee, I will speak for us unless one of you has a dissenting opinion on a matter that comes up." Lord Roil turned his cowled head to the left and right, ensuring all his co-consuls nodded in affirmation. Victor got the impression that this had already been agreed upon before the meeting had begun. He glanced at Ranish Dar, wondering if he should react, but the black stone-fleshed man sat almost like he was in a trance, his eyes half shut and the white fire of his eyes subdued.

The advocate's plump, jelly-like lips opened, and he spoke in an odd liquid voice that made Victor want to clear his throat. "We accept your appointment as spokesperson, Lord Roil."

"It was not brought forth for debate." For the first time, Victor saw a spark of light in the smoky depths of that cowl, and he wondered if it was one of Lord Roil's eyes flaring with Energy. "I will now outline the charges. Victor Sandoval, student of Ranish Dar, you are accused of causing great damage to the Vault of Valor, resulting in a loss of revenue to the City of Sojourn and an unquantifiable loss of Energy and System-generated awards to Arona Moonshadow. How do you plead?"

Hearing that Arona was not summoned as a co-defendant but as a victim, Victor almost lost control of his mouth. In fact, he inhaled sharply and would have barked an outraged laugh if Dar hadn't bumped him in the ribs with a boulder-sized elbow as a warning.

The advocate was quick to speak, though, forestalling any protest from Victor. "Victor Sandoval is not guilty of any intent to harm the city's property and, further, cannot be held responsible for the System's judgment with regard to Arona Moonshadow. The System provided the award it felt she deserved, a single chest, and the System chose to withhold any Energy gains not only from Arona but from Victor, as well. One could argue that we have a case against the city for failing to provide the promised awards of the competition."

"Outrageous!" Yon, the crow-headed man, squawked. Lord Roil held up a long flowing sleeve and turned his cowl toward him until Yon closed his beak and sat back, his feathery arms folded over his chest.

"You would try to countersue the council on the grounds that we have a say in the System's judgment?"

"If you think Victor can influence the System or should be held liable for that very same judgment, does the logic not flow?" The advocate's voice was even, but Victor could hear a hint of "gotcha" in his tone.

"There is a flaw with your comparison, Advocate," Roil said, some wisps of smoke escaping his cowl. Was that because of his breath? Was there a breathing body behind all that smoke? "Victor Sandoval caused the damage.

The System withheld Energy from him and Arona because it used that Energy to stabilize the damage. Further, the penalty charged to the city for the dungeon's repair resulted from the damage he caused. Can you not see how he, logically, is the responsible party?"

"If we are going to boil the bone, then let us get the marrow out," the advocate said, gently and silently tapping the table with one of his squishy fingers. "Arona and her allies ambushed Victor. If he had not had to defend himself in a five-versus-one contest, he would not have had to utilize his most destructive powers. Should the blame not be laid at the feet of all participants in said battle? Considering he was not the aggressor, I feel it's generous that Victor would be willing to share one-sixth of the penalty."

Roil nodded. "This has been considered, but the damage done to the dungeon comes down to poor judgment. Any person with good intentions would know that unleashing an earthquake-causing Energy ability in a dungeon level made entirely of stone and built like a cavern with thousand-ton stalactites dotting its ceiling was a poor choice. Such a move was not only overtly destructive of the dungeon's framework but also self-destructive. Does Lord Dar not agree that his charge should be more respectful of the council's property and of himself? Does he think it wise that his student would throw away his own well-being for the vanity of pride and the refusal to keep his destructive instincts in check?"

Victor knew what was coming next. The advocate and Dar had already prepared him for the concession they were willing to make. Still, when the advocate spoke up, Victor found himself clenching his fists in anger. "Lord Dar agrees that his student showed poor judgment, but he disagrees that the fault lies entirely at his feet. Victor was unaware that a dungeon could be permanently damaged. He comes from a world with few dungeons, and those are not managed by citizens. They are naturally occurring System-managed dives. My client agrees to pay a portion of the damages but feels the council, in its wisdom, should bear the brunt of the expense. It was the council who designed this activity, and it was the council who failed to warn the entrants of the dungeon's fragility."

To Victor's surprise, Lord Roil's cowl moved in a slow nod. He shifted his focus to Arona and asked, "What say you, Lady Moonshadow?"

Victor looked at her closely, watching her dark eyes shift up from where they stared at the table. A pink flicker of her tongue on her black-painted lips betrayed some nervousness as she quickly glanced at Victor and then turned back to the consuls. "Lords and Ladies of the council, I seek no reparations. I cannot blame this man sitting here for fighting with everything he had. I am sorry I wasn't allowed to finish the dungeon, but I recognize no malfeasance on his behalf."

Lord Roil's cowl shifted to the left, awaiting acknowledgment from the consuls on that side. When they both nodded, he turned to the right, and when Yon and the elf nodded, he turned to face Victor. "Victor Sandoval, do you wish to speak on your own behalf before I render the committee's decision?"

Again, Victor had been instructed on this matter; it was common practice for the accused to be given a chance to speak, regardless of advocacy. Dar had told him what to say, and Victor found the words easy enough; his pride had retreated in the face of so many powerful auras. "Lords and Ladies of the council, I simply wish to apologize. As my advocate indicated, I had no idea that anything I did in that dungeon could damage its structure. I was pushed to the point of breaking by the challenges offered, and it didn't occur to me that I should withhold my strongest abilities. I ask for your mercy in your decision."

As he finished, something deep in his chest rebelled, and Victor had to press his lips together in a thin line to keep from frowning or growling. He hated being obsequious, and he really didn't mean the words; he wasn't truly sorry, and he hoped the lip service he gave to the consuls would be enough if they could sense his lack of remorse. He wouldn't have agreed to say those things if the advocate hadn't assured him that the council would go easy on him out of respect for Dar. It hadn't hurt to hear Arona's statement first; she'd been surprisingly cool about the whole thing. Had she known she wasn't here as a defendant? He supposed it made sense.

"Very well. Hear our judgment: Victor Sandoval, in lieu of imprisonment, fines, and reparations to Arona Moonshadow, you are charged with completing three tasks for the Council of Sojourn. A majority of the current consuls must decide upon each task, and you must remain living in this city until you've accomplished this penance. Are there any objections?"

If Victor had been grasping coals in his hands, he felt like he'd have made some new diamonds as he listened to the decree. It was all he could do to clench his jaw and refuse the Quinametzin in him the chance to curse or yell. He'd been hoping to pay some Energy beads and be done with this bullshit, but now he was tied to some nebulous "tasks"? As he fumed and tried to make sense of it all, Dar pushed his chair back and stood. For the first time, the giant spoke, his voice grinding out with unchecked volume, forcing more than one of the consuls to flinch. "Very well. The council knows how to reach me. I will receive the requests for my student's services and judge whether they are appropriate. Do you object?"

"Do not overstep, Ranish Dar," Roil hissed. Though his voice was soft, it cut like a knife with the force of an aura that blanked Victor's mind and made him instantly forget what he'd been angry about.

Dar pressed his palms on the ivory table, leaning forward into that aura, his eyes suddenly blazing like twin suns. "Is it overstepping to look out for the welfare of my student? I will have a say in these tasks, or there will be a need for further inquests. What say you, Roil?"

The cowled figure faced the fire of Dar's eyes for several long seconds and then nodded. "Very well. The matter is settled." Then he abruptly stood and glided out of the room, slipping through a side door before the other consuls had even managed to stand.

"Come," Dar said, clapping Victor on the shoulder. Victor started to stand, but then Yon opened his beak and squawked.

"What a farce! You were lucky this time, Dar."

Dar turned to regard him as Victor moved to stand by his side. The other consuls had all stopped in their tracks, eyeing the seven-foot crow-like man and the towering, seething, statuesque Dar. "There was no luck involved, bird. Speak to me again with such an unfettered tongue, and I'll issue a challenge."

Yon's beak closed with a *click*, and Victor wasn't alone in his smile as Yon turned to make a hasty exit. Everyone else started moving again, and the advocate broke the silence by saying, "I'll go to the admin office to get this settlement recorded on a legal decree."

"Good. You earned your pay, Advocate." Dar pulled the door open for him, and then Arona stepped forward.

"I'm sorry I was involved in this, Lord Dar."

"Nonsense. It wasn't you or your master who put you into that position. I fully blame Roil and the three or four others on the council who hold various grudges against me. Your words here earned you a favor from me. Use it wisely."

Arona's pale sharp-boned face lit up with undisguised pleasure, and she bowed very low. When she straightened, she nodded to Victor and said, "I'm sure we'll meet again." Then she slipped out the door, and Dar threw an arm over Victor's shoulders, guiding him out.

"It wasn't bad; three tasks requiring my approval—it's nothing. I'll be sure the demands will convey good learning opportunities for you."

"I guess." Victor sighed. "It was hard to sit there and take all of that. This whole thing feels like a bad joke."

"That's how politics work, Victor. I won some clout with your performance in the dungeon, and my enemies clawed a little back with this inquest. You're unfortunately a pawn at this stage of your life. Stick with me, and I'll teach you to be a player." As they walked through the lobby, Dar, apparently in a good mood, continued to speak loudly, his voice almost jovial. "It's time you visited my lake house. There's someone there I'd like you to see; she'll provide a learning opportunity for you."

"Yeah?" Victor was tired of surprises, so he pressed for more details. "Who?"

"You know her—the Fae girl who switched sides on you in the dungeon. Your terror-born alter ego infected her with a creeping dread that has left her broken. I thought you might want to learn how to remove such an affliction. Did you have other plans?"

"Nope. My friends have all gone into one dungeon or another—well, all but one, but I'll meet her later if that's okay. I wouldn't mind seeing Sora, and yeah, I wouldn't want to think of her dealing with some mental trauma I caused. Besides"—Victor grinned and picked up the pace, heading for the black-lacquered flying carriage Dar had picked him up in—"she has a cloak I might try to buy off her."

"Ah, is that so? Your elusive fifth piece of the set?" Victor could hear the humor in Dar's voice.

"That's right. I won't, like, refuse to help her unless she gives it to me, but I might drop some hints afterward. Maybe she'll be generous."

"Perhaps, but you're a man of means. Don't be afraid to open negotiations. Now, get into the coach. I'm weary of these robes and want to walk in the warm sands of my beach before the sunset."

"Is it far?" Victor craned his neck, trying to spot the sun past the towering crystal buildings all around. As far as he could tell, it was still just a little past noon.

"Not too far. Not as the crow flies. I should have a teleportation platform installed, but I've only had the house for a few years and haven't spent much time there." Dar grunted as he climbed into the opulently appointed coach behind Victor, sitting with his back to the front end, facing Victor, who had taken a seat across from the door. "I rather enjoy the need to travel there by conventional means, if I'm honest. It adds to the notion that the home is meant as a retreat."

"Yeah." Victor smiled and leaned back, enjoying the sensation as the carriage lurched into motion. Dar's driver apparently knew what was expected of him. Victor was looking forward to staying in one town for a while and learning from someone who was a recognized master of spirit Energy. He might have to contend with the annoying politics of Sojourn, but there was a lot in the city for him to do and experience, and it was good for Valla and the others, too. Besides, those guys could travel back and forth to Fanwath if they wanted; they weren't tied there like he was. Was he, though? "Do you think I can travel at all, or will the council get angry?"

"Oh, I'm sure there will be some travel in store for you. Or did you mean for your own ends?"

"I wouldn't mind visiting my lands on Fanwath now and then."

Dar chuckled and shrugged. "We'll arrange something."

Victor's smile broadened, and he let his eyes drift closed as the coach hurtled through the air. He hoped Valla and Lesh were doing well in their dungeon. They planned to take it slow, and their window was for a week, so he didn't expect them anytime soon. He'd warned everyone about the potential of his enemies from the contest seeking to harm him by using them, so they were all on the lookout, but everyone should be fairly safe in their dungeons, other than Lam. He opened his eyes and turned to Dar. "Can we send someone to pick up my friend? She'll be alone after our other friends enter a dungeon."

"You want her to come to the lake house?" Dar's weird stony lips turned down while he contemplated it. "Why not? It's a big place, and I've plenty of food. Is she one of the insect-like ones?"

"Heh." Victor couldn't imagine Lam would like that description. "She's the one with the golden wings."

"I'll send someone for her."

Victor nodded his thanks and closed his eyes again. With that settled, he really didn't feel stressed about anything, and he hadn't slept much the night before. He tried to keep thinking about his plans—the things he wanted to do and learn—but his mind had other ideas, and soon, he was drifting off into a deep untroubled slumber.

Status				
Name:	Victor Sandoval			
Race:	Quinametzin Bloodline: Epic 1			
Class:	Herald of the Mountain's Wrath: Legendary			
Level:	65			
Breath Core:	Elder Class: Improved 3			
Core:	Spirit Class: Advanced 8			
Breath Core Affinity:	Magma: 9		Breath Core Energy:	2200/2200
Energy Affinity:	Fear 9.4, Rage 9.1, Glory 8.6, Inspiration 7.4, Unattuned 3.1		Energy:	25307/25307
Strength:	430	Vitality:	560 (616)	
Dexterity:	190	Agility:	213	
Intelligence:	172	Will:	613	
Points Available:	0			
Titles & Feats:	Titanic Rage, Ancestral Bond, Flame-Touched, Greater Titanic Constitution, Titanic Presence, Desperate Grace, Challenger, Elder Magic, Born of Terror, Battlefield Awareness, Battlefield Presence, Aura of Command, Epic Quinametzin, Mountain's Resilience			

Skills:	
System Language Integration	Not Upgradeable
Spirit Core Cultivation Drill	Advanced
Breath Core Cultivation Drill	Advanced
Cooking	Basic
Animal Taming	Basic
Unarmed Combat	Basic

Knife Mastery	Basic
Spear Mastery	Basic
Bludgeon Mastery	Improved
Axe Mastery	Epic
Grappling	Advanced
Sovereign Will	Advanced
Titanic Leap	Improved
Aura Veil	Basic
Spells:	
Iron Berserk	Epic
Inspiration of the Quinametzin	Epic
Channel Spirit	Improved
Enraging Orb	Basic
Globe of Insight	Improved
Project Spirit	Improved
Dauntless Radiance	Basic
Heroic Heart	Basic
Spirit Walk	Basic
Tether Spirit	Basic
Harsh Light of Justice	Improved
The Inevitable Huntsman	Improved
Aspect of Terror	Advanced
Imbue Spirit	Improved
Honor the Spirits	Improved
Titanic Aspect	Basic
Alter Self	Improved
Energy Charge	Basic
Banner of the Champion	Basic
Wild Totem	Advanced
Impart Nightmare	Improved

Guard Ally	Basic
Volcanic Fury	Basic
Wake the Earth	Basic
Roots of the Mountain	Basic

ABOUT THE AUTHOR

Plum Parrot is the pen name of author Miles Gallup, who grew up in Southern Arizona and spent much of his youth wandering around the Sonoran Desert, hunting imaginary monsters and building forts. He studied creative writing at the University of Arizona and, for a number of years, attempted to teach middle schoolers to love literature and write their own stories. If he's not spending time with his dog, you can find Gallup writing, reading his favorite authors, or playing *D&D* with friends and family.

Podium

DISCOVER MORE

PodiumEntertainment.com

www.ingramcontent.com/pod-product-compliance
Lightning Source LLC
Chambersburg PA
CBHW030920120726
47906CB00002B/413